D0626910

He answered on the second ring, businesslike and clipped. "Forbes."

"Hello. It's Alexandra Forrest."

"Alex?" His tone changed with gratifying speed to unbusinesslike and sexy.

She rolled her gaze. "Yes, Alex."

There was a short pause as she tried to work out what she wanted to say. In the background she heard traffic noises. He must be in his car.

He took care of the awkward pause by saying, "Are you taking me up on my offer to take you to dinner?"

She drew a deep breath and felt the oxygen pump to every erogenous zone in her body. "No. I'm taking you up on your offer for sex."

The second pause was a lot longer than the first and she enjoyed every nanosecond of his obvious shock. But he rallied fast. "Great. When?"

Alex was a great believer that there's no time like the present. "How about now?"

"I'll be there in sixty seconds."

"Sixty seconds?" There was a good five miles between her place and the cottage he was renting. Unless he had supernatural powers . . . She heard a truck go by on the street outside her place and then heard its faint echo from the phone clasped to her ear.

It was her turn for shock.

BOOK YOUR PLACE ON OUR WEBSITE AND MAKE THE READING CONNECTION!

We've created a customized website just for our very special readers, where you can get the inside scoop on everything that's going on with Zebra, Pinnacle and Kensington books.

When you come online, you'll have the exciting opportunity to:

- View covers of upcoming books

- Read sample chapters

- Learn about our future publishing schedule (listed by publication month *and author*)

- Find out when your favorite authors will be visiting a city near you

- Search for and order backlist books from our online catalog

- Check out author bios and background information

- Send e-mail to your favorite authors

- Meet the Kensington staff online

- Join us in weekly chats with authors, readers and other guests

- Get writing guidelines

- AND MUCH MORE!

Visit our website at
http://www.kensingtonbooks.com

NANCY WARREN

Drive Me Crazy

Kensington Books
KENSINGTON PUBLISHING CORP.
http://www.kensingtonbooks.com

KENSINGTON BOOKS are published by

Kensington Publishing Corp.
850 Third Avenue
New York, NY 10022

All Kensington titles, imprints and distributed lines are available at special quantity discounts for bulk purchases for sales promotion, premiums, fund-raising, educational or institutional use.

Special book excerpts or customized printings can also be created to fit specific needs. For details, write or phone the office of the Kensington Special Sales Manager: Kensington Publishing Corp., 850 Third Avenue, New York, NY 10022. Attn. Special Sales Department. Phone: 1-800-221-2647.

Kensington and the K logo Reg. U.S. Pat. & TM Off.

First Trade Paperback Printing: February 2004
First Mass Market Paperback Printing: January 2005
10 9 8 7 6 5 4 3 2 1

Printed in the United States of America

Acknowledgments

In spite of what we authors like to think, we are never solely responsible for our books. There are the librarians whom we pester with bizarre questions, the friends of friends who might know something about some obscure research fact without which we can't go on, our families, and our colleagues.

DRIVE ME CRAZY was typical. I had help from so many sources that I can never thank them all, but some do deserve special recognition. I am especially indebted to an Oregon police officer who cannot be named, but I hope she knows how very much I appreciate her patient explanations about police procedure, murder investigation, and day-to-day life on the beat.

I adore librarians. They know such a lot, and what they don't know they can find out. I loved having a librarian heroine in this book, and I hope she put to rest a few stereotypes. Thanks to my librarian on the inside, Michelle Olson, for all her help and wonderful stream-of-consciousness letters about what librarians do all day. Thanks also to Galaxie Library, Dakota County, Minnesota.

I want to thank my brilliant editor, Kate Duffy, from the bottom of my heart. She is three of my favorite things: she's smart, she's funny, and she cares. This time, I really made her work!

And I'd have to use the same three attributes for my

agent—smart, funny, caring Robin Rue, who makes everything seem so easy.

My faithful and patient family put up with me on deadline, have all learned how to cook and clean, and can usually figure out where I left the car keys. Rick, James, and Emma, you are the best.

And, finally, to my readers who asked for a bigger book, here it is. I hope you enjoy. Come and visit me on the web at www.nancywarren.net. You are always welcome.

Chapter 1

Duncan Forbes knew he was going to like Swiftcurrent, Oregon, when he discovered the town librarian looked like the town hooker. Not a streetwalker who hustles tricks on the corner, but a high-class "escort" who looks like a million bucks and costs at least that much, ending up with her own Park Avenue co-op.

He loved that kind of woman.

He saw her feet first when she strode into view while he was crouched on the gray-blue industrial carpeting of Swiftcurrent's library, scanning the bottom shelf of reference books for a local business directory. He was about to give up in defeat when those long, sexy feet appeared, the toes painted crimson, perched on do-me-baby stilettos.

Naturally, the sight of those feet encouraged his gaze to travel north, and he wasn't disappointed.

Her legs were curvy but sleek, her red-and-black skirt gratifyingly short. The academic in him might register that those shoes were hard on the woman's spine but as she reached up to place a book on a high shelf, the man in him liked the resulting curve of her back, the seductive, round ass perched high.

From down here, he had a great view of shapely hips, a taut belly, and breasts so temptingly displayed they ought to have a "for sale" sign on them.

He shouldn't stare. He knew that, but couldn't help himself—torn between the view up her skirt and that of the underside of her chest. He felt like a kid in a candy store, gobbling everything in sight, knowing he'd soon be kicked out and his spree would end.

Sure enough, while he was lost in contemplation of the perfect angle of her thigh, the way it sloped gracefully upward to where paradise lurked, she looked down and caught him ogling. Her face was as sensual and gorgeous as her body—sleek black hair, creamy skin, and plump red lips. For that instant, when their gazes first connected, he felt as though something mystical occurred, though it could have been a surge of lust shorting his brain.

Her eyes went from liquid pewter to prison-bar gray in the time it took her to realize that he hadn't been down here staring at library books. What the hell was the matter with him, acting like a fourteen-year-old pervert?

"Can I help you with something?"

Since he'd been caught at her feet, staring up her skirt, he muttered the first words that came into his head. "Honey, I can't begin to tell you all the ways you could help me."

The prison bars seemed to slam down around him. "Do you need a specific reference volume? A library card? Directions to the exit?"

The woman might look as though her photo ought to hang in auto garages reminding the grease monkeys what month it was, but her words filled him with grim foreboding. He was so screwed.

"You're the librarian?"

A ray of winter sunlight stole swiftly across the gray ice of her eyes. "Yes."

"But you're all wrong for a librarian," he spluttered helplessly.

"I'd best return my master's degree then."

"I mean . . ." He gazed at her from delicious top to scrumptious bottom. "Where's your hair bun? And bifocals? And the crepe-soled brogues and . . . and the tweeds?"

If anything, her breasts became perkier as she huffed a quick breath in and out. "It's a small mind that thinks in clichés."

"And a big mouth that spouts them," he admitted. God, what an idiot. He'd spent enough time with books to know that librarians came in all shapes and sizes, though, in fairness, he'd never seen one like this before. He scrambled to his feet, feeling better once he'd resumed his full height and was gazing down at her, where he discovered the view was just as good. He gave her his best shot at a charming grin. "I bet the literacy rate among men in this town is amazingly high."

"Is there something I can help you with?"

So much for the charming grin. "Yes. Art."

If anything, her gaze froze deeper. If he came back here, he'd have to remember long underwear and a hot water bottle. "As in, you'd like to show me your etchings?"

Couldn't blame her, he supposed. She probably got hit on all the time. And he hadn't exactly come across as suave. "As in, where's your art section?"

"Photographic? Plastic? Sculp—"

"Paintings. Impressionist through modern."

She glared at him as though waiting for the punch line to an off-color joke. When none came, she snapped, "This way."

She led him past rows of books lined up with military precision, though it was her much more alluring backside that held his attention. He shrugged. If she didn't want men looking, then what was she doing dressing like that?

"There you are." She indicated a section small enough that he deduced Swiftcurrent, Oregon, didn't rate fine arts all that highly.

"Thank you." A quick glance told him he wouldn't find anything of interest. The art books were standard small-library fare, enough for a grade-nine essay on "my favorite artist." Needless to say, his book on Gauguin wasn't on the shelves.

"Anything else?" How could a package so hot emit sounds so cold?

"Yes." He turned back to her. "Newspaper files. Are they on computer?"

"For which paper?"

"The local one." Damn, he'd forgotten the name.

"The *Swiftcurrent News*. Yes. We have files going back twenty years."

"On computer?"

His hopeful entreaty was met with a bitchy smirk. "Microfiche."

He might have known.

"If you plan to take anything out of the library, you will of course need a library card, Mr. . . . ?"

His ego might wish she were asking his name for personal reasons, but he wasn't that stupid. She was worried he might pilfer one of her precious books.

"Duncan Forbes."

She nodded, and pointed to a corner. The library was all on one level, small enough that he could see from one end to the other without squinting. It was part of a fairly new-looking municipal building constructed of river rock and cedar that also contained city hall and the police department. The complex was set in a paved courtyard with a few trees in stone tubs. Across the pedestrian-only square was a row of retail places: a café, a health food store, and an outdoor equipment outlet he'd already patronized.

He felt the urge to head back over to check out more climbing grips. Instead, he followed the icy but sexy librarian once more.

Duncan took a seat in front of the microfiche reader in the area marked Periodicals.

"Which issues of the *Swiftcurrent News* do you require?"

Man, her looks were at odds with her personality. She talked like a fifty-year-old spinster. "Every issue for the past six months."

With a frown at him, as though she were trying to think of a reason to refuse, she finally slipped a stretchy red thing like a coiled telephone cord from around her wrist and fitted a key hanging from it into the lock of the cabinet below the fiche reader. After carefully removing a plastic file box as though it contained the CIA's most secret files, she relocked the cabinet and placed the box at his elbow.

She walked away then, but he felt her eyes lasering into his back as he set up.

He was familiar enough with microfiche that he didn't have to ask the ice queen for anything. Not that it was completely her fault they hadn't hit it off right away. Tact had never been his strong suit.

"Should wear a pair of support hose at least, and a cardigan," he mumbled to himself as he flipped through the fiches and started six months back.

A couple of months earlier, an intriguing rumor had reached his ears that a certain art and antiques dealer, Franklin Forrest, had some information on a Van Gogh missing since World War II. The source was reliable:

Duncan's Uncle Simon, who had better underground connections than the London tube the old man rode every day.

Since the family that was the rightful owner of the missing Van Gogh landscape was among Duncan's clients, he'd cleared his schedule as quickly as he could and followed the rumor out west.

Before he contacted Franklin Forrest, Duncan wanted to get a feel for the place where the man lived and worked, see if he showed up in local news clippings.

He squinted at the blurry image on the screen and adjusted the focus, then began to read.

Within half an hour he received worse news than he could have imagined when he stumbled across Franklin Forrest's obituary.

Forrest had been an art student in Paris when the Nazis invaded Poland and, according to the rumor that had brought Duncan here, had known the young man who'd supposedly hidden the Van Gogh—a Frenchman and a fellow art student who was later killed fighting for the Resistance. Now Forrest was dead and with him the first faint lead to the missing painting's whereabouts in more than half a century.

Shit. *Shit, shit shit!*

Automatically, Duncan started scribbling notes even as he tried to take in the depressing probability that he'd come all the way to this backwater for nothing.

Mr. Forrest had been an old man, more than eighty when he died, but still Duncan couldn't believe his bad luck. He'd missed the man by a mere two months.

Shit.

"Mr. Forbes!"

The sharply shouted accusation made him jump a mile. He glared at the red-faced librarian standing over him like *Playboy's* version of the wrath of God.

"Aren't you supposed to whisper in a library?" he asked. "You damn near gave me a heart attack."

"What do you think you're doing?" Her voice vibrated with loathing.

"Research, sister. What do you call it?"

"I call it defacing public property."

He blinked, then followed the accusing line of her arm right down to her red-painted fingertip, which pointed, like a blood-tipped arrow, to the open reference book on which he'd mindlessly scribbled notes.

"Shit. I mean damn. Sorry. Forgot it wasn't my own book."

"Apparently."

"Hey, it was just a mistake. I'll replace the book."

"You certainly will. Come this way."

"Wait, I'm not—"

But he was wasting his breath. She snapped the book closed, picked it up as though he weren't worthy to touch the thing, and marched to the checkout desk.

He followed. "Now, just a damn minute. I still need that book."

"That's lucky. Because you're purchasing it."

Fair enough. He was willing to buy the book. He wanted his notes. He pulled out his wallet and waited as she ran the bar code through a scanner. He wondered sourly why they could computerize that and not the newspaper archives.

She pushed a lot of buttons on her computer/cash register combo while he stood there feeling like a kid who'd just pulled detention.

At last he heard the whir of a printer.

"That will be one hundred and forty-eight dollars," she said crisply. "How do you wish to pay?"

What did she take him for? "A hundred and forty-eight bucks?" He glared at her and grabbed the book, flipped it over. The price was printed on the back cover. "Look. Right there is the price. Forty-one dollars."

"That's right." She sounded cheerful for the first time since they'd met. "Forty-one for the book," she said in her clear, musical voice. She grabbed the print-out and slapped it in front of him. A couple of older women strolled by and shot him a suspicious glance. He gritted his teeth.

"Plus a seven dollar restocking fee." She pointed to the last item with relish. "And a one hundred dollar fine for defacing municipal property."

He placed both hands on the desk and leaned forward until he was close enough to see the flecks of gold in the center of each iris, close enough to smell—he wasn't sure what. Jasmine, maybe. Some kind of flower much too sweet to lend its fragrance to this woman.

"You don't have the authority to issue fines."

She didn't appear remotely intimidated as he towered over her, or ruffled by his temper. "As a matter of fact, I do. But, if you like, I can call city hall and have Sergeant Perkins issue you the ticket, or if he's not in, the chief of police himself will take care of it. Then you'll be escorted next door to pay your fine and it's up to the law enforcement officer whether he wants to add vandalism or public mischief charges. Those carry jail time." She shrugged elegant shoulders. "Up to you."

He pulled out his wallet and glared at her. "I don't suppose you take credit cards?"

"Cash or check." She glanced at him. "Certified."

It was obvious she was hoping he had neither, so she could toss him in jail.

He dug out bills, glad he'd hit the bank yesterday, slapping three fifties down. While he waited for his change, he tapped his fingertips on the countertop. Everything was all neat and orderly, color-coded and

Dewey-decimaled within an inch of its life. A small brass-and-wood plaque read A. M. Forrest, Head Librarian. Not so much as a finger mark smudged its shining brilliance.

His fingers stopped tapping. *Forrest?* There was only the one librarian that he'd seen. Was it possible that the ice bitch's last name was Forrest? In a town this size, chances were everyone who shared a name was closely related. He recalled the obituary. There had been two granddaughters. One was Genevieve, Germaine, something with a G. The other was . . . Alexandra. That was it. A. M. Forrest looked to be in her late twenties, which put her about the right age to be one of Forrest's granddaughters.

This day just kept heading south. Inside his head he shouted every foul curse he'd ever heard. He kept his lips firmly clamped, though. Let one of those curses escape and the librarian would have him locked up on death row.

While she meticulously counted out his change, he decided to find out if his dreadful suspicion was true. "A. M. Forrest," he said as pleasantly as a man who's paying a punitive fine for an honest mistake could. "What's the A. M. for?"

She paused and he kept right on looking at her, his brows raised. She must know if she didn't tell him he'd find out easily enough what her name was. "Alexandra Michelle."

He was never sorrier to have made a correct assumption. Well, if she was the granddaughter of Franklin Forrest, and a remaining link to the man he'd hoped to see, he was going to have to grovel himself into her good books. He'd traveled a long way. If she knew anything about her grandfather's affairs, there was hope he could still salvage some scrap of information from his trip. He swallowed his annoyance. "Can I call you Alex?"

"You can call me Ms. Forrest."

His lead on the Van Gogh, already slim, was hanging on by its teeth. He picked up his book and strode for the door. Damn it, Uncle Simon's connections were amazing and he wouldn't pass on information to Duncan unless he were convinced it was true.

As much as Duncan was tempted to take his extremely pricey library book and blow town, he'd be a lot smarter to hang around for a bit and discover whether Franklin Forrest had somehow left his knowledge behind.

He glanced back to find the frosty Forrest granddaughter watching him, obviously not planning to let him out of her sight until he was off the premises.

It was clear from the obit that Forrest, a widower, was close to his two granddaughters who lived here in town. He'd bet his hundred-and-forty-eight-buck book that if anyone alive knew what Louis Vendome had done with the Van Gogh in that crazy time after France fell, it was the librarian or her cousin.

A. M. Forrest probably thought she was rid of her book-defacing patron, but she'd find out differently, very soon.

In fact, why spoil the anticipation?

Almost at the double doors leading outside to the town square, he turned. "What time do you open in the morning?"

Her look of horror was almost worth the hundred and fifty bucks. "You're coming back?"

"Oh, yeah."

"Why?"

Libraries were supposed to be free for anyone to enter, but instead of calling her on it, he decided to give her part of the truth in hopes it would improve her opinion of him. "I teach at a university back east. I'm on sabbatical, writing a book, and plan to do a lot of work here in the library."

Her eyes widened to the point he was afraid her eyeballs might roll out of her head. *"You're* a university professor?" She stared at him and then at the book he'd just been forced to buy.

"It's a small mind that thinks in clichés," he reminded her. "What time tomorrow?"

She was still staring at him as though in shock. "N-nine o'clock."

He let his gaze dwell insolently on her mouth. "It's a date, then. *Alex.*"

She swallowed, a convulsive jerk of her throat. She might have the personality of a death camp matron, but that didn't prevent the impulse to run his lips over her long, smooth neck, his tongue along the strong hint of cleavage revealed by her tight black sweater.

He trod slowly back to her, enjoying the way her eyes darkened and her breath jerked in her chest.

He leaned once more over the counter, much more slowly this time, until he was close enough to catch another tantalizing whiff of jasmine, close enough to see her lips tremble slightly as they slipped apart.

Close enough to kiss her.

He spent a moment enjoying her reaction to his nearness. Not all ice, was she? Oh, no. There was warmth and passion under the surface. He derived a perverse pleasure from watching the pulse in her throat kick up.

For one more moment he stayed there. Still, silent, and so far in her personal space he was practically sharing her underwear.

Then he grabbed the printout off the counter. "Forgot my receipt."

Chapter 2

A lex was never late for work, but this morning she
made sure to arrive extra early. She was determined
to have the library fully operational when—and if—the
odious Duncan Forbes arrived. She couldn't keep him
out, unfortunately, since this was a public building, but
she could certainly keep a close eye on him and his roving ballpoint.

Not to mention his roving eye.

She unlocked her office, booted up her computer,
and started the coffee, as she did every morning. She
measured the coffee carefully, using the rich, dark rain-
forest blend she purchased from the Italian café in her
neighborhood. As she wiped a trace of spilled coffee from
the white counter in the tiny coffee room, she thought
about Duncan Forbes as she'd been doing with annoy-
ing frequency since yesterday.

There was something about him she didn't trust.
She'd been so flabbergasted when he'd announced he
was a professor that she'd let him go without challenging him. But if he were an academician writing a book,

why wouldn't he go to one of the university libraries at Eugene or Portland or Corvallis? Even a big city library would make more sense. She did her best with a limited budget, and the Internet brought instant access to all kinds of research, but Swiftcurrent was still a very odd choice.

She wondered what he taught. Wished she'd had wit enough to ask him. Outdoor recreation, maybe, or forestry. Something that kept him outside a good deal.

Forbes didn't look like a professor of anything. She tapped her fingers against the once-again immaculate counter as she tried to decide what he did look like. His image appeared in her mind immediately, and as clearly as though he stood in front of her. Brown hair streaked with blond, weathered skin, squint lines around the eyes, as though he'd spent a lot of time in the sun.

His clothes were rumpled casual in natural fabrics. He wore rugged leather walking shoes and he'd carried a sturdy canvas pack.

A wanderer, that's what he looked like. She imagined that sun-streaked hair blowing in the wind, the blue eyes squinting at the horizon, and smiled to herself. Not just any wanderer. A pirate. A modern-day pirate with plunder in his blood, who took without asking. He'd certainly helped himself to the view up her skirt without permission.

That had been bad enough. Worse had been the dizzying rush of attraction she'd felt when she'd first caught him eyeing her with his deep blue pirate's gaze. For one wild second she'd imagined she'd quite like to be plundered.

She slapped the counter as though the white laminate were having the inappropriate impulses. A footloose pirate was exactly the kind of man she didn't need complicating her life.

Leaving the coffee room, where heavenly smells were already beginning to waft, she headed for the books.

While the computer was booting and the coffee brewing, it was her habit to walk through the quiet library and make sure all was in order. The cleaners had been in last night. She still shuddered at the memory of the night they'd left behind a spray bottle of window cleaner and a couple of sixth grade hooligans had found it first.

Stepping out from behind the checkout desk, she decided that if Mr. Forbes returned today, she'd remind him of all the superior research centers in other parts of Oregon.

The man was sexy as hell in a sleepy, rumpled way, but she'd be busy for the next few months with her own agenda. She'd given herself until the summer to get her grandfather's life story from audio tape to print and her grandparents' house sold. Once all that was done, she'd help hire her replacement and then she was out of here. She'd find a job in a big, exciting city where anything was possible and people were too busy to gossip about her and her cousin.

The only reason she'd come back to Swiftcurrent was to look after her grandfather once her grandmother passed on. Now that he was gone . . . The pang of grief was a small, sharp pain in her chest. She rubbed it, feeling the outline of the necklace Grandpa had given her for her twenty-first birthday.

He'd been an old man who'd lived a good life, but still it was hard to believe she'd never see him again.

She shook off her gloom. It was time to get back to her life plan. Marriage before she was thirty-two—well, it was her modified plan. Originally she'd planned to be married by thirty, but since her big birthday last month, she'd had to adjust her life map. She still hoped to have her first child before she hit thirty-five and her ovaries started emitting warning signals.

For her plan to work, she needed to move to a bigger city where she might actually find a decent, well-educated man in her age range with good eyes and strong teeth, who was good in bed and a good conversationalist. In Swiftcurrent, you could find up to three of those attributes in any one single guy. But Alex was particular. She wanted them all.

She had one other unshakable requirement. He had to be a stay-put kind of man. She wouldn't put her kids through the vagabond life she'd lived.

Besides, a move out of Swiftcurrent was a move away from her troubled cousin. The familiar feeling of helpless frustration smacked her at the thought of Gillian, so she put that thought firmly away, the way she'd put a damaged book in the basement storage room.

She loved the first luxuriously peaceful minutes of the day. Everything was as quiet as a library should be and in perfect order. She walked among the stacks, breathing the smell of books. The paper and glue, old leather and dust. The smell of learning. She loved being alone with volumes crammed with ideas and knowledge, waiting to be explored. She stopped to straighten a row in the children's section, then noticed that the Goosebumps were out of order and took a moment to numerate them correctly.

If there was a phrase that made her cringe, it was the young mother telling her child to "put that book back where you found it." In her experience, toddlers who hadn't mastered the toilet weren't ready for the finer points of Dewey decimal.

It wasn't a big library, but she was proud of how many resources she could offer the people of this small town. There were two computers with Internet access, plus books for all ages, which she updated twice a year. She'd be able to offer an extra hundred dollars' worth, thanks to Mr. Forbes, she thought, as she strolled down Antiques and stepped around the end to the next aisle.

Where she stopped in her tracks and slapped her hand over her mouth.

This morning, there were no stray cloths or bottles of cleaning solution littering the library.

There was a man lying facedown on the floor.

For a stunned second or two she simply stood and stared.

His feet were toward her, so the first thing she noticed was black shoes with crepe soles. He wore navy slacks and a navy windbreaker. His neck was ruddy and his thick hair more salt than pepper. His arms were on either side of his head, almost as though he were about to do a push-up. A heavy gold ring with a dark red stone adorned the ring finger of his right hand.

She noted all this in the instant it took her to realize that something was wrong. Very wrong.

Her first thought, that a homeless guy had somehow sneaked in and slept here all night, she quickly dismissed when she saw the decent clothes, crisp lines of a recent haircut, and the ring. In the next instant, her skin turned clammy. He looked awfully still and he slept without a sound.

And what was that smell?

Dropping to her knees beside him, she put a trembling hand to his shoulder and squeezed. "Sir?"

No response.

Nausea rose, but still she managed to put two fingers to his neck in search of a pulse, only to draw them back with a helpless moan. His flesh was as cold as marble and almost as stiff. There was no pulse that she could detect.

For the first time she understood the term *stone, cold dead*.

She crouched over the man, scrubbing the fingers that had touched him against her thigh.

Help. She had to get help. There was a phone in her office, but she wasn't near brave enough to hang around having a tête-à-tête with a corpse while she waited for the police. She'd run next door and get Tom or the chief. They'd know what to do.

Run being the operative word.

She took off at a sprint. She barreled through the library, rounding the corner so fast she put out a hand to hang onto an end cap and knocked *Interior Decorating for Beginners*, Third Edition, onto the floor.

It was an indication of her level of panic that she didn't even consider pausing to reshelve the book sprawled untidily on the floor, but kept running.

Only to smack into something warm and hard.

That grabbed her.

She screamed, horror-movie visions of psycho killers overcoming her common sense. Strong arms tightened, and she bucked and struggled wildly. Kicking, scratching, squirming—fright lending her supernatural strength.

Her fist connected with flesh in a satisfyingly deep jab.

Immediately, the arms released her. "Ow! Alex! It's me. Duncan Forbes. Hey, what's wrong?"

The voice. She knew the voice. As the words penetrated the veil of terror covering her senses, she stopped struggling and drew a breath, focusing on the strong, rugged planes of the face in front of her. She'd think about how foolish she'd acted later. For now, even a book defacer was a comforting presence in comparison to a psychotic murderer.

"He's dead," she said in a small voice, pointing, ashamed to note that her entire arm trembled.

"Dead? Who's dead?"

"The man. On the floor. Between Art and Home Decorating."

Duncan Forbes didn't look all that shocked by her explanation. He had, she realized, eyes that had seen everything, broad shoulders that encouraged a woman to lay her head—and her problems—there. There was a solidness to him. If there was trouble he'd get to the bottom of it. A fight to be fought, he'd fight it. A dead man on the floor, he'd deal with it.

For a woman who already had too much weight on her own shoulders, such a man looked tempting indeed.

Duncan Forbes gave her arms a brisk rub. "You okay?"

She nodded. *Liar.*

"Wait here," he said, and headed off to investigate. Now that Duncan Forbes was here, she didn't feel such a strong urge to run, and she realized she couldn't leave her post. Forcing herself to march back through the door and into the library, she walked straight to her office and phoned the sergeant.

"Tom's across the street getting donuts," Raeanne Collins, the police department receptionist, told her in a cheerful tone. "He'll just be a minute. Want him to call you?"

"No. Ask him to come straight over. I'm closing the library so he'll have to use his master key or knock."

"Oh, my gosh! You didn't close that time you had pneumonia. Were you all robbed?"

If Alex told gossipy Raeanne there was a dead man in her library, the entire county would know about it long before Tom made his choice between cream-filled and sprinkles.

"No. We weren't robbed. There's a . . . situation I'd like his advice about."

"Is there anything I—"

DRIVE ME CRAZY 25

God, no. "No. Tell Tom to bring me over a cinnamon sugar." The very idea of a donut was enough to make her gag, but her request would squelch Raeanne's curiosity.

She locked up the library, then reluctantly went back to the dead man.

As she dragged her feet back to the spot, she braced herself to face a deceased man facedown on her floor, but even so she suffered a second shock.

"What are you doing?" she shrieked.

So much for her ridiculous fantasy that a man who scribbled on library books could be counted on in an emergency. The fool had flipped the corpse onto its back.

"I was checking to make sure he was dead."

Oh. The man had no pulse and felt like a slab of granite. That had been good enough for her. "Is he?"

Duncan Forbes glanced up. "Oh, yeah."

Something about the way he spoke made her look at the body again, and the minute she did so, she wished she hadn't. There was a ragged hole in his chest that appeared black and crusty and from it spread a dark, oily stain that had to be blood. The swarthy, middle-aged face was hideous in its final grimace.

"Oh, God. He was . . . he was . . ." She slapped a hand over her mouth as nausea choked her. The sickly smell of blood and death was worse, now the corpse was faceup.

Ignoring her distress, Forbes calmly completed her sentence. "Murdered. Yes. Recognize him?"

She forced herself to look at the man, really look at him. "No." She swallowed. If the stranger could be matter-of-fact, so could she. "Why would anybody murder a man inside a library? It doesn't make sense."

He shook his head. "Nobody did."

"What? You think he killed himself in here?" She glanced around. "Where's the gun?"

"He was murdered, all right. But not here."

How did Forbes know that? Who was he anyway? Two strangers came into her library within twenty-four hours, one live and one dead. Could it be a coincidence? Damn, she wished Tom would hurry. As one of the only bachelors in town young enough to sport a good head of hair and his own teeth, Tom was popular and prey to matchmakers of every description. She supposed even getting donuts involved chitchat—especially since Val at the donut shop had a single daughter she'd been trying to fix him up with for years.

Meanwhile, Alex was stuck in here. For all she knew, the live stranger had killed the dead one. She rubbed her chilled arms. "I called the police."

"Good."

Silence stretched and she couldn't stand it any longer. She wished someone would come in, if only to return a book. But, of course, they wouldn't now that she'd closed the library.

"How do you know he wasn't killed here?"

"Not enough blood. He was shot first, then dumped here."

"Is that why there was no bullet hole in the back of his jacket?" That's why she hadn't noticed right away that he'd been shot.

"That would be my guess. He was shot, bundled into the jacket, and brought here."

Great. Just great. They couldn't dump the body in Earl's Pizzeria, or Val's goddamn donut shop, no. The murderer had to put the dead guy in *her* library.

"Why? Why would anyone put a body here? Where I'd be bound to find it?"

The look Duncan Forbes sent her was piercing. His eyes were a deep, earthy blue. Not cloudless skies, or limpid-lakes blue, but the blue of lapis dug out of the ground.

"I've been wondering that myself," he said. "Do you have any enemies?"

Besides you? she almost answered, but she couldn't return a flip answer to his question, given the circumstances. "What are you suggesting?"

"I'm trying to figure out why the killer dumped the body here, where you were obviously going to be the first one to stumble over it. Why?"

The chill spread from her arms and danced down her spine. "Of course I don't have enemies. Anyway, I fail to see how putting a dead body in my library is punishing me."

"Maybe it's a warning, or message of some kind. Are you in any kind of trouble?"

He continued to gaze at her with concern and a measure of disbelief, which immediately had her stretching to think of anyone who might wish her harm. Winnifred Pouch, who'd been an unsuccessful candidate for a part-time librarian's job, had been pretty upset with her. When she'd taken to traveling a hundred miles to have her hair done rather than entrusting it to Katie's Kut 'n' Kurl, Katie had made her feelings known to everyone in town who wanted to listen, but that was as far as she could stretch in search of enemies.

She and her cousin Gillian had had some major-doozie fights in their time, but they were family. That was different. Anyway, who was Duncan Forbes to be giving her the willies? If what he'd told her was true, he was a college teacher, not a cop. Obviously, the man was having the first bit of excitement in his humdrum life and it had gone straight to his head.

"Anything you want to tell me before the cops arrive?"

"Like what?" The only thing she wanted to tell him was good-bye. But before she got the chance, Tom Perkins arrived. He called her name and she answered with relief, "Over here."

She'd known Tom since they were teenagers. A solid, good-looking kid who excelled at sports and won sportsmanship awards and had only ever fought once as she recalled—when a handicapped kid got picked on—Tom had the perfect job. However, if there'd ever been a murder in Swiftcurrent, she hadn't heard of it. Didn't look like Tom had had much truck with murder, either. He turned pale gray at the sight of the dead man and sweat broke out on his forehead.

"Holy mother of God," he said. "Somebody shot the poor schmuck right through the heart."

Alex hadn't thought about it in such graphic terms, but the hole was in the left side of the corpse's chest. Yep, *right through the heart* pretty much summed it up.

Once Tom had pulled himself together, he took charge and Alex was happy to shift the responsibility. He checked for vital signs, but it didn't take long to confirm the guy was dead.

Tom considered the man staring sightlessly up at him and made a quick visual scan of the area. "Did either of you move the body?"

"I flipped him over to see if he was dead," Forbes said in that same cool, matter-of-fact tone he'd used on her.

"And you are?"

"Duncan Forbes. I arrived in town yesterday. I'll be in Swiftcurrent for a few weeks writing a book."

Tom's stare told them both what he thought of civilians interfering in crime scenes, but he didn't say anything. He squatted, slipped on surgical gloves, and went systematically through the dead man's pockets. They yielded nothing. No wallet, no ID, not so much as a stick of gum or candy wrapper.

"I want you both to go into Alex's office and wait there for me. Don't touch anything on the way."

She nodded. He got out a cell phone, while still crouched over the body, and she knew the quiet library would soon be a lot busier. "Bert, we've got a homicide," she heard him say, obviously talking to Chief Bert Harmon, a hefty southerner who did the administrative work and left Tom to handle law enforcement. "We're going to need a Major Crimes Team. Can you start calling them in? I'll call the M.E."

She shuddered at the thought. Because Swiftcurrent's population of 7,500 wasn't large enough to support much of a police force, the area shared resources. She knew Tom had been called out to help in other towns when people went missing or a major crime occurred. Obviously, it was now Swiftcurrent's turn to call in the team.

"Yes," Tom continued, "the area's secure. No. Victim's a stranger. No ID. Right, Bert. When you come over, can you bring the camera?"

He glanced over at Duncan and his gaze hardened. "I'm not sure. Maybe." She didn't want to think about what question he was answering.

Chapter 3

Duncan glanced at his pale companion. So she did go by Alex. The shortened name suited her. It was crisp and businesslike but with a hint of the more exotic and oh-so-feminine Alexandra. "Are you okay?"

"I'm all right. It's just hearing Tom call it a homicide makes me feel a bit weak at the knees."

Her eyes were soft now, the gray of mourning doves and gentle rains.

When he'd first arrived, the sergeant had looked as though he might toss his cookies and mess up the crime scene, but he managed to pull it together. He might not be all that familiar with murders, but he knew the drill.

As he and Alex made their way to her office, he glanced around but nothing seemed out of place. Was it a coincidence that the body had been placed in the art section? Duncan didn't believe so.

Once in her office, he took a moment to look around. Her workspace was as efficient as he would have guessed. Neat and well organized. A computer already humming. She must have come in here first, then, before discovering the body. The scent of coffee reached him and he realized she'd started that as well, in what must be her daily routine—before her day went all to hell.

While she sank into her desk chair and stared blankly ahead to her computer screen, he slipped quietly out of the office and followed his nose to the coffee machine. He poured two mugs and brought them into her office. "You take milk and sugar?"

Alex clasped the mug in her hands, obviously needing the warmth, but didn't sip. "Do you mind? There's skim in the fridge."

He fetched the milk and watched her add a healthy dose. Then she sipped and nodded, sending him a small smile and pushing the carton back his way. Obligingly, he returned the milk to the fridge.

Sipping his own coffee, he returned to her office and sat in a visitor's chair that was too small for his frame. The blond wood dug into his back just below the shoulder blades and the too-short seat cut off the circulation in his thighs.

At least she brewed decent coffee, he thought, as he scanned her office, disappointingly lacking in clues about her life. No photos, stuffed toys, dishes of candy. The only personal touch—if you could call it that—was a framed copy of her master's degree in library sciences, from the University of Illinois.

He was lost in his own thoughts, and it seemed Alex was, too. She pretended to check her e-mail but he thought she was staring at the screen to avoid having to talk to him. "Don't delete any e-mails. Just in case," he warned her and finally saw some animation in her pale face when she glared at him.

That was more like the woman he'd met yesterday. She must be getting over the shock.

A portly, older, uniformed officer arrived with a camera and video recorder and a black plastic case. For fin-

gerprints, Duncan guessed. "That's the police chief,"
Alex informed him. "Bert Harmon."

After a while, Perkins came into the office with another uniform. In the hour or so since they'd found the
body, about half a dozen officers had arrived, including
two plainclothes guys who looked like FBI.

"Alex, would you mind going next door and giving
your statement to Detective Remco here?"

She nodded and rose, tossing a questioning look his
way.

"I'm going to take Mr. Forbes's statement right here."

Duncan pulled out his wallet and dug out a business
card from Swarthmore. It gave his position—Associate
Professor, Art History—and the usual contact info.
Duncan pulled out a pen and added his cell number. As
he handed it to the sergeant, Alex tilted her head as
though to read it, so he scribbled his cell number on a
second card and handed it to her.

"I'm currently on sabbatical from Swarthmore, writing a book. I came here looking for a quiet place to
write."

Perkins scratched his chin with the top of a ballpoint. "You're writing a book about art?" From the in-
flection in the man's voice, he was questioning either
Duncan's sanity or his masculinity. He wasn't certain
which.

"Yes."

Alex left, but not before he'd caught her blink of surprise. She either hadn't believed him, or thought he
taught at some McCollege in the hinterlands. What a
trusting woman.

Perkins pulled out a small tape recorder and a notebook. "We don't have fancy interview rooms next door,
so I'd just as soon take your statement right here."

"Fine by me."

The sergeant started the recorder, gave his name, Duncan's name, and the date and time of the interview.

"Where are you staying while you're in town, Professor?"

"Riverside Cottage Suites. Unit eight."

The sergeant nodded. "You'll need to stay in town while we investigate."

"I'll be around for a couple of months, most likely." He'd decided to spend a bit of time with Forrest's granddaughters and anyone else in town who might have known Franklin Forrest. Dig around a little. Try and find clues to the missing painting while writing his book as cover.

"Do you have any other ID on you, Professor?"

And so the tedious interview began. The cop might be the plodding, methodical sort, but he wasn't stupid. His gaze was penetrating and his seemingly idle questions anything but. Duncan wasn't stupid, either. With no decent suspects on the horizon, he, the stranger in town, was the perfect guy to pin the murder on.

"It's quite a coincidence, you and the dead guy both showing up in town on the same day."

"Coincidences happen."

"Cops hate them." Perkins scratched the back of his head. "Why'd you move the body?"

"I didn't move it. I flipped it over to confirm the guy was dead. Can't give CPR to someone's back."

"He was pretty far beyond CPR." Perkins leaned forward and sent Duncan a man-to-man look. "We've got a problem. When you rolled the body over, you got your fingerprints on him. That doesn't look good for you. If there's something you want to get off your chest, now's a good time."

"Are you planning to arrest me?"

"Why don't you tell me what really happened."

He couldn't blame the guy. He'd have acted the same in his shoes.

"I arrived at the library right after it opened because I wanted to get an early start on my work. Ms. Forrest came running out of the library and told me there was a dead man inside. We came back inside together."

"Did you know the victim?"

"No." It was true enough. They'd never been introduced.

"Were you ever alone with the body?"

"Yes. When Ms. Forrest went to her office to phone you. She was gone about three minutes."

"What did you do while she was gone?"

"I told you. I turned him over to confirm he was dead."

"Anything else?"

Sergeant Perkins wasn't going to like this, but he'd find out as soon as the forensics report came in. "I checked for ID."

"Did you find any?"

He narrowed his eyes. "No."

"Professor, could I have your permission to search that backpack you've got there?"

There was silence as they stared at each other. The tiny sound of the whirring tape was audible. If he refused he looked guilty and they'd get a search warrant. "All right."

"And would you mind emptying your pockets for me? It's just routine."

Yeah, right.

He passed over his backpack and made noisy work out of dumping change out of his pockets along with his wallet, Swiss army knife, and keys.

The sergeant opened his pack and went through it pretty thoroughly. He opened the laptop computer but didn't try to boot it up. If he was disappointed not to find the dead man's wallet or the gun that killed him, Perkins hid it well.

"Thanks for your cooperation," he said, after he'd flipped through Duncan's wallet and returned everything.

Perkins leaned back and put an ankle over one knee. "So, what's your book about?" he asked.

"The history of a few famous French Impressionist paintings." In fact, the book was about how those paintings had gone missing, and the story of their recovery. One day, he hoped the story of Van Gogh's *Olive Trees and Farmhouse* would be a chapter, but that one was still being written.

Alex drank three cups of coffee, not because she needed any more jitters in her system, but for something to do. After the initial drama and adrenaline rush of finding a dead body between Picasso and Martha Stewart, the business of documenting the evidence and seeing the body off the premises took on a tedious life of its own.

By the time the grim lump was trundled out of the building on a stretcher into the coroner's van, it was almost two o'clock. A team of half a dozen people, most of them called in from the county sheriff's office and state and local agencies, were busy out in her library, while several more officers searched outside.

Remco was a hard-eyed detective she'd never seen before who never stopped moving as he interviewed her. A foot tapping here, fingers drumming his knee there, now shifting in his chair as though it were uncomfortable, then rubbing his stomach as though he had an ulcer. And his questions came fast and sudden, making her feel tongue-tied and guilty, as though she'd committed a terrible crime, not discovered one.

"Did you know the victim?"

"No."

"Had you ever seen him before today?"

"No."

"When did you first meet Duncan Forbes?"

"Yesterday."

"Do you own a gun?"

"No!"

Had she heard anything? Seen anything? Seen anyone? Noticed anything out of the ordinary when she arrived this morning?

"No." Just the dead man.

By the time Remco was done with her she felt light-headed and her mouth was so dry her tongue felt like flypaper. So she drank more coffee. And waited.

"When can I reopen the library, Bert?" she asked the chief when she passed his open office door. She could already see paperwork piling up on his desk.

"The forensics boys should be done today. I'll call you when they're done and you can get the cleaners in tonight and open tomorrow, probably." His kindly face squinted as he glanced at his paper-strewn desk. "Next day at the latest."

At the thought of what the cleaners would be working on, she shuddered. Since no one had told her she could leave, she headed back to her office in the library and waited some more.

As did Duncan Forbes.

Finally, Tom came into her office, where she'd been pretending to work and her companion had watched the investigation going on outside her office window.

"Sorry we had to keep you so long, Alex," he said. "You're free to go."

"You, too," he said to Duncan Forbes. "Remember, don't leave town without checking with me first."

"I'm not going anywhere."

As they finally left her office, he asked, "Are you hungry?"

Amazingly, she was. "Starving. Though it seems kind of tactless under the circumstances."

"We can be tactless together. Come on, I'll buy you lunch." He sent her a grin that was far too attractive for any scruffy art professor. "I've still got a few bucks left after paying my fine. And by the way, thanks for not telling the cops I'm already a felon in Swiftcurrent."

"You should be too ashamed to bring up that incident," she said, trying hard not to respond to the infectious grin, but so happy to forget the awful morning for a few minutes that she was willing to forgive him his lapses in judgment yesterday. "And you a teacher, too."

"I want to talk to you."

In her experience, when men said they wanted to talk to her, they wanted to take her to bed. And, in spite of a certain sexual appeal that pulled at her, Duncan Forbes was not a contender. She had a busy few months ahead of her and no time for an affair with a rulebreaker. He was so not her type.

But the alternative was going home to an empty apartment and brooding. And as little as she liked the virtual stranger in front of her, he had the attraction of having shared today's ordeal. He was the one person she could hash it all over with without having to explain the details. If she got hit on in the process, she could squash him easily enough. She'd had plenty of practice.

"All right."

"This is your town," he said, not seeming remotely surprised that she'd agreed to eat lunch with him. Of the two of them, she bet she was more shocked. "Where to?"

They walked to the main doors and she peeked out. The middle of the afternoon wasn't the social high point of the day in downtown Swiftcurrent. Most people were at work, at home with kids or at the grocery store. But it was a small town. They hadn't had a murder since . . . since never, that she knew of, so it wasn't surprising that many of the town's curious had managed to find their way downtown. On the other side of the yellow crime scene tape, a small crowd was gathered, talking in hushed voices as though in church. Or in the library itself.

If she and Duncan passed through the second set of double doors she'd be as good as mobbed. There was even a TV crew and Dash Trembley from the *Swiftcurrent News* hanging around out there.

"We'll go out the employees' entrance," she said, backing away from the main doors. "We could go across the way to Elda's Country Café where the food's pretty good, but we'd be surrounded in seconds."

A grimace from her companion had her nodding. "If we want real food, we drive past all the fast food franchises along the highway till we hit Delaney's, a steak place, where with luck no one will know about the murder."

"Done. But my vehicle's at the cottage where I'm staying. I walked up."

"My car's out back." She turned and led the way, already rooting in her bag for her keys. She had a sudden craving for a Delaney's steak sandwich. If ever there was a time for comfort food . . .

They reached her blue Ford compact and got in without attracting notice. But as she pulled out of the municipal employees' lot, she caught the startled gaze of Mildred Wickerson peering in the window at Duncan, and then at Alex, as though she couldn't believe her eyes.

"Well," Alex muttered, "this will be all over town within the hour."

She knew she'd been heard when her companion said, "Is that a problem for you?"

"Hmmm?" She turned onto the highway and then glanced his way.

"Is there a husband or significant other who won't be too pleased we're having lunch together?"

"If that were an issue, I'd hardly be here." And if he were trying to gauge her marital status he was going to have to come right out and ask.

Which, rather surprisingly, he did. "So, are you?"

"Am I what?"

"You're too smart to play dumb. Are you married?"

"No."

"Involved?" She didn't like the spurt of . . . something his line of questioning evoked.

"No."

A McDonald's, Wendy's, and Arby's flashed by in a blur of primary colors and parking lots scattered with family vans.

"Why not?"

She laughed. She couldn't help it. She laughed out loud and it felt good after all the dismal seriousness of the morning. "That's a personal question."

"They're more interesting than impersonal ones."

She shook her head and kept driving, the dark brown wood siding and the deep red sign announcing that Delaney's was just ahead.

"Well?"

She pulled smoothly off the highway and into Delaney's parking lot, pulled up close to the building and cut the engine before turning to him.

It hit her then, what a truly attractive man he was. Here in the close confines of the car her skin prickled as she found his blue eyes staring at her. His skin had the rugged look of someone who spends a lot of time outdoors. A couple of grooves tracked from his cheeks to a square jaw. His mouth was shockingly at odds with the rest of his face. It was sensual and belonged to a man who loved to talk, loved to eat exotic foods, a man who loved to kiss.

It was obvious he hadn't simply been making idle conversation and she needed to be clear that she wasn't interested.

"Mr. Forbes—"

"Come on. We've faced each other over a corpse—I'm pretty sure that automatically puts people on a first-name basis. It's Duncan."

"Duncan. I have known you for less than a day. In that time I have not grown to like you particularly."

He simply stared at her, waiting patiently for her answer. In spite of herself, her lips twitched. "Inside."

As she'd hoped, Delaney's was close to empty. They slid into one of the anonymous, high-backed red leather booths and she felt a little of the morning's tension slide off her shoulders.

Harold, the owner and maître d', handed them menu folders in the same color—probably the same fabric—as the booths. It was that sort of place. Nothing ever changed. There was rice mixed with the salt in the shakers, six pages of menu items, including Greek, Italian, and recently some stir-fries, but everyone came to Delaney's for the steaks.

"Steak sandwich," she told Harold, not bothering to open her menu. "Medium rare, on sourdough. Blue cheese dressing on the salad."

"Sounds good. I'll have the same," said her companion.

"Anything to drink?"

"Perrier and lime."

Duncan Forbes opened the wine list. He ordered a bottle of something that sounded French and expensive.

"The bottle, sir?"

"Please. And bring two glasses."

She smiled rigidly until Harold—who must be bliss-fully unaware of the morning's discovery at the library since he hadn't asked a thing—took their menus and disappeared. "I don't usually drink wine at lunchtime," she said.

"Neither do I. But there's nothing usual about today. I think we both need a drink." He rubbed a hand across the back of his neck. "God knows I do."

Maybe it was that oblique admission that he was as shaken as she by their grisly discovery that made her shut up and let Harold place a wineglass in front of her.

"Nice day," he said as he went through the business of uncorking the bottle.

She wanted to giggle so badly her throat tickled with it. *Nice* was not how she'd describe her day so far. *Nice* had nothing to do with dead bodies shot through the heart, with police teams, with wondering if she'd ever forget the sight of that gray, slack-skinned face that had stared sightlessly up at her.

Ever seen him before? Detective Remco had asked her just as Duncan had.

Being a woman who was always careful with facts, and who believed passionately in the importance of careful research and the truth, she'd taken an extra minute to study the dead man's face, but all her extra study only confirmed what she'd known at first glance.

The man was a stranger.

"Having a day off?" Harold asked as he poured the wine.

A beat passed. If she told him the news it would end the relative peace of this place. "We're just in for a late lunch," she said.

She watched the rich, red liquid fill the glass deep and sparkly as garnets and decided there were times when a glass of wine at lunch was a very good idea.

She sipped and sipped again. "This tastes expensive."

"You know wines?"

"I'm no oenophile, but I managed to graduate from wine in a box."

He touched his glass to hers. "Drink up." He watched until she'd downed more of the wine. "I'm still waiting for the answer to a very simple question. Is there a man in your life?"

Not since Grandpa died, she thought with a pang, wondering when she'd stop missing the man who'd taken the place of her father in many ways, who'd given her a stable home, who'd taught her about art and antiques, about history. They'd been friends and recently they'd become colleagues. But of course, Duncan Forbes wasn't interested in her relationship with her eighty-two-year-old grandfather.

"No. I'm not involved with anyone. And, just so we're clear, I'm not interested in getting involved."

Those blue, blue eyes studied her and she had to force herself not to lick her lips. God, he was gorgeous in that rumpled, intellectual way. There was a craggy line between his eyebrows as though he'd ruminated over plenty of thorny scholastic puzzles in his time. "Why not? Don't you like men?"

His arrogance staggered her. "I don't like you."

He didn't beat his chest, storm out, or even look hurt. He sipped his wine, his gaze never leaving her face. "Maybe I'll grow on you."

Maybe she'd get gangrene.

Their food arrived and she could have kissed Harold for his timing. She sliced into her steak and found it as sizzlingly perfect as always.

Like her, Duncan ignored the salad and went for the meat. After an enormous bite, which he demolished rapidly, he said, "You were right. This is great."

"Best steaks in town."

"Did you know him?"

Him, today, could only refer to one person. The recently deceased.

Her brows pulled together. "I told you I didn't know him. I never saw him before today."

"Well, you told the police that."

If he wasn't careful, Duncan Forbes was going to wear his far-too-expensive wine all over his rumpled Eddie Bauer special cream denim shirt.

"I have no reason to lie to the police, or you, or anyone. I did not know that poor man."

"Okay. Then why do you think somebody put him there for you to find?"

She shook her head. In the back of her mind, like a dull headache, the same question had plagued her for hours.

Why?

"I wish I knew." She gazed up at him, not wanting to trust him, but feeling at least on some level she could talk to him. He barely knew her, had arrived in Swiftcurrent all of one day earlier, and yet his assessment of the situation exactly coincided with hers. "You think whoever put him there knew I'd find him?"

"It's the logical conclusion. From what you told Dudley Do-Right in there—"

"Sergeant Tom Perkins." And she would not even smile at the uncomfortably exact comparison Forbes had made between their local sergeant and the upright cartoon character.

"—the cleaners finished around ten last night. There was no stiff on the floor when they left."

She nodded.

"Who else might be expected to be in the library to find the guy? Other librarians?"

She shook her head. "I always open up. I'm the only full-time librarian in town."

"Anybody else in city hall?"

"A couple of people have keys to the library, but they wouldn't go in first thing in the morning. There'd be no reason to."

"So, we have to assume whoever put the body there knew you'd find it. And do you think it was significant that the body was in the art section?"

"You think the killer was an art lover?"

He put down his knife and fork and contemplated her. "Honey, I don't know squat about this town, but I think you need to watch your back."

She repressed a shiver. "I think a couple of creepy guys had an argument and one shot the other. It could have happened anywhere and the body was tossed into the library to get it out of plain sight while the killer or killers drove off. They're a thousand miles away by now." She started on her salad. "Are you trying to scare me so I'll throw myself in your arms for protection?"

His eyes crinkled all too attractively when he almost, but not quite, smiled at her. "I never resort to cheap tricks to get a woman in bed. You'll get there in your own time."

Don't even acknowledge his colossal arrogance. You'll only encourage him. "How's your steak?"

"Fantastic. So, tell me what a woman like you is doing in a dinky little town like this?"

Maybe it wasn't the change of subject she'd prefer, but she could live with it. "It was my grandparents' home. My father's an executive with an international oil company so we moved around all over the world. By my mid-teens I'd lived in the Middle East, Africa, South America, and all over Europe. I was sick of it, so I came here to live with my grandparents. After grad school, my grandfather wrote that the librarian job was open, so I applied."

"You with your master's degree."

So, he remembered that. "Yes."

"Don't you think you're overqualified?"

"A little. But a good job in a small town is tough to find. And I needed to be here to look after my grandfather after my grandmother was gone. He passed away a couple of months ago." She blinked suddenly and took a sip of wine.

"I'm sorry." He touched her hand, and the warmth felt good. "Did your parents retire here?"

"No. They're in Europe. Stateside, there were only my grandparents, my aunt who's living in a hippie commune in Montana, and my cousin and me."

On top of a bad day, she didn't want to think about her pathetic family story. "Grandpa was pretty old, but he was in such good health that it was a shock when he died suddenly."

"Was he ill?"

"No. A heart attack." She sighed. "They practically brought me and my cousin up. Well, her mom abandoned her not long after she was born. Mine relied on nannies until I was old enough to fly home for summers."

"How old was that?"

"Eight. I spent every summer here. It was a lot more like home than the apartments we lived in. We moved at least once a year, sometimes twice, so this was the only real home I ever knew."

"Sounds miserable."

She smiled. "Sounds like I'm whining. I don't mean to. It's just hard on a kid to have no roots. When I was sixteen, I rebelled and finished high school here."

"Do you ever see them?"

"My parents? Oh, yes. I joined them for Christmas last year in Prague." And she'd never make that mistake again. *Alexandra, that dress is vulgar. Darling, you've got too much cleavage for décolletage.*

On New Year's Eve she'd had her navel pierced.

Chapter 4

"Why do you dress that way?" Duncan asked.

She'd driven him back to the summer cottage that he'd told her he was renting by the month since it was off-season. She'd left the car engine running and thanked him for lunch, but he seemed interested in carrying on their chat and, once again, asking her a very personal question.

She glanced down at herself—not that she'd forgotten she was wearing the rose drawstring off-the-shoulder silk top and hip-hugging black leather skirt, but to try and see it through his eyes. "What way?"

"Sex on heels."

She chuckled softly. It had started out as a childish rebellion, she supposed. Provocative clothing got her noticed by her mother, who was a brilliant entertainer, perfect corporate wife but a lousy mother, and by her father who never stopped climbing the corporate ladder long enough to look around him. Maybe he thought if he climbed fast and far enough, he'd get to heaven without the bother of dying first.

She hadn't shocked so much as irritated her parents by her flamboyant dress code, but by the time she realized her plan hadn't worked, she'd grown into herself and she liked the way she looked. Apparently, so did Duncan. "You noticed."

"Every man noticed from the forensics guys to the old geezer at the steak house. It makes me wonder about you." He shifted so his body was turned toward her, and there was a lazy glint in his eyes that teased. "There are two reasons a woman dresses like that."

She lifted her brows. The single glass of wine she'd allowed herself had dulled the horror of the morning, but the memory of that poor man hovered like a threatening storm, so it was nice to have her mind taken off her troubles, even if it was in a criticism of her wardrobe. "Okay. I'll take the bait. What are the two reasons?"

He gazed down at her in a way that suggested he was more concerned with what was under her clothes. In spite of herself, the intensity of his inspection had her nipples tightening.

He said, "You could be totally at ease with your body, and dress that way to celebrate your sexuality and your pleasure in your own skin."

She didn't say anything, but she kind of liked that view of things. "You mentioned two possibilities."

"Or, you could be so insecure, you project that sex goddess image as a smokescreen. You could secretly be terrified of men. You could hate sex." He leaned closer and whispered, "You could be frigid."

"I could be faking who I am?" She was more than a little irked at this second possibility, but refused to show it. Instead of wrapping her arms around herself in annoyance, which was her first impulse, she deliberately edged her elbows open a little more. Body language for *I'm so comfortable in my body I can hardly stand it.*

"And?" she asked.

"And?" he parroted back, the disturbing glint in his eyes more pronounced.

"Which do you think is the reason?"

He rubbed his jaw, half narrowed his eyes, and let his gaze roam her body. His blatant assessment of her attitude to her own sexuality struck her as offensive, inappropriate, and annoyingly enticing.

"I don't like how long it's taking you to decide."

"I'm an academic. I'm trained to research a thesis, not jump to conclusions."

She'd forgotten he was a professor. He was too sexy for academia, and far too sure of himself. Also, she was in no doubt that he was more than comfortable with his own sexuality. He was so potently male he damned near hummed with it. She wouldn't be so aggravated if she weren't picking up his frequency like a tuning fork.

He wasn't her type and he irritated the hell out of her, but it didn't stop her body from reacting to the raw animal appeal of the man. "Research . . ." She let the word trail off her lips. "You mean you'd ask around about me? Interview former lovers?"

His gaze narrowed further. "Secondary sources—as you, being a librarian, should know—are notoriously unreliable. I prefer firsthand research."

She couldn't help the smile that tugged at her mouth. He could both insult and intrigue at the same time. "That is certainly an original come-on."

Right now, she could do what he thought he'd manipulated her into, which was proving her sexuality to him in no uncertain terms, or she could take a turn at his little game.

She let her gaze run up and down the length of his body. "What about you?"

"Me?"

"You dress casually to the point of sloppiness. Your hair's not combed and I don't believe you and your razor are on the most intimate terms. You play up the whole absentminded professor routine. You've got a sleepy sexiness that makes a woman wonder if you'd put any effort into an . . . intimate situation."

"That's what you think?"

"It's one possibility. Or is the absentminded professor a front?"

His eyes gleamed with quick humor as though the *I'm such a babe magnet I don't have to iron, shave, or even match my socks* routine was a kind of private joke.

Whatever. Some instinct warned her to stay away from this one, and she respected her instincts.

"Well, I know one thing," he said in that sleepy, sexy way.

"What's that?"

"You've been thinking about me in the last twenty-four hours as much as I've been thinking about you. But I'm still not convinced you're not frigid."

She determined to put him in his place and wipe that altogether-too-smug grin off his face. He wanted to play games? Fine. Frigid, huh? She'd show him frigid.

Shifting her body so their knees almost touched, she settled herself to her best viewing advantage. She knew her body had an atavistic desire for his and that her nipples were broadcasting the fact, so she leaned back enough that her chest was prominently in his line of vision.

"I'll save you the research," she said. "I love sex. I love everything about it." She breathed deeply, pulling up random images and memories, letting her sensual nature off its leash. "I love the warm feel of a man's body sleeping beside me in the night, the smell of his skin when it's silky with arousal, kissing when you're so hot and sweaty your lips slide around."

She stopped to lick her lips, stifling the urge to climb into his lap and show him exactly what she meant. She stared into those lapis lazuli eyes, already darkening and clouding with desire. Ha! "I love the hard driving, when you're both so excited you can't fill your lungs fast enough, and staring deep into a man's eyes when we climax together and it feels as though we've swapped a little of our souls."

She had to pause a second to draw breath and remind herself not to squirm on the faux-leather car seat. She pretended she'd gone for a dramatic pause, then finished with, "I love lying naked, afterward, still pulsing with pleasure. Waiting for my partner to recover for round two."

She leaned even closer and used the huskiness that had crept into her tone to taunt him further. "Because there's always a round two, and three, and four. I . . ." she let her fingernail flick the top button on his shirt, "am," flick went the second button, "insatiable."

Duncan's temperature seemed to be rising. He appeared flushed and his breathing was rapid. She forced herself not to imagine him thrusting hard and deep inside her, him staring into her eyes while their bodies exploded with pleasure, him connecting with her in that deeply intimate way.

After a long, long moment when she felt her blood pound and her body throb with wanting, she knew she'd made her point and she'd better get out of there before she proved beyond words how far from frigid she was.

She glanced at her watch, pulling her librarian's tone out like a theatrical prop. "Thanks for lunch. I need to get going."

"Have dinner with me tonight," he said, his voice barely his own.

She stifled a smirk of satisfaction. She'd made her point. She loved sex. But did he think she was going to fall into his bed because he had some basic animal appeal? She hoped she had more sense. "No, thank you."

"Are you busy tonight?"

"No. Just not interested."

"You should reconsider. You'll feel a lot less slutty if you go out with me before we have sex."

His arrogance had her blinking. "Believe me, that is never going—"

She got no further. Strong arms pulled her forward and he kissed her. Hard.

Her instincts had been right on, she realized, as the full impact of the kiss hit her. This man, with these firm, sensuous lips, was going to be trouble.

"My cell phone's on my business card," he said when he pulled away. "Call me anytime."

"I wo—"

She wondered why she bothered trying to talk to the man if every time she opened her mouth he was going to cut her off by slapping his lips on top of hers.

Then she became overwhelmed by the sensation of his mouth moving on hers, of his tongue tricking her into a response she didn't want to show. But how could she help herself? There was some powerful chemistry here.

She felt his hands in her hair while his tongue teased and promised. In spite of what she'd told herself about staying clear of him, her body strained closer to his. Her hands reached for him as though they had their own agenda: his shoulders, muscular and broad; his chest, firm and wide; his back, long and sturdy. She gave up and leaned all the way in so her chest brushed his, making her moan softly as sharp pleasure ignited in her nipples and spread.

Her fingers found their way into his messy hair, which was thick and gorgeous to the touch. Her mouth opened greedily and she licked at his tongue, sucked it, wanted more.

Dizziness began to invade her senses and there was

some kind of humming in her ears when she finally managed to drag herself away.

"The hell with tonight. Come in with me now." His words were hoarse, his breathing ragged, and his lips wet from kissing her.

Oh, she wanted to go in with him, and badly. He felt so warm and strong and dangerous she wanted to ignore her instincts of self-preservation and follow this powerful attraction to its logical conclusion; but she hung on grimly to enough sense to shake her head. Her to-do list was full and there was no room on it for a mindless affair with an obnoxious book scribbler she'd known for twenty-four hours.

She shook her head.

He ran a hand through the hair she'd already mussed, tangling it further so it looked as though he'd just crawled out of bed. "It's inevitable. You know that as well as I do. One day very soon I'm going to be driving inside you until you scream with pleasure."

She couldn't speak, only stare into his mesmerizing eyes.

"And you will scream. That I promise."

A hand on her knee, a gentle pat as though she were his aged great aunt, and he was gone. But the sight of that hand stayed with her. She noticed the long fingers, the elegant square of the palm.

And as he'd pulled his arm away she'd seen the streak of red on his shirtsleeve and on his wrist, as though he'd washed blood off his hands and missed some.

Cold and shaken, she put the car into gear and reversed. Probably he'd gotten blood on himself when he turned the corpse. But even as she tried to convince herself, she went heavy on the gas and kept glancing in her rearview mirror all the way home.

Chapter 5

The phone rang as Alex was swilling with mouth-wash for the third time. She'd brushed her teeth, even brushed her tongue, and flossed as though it were a competitive sport.

She'd kissed a man with blood on his hands. Oh, God. Right now, she wanted nothing more than a hot, hot bath to wash every bit of her that had been in any kind of contact with Duncan Forbes, or even thought about coming into contact with him.

But it seemed bubbles and soothing aromatherapy would have to wait.

She grabbed the phone before her recorded message kicked in, assuming it was the police. "Hello?" She hoped it was Tom. It would be easiest to tell him about the blood on Duncan Forbes's hands.

A deep, racking sob was her only answer.

Oh, no. She wished with fierce desperation that she'd left the phone ringing. Not today. Not now.

The sob ended on a series of hiccups, like a stone skipped across water.

Knowing she couldn't hang up, and that the call was going to be a long one, she propped the receiver between her ear and shoulder and headed for her bedroom to take off her clothes. "Gillian?" As though she had to ask. Who else ever phoned in mid-sob?

"Eric wants to get back together."

Dead bodies could litter Swiftcurrent like fallen autumn leaves and they wouldn't divert Gillian from her personal crisis—whatever that week's crisis happened to be.

With anyone else, an estranged husband wanting to get back together might be considered good news. But with her cousin, everything was disaster and heartache. Good news, bad news, it didn't matter. Had the drugs done this to her or had her overwrought personality drawn her to the drugs?

Alex realized a full minute had passed without anything but sobbing and hiccup noises passing across the phone line. Clearly, something was required from her. She ought to be more sympathetic; the woman's husband had just left her, but over the years, Alex's stock of sympathy had worn thin. Gillian brought most of her problems on herself.

"Oh, really?" was about all she could manage.

For once, *she'd* like someone to lean on. Someone close enough she could call and say, *I had a shitty day. Found a dead body and it went downhill from there.* But there was no one. That's why she'd made such an error in judgment and gone to lunch with a man with another's blood on his hands.

She shuddered.

She slipped off her skirt. Tom would most likely agree with her that the obvious cause was from flipping the body. Still, that might give them enough suspicion to test Duncan Forbes for gunpowder residue. She'd seen that on *CSI.* It was amazing how much evidence a killer left behind. Surely, she hadn't kissed a murderer . . . had she?

"So what do you think I should do?"

Alex forced her concentration back to the phone call. "About Eric wanting to get back together?"

"Ye-e-es," Gillian wailed.

Hope flickered, but not brightly, at the thought that her ditzy cousin might be reunited with the man who'd kept her more or less stable for almost a decade. It wasn't a beacon of hope, more like a twenty-five-watt bulb on its way out. Eric had surprisingly turned out to be the one strong influence in Gill's messed-up life. It was only once he'd left, after seven years of marriage, that Gillian had taken to calling Alex. Prior to that, their relationship had been rocky at best. They were cousins, but classic good girl/bad girl opposites.

She jammed the phone between her ear and shoulder while she freed her hands once more to pull off her pantyhose.

"Did he tell you he wants to get back together?" Or was it a cocaine mirage. The irony of Gill and Eric's relationship was that drugs had brought them together and, when Eric cleaned up and Gill didn't, had driven them apart.

She pulled on the stretchy black pants she used for yoga, spread the toes of her bare feet in relief after having had them squished in dress shoes all day, and peeled the blouse over her head.

"I'm so confused," her cousin sniffled on the other end of the phone. "I'm not good on my own. I'm not strong like you."

Yeah, well, she was tired of being strong. Tired of being leaned on. "Take him back, then."

"I can't. Look—do you think we could go to a movie or something one night?"

All of a sudden, Alex saw Gill as she'd been before she ran away to L.A. in her senior year. She'd been so pretty and carefree. She could have any guy she wanted, with her luscious body and wild-child ways, and mostly she'd had them.

She'd developed a crush on Tom Perkins, Alex remembered now. One of those violent teenage crushes, but he hadn't been interested. He was probably the only man who ever said no to Gill. It must have been seeing him today, and now hearing from her cousin, that brought that memory back. She bet Gill didn't even remember that intense teenage crush.

Then Gillian left home. She left a note saying she was going to L.A. to find work as an actress.

What she'd found was drugs.

And Eric.

"Look, Gill. Make yourself some tea or something. Of course we can go to a movie. I'm pretty tied up this week. How about one night next week?" Tomorrow, she'd probably forget they'd ever had this conversation. Poor Gillian—when she wasn't driving Alex insane, she was pathetic. When they'd been younger, Alex had actually been sort of jealous of her gorgeous, sexually confident, utterly unrestrained cousin.

Now that she'd outgrown her own insecurities and come into the woman she was meant to be, she no longer felt intimidated by the easy sexuality of her cousin. Her lack of discipline and her chemical dependencies had messed up her life so badly that now Alex felt sorry for her.

"Can I come over tonight? I need to talk to you about something."

Right. They had decisions to make about the estate. But not tonight. She wasn't up to it. "I'm really beat. I had a rough day. Can we make it tomorrow?"

There was a pause, and a soft, "Sure." The one word

contained a touch of hurt, and guilt mixed with the frustration that gushed from deep inside.

She picked up the phone again and called the non-emergency police line. It wasn't quite five and Raeanne was still at her desk. "Can you get Tom to call me when he gets a minute?"

"Oh, my gosh. He's pretty busy with the murder investigation right now."

Raeanne was as excited as a gossip columnist in the middle of a juicy scandal. "Of course. I understand. I'll give you my cell number and he can call me when he gets time."

Having done her duty, she did a few yoga stretches to bring peace and serenity. It was an abject failure, but she couldn't blame the yoga. She didn't think much short of a lobotomy could bring peace and serenity tonight.

The walls of her apartment were closing in on her. She needed to do something to take her mind off her troubles. If she lived in a big city, she'd have more friends her own age and a whole lot more things to do and places to go. Instead, for fun and excitement, she called Myrna, the circulation clerk, to tell her not to come in tomorrow and spent fifteen minutes telling her about the murder.

That done, she couldn't relax enough for that hot bath she'd promised herself. She was too jumpy yet. She played a Diana Krall CD and decided to rearrange the linen closet. But she discovered, on opening the door, that it was perfectly ordered. She'd cleaned it out only a couple of weeks ago.

Her next stop was the kitchen. She was still full from lunch, so she poured herself a glass of milk and washed an apple, then peeled it in one long, tidy swirl and sliced the fruit into four precise quadrants which she placed on a plate. It wasn't really enough for a balanced meal, so she cut four slices of cheese and buttered a slice of whole wheat bread.

A meal didn't have to be large, but she liked to think it contained all the required food groups.

While she ate at her kitchen table, using a linen napkin and placemat—because she was also a big believer that a single woman needn't live like a slob—she flicked on the small TV to catch the news.

The murder was, predictably, the top story. Tom was interviewed, looking solid and impassive and giving out no information but that an unidentified man had been found dead in the library. An investigation was under way.

He didn't comment on anything, right down to who had discovered the body, for which she was thankful.

Tidying her dinner dishes took all of a minute and a half. She wiped down all her cabinets and the counters. Managed to impose a tiny measure of order in a world of chaos by swapping the cinnamon and the cardamom in her spice rack, which had somehow got switched out of their normal alphabetical order. Then she brewed a pot of chamomile tea, which was supposed to be calming.

She had a couple of children's books she wanted to read so she could classify them properly, but her mind wouldn't settle. And the tea didn't calm or soothe her tonight. Her mind dashed in a disorganized fashion from the dead man to Gillian's call and, most often of all, to the kiss Forbes planted on her.

It had been steamy and erotic and she'd responded with all the passion of a woman starved for steamy and erotic.

Worse. She'd kissed a man with blood on his hands.

She rose so fast the calming, soothing chamomile tea splashed everywhere. She had to get out of here.

Before she'd finished gathering her keys and purse, she knew where she was going. To her grandparents' house. Foolish it might be, but her instinct was to run home—or, as she'd told Duncan Forbes, to the only home she'd ever really known.

She'd been helping her grandfather with his memoirs when he died. Fortunately, he'd preferred talking to writing, and he'd completed the telling of his life story on tape up to his official retirement five years earlier.

She sniffed and blinked rapidly. The book wouldn't get written if she didn't carry on. It was her monument to him. Of course, the memoirs of an ordinary man who'd lived an ordinary life weren't going to be the stuff of bestseller lists, but she'd already decided to donate a copy to the city's archives whether they wanted it or not. She'd also have one copy bound and indexed in the library system. Franklin Forrest would have gotten such a kick out of that.

She could have brought all his papers and the tapes to her own home, but she'd left them at his house. She convinced herself it was because he had a bigger desk and a larger study than she did, but in truth, she still felt his presence in the house where he'd lived since returning to the States after the war and marrying.

Her mother and her aunt had grown up in that house. Her cousin had grown up in there, and, in many ways, Alex had also grown up in the old Victorian.

Once she'd moved permanently to Swiftcurrent, her grandpa had hired her to help him on weekends and in the summer. In his poky, dusty antiques and art shop, she'd learned more about art than she'd ever learned touring the greatest galleries of the world. She'd inherited her grandfather's passion. Not that she could paint or draw, as he did, but her organizational skills were superb. She catalogued, recorded, and filed. It was in working for her grandfather's store that she discovered her true calling. She was a born librarian.

She pulled on a hooded black sweatshirt and ran lightly down the stairs and out the back door of her apartment building to the parking lot.

Soon she was driving through the quiet roads to her grandfather's house. As she drove past the central municipal building, she shuddered, thinking of the body now resting in a steel cubicle in a morgue somewhere.

She pulled into the gravel drive of the two-story shingled house, its original yellow paint faded to pale butter, moss clinging to the roof edge like bushy eyebrows. She felt the familiar pang of loss. It had been almost two months—when would she grow accustomed to her grandfather's death?

In a gesture of self-comfort, she rubbed the gold necklace he'd given her for her twenty-first birthday. It was in the shape of a key. *The key to your heart,* he'd said, and she always wore it on a chain just long enough so it did rest near her heart. How she missed him.

Sighing, she stepped out of the car. She and Gillian, his two beneficiaries, were going to have to make some decisions about what to sell and what to keep.

Strangers would soon be living in this wonderful house where all her best memories were stored. The house cried out for a family, for kids to climb the apple and cherry trees, a dog and laughter and backyard barbecues—not something a spinster librarian or a chemical-dependent, recently separated woman could provide. Besides, Alex would be leaving Swiftcurrent soon.

Chapter 6

Duncan was pissed.

If there was one thing he hated it was being made a fool of, and somebody was doing a fine job. What the hell was going on? This backwater might look like *Mayberry RFD* but it had the undercurrents of a Stephen King novel.

He drove slowly through the unfamiliar, barely paved roads, squinting at street signs as they were briefly illuminated by the headlights of his tan midsize rental car. The town didn't seem to have a map and he couldn't ask for directions to the deceased Franklin Forrest's home. Not when his purpose in going there was to engage in some quiet breaking and entering.

Everyone who'd questioned Alexandra Forrest today had wanted to know if she recognized the dead man. To each of them, including him, she'd denied ever seeing the stiff before.

Perkins had asked if he'd known the man, not if he recognized him, which had saved him from having to lie to the cops. He knew what the stolid sergeant would soon discover. The stiff, Jerzy Plotnik, was a small-time drug dealer and fence. He wouldn't have come to Duncan's attention except that he sometimes worked for an on-the-surface-reputable art dealer in L.A. who also dealt, far more lucratively, in high-level, black-market art. The kind of deals Mendes brokered were never heard of at Sotheby's or Christie's, and the treasures that changed hands usually ended up in a secret vault.

It couldn't be coincidence that Duncan Forbes and Jerzy Plotnik had both ended up in Swiftcurrent, Oregon, at the same time. It had to be the Van Gogh.

But why was Plotnik dead? A guy who'd hung on the fringes of organized crime, Jerzy was a small eel swimming with piranhas, but as long as he was useful, there was no reason to get rid of him.

Jerzy had either tried to double-cross his boss, Hector Mendes, or he'd screwed up.

Duncan wished he could buy into Alex's theory that the murder was a random act of violence, and the placing of the body in a Swiftcurrent library a coincidence. But Duncan believed Jerzy Plotnik's corpse had been planted in Alexandra Forrest's path for a reason.

If Duncan's Uncle Simon had heard the rumor about the Van Gogh, it was likely Mendes had heard the same whispers. That could explain how Plotnik ended up in Swiftcurrent, but not how he ended up dead, who killed him, or how Alex fit into all this.

He had a feeling the librarian in sex kitten's clothing was playing him for a fool and he didn't like it.

Beneath his anger, excitement bubbled. His left foot was doing a kind of tap dance against the floor as he drove. For it occurred to Duncan that maybe more than a rumor was hidden in this seemingly tranquil backwater.

What if the painting itself was here?

Grandpa wouldn't take a priceless Van Gogh to the

grave with him. He'd have had an accomplice, and who better than the lovely granddaughter?

Shit, but she'd played him, with her lush body and prissy attitude. As his headlights cut tunnels of light through the darkness, his eyes narrowed on a sign in dire need of repainting. Lavender Lane crossed Larkspur Drive. Duncan was no botanist, but he had a feeling Primrose Avenue, where Franklin Forrest had lived, must be close.

It was a long shot that the painting would be right in the house, but in his career Duncan had seen crooks do stupider things. Even if the painting wasn't there, he could get the lay of the house. See if there were any clues.

He didn't think Alex could be on to him, at least not yet. She believed him to be exactly what he was—a professor working on a book. He'd made no secret that his attraction to her was sexual. At first he'd hoped she might remember some of her grandfather's stories from the war. Perhaps through those he could piece together where Forrest's good friend Louis Vendome had hidden the painting. He, like most art historians, had imagined the painting still safely hidden from the Nazis, the young man who'd hidden it killed before he could reveal its hiding place. That was the best-case scenario.

There was also the possibility that it had been accidentally destroyed, lost, or looted. He'd hoped maybe Franklin would have left a diary or a journal, letters home, something that would lead Duncan another small step on his journey to solve the mystery of the missing Van Gogh. The family who'd owned it had contacted him almost a decade ago when he'd had his fifteen minutes in the sunshine of celebrity for a big find.

He'd tracked an old master "purchased" by the Nazis

in the late 1930s, when they'd forced wealthy Jewish families to sell their treasures for ridiculous prices. He'd finally found the Rubens tucked away in an obscure American gallery. He'd helped prove its provenance and then returned the painting to the industrialist's descendants. Duncan wasn't much of a crusader, but there was a certain satisfaction in righting the wrongs of history.

His arrangement with such clients was that he'd take a fee if he found the art. Some quests were successful, but many weren't, and often it took years of patient investigation, dealing with uncooperative governments, criminals of one sort and another, and galleries who turned a blind eye to shady dealings in the war years.

He also helped solve more recent thefts, such as the Van Dyke portrait he'd restored to the English marquis from whose ancestral home it had been lifted.

Solving puzzles—that was partly what drew him to his work. He also loved the cloak-and-dagger intrigue, and the occasional heart-pounding danger. And he didn't mind the fat fees that had made him rich.

Duncan's own family connections to crime had advantages. He might walk on the right side of the law, but he used the skills passed on by his larcenous forbears. He'd broken into the secret vault in Bermuda where the pilfered Van Dyke was hidden and stolen it back.

He shifted a little, as the remembered adventure caused a twinge in his thigh. He'd been shot on his way out of the villa at a dead run, the canvas tucked under his arm. Was the Van Gogh landscape going to be as easy to return to its rightful owners? After ten years of blank walls and dead ends, it seemed he was going to find *Olive Trees with Farmhouse.*

There was a solution that no one connected with the story had ever considered. Franklin, the American art student and friend of Louis Vendome, had stolen the painting for himself and brought it home as though it were a worthless print from the Louvre gift shop.

Duncan had a black-and-white photo of the piece, painted in the last year of Van Gogh's life, when he'd painted masterpiece after masterpiece with manic frenzy, almost as though he'd known his days were numbered. The photograph, taken before color photography was invented, was vague with age, the blacks shifting to gray. The very grayness of the indistinct photo spurred him on. He itched to see the original in all its colorful, summer-in-the-south-of-France glory.

Depending on its condition, that painting would be worth tens of millions.

He sighed as he discovered Petunia Place was a dead end and made a U-turn. He was going to have to stay close to Alex, not only in hopes of finding out what she knew about the Van Gogh, but to protect her as best he could from whoever had killed Jerzy Plotnik.

Sex was the quickest and most pleasurable path to get close to her. He'd have preferred it if she were innocent, but he wasn't going to fool himself. He'd sleep with that woman because she turned him inside out. When he held her in his arms, tasted her mouth, and felt the promise of ecstasy in her willing body, he didn't care how entangled she was in stolen goods. In fact, he thought with a wry twist of his mouth, a larcenous looker was exactly the kind of woman his family would most approve.

Primrose Avenue turned out to have no street sign, but fortunately someone had commissioned a painted metal plaque picturing a basket of primroses and the address: 273 Primrose Avenue. A couple of houses over, and there was 245.

Duncan drove slowly past, but the big old Victorian had that uninhabited look that all the lawn services and timer lights in the world couldn't disguise.

No cars in the gravel drive. One light burning in the upstairs hall. A newsprint flyer had suffered rain and wind damage. Its damp sheets clung, with a few wet leaves, to the front steps.

He drove around a couple of streets, found a lane that let him see into the back. Open drapes. Nothing stirring. On either side the neighbors were safely ensconced behind closed blinds and drawn drapes, most likely watching TV.

He parked a couple of blocks over under a spreading, leafy tree and made his way back. He wore black Levis, hooded sweatshirt, and sneakers. Having learned from the best, he didn't skulk around the back but walked boldly up the front path. No one challenged him and the lock didn't remotely test his lock-picking skills. He wasn't further tested by an alarm system, since there wasn't one.

Feeling vaguely disappointed that his B&E skills hadn't been stretched, he shut the front door quietly behind him and stood still for a moment, listening.

The house was silent. It smelled shut up: of stale air, dust, and a little bit of old man.

"Where did you put it, you sly old bastard?" Duncan muttered. But only silence as dense as the grave answered him.

From within his black jacket he pulled out a penlight. As he played the tiny beam around him, he found he was in a hall so dark and somber he suspected the decor was original Victorian.

He turned to his right and started with the parlor, checking the pictures on the walls first. For all he knew, Franklin Forrest had displayed an original Van Gogh in his front room. A smile tugged at Duncan's mouth. He had reluctant respect for a thief with that kind of balls.

But a quick tour showed him the art was mostly Victorian prints. One reasonably decent oil from the period held pride of place over the mantel. An embroidered sampler with a schmaltzy saying surrounded by twining hearts hung over an overstuffed, high-back chair with an embroidered footstool placed in front.

Rapidly he checked behind the frames for a wall safe. Nothing. Shielding the light, he crept to the dining room. A decent still life—early-to-mid-eighteenth century—hung over a burled walnut buffet. No Impressionists. No wall safe.

He headed for the back of the main floor and discovered a TV room, a big old kitchen that looked like a set for a fifties family sitcom, and a den/library/gentleman's study that smelled of pipe tobacco.

Duncan's knee twitched. Here was where the old guy had spent most of his time. The room felt warmer, more lived in and less rigidly tidy.

He stepped inside and wished he dared turn on a light but knew he couldn't risk it. This wasn't a big city where nobody knew his neighbor's name, much less cared if there was an unauthorized stranger in the house; this was Hicksville.

After a quick inspection of the walls, he headed for the big oak desk and slid open the top drawer. He heard a car crunch over the gravel drive and flicked off the penlight, muttering a curse.

Maybe it was someone turning around or something, but as he waited, backing stealthily to the wall, he heard a car door slam. By the time he heard a key scrape in the front door lock, he'd run out of time to leave. He dove behind an ancient leather couch, curious to discover who else was spending time in Franklin Forrest's house.

Alex shut the door to her grandfather's house and sadness joined her like a pensive ghost. She didn't shudder. She felt no fear. Her grandfather had died here in the house he'd loved just as he would have wanted.

She wished she could see her grandpa's ghost. She'd

love to see him one more time, to indulge in one of their rambling discussions, and she'd love his advice on what to do—about this house, her future, the mess of Gillian's marriage. Though she couldn't do that, of course, even if he were here. She, Gill, and Eric had all agreed to keep the marriage disaster from him. Eric was the son Franklin Forrest never had and he'd been so proud of him, it would have broken his heart to know Eric and his troubled granddaughter were no longer together. He would have worried about Gillian.

Now that was another legacy that had fallen to Alex—worrying about her wayward cousin. Although she wasn't as soft as her grandfather. She was firmly in the pull-yourself-together camp of human psychology.

Even as she drew in a breath of stale air, she imagined the presence of a living, breathing man and, flipping on the hall light, went straight to her grandfather's study, where she felt close to him and could work on his legacy.

She opened the desk drawer where the tapes were neatly stacked in chronological order. Franklin Forrest had dictated his memoirs onto tape and it was her job to transcribe the notes to computer. He'd only made it to the early 1990s in the story of his life, but by then, most of the significant events had already happened.

In the last month, in the sporadic hours she'd spent transcribing, she'd managed to get two tapes done—his account of his childhood and early years in Oregon. She reached automatically for the third, the next in line chronologically, and realized she didn't have to be quite so rigid. She almost blinked at her own audacity, but she could rearrange computer files to her heart's content. She decided to skip to the tape after the war years, knowing it contained his account of meeting and marrying her grandmother.

She slipped the cassette into the player and pushed "Play." The creaky old man's voice filled the room and a wave of grief hit her so suddenly she had to grab a tissue. It was silly. He'd lived a good long time and he hadn't endured a lingering illness. He was probably enjoying an afternoon rest when he'd suffered a heart attack right here in this room. She should be so lucky.

But then she wasn't crying for him, she realized with a sniffle. She was crying for herself. Because she missed him.

Tossing the tissue in the trash, she got to work and let her grandfather's voice lull her as he talked of seeing the woman he would marry. "She was my heart," he said gently, "and my greatest treasure."

Alex grabbed another tissue and then her fingers had to race to catch up with his next words. She loved listening to his stories of courtship and marriage—they sounded so safe and happy on this day when she'd faced violence and death.

And passion. She licked her lips recalling, and then swiftly banishing, Duncan Forbes's kiss.

She was typing up the details of her grandmother and grandfather's early marriage. The decorating of the house that was already old, even then; their first car, a Ford Packard. She could almost see her grandmother through her young husband's eyes as she sat contentedly rocking on the front porch, her needlework in her hands. Their grandmother's work adorned samplers, footstools, cushions, household linens and they still used the communion cloth she'd done in crewel-work at the Swiftcurrent Presbyterian church.

Alex started when her cell phone rang, pulling her sharply forward half a century.

She scrambled in her bag for it and answered.

"Hey, Alex. How are you holding up?"

"I'm okay, Tom. Thanks for calling me back."

"No problem. I guess you're wondering about when you can open the library. We're going to need another day. You can open the day after tomorrow. Okay by you?"

"Yes. That's fine."

"Do you want to book the cleaners for tomorrow night?"

"Yes. If you're sure . . . I mean, did you interview the cleaners?"

"Of course we did. Mrs. Rodriguez went straight to the hospital after they finished cleaning the library, and her husband did one more job and then joined her there. Their daughter gave birth to a nine-pound baby boy right around the time of the murder. They were there along with nurses, family, and friends. All right?"

It was hard not to worry. She was suspicious of everyone from the cleaners to a visiting art professor. And on top of all that, now she had to feel guilty that she'd been too preoccupied to know that the Rodriguezes' first grandchild had entered the world.

"Look, Tom. I'm not sure if this is important, but . . ." It was harder to tattletale on a man she'd kissed passionately than she would have believed.

"Go ahead and tell me. If you think it's important, it probably is."

"It's about Duncan Forbes. As I was leaving him today, I noticed he had a streak of blood on his wrist and the sleeve of his shirt. He probably got it when he turned the body, but . . ."

She heard a creak and pop from the direction of the old couch on the other side of the office. She started, then realized she was hearing the normal noises of an old house settling for the night. She shook her head. Her crazy day was making her fanciful.

"Thanks," Tom said grimly. "I'll check it out." Suddenly, she didn't feel that she'd been fanciful at all. Obviously, Tom had his eye on Duncan. She ran her tongue around her mouth, wishing she had her mouth-wash with her to rinse out even the memory of those kisses.

She was past the halfway point in the tape, and she was pretty sure she was about to find out that her grandmother was pregnant with her own mother, when someone knocked on the door.

Neighbors? Polite burglars?

She crept soundlessly out of the study and into the dining room where she could see the front porch without being seen. And then quickly went to open the door.

"Eric," she greeted him with pleasure.

As always when she saw him, she was amazed at how well he'd cleaned up, the long-haired, loose-limbed boyfriend Gill had brought home with her from California, and who was now as clean-cut and polished as the businessman and politician he'd become. He'd taken over Forrest Art and Antiquities when her grandfather retired—and had pleased the older man no end when he refused to change the name of the store. In the last election, he'd also won a seat on the city council.

The transformation suited him, and she had to admit her grandfather's faith had been justified. The modest mail-order venture her grandparents had added to the retail portion of their business had blossomed with the advent of the Internet and online auctions. Eric was busy enough to employ a fulltime staff of two to work with him.

"What are you doing out this way?"

"I drive by if I'm in the area to make sure everything's all right. I saw your car out front."

"Well, come in."

"Thanks. I wanted the opportunity to talk to you about something."

Chapter 7

Hidden behind the big leather couch, Duncan felt as though he were locked inside a very old trunk. Forty minutes of crouching was enough for any man and he'd thanked the powers above when the doorbell sounded and Alex left the room, thinking he'd hightail it out of there.

If he knew the stolid sergeant, he'd only stop to iron his uniform before heading out to interview Duncan Forbes about the "blood" on his forearm. He hadn't noticed the streak himself until he'd climbed into the shower late this afternoon. He ought to be there to explain to the sergeant when he called.

But, perversely, the minute he heard a man's voice at the front door and Alex's friendly reply, Duncan made do with a quick stretch and refolded his limbs. He took a chance they'd be too busy chatting to look behind the couch and eased his way to the end where he could eyeball the doorway.

Sure enough, the two who came in weren't looking

in any corners, but at each other. And with obvious affection.

He stifled a quick flare of annoyance. Oh, the sexy librarian had played him, all right. No man in her life, huh? He disliked the smooth-looking blond man with the politician's smile on sight. He'd bet his left nut the guy was trying to look down her top. He knew, because he'd had his head bent that exact same way for most of the day, trying to do the very same thing. Yeah, men are pigs, but it takes one to know one.

He stuffed himself back behind the couch and eavesdropped shamelessly.

"I'm sorry I can't offer you a soda—all we have is water," Alex said.

Leather squeaked as she seated herself on the couch, not a foot from his head. What was she talking about? He'd spotted a crystal decanter that glowed gold in the light. Scotch, and a good one, he guessed. He'd been salivating over it as he crouched back here, his throat getting drier and drier in the dust.

The man sat beside Alex, of course, and Duncan was only happy he didn't have to be further tortured by the sounds of ice clinking in drinks while he performed his impression of an earthworm rolled up at the side of the road, slowly drying out in the sun.

If they started going at it, his predicament was going to get a lot worse, and fast. He wanted to be the man rolling on the couch with Alex, not stuck between the creaky old chesterfield and the wall when the former started rocking with passion.

"I don't want a drink. I wanted to see you."

Here we go, thought Duncan, wondering what he could use to stick in his ears so he wouldn't have to listen to a woman he desired putting out for a guy who belonged on a toothpaste commercial.

"Why?" She sounded surprised, which had to be good. Maybe she wasn't as fixated on a roll on the couch as her boyfriend.

"I should have been there for you today. I wanted to, tried to get in the library, but they wouldn't let me in. I even pulled the family connection, but no dice. *Sergeant's* orders." He snorted. "Jumped-up Boy Scout."

"I'm sure Tom was only doing what he thought was right. He had to secure the crime scene."

"For Christ's sake, I wasn't going to mess anything up. I'm a city councilor and a relative. I only wanted to be there for you. It must have been hell."

And nice of you to remind her of that and put her through it again, Duncan thought. The man sneezed—once, twice, three times—and each time Duncan felt his head squished against the back wall. Then he felt the load lighten and the sound of a nose blowing.

"Have you been around a cat?" Alex asked.

"Or something. I've got so many allergies I can't keep track."

"It's nice of you to worry, Eric. Thanks. I never want to go through that again. But I'm fine."

"That's why you're sitting here in this old house alone." Duncan heard the squeak of a spring and felt the sofa shift. He guessed *Eric* was taking her hand. Or getting ready to maul her. Family, he'd said. What family? He thought she didn't have anyone locally but a cousin. A female cousin.

"Well, there are things to do and . . ." Alex laughed softly, but with a sad note running through it. He could imagine her eyes sparkling. "You're right. I ran straight to Grandpa."

"Next time, come to me," the man said in a nasal tone, and then blew his nose again.

There was a short pause. "Thank you, Eric."

Behind the couch, Duncan rolled his eyes.

"No. I mean that. You seem troubled. If there's anything you want to talk about . . . any way I could advise you. Franklin—well, he was like a father to me, you know that. I'd like to feel I could pay him back in some way by giving you a shoulder to lean on."

A cock to suck on. Slimy bastard.

"Thanks—there *is* something preying on my mind." Duncan's ears perked up, hoping she'd reveal to Mr. Toothpaste the whereabouts of the painting. Once he knew the Van Gogh's location, it was game over.

There was a pause and he waited with growing excitement, his leg muscles already tensing, ready to run for the treasure. He slowly breathed the smells of dust and old man, until he heard her voice again. "Why anyone would put a dead man into my library."

To scare you into revealing the whereabouts of the Van Gogh?

Mr. Whiter-than-white said, "What are you saying? He didn't die there?"

"No. The police think he was killed somewhere else and moved." Duncan heard the slight tremor in her voice, and then nothing as both speakers paused.

"Do you have any idea why someone would do that?"

"No."

"Do you know who the man was or why he was there?"

"No. I'd never seen him before. It doesn't make sense."

More silence.

"Well, maybe someone will come forward who knew him or saw something. I'm sure they'll get whoever did this, Alex. But in the meantime, if you think of anything, or remember anything, anything at all, you can come to me day or night."

"It's good to know there's someone in town I can trust. But we need to change the subject now. I'll never sleep if I start obsessing over that poor man."

"Right. Of course." There was a pause. "Have you talked to Gillian lately?"

Another heavy pause, dripping with unspoken meaning. Conversation between these two was like a Bergman film. "Yes. She called me earlier this evening." Alex made a sound between a sigh and a groan. "My day's been one high point after another."

What about the lunch with an exciting new man in town? What about the scorching kisses and the fact that you're about to have the affair of your life, babe?

A heavy sigh. "Don't spare me. Did Gill sound whacked out?"

Alex spoke in an expressionless tone, like someone delivering bad news and trying hard not to have an opinion about it. "She said you wanted to get back together."

The couch jerked and he heard footsteps pacing. "Oh God, Alex. I don't know what I'm going to do. She needs help, more than I can provide."

"So it wasn't true."

"I'm sorry. I know it's making your life even tougher that Gill and I broke up. Maybe if I'd known Franklin was going to . . . that there wasn't much time left, I'd have stuck with the marriage longer. Well, I didn't. It was hell walking out on her, you have to know that, but I've propped her up for eight years. The drugs, the booze, the lies . . . I couldn't take it anymore. I dropped by a couple of days ago to see how she was holding up. She wasn't as close as you were to Franklin, but well, he was always so good to her."

"Yes. Yes, he was."

"She was high as a kite. I guess in her deluded brain

she thought me dropping by meant I wanted to get back together."

"I'll be honest," Alex said. "A part of me hoped it was true, even though I didn't believe her story. You helped her a lot. It's been years since she's made a fool of herself in public or showed up drunk or high at a family function."

"I hoped we could get clean and sober together. But she never stuck to the program."

"I'm so sorry. But thank you for not letting Grandpa know. At least he died happy, and thinking Gill was taken care of."

"I'll still do everything I can for her. I won't let you take on the entire burden of your cousin."

"You've got your business to think of—and your political career. The next mayor of Swiftcurrent needs to be squeaky clean."

"I haven't decided if I'll run for the mayor's job yet, but I appreciate the support."

God, Duncan was going to puke if he had to listen to much more of this. Were they lovers? Was that the real reason this guy had left his wife? The woman who had to be Alex's cousin and obviously the skeleton in the Forrest family closet. One of them, anyway.

The two didn't sound like lovers, but the way Mr. Smarmy had been checking out Alex's cleavage, he wanted her buck naked and writhing beneath him on this very couch.

But it turned out sweaty sex on the old couch, with Duncan's head getting smacked rhythmically against the wall, wasn't on the agenda tonight.

"Alex, I've been wondering . . . this isn't easy for me to tell you, but we're going to have to sell the house."

"This house?"

"No. No. Your grandfather left this place to you and

Gill. It's nothing to do with me. I'm talking about my house. Gill's and mine. Now that we're going ahead with the divorce, it's got to be sold."

"But that's Gillian's home . . . With her problems, and the breakup, doesn't she need stability right now more than anything?"

A heavy sigh—that was going to be dynamite if this guy ever went into serious politics—issued with slow expulsion, sounding as though it came straight from his heart. "I hate to sell the house from under her, but it's inevitable. There are debts."

"Oh, Eric, no. Her drug habit?"

"I didn't say that."

Hah, what a prince.

"You didn't have to." Again the couch rocked, and Duncan bet that the woman was treating her cousin's ex to a big, lay-your-head-on-my-shoulder hug. "Every time I start to think maybe there's hope . . ."

"It's embarrassing to admit this to anyone, but I need the cash to pay off the debts. The place needs painting and the carpets have to be cleaned before it goes on the market—then there are the realtors coming through. I'm sure you can appreciate, that is, under the circumstances, it would be better if she wasn't there."

"I understand." Another Bergmanesque pause for deep contemplation of the human condition, while Duncan tried not to contemplate his own all-too-human incipient emphysema from inhaling dustballs all evening. "Where will she go?"

That heart-tugging sigh again. "Could she stay here for a while?"

"Here?" Alex sounded horrified. "In Grandpa's house?"

"I know it's an imposition, but it is half hers and, frankly, it's all I can think of. I thought of a few places downtown but—"

"With her history, no one will rent to her."

For all her *milk of human kindness* posturing, Ms. A. M. Forrest was amazingly reluctant to let her soon-to-be-homeless cousin into the home of which she was now co-owner.

Interesting. Could it be there was something here Alex didn't want her cousin stumbling over? Something about seventy-two and a half by ninety-two centimeters covered with bold swirls of color and signed *Vincent?*

"But I want to get this house ready to go on the market."

"You're selling?" Eric sounded appalled.

Duncan wasn't thrilled, either. Damn, he needed to find that painting.

Of course, no man succeeded in politics without some pretty sophisticated persuasive abilities, and Mr. Toothpaste didn't stint. Whether she wanted to do a favor for this guy, who seemed awfully close for a cousin-in-law, or to help out the cousin with the little chemical abuse problem, Duncan wasn't certain, but within five minutes of her horrified reaction to the idea, Alex agreed to let her cousin move in.

"But it's only for a few months until she finds something else. And I'm operating on a zero-tolerance agenda. I mean it, Eric. I won't have our grandparents' home the site of drug and alcohol abuse. It would be so disrespectful."

"I'll explain that to her, naturally. Thanks, Alex. It will help me out enormously. Um, maybe we'd better keep away temptation . . ."

"I'm not—oh, you mean Grandpa's whiskey decanter. It's the only alcohol still in the house. It reminds me of him to see it sitting there."

"Would you like me to—"

"And risk your teetotalling reputation?" She laughed lightly. "No. I'll take it to my place. But thanks."

Duncan felt like leaping to his feet and offering to

take the decanter off her hands. A good, thorough soaking with single malt was the best cure he could think of to clear the dust from his tongue, and the treacly sweetness of tonight's overheard conversation from his gullet.

"Look, I know this place is half hers, but can you give me a week? I'd like to finish transcribing these notes. I . . . I like to do the work here."

"A week."

"Maybe less. The library will open again day after tomorrow, and I've got the evening book club Thursday night. Other than that, I'll have lots of time to devote to these tapes."

"Well, I do have some good news. Forrest Art and Antiques is going to pay to publish a thousand copies of Franklin's memoirs when you finish them. We'll donate them to libraries, university archives, and schools."

"Oh, Eric, you don't have to—"

"Yes, I do. It's my memorial to the man who turned my life around."

Where did this guy come up with these lines? Daytime soap operas?

"I'm touched. I know Grandpa would be so honored. Thank you."

"No more. Please. I promise I'll keep a good eye on Gillian while she's here. I'll stop by regularly to make certain she's all right and respecting your wishes." He sighed. "But if things don't improve . . ."

"Yes?"

"Well, we may have to consider a rehab clinic. And I doubt she'd go willingly."

"Oh, poor Gillian. I hope it doesn't come to that."

"Me, too. But I want you to be prepared," Eric said.

"Well, I guess I should be going."

"I'm done here for tonight," she said in a subdued tone. "I'll see you out."

Duncan gave them time to leave, stopping only to scoop the tapes out of the drawer and pop them in the dark cloth bag he'd brought along just in case. He'd prefer it if he was sliding the Van Gogh into the bag, but the tapes might hold some clues apart from the incredibly boring story of the old guy's courtship and marriage that had had Alex sniffling.

He'd have the tapes copied and back in that drawer by tomorrow night.

Then he realized that the sergeant was probably staking out his place at this very moment, possibly with a search warrant. Getting caught with Alex's tapes was not a smart idea. Reluctantly, he returned them to the drawer exactly as he'd found them. He'd come back when she was at work, and before the loser cousin moved in.

And now he had a deadline to search this house thoroughly. If the Van Gogh was here, he'd find it. He had a week.

Duncan slipped out of the back door and sprinted for his vehicle so he could confirm that Alex drove straight home. Preferably alone.

He tried to be philosophical about the fact that she could be having an affair with her cousin's ex—hell, maybe she was the cause of the split. But when she pulled into her building's parking lot alone and went up to her apartment, still solo, he let out a huff of relief. It wasn't that he cared about her morals, he told himself, simply that he didn't share women. If she was humping the toothpaste ad, he'd have to leave her alone. And that would be a tragedy.

Having seen Alex safely inside her apartment and the lights on, he sped on over to his place until he hit the Riverside turnoff. Then he drove slowly down the dark, rutted lane to his cottage, not wanting to startle whatever posse the stalwart sergeant had assembled. But he eased all the way up to his parking spot behind his temporary home and still saw no cops.

He was a little disappointed in Sergeant Tom. He'd expected, from the look of the man, that he'd follow up every lead like an eager bloodhound. Duncan could have brought the tapes with him after all.

His car door made a loud thunk in the quiet, almost-deserted cottage complex. The owners seemed to be the frugal sort who didn't see the point in wasting energy burning lights off-season when there were no guests to speak of, so the dark was thick and damp with the smell of freshly rained-on cedar trees. His boots shuffled gravel as he approached his doorway while the river whispered its midnight secrets in the background.

His key scraped over the lock in the dark and he was just reaching for his penlight when a voice said, "Where've you been?"

"Jesus!" He jumped and only barely hung on to the keys. "You scared the shit out of me." He turned to glare toward the direction of the voice, which was a few feet from the door and downwind.

The bright light of a heavy flashlight, the kind that doubles as a billy club, snapped on, half blinding him in the night.

Duncan managed to get the door open and turn on a couple of his own lights. "You might as well come in," he said and stomped inside.

Perkins followed, still holding the flashlight, his gun in easy reach. A second uniform appeared at the doorway.

"What can I do for you?"

"We came by earlier with a couple more questions but you were out. We've been waiting over an hour."

"If I'd known we had a date, I'd have rushed home."

"Where did you go?"

"I grabbed a bite to eat at the roadhouse just outside town and then I went for a drive. Clears my head."

The sergeant gave him an impassive cop's stare designed to intimidate. They'd check, and find out he'd been at the roadhouse. He was a stranger in a small town. He was bound to be remembered.

"Alone?"

"Yeah."

"Do you mind if I take a look at the clothes you were wearing this morning?"

"Why?"

"The forensics guys want to get a fiber match. Then, if they find a thread, say, on the dead man's clothing, they can confirm whether or not it came from your clothing. It's just routine."

Duncan leaned against the pale green lino counter of his tiny kitchen and then shrugged. Perkins wasn't much of a liar, but he'd seen worse. "Sure. They're in the bedroom, on the chair."

Perkins jerked his head and the young no-name officer trotted off to pick up his dirty clothes.

"You'll get these back," Perkins said when the young fellow jogged out with the clothes already in an evidence bag.

"Don't bother returning the shirt. I got red paint all over the sleeve. It's ruined."

Their gazes connected for a split second. Perkins said, "Take those out to the car—I'll be there in a minute."

Duncan raised his brows a fraction as the sergeant moved into the tiny living area adjacent to the kitchen. "You paint?"

"I dabble." Following Perkins, he knelt to where he'd stored his painting stuff behind a chair and dragged out his box of brushes and paints and the small oil he'd started the other night. He'd never be an artist, but the hobby relaxed him and allowed his mind to wander, bringing him some surprising insights.

He was about to explain to Perkins which colors he'd used on the rather uninspired still life, but he saw the sergeant's attention had wandered. He was looking at the climbing gear laid over the couch, including the new carabiner and chalk he'd bought yesterday. His harness and ropes were laid out alongside them.

"You climb?"

"Yep. It's one of the reasons I chose to come here to write my book."

Perkins nodded to the bag with the logo of the Swift-current Outdoors Store on it and sent him one of his trademark impassive glances. "I'll take you up when I get a day off. Show you the best spots to climb around here."

It sounded more like a command than an invitation.

"That's great. But I can hire a guide. Don't want to take you away from the investigation."

"You've been very cooperative. It's the least I can do for a new climber in town. I'll give you a call when I get a day off."

Smooth, Duncan thought as he saw the sergeant off the premises. Very smooth. Wasn't that something to look forward to? Rock climbing with the man who wanted to jail him for murder.

"Hey," he said when Perkins took the first step out into the dark night. "Off the record? We're on the same side."

There was a pause and he heard stones rub together as the heavy boots turned on the gravel. "Off the record? You mess with Alexandra Forrest and I'll break your balls."

Chapter 8

_____

T he next morning, Duncan was leaning against his car, which was parked right outside Alex's place when she came down. It was a sunny, crisp day and he was pleased to see he'd guessed right by waiting at the front entrance to her apartment building. She was walking to work.

He allowed himself a moment simply to enjoy the sight of her in low-slung black pants that hugged all the places he wanted to, high-heeled boots, and a black pea jacket with a bright red scarf at the neck. Then she spotted him and he instantly donned a mask of righteous indignation, crossed his arms, and straightened.

She hesitated before letting her apartment door swing shut behind her, as though debating whether to turn tail and bolt. A slight flush mounted her cheeks. He wasn't certain whether it was because she was recalling the way they'd steamed up the windows of her car last time they'd been together, or because she was worried she'd been swapping spit with a murderer.

"It was paint," he told her, striding forward. Better get her last objection overruled first.

"I beg your pardon?" She gave him that snotty, frigid tone she'd first used on him.

"Thanks for running to the cops, telling them I was a murderer, but it was paint you saw on my shirt. Not blood."

She didn't bother to deny the charge, but he saw some of the stiffness leave her shoulders. "Paint. What were you painting?"

"I'm an art historian. What do you think I was painting? The side of a barn? Pictures. I paint pictures."

The quick flash of relief he saw in her eyes made him glad he'd followed his instincts and confronted her with the truth. She turned him on with her cold, bitchy routine, but she turned him on a hell of a lot more when she was warm and willing.

"Bloodstains," he explained, "would be brown, not red. Air oxidizes the blood so it turns from red to brown. Dudley Do-Right won't be able to arrest me quite yet."

"I did what I thought was right," she said, still as high and mighty.

"Did it occur to you to mention the matter to me rather than the cops?"

She laughed suddenly. "Just like a movie-of-the-week character. A stranger comes to town the day of a murder. A girl, seeing a suspicious red stain on the stranger's arm, asks him where he got it. Poor dame never makes it past the first commercial."

She was right, of course, and mostly his big performance was to let her know he'd been checked out by Swiftcurrent's finest, and so far exonerated.

He let himself enjoy the sparkle in her eyes, the color being whipped into her face by the crisp breeze, and the red, red lips that kissed as though she'd been practicing for centuries.

Her color grew deeper. "I'm going to kill Tom. How could he—"

"He didn't. But who else would have noticed except you? I never went anywhere that day but with you."

"Oh."

"So," he said, shifting closer, "do you want to come and see them sometime?"

"What?"

"My paintings."

She laughed for the second time. This time she was a lot warmer about it. "Does that line ever work?"

"You'd be surprised. Think about it." He leaned forward and tucked the red silk scarf fluttering at her throat more firmly under the lapel, taking his time about it and running his index finger down the line of her throat so she shivered.

"Can I walk you to work?" he asked.

"No. How did you find out where I live?"

"You're in the phone book. Want a ride?"

"No."

"Okay, see you at the library."

She glanced at her watch. "It won't be open for half an hour."

He knew that, just like he knew he'd be there when the doors opened. He didn't want Alex alone in there where she'd stumbled over a corpse forty-eight hours ago. It was bound to be tough on her emotionally, but worse, he had an uneasy feeling that she could be in danger.

"That's okay," he said. "I'll stop at Elda's for coffee and get started on the new Allende novel. I need to have it read by tomorrow night."

She'd taken a step away from him; now she swung around so sharply her red scarf floated free again. "Are you thinking about coming to the Thursday night book club at the library?"

"That's right. I met a couple of the women yesterday. Mrs. Markle and . . . I forget the other one's name. Her sister, I think."

"Bernice Johnson," she said through gritted teeth.

"That's right. They made the book club sound so good I decided to join. It's always good to stay on top of current literary trends."

"Mrs. Markle thought *Life of Pi* was a recipe book," she informed him.

He laughed. "Imagine."

"And when we chose *The Lovely Bones,* I'm almost certain I heard her and Bernice discussing soup stock."

He was still chuckling when he got in his beige rental car and headed for Elda's.

The first day the library opened after the dead body was discovered was an unusually busy one.

Alex would love to think it was the thrill of reading and joy of knowledge acquired through books that had drawn the crowd, but she knew it was ghoulish curiosity.

Well, she figured, every disaster contained the seeds of opportunity, and she marched forward with a bright smile on her face.

"Mrs. Bates," she said to an older woman standing gossiping in the architecture section. "It's so nice to see you back. I've got a new Irish novel I think you'd enjoy reading."

"Well . . . I . . ."

"And we'd better check and see that your library card hasn't expired. Now that we've gone to computer, the old cards don't all work." Swiftcurrent's library circulation system had been computerized in the mid-80s, but she made it sound like last month.

Once she'd released Mrs. Bates, now clutching a shiny new library card and two novels Alex judged would appeal to her, she searched out a new victim.

"Well, Al Garfield, I didn't know you were a bibliophile," she said to the fresh-faced garage mechanic who'd removed his baseball cap, presumably out of respect for the recently deceased.

"No, ma'am," he said. "I'm a Christian."

A snort of ill-suppressed amusement had her glaring over her shoulder only to find Duncan Forbes ostensibly searching for a book but obviously eavesdropping, his eyes twinkling as he glanced her way. And what on earth was he doing back here, hanging around with the other ghouls near the site where they'd found the body, she wondered, even as she struggled not to twinkle back.

She returned her attention to Al Garfield. "Let's get you set up with a library card. I don't believe you have one." In fact, if he'd ever set foot in her library before this morning, he'd done it while she was on her lunch hour.

"Well, I don't . . ."

"It won't cost you a thing and you'd be amazed at the resources here. There are magazines, videos you can borrow, and, of course, books."

"Oh, well. Videos, that's cool. Do you have DVDs?"

"Of course," she replied, thinking she'd grab patrons any way she could. DVDs were a start, and if she had her way the young man filling out his library card application would be reading entire novels by summer—Hemingway and Faulkner by this time next year.

They didn't realize it but the nosy, the curious, and the gossipmongers helped her get through a day she'd dreaded. While the stacks were crowded, while she was culling through them like a border collie rounding up stray sheep, looking for new patrons and pressing books and magazines on those who visited rarely, she was able to take her mind off the last day she'd been here.

Even if the barely suppressed carnival atmosphere and the constant whispering irritated her librarian's sensibilities, she made the best of her opportunities with guys like

Al who'd normally eat live cockroaches before they'd visit a public library.

She was reminded forcibly of the tragedy, however, when she spotted Tom wandering around the stacks in his uniform. For a blank second she wondered if he'd come in search of a book, when she realized he was on duty. He wasn't looking at the books, but at the people. A shiver ran down her spine as she realized he was doing the equivalent of showing up at the murder victim's funeral and scanning the mourners—hoping the killer had shown up.

He didn't speak to her, beyond a quick "Hi" in passing, but she saw him glance at Duncan, who was reading his book club novel in one of the easy chairs near the library's main entrance. He took a step in that direction, then seemed to change his mind.

She invited him into her office and immediately asked, "Have you gotten any leads on who killed that man?"

He shook his head. "I sent the victim's photo out. We ran the fingerprints through the AFIS database and immediately found a match, and a criminal record. His name was Jerzy Plotnik. Name mean anything to you?"

"No."

"He was a minor criminal. A bit of drug dealing, some theft, hung on the fringes of organized crime. He roughed a few people up. He was from L.A. That's all we have."

"No suspects?"

She saw him glance toward where Duncan still sat, but shook his head. "No."

"I'm sure it was a random thing and the killers are long gone."

"I hope so." But he glanced through her window to the busy library. "Have you seen anything out of the ordinary today?"

Alex turned to find she wasn't the only one in her family blushing hotly.

Just what she didn't need today of all days was more stress. "Gillian." Her cousin had been in the library fewer times than Al and his bill cap, so Alex wasn't fooled that she was here for a good read. In fairness, she didn't think she was here out of ghoulish curiosity, either. She must be here about the house.

"Gill. How are you?" Eric said, gentling his voice as though a wounded wild animal had wandered into the place.

"I'm all right," Gill said in her soft voice. She looked all right, too, Alex was relieved to see. Her eyes and speech were clear, her hair shiny, and she was wearing one of her usual flowing outfits. Hippie chic.

She lifted her hands to fiddle with her hair in an old nervous gesture, and Alex noticed her fingers trembled.

Alex still hadn't recovered from the fact that Duncan had taken it upon himself to get her lunch. Or that he'd announced it in front of Eric, who must be thinking . . . well, right now he was probably thinking about Gillian, who, for once in her life, had actually eased over an awkward situation instead of creating one.

"Why don't you come back to the shop with me, Gill. There are some papers—"

"I came to see Alex . . ." She shot a quick glance of alarm at Alex, who nodded reassuringly. Of course it had to be tough going through a divorce from the man who'd been your anchor for a decade, but it was the right thing to do.

"After you're finished, come on back and find me. We'll talk." The antiques shop was only around the corner. A five-minute walk at most.

Gillian took a deep breath, nodded, and followed Eric.

"You didn't tell me your cousin was a babe," Duncan said as he placed a hand at the small of her back and urged her to her office.

"I'll introduce you next time," she said, speeding her pace to evade the warm hand on her spine. "She's newly single."

"Don't be ridiculous. I don't want to sleep with her. I want to sleep with you. But looks run in your family."

They got to her office before she could think of a retort that conveyed all she wanted it to: *One, I'm never going to sleep with you; two, I don't look a bit like my cousin; and three, don't ever treat me like we're intimate in front of people I know.* Since nothing sufficiently comprehensive and crushing sprang to mind, she ignored his remark completely.

He set the bulging brown paper sack on her desk. "There's your lunch."

"That was very—"

"Nice of me, I know."

"Actually, I was going to say, *interfering. Officious,* even."

"Nonsense. I did it for my own purposes. I'm a very athletic lover. You'll need your strength if you're going to keep up."

In spite of the warmth that stole through her, she wanted to smack him. "I'm not—" She closed her lips hard before going on, recalling what had happened the last time she'd claimed she wouldn't be sleeping with him.

Humor danced along with the sexual allure in his eyes. "You're learning." He took the seat opposite her desk and reached for the bag.

"Thanks," she snapped, "but I can feed myself."

"My lunch is in there, too."

She gaped at him, and then at the window that overlooked the library. "You can't eat in here."

"Why not?"

"People will see us. It will give them more to talk about than the dead guy."

He shrugged, leaned over and closed the blinds.

"Would you stop that? Now they'll think I'm—we're . . ." She snapped the blinds open and rolled them up, while Duncan opened the paper sack and retrieved two cans of juice. Orange for him. Apple for her.

She would have chosen apple—if anyone had asked.

He handed her a submarine sandwich wrapped in waxed paper. "I got you ham and cheese," he said, taking out a second sandwich, "but there's turkey if you prefer."

She wanted to grab the turkey, but the truth was she did prefer ham and cheese. She bit into it, chewed and swallowed. "There's no mustard in this sandwich," she said.

He stopped chewing. "You wanted mustard?"

"No. I hate mustard. But you don't know that!"

"Beauty of a small town," he said, sitting back and looking smug. "I asked Elda what you usually have."

Of course he had. He'd wandered across the street to gossip central and ordered her lunch, no doubt in a loud, booming voice.

She'd have poked him in the eye with her sandwich, but she was too hungry.

"Your cousin looks pretty good for a junkie," he said as he munched.

She felt as though she'd been kicked. "How did you know she's—"

For a second he stopped mid-chew and stared at her. "Sorry. Like I said, it's a small town."

So, he'd talked more than book club with the sisters. Of course, she knew that Gill was often the subject of gossip, but she'd have protected her self-destructive cousin from strangers knowing if she could have.

"Are you worried addiction runs in the family?" she asked him, though why she should care for his opinion, she had no idea.

"Don't be an idiot or you won't get dessert."

She groaned. "Don't tell me Elda made her white chocolate and macadamia nut cookies today?"

"She did."

"I am almost ready to forgive you for scribbling on one of my library books."

He snorted. "I paid for that book three times over. If you've forgiven me, does this mean I can bring pens into the library now?"

"I'm grateful, but not that grateful." He'd thought she was joking when she confiscated his pens on arrival this morning. After a fierce argument, she let him keep a single pencil, figuring she could always erase pencil scribbles.

"Why don't I come over tonight?" he said as she moaned with pleasure halfway into her first bite of cookie.

"You think you could compete with white chocolate macadamia nut cookies?"

"I'm such an egotist."

Since that was pretty much her assessment of his character, she kept her mouth shut, enjoyed her cookie, and tried to convince herself it was better than sex.

Her quietly blissful chewing was interrupted by Gillian, who halted in her office doorway. "Oh, I'm sorry. You're—"

"I was just leaving," Duncan said, rising out of the single chair as Gillian entered the small office. He held the back of the chair and motioned Gill into it like a maître d' at a fancy restaurant.

"Want a cookie?" Alex said.

"Elda's white chocolate and macadamia nut?"

A nod, a shared glance of ecstasy, and the two were munching happily.

"So, how are you doing?" Alex asked around a mouthful.

"Okay. Sorry I lost it on the phone the other night."

When Gill was like this, sensible and in control, Alex remembered how much she liked her. She only wished she were like this more often. "It's okay. I know you need someone to talk to sometimes."

Her cousin nodded and flipped her hair over her shoulder. It caught the light and gleamed like rich honey.

"I'm pretty busy today. I can't chat for long."

Gill pulled in a full breath and straightened her spine. "I want to help."

"Okay. Help with what?" She was hoping she'd help with the garden in the old Victorian. Gillian had always had a flair for growing things and their grandmother's pride and joy garden was a bit of a mess. She had a feeling the roses needed to be pruned before summer. Or was that at the end of summer? She couldn't remember, but Gill had always been good with plants.

"Here in the library. I want to volunteer."

Alex felt as though she'd developed a sudden case of tinnitus. She knew it was Gill's announcement that had the Westminster chimes ringing inside her ears, only they were hideously out of tune. About as discordant as her library would be if an addict starting messing with the books.

"I'm, well, I—"

"Please, Alex. I need to do something now I'm alone. I can't sit in the house all day—I'll go crazy."

"But you never even come into the library to take out a book. Why do you want to volunteer here?" The minute the words left her mouth the answer came to her. Of course, she wanted to be close to Eric. Her needy, clinging cousin wanted to plant her kudzu vine roots in the area where her ex worked now that he'd hacked himself free on the home front.

Gillian blushed, a telling sign. "I tried to volunteer with Meals on Wheels and Reading to the Blind. They both turned me down. I'm going to have to get a job, and no one will ever hire me if I can't prove I'm a reliable volunteer."

Are you? Alex wanted to say, but didn't. Her shoulders felt tight as she thought for a minute. There was no way she could tell Gill she didn't have need for volunteers, not with the poster on the wall appealing for them.

Eric was going to have a cow.

But Gill needed a few extra chances, and at least at the library Alex could keep an eye on her cousin. "All right. I can give you a few hours a week. But it won't be glamorous. You'll start by cleaning the baby board books—getting the dried arrowroot cookie and baby body fluids off. If you still want to be a volunteer after you've done that, we'll talk."

"Great," Gillian beamed as though she'd just been offered the chairmanship of IBM. "When do I start?"

"Tomorrow," Alex said, hoping to hell she was doing the right thing.

Chapter 9

Alex paced her apartment, almost tripping as she tried to undress and pace at the same time. She wished for a moment that she smoked, just for the distraction.

She also wished the library weren't a public building. Day after day of going to work—watching Duncan Forbes arrive on the dot of nine, sometimes already standing outside waiting when she opened the doors, was wearing on her nerves.

If only he'd be obnoxious, or deface a few more books, she could keep him out. But Duncan Forbes was the model library patron. If you discounted the way he kept undressing her with his eyes, taunting her constantly without ever saying a word. And when he spoke, he made the simplest declarative sentence sound like a come-on.

Since he was always her first customer, he had his choice of the limited seating and he chose the table and chairs with the best view of her office and the book counter.

No wonder she was thinking about him so much—the man was forever shoving himself within her field of vision.

She had to do something about him. But what?

If she didn't feel the prickle of attraction every time their gazes met, she wouldn't mind so much; but she did—an attraction so hot she was amazed the desiccated pages of older library books didn't burst into flame.

Sometimes he disappeared for a few hours at a time. She had no idea where he went, but she knew instinctively when he left, and she felt the moment he returned. It was driving her nuts.

He'd invaded her library, her book club—she still gritted her teeth when she recalled how he'd charmed all the women in the club as though they were his own personal harem. Worse, he invaded her dreams, so she woke each day increasingly cranky and sexually unfulfilled.

His words taunted her as much as his presence. When he wasn't outright telling her she'd soon be sleeping with him, his glances were sending the message subliminally. She'd thought Gillian might give his thoughts a new direction, but, apart from a cheerful hello to her newest volunteer, he hadn't shifted an iota of his attention from Alex.

And Gillian was another reason she was pacing. She'd volunteered twice, and done just fine. She'd cleaned the gross baby books, then cleaned the CDs and DVDs, then dusted the books without complaint and without messing anything up. She'd helped out at toddler story time and seemed to enjoy it, but Alex wasted so much of her attention checking up on her cousin that she got even less done when her new volunteer was around.

Between worrying about Gillian, wishing the team of detectives could solve the murder, and feeling as though her clothes were being peeled off every time Duncan glanced her way, she was becoming in desperate need of a little tension release.

The last thing Duncan Forbes had said today when he left the library was, "Call me."

She snorted in the quiet of her apartment. As if.

Except that she really, really wanted to.

Swiftcurrent had a lot to recommend it. It was safe, quiet, clean, and neighbors looked out for each other. It was close to recreation—there was fishing, river kayaking, hiking, climbing at her doorstep and only a couple of hours' drive had her at the spectacular Oregon coastline. She was also close enough to Portland that she could shop, get her hair cut, have her city fix any time she felt like it.

But one huge drawback to Swiftcurrent, and the main reason she was planning to leave, was its lack of interesting single men. Apart from Tom Perkins, who was a nice man but not her type, there really wasn't anyone.

That had to be why Duncan Forbes was getting to her.

She didn't even like him all that much. Even when he was doing something nice for her, like bringing her lunch the day she was too busy to leave, there was an accompanying attitude, as though it were all part of some grand seduction, that drove her crazy.

But when he wasn't irritating the hell out of her, he was attracting her with his combination of rugged outdoor pirate looks and the studious concentration he exhibited when he was tapping away on his computer, checking something on the Internet, reading, or making notes. Somehow, he'd become a part of her life in almost every way but the one she most wanted.

What if she simply did as he suggested? Called him on his cell and suggested . . . what? A movie? There was one movie theater in town which showed two new films a month. *New* being the biggest stretch of a word she'd ever seen. The film currently playing had won the Oscar for best picture last year.

Dinner? There was the steak house and one gourmet place in a country inn half an hour outside town. That was it. Besides, she didn't want to contribute to the gossip in Katie's Kut 'n' Kurl, the grocery store, or Elda's Country Café. She probably generated enough gossip without doing anything; Lord help her if she actually gave them fodder.

She finished undressing and jumped in the shower, noting how sensitive her skin felt under the cascading water, her nipples pebbled, desperate for any action at all, even the water sluicing over them. How pathetic.

She might as well face the truth. She didn't want to see outdated movies or eat restaurant meals. She could do those things any day with a number of women friends.

She wanted sex.

With Duncan Forbes.

And she wanted it now.

Once she was out of the shower and wrapped in her terry cloth robe, she'd made her decision. Men like Duncan Forbes didn't come to Swiftcurrent every day. Passing him up would be like not ordering the latest reference books for the library—and that was practically a crime.

She picked up the phone, recalling his earlier comment that she'd feel less slutty if she dated him first. The gorgeous truth was she could eat a meal with the man, go home alone, and be assumed to be having an affair; or she could skip the meal, jump his sexy bones and, unless he blabbed, no one in town would know. Keeping a secret in Swiftcurrent took cunning and guile, but she'd been doing it one way or another since she was fifteen.

A small smile curled her lips. She'd trade battered oysters and coy glances for orgasms and secrecy any day.

Since his card was sitting on her desk beside the phone, it took her no time to dial his cell number. He answered on the second ring, businesslike and clipped. "Forbes."

"Hello. It's Alexandra Forrest."

"Alex?" His tone changed with gratifying speed to unbusinesslike and sexy.

She rolled her gaze. "Yes, Alex."

There was a short pause as she tried to work out what she wanted to say. In the background she heard traffic noises. He must be in his car.

He took care of the awkward pause by saying, "Are you taking me up on my offer to take you to dinner?"

She drew a deep breath and felt the oxygen pump to every erogenous zone in her body. "No. I'm taking you up on your offer for sex."

The second pause was a lot longer than the first and she enjoyed every nanosecond of his obvious shock. But he rallied fast. "Great. When?"

Alex was a great believer that there's no time like the present. "How about now?"

"I'll be there in sixty seconds."

"Sixty seconds?" There was a good five miles between her place and the cottage he was renting. Unless he had supernatural powers . . . She heard a truck go by on the street outside her place and then heard its faint echo from the phone clasped to her ear.

It was her turn for shock. She strode to the window, snapped open her California shutters, and stared out at the street. Sure enough, the beige rental she'd seen outside his cottage when she'd dropped him off was at this moment parked across the street and Duncan Forbes was sitting inside it with his phone to his ear.

He glanced up and even across a road and through

two windows the force of his gaze sizzled her where she stood. "What are you doing there?"

"Coming to see you."

"What a coincidence," she said faintly, but he'd already disconnected.

Now that he was on his way, she was less sure about her great idea. Sex with Duncan Forbes? What if it was awful? She'd have a terrible time giving him the brush-off if he insisted on showing up at the library every day.

She paced once more, too wired to care she was in her robe, her hair a wet mop brushed back from her face.

A knock sounded on the door and reflexively she checked her watch. Fifty-four seconds.

She made him wait another fifty-four while she dashed to the bathroom and applied lip gloss and a tiny dab of perfume behind her ears. Then she answered the door.

He looked more gorgeous than ever with the carnal gleam in his eye and a certain energy pulsing around him that had her response system on full alert. "Is this a social call?"

"No. Business," he said, stepping inside.

Her brows rose. "What kind of business do we have together?"

"Unfinished business." And he pulled her to him and kissed her.

With a little moan, she let go, let her head flop on his shoulder, her lips part, and her body close in on what it had craved since the first moment she'd caught him looking up her skirt, both boyishly disconcerted and appreciatively grown up.

And every minute they'd spent together, between then and now, she realized, had been a kind of mental foreplay. They'd been toying with each other at the library each day, swapping scorching gazes, the ions of the air around them so charged she was amazed her pores didn't steam.

"I have wanted you since the first second I saw you," he said, echoing what she'd been thinking.

"Me, too," she finally admitted.

After two weeks of foreplay, she was as aroused as she'd ever been. Her body shot from zero to incendiary the instant he touched her. He pulled the robe's tie with a quick jerk and she moaned, deep in her throat.

His hands plunged beneath, cupping her breasts, which showed their gratitude for the attention by hardening immediately, the sweet ache spreading. Her nipples were almost painfully pinched by desire and as he touched and stroked them, they grew even more sensitized, sending darts of excitement everywhere.

He never stopped kissing her, his mouth hungry on hers, his tongue demanding a response, which she eagerly gave. She was one open garment away from naked. He wore far too many clothes. She could help him solve that problem, which she did by attacking the buttons on one of his endless creased, natural-fiber shirts.

The linen, or hemp or whatever it was, radiated heat from his body as she unbuttoned him with urgent haste. He was still way ahead of her. She'd barely revealed his belly, hardly taken in the sight of a nicely muscled, satisfyingly hairy chest, when she felt a hand slide down her belly and between her legs.

"No, wait," she gasped, even as she slipped her feet wider apart to give him easier access.

"You're so wet," he murmured against her lips.

Oh, and she was going to get a whole lot wetter, and fast, if he kept touching her like that.

Her hands were trembling so badly she fumbled the last few buttons, her whole attention focused on the sensation of his spread fingers sliding back and forth across her lips, so poutily eager they were practically kissing him back. She felt them swell and grow heavy, as he used two fingers to massage the outer lips and with a lighter touch, stroked her clit with his middle finger.

She was going to come so fast he'd think she was starving for a man. Which would be the absolute truth, but a woman had her pride.

But what was pride compared to the orgasm she felt building inside her like a tsunami?

The force of the wave seemed to start in her toes, travel up through her feet, her ankles, calves and thighs. Completely losing coordination, she ripped the final button, pulling him against her so their chests rubbed.

She was trembling all over, trembling so badly she couldn't tell him, couldn't stop the wave that built, crested, and seemed to hold her aloft, timeless, motionless, perched on the edge. In the distance she heard panting and tiny whimpers and knew they came from her mouth.

"Let go," he said, his voice low and rough in her ear. "I'll catch you."

She might have still hung on but the sneaky devil brought his other hand into play, thrusting two fingers inside her even as he picked up the pace with the rubbing hand.

Alex had never fainted in her life, but she felt close to it now. There wasn't enough oxygen in her system to supply her overworked lungs, her pounding heart, and her engorged clitoris.

He pushed inside her and stroked her at the same time and she cried out as the wave broke and literally knocked her off her feet.

He must have quick reflexes and great coordination, for she'd hardly begun to sag when he'd shifted, throwing one arm around her back and the other underneath her collapsing knees.

"I've got you," he assured her as he hefted her into

his arms as though she weighed no more than the rag doll she was currently imitating.

She felt wonderful—weightless, drowsy, and bobbing along on a warm ocean current. When she came back to herself, she realized she actually was bobbing. He was walking with her in his arms and his destination was her bedroom.

Good.

Fortunately, her neatnik inner librarian snatched at the very expensive bedcover she'd ordered over the Internet from New York, flipping it back so that when he lowered them both to the bed, she sank onto her equally self-indulgent matching Egyptian cotton sheets. Thread count in the millions.

She only felt the cool, luxurious cotton against her calves and feet and she frowned, realizing she was still cocooned in her white terry robe. This wouldn't do. But she was really much too lazy and heavy with reple-tion to put the effort into taking the thing off.

Her energies were needed to watch Duncan Forbes strip, which he did with economical and flattering speed. That haste had to mean he was as anxious to be inside her body as her body was to welcome him. Already, the post-orgasm pulsing was turning into pre-penetration pulsing.

His shirt was floating to the floor as white as a flag of surrender, and she took a moment to enjoy the muscu-lature of his shoulders and chest. The man was buff. He didn't get like that spending day after day at a library— or teaching.

"How do you keep in shape?" she asked idly.

He grinned at her, his hands busy unzipping and shucking his khakis. "Rock climbing. It was one of the draws of this area."

He was down to briefs, striped gray cotton, but she

tried not to peek or to imagine what he would look like without them.

Rock climbing. They were talking about rock climbing. She lifted her brows. "I haven't seen you do any rock climbing since you've been here."

"Honey, I've been too busy storming the citadel."

She gave him her best librarian frosty stare. "Is that some vulgar expression for—"

"Fucking your beautiful brains out? Oh, yeah."

"Well, you haven't done it yet," she said, trying unsuccessfully to keep the smile off her face. His briefs went the way of the rest of his clothing and the smile froze.

Oh, my God. The man was hung.

She knew she was staring, mesmerized by a jutting penis that made her gooey and soft just thinking about how far inside her it would reach, all the delightful spots it would stroke along the way.

"Better get right to it, then," he said and took the step that separated them.

Naked, her body cried out. *Have to be naked.* Right, the damn robe. Not even caring if she looked desperate and ungainly, she rolled and twisted until she was free of the confining terry cloth.

Instead of helping her, Sir Galahad just stood and watched.

"Thanks for the helping hand," she muttered as she tossed the robe aside.

"You are more gorgeous than I'd imagined in my wildest fantasies," he said softly, making her forgive him immediately for standing there watching her struggle.

She knew she had a good figure, and didn't waste a lot of time on false modesty, but she'd never felt quite so good about her body as she did at this moment with Duncan gazing at her, unblinking.

As turned on as she already was, the idolatry in his

gaze had her nipples aching and her clit perking up again.

"Get in this bed," she ordered.

He placed a knee on the mattress, then stopped with a groan. "Have to get a condom."

"There are some in the bedside drawer," she said, pointing.

He nodded, and retrieved one. When he would have rolled it on, she stopped him by twitching it out of his hand.

Nothing was shrouding this baby until she was ready.

"Has anyone ever told you, you have a beautiful penis?" she asked him.

He chuckled, "Not recently," he said, wheezing at the end when she wrapped her hand around the warm, hard flesh and squeezed. Oh, he was gorgeous.

She leaned over and kissed him, touching the tip with her tongue. He groaned and his hips jerked. She ran her tongue slowly all around the head.

In that instant, control shifted to her. With one orgasm out of the way, she wasn't as helplessly needy as she had been. She could take her time and torment him a little—not too long, because her own body still required some pretty urgent attention, but she certainly had time for some gentle teasing.

Duncan had yet to experience any relief. He'd been hard when he got to her door and he was harder still now.

His erection jutted from a thatch of rough auburn hair, his scrotum peeking dark and mysterious from below. She licked her lips and took him into her mouth.

Through her lips she felt the fine quivering in his flesh, like the initial tremors of an earthquake, and knew she teased him much longer at her peril, so she swiftly sheathed him.

Just as she lifted a knee to climb on top of him, he

rolled over and pinned her with his weight, gazing down at her with eyes so fiery she ignited all at once. She parted her legs wide, hooked her calves around his hips and tilted her pelvis, knowing she'd need to be as open as possible to accommodate him.

He watched her face, taking hold of his erection to guide it slowly inside.

She gasped at the initial penetration. Oh, it felt so good to be stretched like this. Her body had craved this for too long.

He was as considerate as she could have wished, taking his time, easing into her slowly enough that her body naturally opened for him. Not since her first time had she felt so stretched, opened so wide.

She felt the effort it cost him to go slowly and not plunge wildly into her and she silently thanked him for his restraint. It felt as though he was inside her as deeply as it was possible to go, and still there was more of him. She experienced a moment of panic. This wasn't going to work. There was simply too much of a good thing here.

It seemed as though he read her mind, or perhaps some signal from her body stopped him. He spent a while kissing her, holding his pelvis utterly still. His lips moved down her throat and her head went back on a sigh. She didn't notice his hand move between them until she felt him stroking her hot spot with tiny, circular movements.

She grunted with pleasure, and hardly knowing what she was doing, thrust upward. Somehow, there was room and he was all the way inside. So deep inside her their hipbones touched.

"You okay?" he whispered.

"Oh, yeah." She smiled up at him and nudged at him with her pelvis, letting him know it was time to move.

Which he did. Slowly.

She grasped his shoulders and matched his rhythm.

"I love this beauty mark," he said, kissing the small black mole just to the right of her left nipple.

A little faster.

She began panting as excitement built inside her.

Faster still until her hands were slipping off his sweat-damp shoulders and her eyes were losing focus.

Somehow she felt he was still being polite and there was no room for politeness in this bed at this moment. Unable to articulate her message, she grabbed his butt and pulled him into her, harder, faster.

With a groan, he let go. He was pounding her, slamming into her, and she was arching up to receive each thrust, loving the power, the friction, the sheer size of the man.

The wave was building again, lifting and carrying her to oblivion. Her head tilted back like a sprinter in the final stretch and she felt the moment her climax lifted her and tossed her into the air. She cried aloud, feeling his girth as her inner muscles squeezed and massaged him. A stroke more, two, and he lost the measured rhythm and tossed and bucked with wild abandon.

She rode the final frenzy with him while her body throbbed out the last of her own powerful climax.

"You should come with a warning," she muttered, when she could finally speak. "You could whip cream with that thing."

A low chuckle rumbled through his chest, which happened to be under her ear. "You seemed to keep up okay."

"That's because I'm a special woman."

"You are that."

Chapter 10

Duncan woke on the tail end of an erotic dream that had him panting instead of snoring.

As he came fully conscious he realized his fantasy was fueled by the woman sleeping beside him with her body curled in such a way that her butt thrust into his crotch. He kissed the nape of her neck and she shifted in sleep, her backside pressing against a morning boner so rampant you'd never know it had done stallion service for most of the night.

He grinned to himself. She hadn't lied to him that day in her car. She really did love sex. Creatively and unabashedly. Who'd have known such an unremarkable town could hide such a woman?

A woman with such a nice butt that he took a lazy tour down her spine, licking and kissing until he arrived at the firm twin cheeks and planted a love bite on each. The first made her wriggle, the second had her waking sufficiently to swat him.

"What are you doing?" she asked in a sleepy voice that nevertheless sounded turned on.

"I'm kissing you good morning."

"My mouth is up here."

"I have a lousy sense of direction. I got disoriented."

He placed his hand on her backside, the middle finger along the crease where her cheeks met. "I'll follow this trail and see where it leads."

He felt her body shake with a chuckle, but he also felt a certain warming along her already sleep-warm skin, and a tension was developing in her body that made him grin and ease her legs apart, then roll her lazily to her back.

His good morning kiss soon had her thrashing on the bed until he sucked the orgasm right out of her.

"Can you die from too much sex?" she asked weakly as he kissed his way up the front of her body.

"What a way to go," he replied, entering her carefully in case he really had overdone it with her.

But she wrapped her legs around him and grasped his hips, pulling him into her and increasing the rhythm when he would have taken it slowly.

After they both came and their bodies were slick with sweat, he finally kissed her lips. "Good morning."

She chuckled, then shrieked, which disconcerted him until he realized she was glancing at her clock.

"I have to get to work." She shoved at him.

"You're a civil servant. Nobody expects you to be at work on time."

"I am never late," she informed him primly. He decided it was one of her qualities that most intrigued him: the primness hiding beneath the sexpot.

She dashed out of bed and he rolled to his back, stacking both pillows beneath his head to enjoy the show.

And she did put on a show. He didn't think an efficiency expert could outdo her for a morning routine that wasted not a nanosecond.

The minute her feet hit the floor, she was in fastmo. Kitchen, bathroom, where he heard the shower, and considered climbing in with her. How difficult would it be to make her late for work?

Before he'd made up his mind about joining her, the shower was over and the welcome smell of fresh coffee reached him.

She brought them both mugs of coffee, but instead of climbing back into bed, she plonked his mug on the bedside table and, while drinking hers, went to her double closet and opened the doors.

He couldn't hide his snort of disbelief. "You color co-ordinate your clothes?"

She glanced back in surprise. "Doesn't everyone?"

"No."

"Well, it saves a lot of time. I also arrange according to the season and separate casual from work wear." While she spoke she was pulling things off hangers and in seconds had a perfectly matched outfit at the ready.

Bright blue slacks in some kind of stretch wool, a silky white top, and a fitted jacket.

Her shoes were in boxes and—he blinked in disbelief. "Is that a numbering system on your shoe boxes?"

Even she must have realized it was a little over the top for as she selected one, she got a bit huffy. "I know, I should be more like you. Two boxes. Ratty sneakers and rattier sneakers."

"Well, at least I don't need a card catalogue to find a pair of shoes."

They were in perfect rows, too.

Just as he was thinking she really was too organized to live, she went to a drawer and pulled out underwear that made him almost swallow his tongue. She slipped into a thong, deliberately keeping her back to him and wiggling her butt as she slipped the narrow ribbon of fabric between her cheeks.

"You're torturing me, you know that."

She chuckled, and turned so he could watch her put on her bra, an absurd see-through affair that was about displaying the goods, not supporting them. In less than a minute she was fully dressed.

Another ten minutes and she was pretty much done. To look at her, fastening a gold belt around her waist, you'd think she'd spent the morning in bed with a fashion magazine and a nail file, not that she'd just prepared and eaten breakfast, showered, dressed, done some kind of makeup and hair thing, and cleaned the kitchen all in under half an hour. She'd impressed the hell out of him but he couldn't admit that.

He rose once he felt he wasn't in danger of getting run over by one superefficient librarian, stretched, and since she was clearly close to leaving for work, started shoving himself into yesterday's clothes.

She regarded him for a moment and he felt her debating whether to leave him alone in her apartment. What was her level of trust? He was anxious to find out.

"Look, you can stay for a while if you like. Shower and eat something. Let yourself out when you're ready. The door self-locks."

He was glad he was looking down as he shrugged into his jeans so she wouldn't spot the triumph in his face. She trusted him.

He had no intention of taking her up on her offer, however. He'd come back later for a quiet snoop.

What was the point of having a father who'd devoted his life to crime if you couldn't manage a candy ass lock like the one on her front door?

"No, thanks. I've got fresh clothes at my place. I'll shower there and grab something to eat."

He found his jacket under the bed, shrugged into it, and pulled her to him for one last kiss. She followed him all the way until he opened the door.

"Hey," he said, glancing back. "I had a good time."

She looked like every sex goddess in history as she sent him back a close-lipped half-smile. She didn't say a word. She didn't have to.

"Cocaine addiction is one of the most difficult addictions to treat," Gillian read aloud. "Tell me about it," she mumbled to herself, tossing the booklet aside and flopping her head into her hand. Some days it just felt too heavy for her to hold it up unsupported.

Addiction had ruined the best years of her life.

And her husband's.

Pushing the well-meaning but depressing booklets off the bed, she pulled herself to her feet and staggered to the shower to start another day.

Alone.

Gillian wasn't any good at being alone. She never had been. People had various handicaps and idiosyncrasies, and she'd learned to accept that this was hers.

She wasn't strong. She wasn't brave. She wasn't independent. She needed to lean. A strong man was her first choice, but, as she'd discovered over the years, alcohol and chemicals could give the illusion of strength and safety. At least for a while.

Now she had no one, and she was going to have to figure out how to make a life for herself.

While the shower pounded, she thought of her cousin, Alex, who'd always done everything right. Smart, educated, well-liked. When she'd been younger and clueless about guys, Gillian had been born with the knowledge of a courtesan, there had been some balance at least. Each played to her strength.

Alex was the girl who spent her lunch hours chairing a debating club meeting, or editing the yearbook, while

Gillian had painted her nails and flirted—sometimes a lot more than flirted.

She tried to help her clueless cousin with hair and makeup and Alex tried to help her study, and, in the end, wrote a few term papers that were good enough to help Gill pass school, but not so good that anyone could become suspicious.

Then Alex blossomed into a sex goddess on top of everything else, and the power balance tipped like a teeter-totter when one person gets off. Thump. Gill was dumped on her ass with nothing.

Maybe it was too late to heal the breach that had sprung up between them over the years, but she was short on people she could count on. Alex might be insufferably snooty and her success might snap at Gillian's heels, but she was family, and right now Gill needed her.

She hadn't missed the way Alex watched her like a hawk every second she was in the library. What did she think she was going to do? Snort drugs off the baby books? Freak out in the middle of toddler story time?

One day, she hoped Alex would trust her enough to let her read the stories to the little kids. She'd love that, and she'd be good at it, too. She loved the kids, and when no one was looking she'd sometimes take a break from whatever shit job Alex or Myrna assigned her and sit on the floor to play with the little guys. The moms were only too happy for a few minutes' break, and she loved to spend time with the only human beings in Swiftcurrent who seemed to think she was okay. She loved their round, chubby faces, and their delight in bright colors and pictures. The way they'd squeal and their whole bodies wriggle with delight when they spotted a picture they recognized—dog, cat, cow. Mama.

Eric had phoned this morning and awakened her.

For a moment her heart had spun out of control at the sound of his voice.

She poured a dime-size dollop of herbal shampoo into her hand and lathered the hair she still wore long even though it was a drag to take care of. What had happened to the girl she'd been? The one so full of hope and promise?

While she rubbed shampoo into her scalp, she thought about all the roads she could have taken and hadn't, and the one disastrous path she had chosen.

When she washed out the suds, tears of bitterness washed down the drain with them.

When her phone rang that evening, Alex was snapping clean linen sheets onto her bed. They felt crisp, cool, and sensual and smelled vaguely of flowers. She'd dusted the bottom sheet lightly with lavender-scented body powder, a tip she read in one of this month's women's magazines she'd flipped through before placing it in the Periodicals section.

The first ring had her insides going syrupy. Duncan must be looking for some action. After the way he'd felt her up in the stacks this afternoon, before she smacked his hand away, then tried to trace the path of her thong, well, his call wasn't completely unexpected.

Normally she wasn't a woman to drop everything for a man, but in this case, she was coincidentally looking for some action herself. They could help each other out.

"Hello?"

"Alex, I'm sorry to bother you like this." The syrup immediately hardened to lead. It was Eric, and he sounded shaken.

"Eric, what is it?" All erotic thoughts fled as her heart

trip hammered. Eric only called her regarding one subject. "Is it Gill?"

"I went to see her, to explain about selling the house. She went nuts on me. Attacked me. I tried to calm her down but she was out of her mind. She . . ." He dragged in a shaken breath and Alex got the feeling he was one gasp away from breaking down and crying. "I tried to leave quietly but she followed and she fell down the outside stairs."

For one cowardly moment Alex wished she hadn't picked up the phone. She didn't want this, to be running to her cousin's side, picking her up and dusting her off. Maybe it was hard-hearted, but she'd just started a very promising affair with a guy who wasn't going to be in town more than a couple of months. With sex like last night's, she couldn't afford to waste a minute.

Pity mixed with frustration. "Is she badly hurt?"

"Bruised and shaken, I'd guess. She was so high she probably didn't feel much."

Something inside Alex went snap. Gillian had done so well in the library that she'd foolishly allowed herself to hope that her cousin might turn her life around. Once more that hope was smashed. "This has gone far enough. I'm going to see about getting her into rehab."

"No. Please don't do that. I . . . I promised her. Let's just give her some time. She's got to get over splitting from me, and your grandfather's passing . . . and . . ."

"Maybe it's time for some tough love, Eric." But she was having a difficult time with the concept herself.

"Please, Alex. I wouldn't have called you if I thought you'd turn her in. She's probably fine. She'll fall asleep and wake up wondering why her head hurts. Really. It's not the first time. Forget I called."

Now she felt hard and mean. Gillian's ex-husband was willing to try and help the woman who'd just attacked him, and all she wanted to do was shunt the problem to some clinic. Except she really thought it was the right thing to do. How long could Gill go on like this?

"No. I'm glad you called. Thanks for letting me know. I'll go over and make sure she's okay."

She hung up and smoothed the bedspread over the freshly made bed, but the smile was gone from her face.

As she lifted her car keys, they felt like a fifty-pound pack she was hoisting to her shoulders.

The phone trilled again. "I'm on my way," she said curtly before the wailing could begin.

"Eager to jump my bones. I like that in a woman," said the sexy, sleepy voice that turned her inside out.

She groaned into the phone. "Why didn't you call ten minutes ago? I've got a family crisis to deal with."

"For someone with no family to speak of, you get a lot of that."

"Don't remind me." All day she'd been thinking about him, exchanging X-rated glances. All for nothing. "I'll call you later if I can get away."

"Need any help?"

There it was again, that calm assumption that he could share her burdens. She felt that same rush of relief she had the day she'd flown out the door right into him after discovering the dead body. Suddenly, everything wasn't quite so terrible and the burden of Gill's latest escapade wasn't so heavy on her shoulders. "No. My cousin probably needs a Band-Aid, a box of tissues, and some strong coffee."

"I stay away from girl problems," he said with deep feeling.

"My hero." But she chuckled as she put down the phone, hoping she could get Gill calmed down and to bed and then maybe get herself to bed. With Duncan, and far from calm.

She ran down the stairs, hopped into her car, and drove to the subdivision of newish ranches that Gill and Eric had called home.

Every light seemed to be burning in the house, she noted, as she pulled into the drive.

She'd been irritated when Eric first told her of the latest drama. And that was before she found out she was giving up sex with a man who topped her list of great lovers to babysit an overgrown, rebellious teen.

Alex wasn't in the best of moods when she stomped up the drive and banged her fist on the door. They had a perfectly functioning doorbell, but she needed the physical outlet of pounding something.

She heard Gill sobbing before she saw her. But irritation turned to reluctant pity when her cousin opened the door. There was a livid mark across her cheekbone that was going to be Technicolor bruising in a day or two. Her eyes were red-rimmed, her hair a mess, her jeans torn at the knee. A bleeding scrape showed through.

Her faux-hippie gauzy top also had a tear, exposing the slope of one full breast. The beauty and allure that had broken countless hearts in their time were still there, but they were faded. Those pretty blue eyes that usually sparkled with mischief were watery and lost.

Gill had keys in her hand and a worn denim bag hooked over her shoulder.

Her cousin was just so damned needy that before she said a word, Alex opened her arms and pulled her in for a hug.

While Gillian sobbed on her shoulder, for some reason she remembered her senior year when she, the bookworm with the nerd wardrobe, had been the needy one. She'd been in Gill's room, sniffling with unrequited love for Jacob Koropatnyk, who was now bald, the father of three, and the proprietor of a marine hardware store in Seattle.

Gill had climbed in her window long after she should have been in bed, and collapsed, drunk, on the bed. No. Not drunk, but beyond tipsy. "Whasamatter?" she'd asked.

Alex was just miserable enough, and Gill not sober enough, that Alex had poured out her grieving heart. "I'm so ugly," she'd wailed. "No guy will ever want me."

"You're not ugly. You don't bother." It hadn't come out that clearly, of course, more like one long word with a few sibilants thrown in that didn't belong. But even that pathetic straw of comfort had helped.

Amazingly, Gillian had remembered their conversation the next day and started Alex on the road to discovering her own style. It was hard to turn her back on the woman who'd shared so much of her life.

"Let's get you cleaned up," she said gently. "Eric told me what happened."

Gill pulled away and nodded, raising a trembling hand to her face. "He told you?" she asked in a pitiful little girl's tone.

"Yes. It sounds like you took quite a tumble when you chased after him."

Gillian turned away, her face blooming crimson, and hauled off and kicked the wall, obviously wishing it were her cousin. "Oh, and you always believe everything Eric tells you," she yelled.

And just like that, all the compassion dried up like an autumn leaf in a bonfire. "You ungrateful wretch!" she yelled back. "I'm trying to help you, and I'm telling you right now, you need to get yourself into rehab."

"Would it ever occur to you that everything Eric tells you isn't true?" Gillian was shrieking at the top of her lungs now, beyond hysteria.

I'm the sober, drug-free one, Alex reminded herself, forcing herself to calm down. A deep breath in, a deep breath out. She tried again. "Gill, you need help. Making up stories only makes you look pathetic."

With an angry howl, Gill jumped away. "How can you say that? He . . . he . . ." Then she raised her gaze and the blankness was replaced with a flash of such bitterness that Alex drew back. "Oh, go to hell," Gill shouted, and bolted past her cousin, knocking her bodily away from the door.

"Don't you get in that car," Alex yelled. But, by the time she'd righted herself and realized Gill's intention, it was too late. She raced out behind her, begging her to wait but, with an angry squeal of rubber, her cousin was gone, driving the car as though it were a jet ski.

Alex's first thought was for the innocent citizens of Swiftcurrent who could be out playing street hockey, or walking the dog, and were liable to be crushed by a woman driving under the influence of God knew what.

She bit her lip for a moment, thinking of how many times Eric had been through scenes like this, but he'd always managed to keep them quiet. Well, she'd blown it and instead of soothing her cousin as she should have, she'd allowed Gill to provoke her.

She wasn't going to race all over town in pursuit—a chase would only urge her cousin to drive faster, putting more people, including her fool self, in danger.

She fingered her cell phone, then, firming her jaw along with her resolve, punched out a number.

"Tom, it's Alex."

Gillian didn't even know where she was going. Her face felt raw, burning with pain and tears. She'd rubbed mascara in her eyes somehow and that made it harder to see. She had only one destination in mind. The hell out of here.

She'd been sobbing so long she'd reached the hic-cup stage, little puffs of breath that sounded childish and pathetic. She wanted a cigarette, but her hands were shaking so badly she'd never manage it. She should pull over, but it was easier to keep on driving.

There was half a tank of gas in the boring gray sedan Eric had insisted on. The orange Mustang she'd had her heart set on was too wild, he told her. Like she'd ever been anything else in her life.

She had maybe fifty bucks in her wallet, Sheryl Crow howling out of her CD player. She'd left town before with a lot less. She smiled sadly. Maybe this time she'd do a better job of running away.

But, of course, luck was no more with her today than it ever had been. Before she'd cleared the city limits, she heard a siren behind her and in the rearview mirror saw the flashing lights headed down the same road she was.

She pulled over to let the police car by, thinking at least now she could light up a smoke. Cigarettes never completely killed the cravings for something stronger, but they dulled their sharp teeth.

She fumbled in her purse for the half pack of Marlboros. They were old and stale because, although she'd quit, sometimes she really needed just one. She knew they were in here somewhere, and because she was busy rummaging, it took a minute for her to realize the cop car had pulled in ahead of her. It wasn't until she recognized the sturdily built man walking toward her, his uniform as crisp as though he were headed for inspection, that she fell in. *Alex.*

"Thanks, bitch," she muttered. Fortunately, there were sunglasses in her bag, so she grabbed them and stuck them on her face, wincing as the frames rested on her swelling cheek. She shook her head so her hair fell forward, licked her lips glossy, and then grabbed for the smokes in the dented pack beneath her wallet.

Tom Perkins stood in front of her door and she made him wait while she finished lighting her cigarette, keeping her hands steady by a fierce act of will. Then she rolled down the window, not bothering to lower the volume on the CD.

"Is there a problem?" she said, careful to give him only her profile, glad the bruising was on her right cheek.

For a long moment he didn't say anything at all, and she was forced to turn slightly, enough to read the expression on his face. She could have saved herself the trouble, though. He didn't have an expression. Probably threw them out with his old football uniforms.

"I was going to ask you the same thing, Gillian."

He didn't raise his voice and she'd pretty much had to lip-read over the music, and with the sunglasses on and the dusk already fading, that wasn't easy. So she reached forward and shut off the music. "Huh?"

"Is everything all right, Gillian?"

"You always called me Gillian. Everyone else called me Gill."

He rocked back on his heels and his hands rested on her open window as though he didn't know what else to do with them. Nice hands. Square, sensible, good-guy hands. "Where are you heading?"

"Was I speeding?" she asked.

"No."

"Is this a social visit?"

He shot her an enigmatic glance. Those same, still-green eyes she'd gone gaga over years ago made her wish quite suddenly that she could turn back the clock to a hot summer's day and live that one day over again. How much might now be different.

He shook his head. "Would you step out of the car, please?"

She just wanted to drive away. Why couldn't they let her be? "Why?"

"Ma'am, I had a report of erratic driving."

"You have known me for twenty years. Give it up with

the ma'am crap. I know who ratted me out and I'm telling you I'm fine."

His eyes crinkled briefly when she got to the *ratted me out* part and she realized just thinking about Alex turned her talk to a childish whine.

"Look," she said, "I'm not drunk, I'm not on drugs, I'm not crazy. Please, can't you let me go?" She hated the way her voice wavered but damn it, all she wanted was one person to believe in her. If it couldn't be her own family, let it at least be this man who'd always been kind to the less fortunate. The lame dog, the bird with the broken wing, why not the chick with the blackening eye?

"Please step out of the car," he said, and opened her door for her.

Gritting her teeth against the humiliation of yet again being thought a liar, she turned off the engine, pushed her feet in their leather sandals to the ground, and stood.

And stumbled.

Chapter 11

Two strong arms grabbed Gillian to stop her going down.

"I am not impaired," she said desperately, yanking herself out of those arms that had rejected her so long ago. "I hurt my knee." She'd forgotten about it, what with the throbbing in her face, and it wasn't until she stood that the scraped and bruised knee came to fiery life.

"Banged your face up pretty good, too," he said.

"You must have aced your detective exams."

"Can you walk to the Cruiser?" He gestured to his vehicle, with the lights still flashing. At least no traffic had gone by, but her luck wasn't going to last forever.

"Why?"

"I need to administer a Breathalyzer."

She wrapped her arms around herself, knowing it was the closest she was going to come to a hug from anyone in this town and, with a shock, felt the loose flap of her top. A glance showed half her boob was on display, and then came the sick knowledge that Sergeant Perkins hadn't even sneaked a peek.

"I have to submit to the Breathalyzer. You can't force me to take it."

"That's right. But I wish you would." For the first time he sounded frustrated.

"Why?"

"Goddamn it, Gillian. Because I believe you. If you refuse the test, I have to take you in based on visuals. I received a report of erratic driving, then I drove behind you for a couple of miles and your speed fluctuated. I think it's caused by emotional distress but it could be booze. You take the test. It comes out negative. I don't have to charge you."

She heard only one part of all that. "You believe me?"

He nodded.

She dropped her cigarette to the ground and stepped on it before letting him take her arm and help her to his Cruiser.

It didn't take long. She blew into a plastic tube a couple of times. He checked her levels and then gave her one of his rare smiles, the kind that turned a serious, impassive face into one of the most attractive she'd ever seen.

"Told ya," she said, feeling a smidgen of her old self surface briefly.

"Have a seat in my office. Why don't you tell me all about it."

She took a deep breath and prepared to unburden herself to the one man who might actually listen. But, after eight years of living behind a barricade of lies, she found she couldn't do it.

"I was upset tonight. About . . . well, it doesn't matter. I fell. Then Alex came over and we argued. I left."

"What did you fall on?" He said it conversationally, but she wasn't an idiot. The man was a cop. Still, he wasn't writing anything down.

"Are you going to make out a report?"

"No. I'm just asking."

"I banged into the front door as I was leaving, then tripped down the cement steps."

He gazed at her for a long moment. "If you need a restraining order against that door of yours, you give me a call."

She nodded, her throat aching.

"Wait here." He walked to her car, locked it, and returned with her bag.

"What are you doing?"

"I'm driving you home. You shouldn't be driving with that knee. I should swing you by emergency."

"No. Please. It's fine. I'll ice it when I get home."

He drove in silence. Confident and understated. His vehicle had one of those air fresheners shaped like a pine tree that she didn't know you could buy anymore. There was no music, certainly no conversation. She fidgeted with the strap of her purse, tugged off the sunglasses and replaced them in their case. There wasn't even static from a radio. "Don't you have a police radio? Like on TV?"

He gestured to a square monitor. "It's all done by computer."

"Cool."

More silence.

"Eric and I broke up." Oh, great. Wonderful social chitchat. She might as well tell him she'd be leaving her window open every night this week in case he wanted to climb in. She clenched her teeth against memory.

"I heard."

The speed limit was thirty miles per hour. He was going twenty-nine. At this rate they'd get to her house by morning.

"Most people would say, 'Oh, gee. Sorry to hear that.'"

A huff sounded, and it was definitely more annoyance than condolence. "I wasn't sorry to hear it."

She'd love to feel her heart leap and imagine he was letting her know he was glad she was now single, but she'd known him too long. What he meant, and what everyone else was too polite to say to her face, was that Eric was well rid of her.

"I'll be better off without him," she said belligerently.

Tom nodded.

She was so shocked she could only stare. And her heart—foolish, silly thing that never learned—leaped in her chest.

"The neighbors are going to love this," she said, when he pulled into her drive. She snorted with amusement. "I haven't been brought home by the cops since I was a teen." She shot him a glance. "Are you going to give me a lecture about responsible behavior?"

"No, ma'am. I'm going to see you safe inside and then be on my way."

"Still the Boy Scout," she muttered to herself.

"Don't be too sure," she thought she heard him say, then decided she was suffering some kind of auditory hallucination.

She managed to get her sore knee to the ground and by gritting her teeth and hauling up on the doorframe, got herself upright, but it was about a thousand miles to her front door. And there were cement steps to surmount.

Well. She hadn't managed to run away, so she was going to have to start facing her problems. With courage. She took a step, and found Tom's arm there, not touching, but handy for her to lean on.

But she'd only this second decided to start standing on her own two feet. She took another step and bit her tongue hard to stop herself from moaning.

With a softly muttered curse, the man beside her said, "Give it up, Gillian," and swept her off her feet and into his arms.

Nothing had ever felt so good. He was solid muscle and she knew he wouldn't let her fall. Her arms looped around his neck and she rested her head against his shoulder. He smelled warm and . . . official somehow. Must be the uniform.

They were at her door far too soon but instead of dumping her there, he took her keys from her and unlocked the door, which Alex must have locked before taking off.

He maneuvered her carefully down the hall and into her living room and settled her on the couch with her feet up.

"Thank you for bringing me—" She wouldn't say *home*. This wasn't ever going to be her home again.

"I'm not done yet. Where's the kitchen?"

"Left, down the hall."

She heard his measured tread and some rustling.

Easing her sandals off, she leaned forward to place them on the floor and noticed the note on the coffee table. A neat, tidy little note in Alex's neat and tidy writing. *"Gillian. Give me a call when you get home."* Hah. Like that was going to happen. And Alex could take her grimy baby board books and shove them up her tight ass. Then there was another line scrawled, not neat at all. "I'm worried about you." And it was signed simply, Alex.

She crumpled the note and shoved it in her jeans pocket. And then Tom was back with a bag of frozen niblets in one hand and a wet facecloth in the other. He wiped her knee with the wet cloth, laid a clean one over the scrape and then rested the bag of frozen corn over the top.

"Pretty efficient."

"I could get you an ice pack for your face, but I kind of think we're too late to stop the bruising."

She grimaced, glad there wasn't a mirror nearby. "Pretty gruesome, huh?"

"I've seen worse." He stood near her, as though unsure what to do with himself. "Can I make you some tea or something?"

She smiled up at him. "No, thanks."

"Can I call someone for you? Your cousin?"

The smile disappeared as though he'd shot it off. "No. I'll watch some television and go to bed."

"Okay if I keep your keys? I'll return your car tomorrow."

He was being so nice to her. But then he'd always been nice to the wounded and helpless. "Thank you."

She thought he'd leave, but instead he moved to the very end of the couch and stood staring down at her with his cop face on. "Who gave you the black eye?"

The back of her throat burned with all the things she wanted to say and couldn't. She shook her head. "I told you. The door."

"There's a dead man in the morgue who didn't die of old age and now suddenly you're banged up. Tell me they aren't related."

She was truly shocked. "No. Of course not."

"Just doing my job."

"Well." She dropped her gaze to her hands, noting a scrape on her thumb she hadn't seen before. "Thank you for believing me earlier."

He didn't say a word, simply looked at her, and once more the years rolled back and she was experiencing the same deep yearning she'd felt back in her senior year.

And he was looking at her the way she wished he'd looked at her when they were young.

"You should have taken me up on my offer to climb in my bedroom window," she said before she could stop herself.

He walked all the way to where the living room joined the hallway and turned. "You shouldn't have run away."

And before she could ask him what in hell that was supposed to mean, the man was gone.

Chapter 12

Duncan jerked as his cell phone vibrated against his hip. He'd turned off the ringer, for obvious reasons. He reached for the phone, the surgical gloves making him slightly clumsy. He checked the call display and shook his head at one of life's little ironies. It was Alex.

"Hi," he said into the phone.

"Hi. Where are you?"

"You sound upset." And she'd sound a hell of a lot more upset if she knew he was currently inside her apartment going through her computer records and e-mails. When she'd headed off to help her cousin, he'd expected her to be tied up for a good long while.

"I am upset. You know what I like to do when I'm upset?"

"I'm hoping I do."

"I like to get laid." Tension crackled in her tone. "I'm on my way to my place. Can you meet me there?"

A silent chuckle shook him. "I'll be there before you know it."

In less than two minutes, he'd shut down her computer and left her apartment. He raced down the stairs, slipped out the side door, jogged a couple of blocks to where he'd left his car, tossed the gloves and his lock picks in the trunk, then removed his Mariners ball cap and the dark windbreaker and tossed them on top of the tool kit. He pulled out an old tweed jacket and shrugged into that. If anyone saw him arrive at her building, he wouldn't want them to clue in that he was the same man who'd just left there.

Then he got into the car, sat and pondered his findings. Alex stocked a lot of herbal tea, but drank mostly strong, dark coffee. She collected erotica in a shelf in her walk-in closet, and then alphabetized it. She kept meticulous financial records on a home bookkeeping program and among her deleted e-mails he'd found some steamy ones from a year back that suggested she'd compensated for a long-distance relationship by having cybersex with the guy when they were apart. The woman was a bundle of contrasts.

But one thing he was certain of. She wasn't hiding a Van Gogh in her apartment, nor had she left any clues as to where one might be.

Alex wasn't the only one who was feeling frustrated this evening.

There was another contrast he wished he hadn't noticed. Her words might be telling him she wanted some raunchy sex, but her tone had been heartbreaking.

What that woman needed was a hug.

He sighed. Hug administration wasn't what he'd have put first on his list, but, in spite of the way he usually acted around her, he wasn't a completely sex-obsessed brute.

He chuckled silently. Not hardly.

When he arrived at her door the second time that night, this time bothering to knock, he reminded himself that being naked within ten seconds was not the priority tonight.

Oh, but he wished it were.

"Hi," she said, in her sultry, come-to-bed tone. To torture him further, she'd already managed to lose her clothes and was robed in a thigh-length, dusky-pink silk gown with overblown roses printed on it. He tried to imagine what combination of paints he'd need to capture the colors of her gown, the sheen of her skin, the deep red of her lips, the pale cream of her cheeks, and the sad, liquid gray of her eyes.

A better artist might translate her beauty to canvas. Duncan knew he never could, so he tried to imprint the image on his memory. He'd seen a lot of Alex since he arrived in Swiftcurrent, but not even after the murder had he seen her so emotionally troubled.

"Hey," he said, kicking the door shut behind him, and suddenly he didn't need to remind himself this wasn't about sex. He simply wrapped his arms around her and pulled her close, where she nestled like a homing pigeon settling in for the night.

"I'm so glad you're here," she said against his chest.

"Rough night?"

She nodded, her hair silky under his chin, but she didn't say any more. He put an arm around her, led her to her bedroom, and tucked her in.

He saw the tension and worry tightening the skin around her eyes and knotting her shoulders. He kneaded the tight muscles slowly and she groaned. He sensed she'd feel better if she talked, so he asked, "What happened?"

The tight muscles in her shoulders quivered, but he kept on kneading them. "Gillian was hurt, and I suggested rehab. Why didn't I bandage her up and give her some support? I could have talked to her about rehab in the morning, when she was herself again."

"Hey, don't beat yourself up. This isn't your fault." No wonder her shoulders were tight—there was too much being dumped on them and it was pretty obvious she had no one to share her burdens.

"I felt like I'd just begun to trust her again, and wham. She's pulled that stunt so many times before. So I lost it." Alex's eyes pinched shut for a moment and he almost felt the flash of bad memory after bad memory from her cousin's past playing themselves in her head. "She screamed off in her car, and I called the cops to go get her. Now I'm worried sick about my cousin, angry with myself for handling her so badly, and on top of that there's an unsolved murder that happened in my library."

"There's nothing you can do about any of that now," he said, admiring her strength and commitment to those she cared about. "You did the best you could."

"Well, it wasn't near good enough."

"Try not to be too hard on yourself. What you need is some sleep." He kissed her lightly and rose.

"Aren't you staying?"

"Yeah." He pulled the toothbrush out of his pocket and waved it in front of her face. "Okay if I leave this in your bathroom?"

"Mmm."

He rinsed his face and brushed his teeth, leaving his toothbrush in the glass beside hers. This was as close as he came to commitment. He'd better make that clear. But not tonight.

He flipped out the bathroom light, entered her bedroom and stripped, crawling into bed with her. She burrowed under his arm until her head was resting on his shoulder, then gave him a quick peck on the lips he imagined a woman married thirty years would give her husband.

He smiled in the dark. He kind of liked it. He

rubbed her back, the bones and muscles fine under the slippery silk.

"Thank you," she said, half sleepy, but with a husky note that had nothing to do with sleep.

"You're welcome," he replied, never changing the rubbing motion on her back.

She reached out a hand and unerringly found his cock in the dark. Then she imitated his rhythm on her back, the slow up-and-down stroke.

He figured he'd been as sensitive as the next New Age guy, giving up sex for a backrub. Now she was getting cruel, tormenting him with those excruciatingly slow strokes that had him hardening within her loose, sleepy grip.

Okay, he could be modern about this. She wasn't trying to turn him on with fulfillment in mind, she was simply patting him the way he was patting her. Perhaps she thought what she was doing might soothe him to sleep.

He felt sweat begin to bead his forehead, and he spent a lot of energy keeping his breathing even, but it wasn't easy. He wanted to flip that woman to her back and take her so badly he could hardly stand it.

She turned to face him and feathered kisses along his jaw.

"I'm trying to be sensitive to your emotional needs, here," he said from behind clenched teeth. "You're not making it easy."

"You came to me when I needed you. For that I thank you. Now I really need something to take my mind off my troubles."

"Alexandra Forrest," he said, rising on one elbow to gaze down at her, "are you trying to use me for sex?"

Her smile might still be a little sad around the edges, but it was clearly a "come to bed" smile. "Yes."

"All right." He took her left hand, kissed the palm

and cupped his balls with it. She took the hint and while her right hand stroked his cock, her left began to squeeze and play with his balls.

And this time when his hand ended the downward stroke on her back, he slid a little lower, all the way over her round, tight ass and cupped and squeezed her cheeks before changing direction and slipping the silk gown up over her hips.

Her lazy stroking picked up the pace and her hips joined in, in silent invitation. He wasn't a man to turn down an offer like that. While she nipped his jaw, he helped himself to one of her condoms, then he scooped up her legs and scooted them over his hips.

Her thighs fell open and while she was still busy stroking him, he returned the favor, slipping a hand down one creamy thigh to where she was open and wet. He stroked her until she was starting to moan and toss her hips, then he slid inside of her as comfortably as though he'd been doing it for years.

It was the strangest damn thing. For new lovers, they'd so quickly slipped into the comfort of longtime partners. He felt as though he knew her body, could gauge her reactions, her level of excitement, even, as earlier, whether she really wanted sex or simply comfort.

As he felt her close around him, hot and wet, he felt her hand creep down between them and cup his balls. Damn, she was the same with him. He'd barely thought how much he wanted her hand there, and it appeared.

Slow and easy turned to fast and furious but he didn't worry anymore; somehow they were on the same wavelength and he knew it was what she wanted.

What he wanted was to be deeper inside her than she'd ever taken any man, deeper than he'd ever delved.

With that in mind, he rolled so he was on top of her, her knees hooked around his waist. He pumped, feeling the way she clung wetly to him as though resisting every time he slid out, then sighing with pleasure when he thrust back inside her. There was barely enough light in the room to make out her features, but he stared into her face anyway, mesmerized by the opening and closing of her mouth in rhythmic, silent cries.

He thrust deep, and still deeper, hard and it wasn't hard enough. Sweat slipped into his eyes, matted his chest, slicked his back so her fingers slid and still he wanted more, dove deeper.

She cried out, clenching against him, her eyes opening blindly, her head tossing as she cried out her climax and as her body milked him, he felt his own orgasm thundering from somewhere deep, rolling up and . . .

He heard a bang, like someone pounding a fist on a wooden door. Had they been so noisy the neighbors were complaining? Even as the thought occurred, he felt the blinding pain in his forehead. "Oh, shit!"

"What happened?"

"I cracked my head a good one against the wall."

"I'll get some ice."

He held her still beneath him, feeling the tiny squeezes pulsing around his swollen cock. "Don't," he thrust almost all the way out and then surged into her, loving her gasp as he filled her.

"Even—" all the way out and this time he poised at the brink, making her wait, before thrusting inside.

"Think—"

"Oh, yes, oh, please," she sighed.

"Of—" and her body was shuddering again.

"It!" they cried out together, while he poured his essence into her body and she milked every drop.

Afterward, while she snuggled against him and drifted to sleep, he gingerly felt the goose egg forming above his hairline.

He suspected her apartment was punishing him for sneaking in here and investigating its occupant, and that he deserved the whack on the head. His snooping had only confirmed what he already knew in his gut. For all she was a mass of contradictions, his librarian bombshell, she also rang true. He'd been watching her closely, clothed and naked and in between. At work, at rest, under stress, in mid-orgasm, and she was always the same person. A woman who craved order, who acted with integrity, whose biggest crime seemed to have been foisting library cards on the unsuspecting.

In his snooping in her apartment, he'd discovered she had a pair of shoes for every fantasy he'd ever entertained. There were cowboy boots to go-go boots, shoes with designers so famous he'd even heard of them, and garish sandals from the local ladies' wear shop.

Her wardrobe was top of the trees call girl, which she paid for out of her librarian's salary. He'd uncovered the startling fact that she paid all her bills before they were due. Her bank balance was respectable but nothing to get excited about. No hidden painting. No sudden large deposits into her bank.

Nothing, in fact, out of the ordinary. He was almost convinced that Alexandra Forrest wasn't connected with anything unsavory. Or if she was, it was without her knowledge.

But his gut also told him that painting was here in town, somewhere.

If Alex didn't have the Van Gogh, then who the hell did?

Chapter 13

Tom Perkins didn't like the information they'd so far received about Jerzy Plotnik, the dead guy found in Alex's library. What was such a man doing in sleepy Swiftcurrent? Who had killed him and why had they dumped his remains in Alex's library?

Tom stood in the middle of the break room, which was doing temporary duty as the case room for the murder. Photos of the dead guy wallpapered the room. Tom was sure he was losing weight since he found he couldn't eat with that morbid corpse staring down at him.

He'd spent ten years as a cop, investigated plenty of murders before getting the job back home in Swiftcurrent, but he never became blasé about violent death.

Tom wasn't a particularly ambitious man. He never dreamed of bigger things, because he loved his job. He didn't secretly hanker for some spectacular crime spree in his jurisdiction so he'd have his picture splashed all over the newspapers, CNN asking him for on-camera updates. He preserved peace and order and he wanted his hometown to be safe for its citizens.

He hadn't wanted a juicy murder investigation, but he wasn't evading his duty, either. He might not have as much experience or education as some of the guys on the Interagency Major Crimes Team to which he'd been assigned, but he had one advantage: he knew this town and its people.

Folders and notebooks littered one counter, more folders were pinned to the walls. They contained reports, interviews, statements. For probably the hundredth time, Tom pulled the M.E.'s report, which informed them that the murder weapon was a nine mm semiautomatic pistol. Common as dirt. The body had been dragged, probably after death, along both pavement and gravel. And didn't *that* narrow it down. There was no skin or blood under the fingernails, no DNA at all that didn't belong to the victim.

There were officers in L.A. interviewing known associates of Plotnik, but they weren't the sort of characters who tended to cooperate with cops. The guy had a girlfriend who hadn't seemed too broken up by his death. According to her statement, he'd said he'd be away on business for a couple of days. She hadn't known where he was going or who else might have gone along. Plotnik had a sister in Michigan, but they hadn't been close. She knew less than the girlfriend and had been only marginally more upset by the guy's death.

All they knew for certain was that he was dead and that he'd been placed, after death, in the library.

Tom replaced the M.E.'s report and dug out the blueprint of the municipal building as though he didn't know it by heart. Whoever had killed Jerzy Plotnik had entered the library easily. The locks hadn't thrown them, the alarm system hadn't tripped them up. They'd waltzed in, placed the corpse, and left without so much as stealing a pencil.

The police had put out an appeal via the newspaper

for any information on the victim, included a sketch and photo. He'd personally appeared on local television asking anyone who'd seen the victim alive in the days before his death to come forward.

No one had. Between them, the crime team had canvassed the grocery store, the coffee shop, every restaurant, inn, motel, or hotel within a ten-mile radius. Nothing. Every gas station. Nothing. In a gossipy town where not a lot happened, a stranger was noticed. But not this one. It was as though the man had simply appeared, dead, in the library.

When he'd asked about a stranger in town, a few people thought he was referring to the art professor writing that book of his.

It was an interesting coincidence that the professor had arrived only a day before the murder. But so far Tom couldn't prove that it wasn't a coincidence. He'd thought he had a clear case of one outsider knocking off another when Alex had alerted him to the bloodstains she'd seen on Duncan Forbes. That would have been the easy solution, and he wouldn't have been sorry to learn that this murder was the result of a couple of outsiders having a fatal argument.

But the blood had been paint, and the guy checked out.

Tom wasn't ready to say it was pure coincidence that the two men arrived in town the same week and he wasn't prepared to say it wasn't. He simply put the information aside and returned to one question he felt would help unravel the entire knot. Why had the corpse turned up in Alex's library?

He blinked slowly as he noted he referred to the place as Alex's library. He bet half the town did that. In the same way they talked about Elda's café, Val's donut shop, and Earl's pizza.

It had been she who'd discovered the body. He dismissed the notion that Alex had killed a man almost before it occurred to him. But, he was a careful man who did a thorough job, so he checked her movements anyway. The M.E. put time of death at around midnight or one A.M. Alex said she'd been asleep in bed at the time. She lived alone and no one had seen her come or go when they shouldn't have. So, technically she could have killed the man, but he wasn't wasting his department's slim resources on that theory.

The arrests for drug trafficking had him scratching his chin. Swiftcurrent, Oregon, didn't have much of a drug problem. There was marijuana—mostly homegrown stuff that turned up in high school now and then in spite of the zero-tolerance policy. A couple of ex-hippies who were red-eyed more often than he liked, but they kept to themselves, turned out a lot of bad pottery they tried to sell in the summer and were mostly harmless. He left them alone.

And there was Gillian.

He frowned slightly and rose from his office chair to go stare out the window, as though the parking lot could give him any bright ideas. Alex's cousin had returned from her time in L.A. thin, wide-eyed, and brighter than a neon sign. Perpetually drunk, high, or crazy, she'd pulled enough stunts to have the staid town on its ears, but she got older, as did her boyfriend. They even got married when her grandfather insisted on it and they settled down.

And there was Eric. Tom had disliked him on sight. He seemed to be in the minority, though. Gill's family had taken to him right away, probably as they saw a way to get Gillian off their hands. And the town seemed as happy to welcome a good-looking, charming young man into its midst as it was unhappy to get Gillian back. They liked him so much they voted him onto city council.

Tom could never figure out why. Was he the only one

who saw the obvious? Gillian had drunk more than she should before she left town. Doubtless smoked some pot, but it wasn't until she hooked up with Eric that she got into hard drugs. Who the hell had introduced her to them if not her boyfriend?

However she'd become hooked, a sneaky but persistent rumor around town had it that while Eric had reformed, she still did drugs.

The usual suspects. Whenever there was trouble, Gillian's name seemed to top the list. He'd check her out because it was his job. But he'd seen a woman in a heap of emotional trouble last night. When she'd begged him to believe her he'd seen—not a woman avoiding the truth, but a woman falsely accused. And a woman who'd been struck.

He had a damn good idea who'd done that to her.

They'd assumed the library had been broken into by thieves sophisticated enough to get in and out without a trace. But the more obvious solution was closer to hand. Eric, as a city councilor, had both the keys and the code. And Eric's wife was sporting a shiner. It wasn't much to go on, but enough so he decided to do some quiet investigating of Eric Munn.

Duncan Forbes joined the mix because he seemed to live in the library, though every time Tom went in the man had his nose in a book or was tapping away on a laptop. Alex would be busy doing whatever she did in her office or out among the books. As far as he could tell there was nothing between them but lust on Forbes's part, which was pretty normal where Alex and men were concerned, and dislike on Alex's. That wasn't normal for her. She was usually nice to pretty much everyone. Forbes had probably acted like an animal. That was the fastest way to piss off Alex.

Duncan Forbes. The first stranger in town. Who had been at the library the day the other man was killed.

Who had met Alex that day. In the library. He owned a gun which was still on the east coast. Had he bought himself a new one out here?

He snorted. *The professor in the library with the gun.* He was starting to feel like a character in a board game. And he was feeling more and more like the not-so-bright detective in the game. The one with the thick mustache and oversized shoes.

Come to think of it, there was something unreal and gamelike about this whole scenario.

Still, in this board game he could move, too. Which reminded him that he and the professor had a date to go rock climbing.

But first, he had to return to Gillian's place. It was time they had a heart-to-heart.

He tossed her keys in the air and caught them. Interrogating her wasn't a task he delighted in, but it had to be done. He should have pressed her last night, but somehow when she'd stared up at him out of that bruised and swelling face he couldn't do it.

He phoned ahead and the tiny jolt in his gut when she answered didn't please him in the slightest. It was like an air raid warning going off in his system.

So he was curt. "I'm going for your car now. Is this your house key on your chain?"

"Yes. The one with the blue stripe."

"Have you got your knee elevated?"

"Yes."

"Don't get up and answer the door. I'll use your key to get in."

"You're coming in?" She sounded surprised.

"I want to look at that knee and make sure I don't have to drag your ass to the clinic."

"That sounds like police brutality."

He squelched the urge to chuckle. "Don't tempt me."

By the time he'd had Raeanne drive him to Gillian's car and had driven it to her house, he'd had time to work out what he really needed to know about her.

And what she looked like naked was not going to be top of the list, he warned himself, even as he recalled the sight of her half-exposed breast last night. He'd wanted all of it and more. That was the trouble with Gillian. She always left him wanting more. He had a feeling she was the kind of woman who always would.

But, regardless of the fact that she'd filled him with lust since before he understood what lust was, he'd do his duty. While he was checking her knee, he'd also be scanning her home for any evidence of violence.

He knocked first and then used her key to enter. "Gillian? It's me." He contemplated identifying himself as Sergeant Perkins, but she'd made him look like a jackass last night when he'd pulled that. "It's Tom."

"Thank you for bringing back my car." Her voice had a quality, both soft and penetrating. She could whisper and he'd hear her across a football field.

He went straight for the living room where he'd put her last night, but the room was empty. All neat and tidy. Not so much as the ring from a soda glass.

With a slight frown he checked the kitchen, and noted the gleaming counters, a floor so clean it could star in a TV commercial.

"Gillian?" he called. "Where are you?"

"Back here."

He followed her voice down the hall and imagined her in the den watching daytime TV, her leg elevated. "I bought you a present."

He stopped on the threshold as though it were the edge of a cliff. Stupid, stupid, stupid. She wasn't watching the soaps or one of those beat-each-other-up talk shows. She was in her bedroom. In bed.

Seeing his discomfort, she sent him a mocking smile. "Don't worry. You're safe from me. I won't jump your bones. I haven't got the energy."

Suddenly he was eighteen again, feeling as thick and oafish as a dim-witted giant.

"I didn't . . ." He cleared his throat. "I thought you were watching TV or something. Didn't know this was your bedroom."

What had he expected her bedroom to be like? Bold and erotic, with artsy photos of naked bodies on the walls and the smell of incense and massage oils. He couldn't have been more wrong.

The bed was pale yellow with flowers and frills and way too many little fancy pillows, every single one of which had its own frill. She was propped up against a heap of these with a book in her lap.

"This is your bedroom?" he asked in surprise before he could recover enough to keep his mouth shut.

"It was the guest room, but I moved in here after Eric left. I wanted a new start."

She wore a short denim skirt, probably to keep the fabric off her sore knee, but he couldn't help noticing how long and elegant her legs were, making her bruised, swollen knee all the more garish. Her bare feet were long and narrow, the toes painted a kind of pinky orange.

A pale blue t-shirt hugged her torso and for some reason it made him think of the torn flap on her shirt the night before that had given him a glimpse of the breasts now safely hidden.

Her long, blond hair hung straight past her shoulders. She'd worn it that way forever. In some ways she hadn't changed at all, but for the absence of that dizzying lust for life that used to sparkle from her eyes. And the shiner. That was also new.

He'd seen plenty of black eyes in his time, delivered some, taken one or two. But he hated to see a bruise like that on a woman, especially on Gillian. The red had faded and spread into purple, yellow, and green. The swelling had almost closed her right eye and discolored one temple as the bruise crept into her hairline.

She flinched slightly under his scrutiny, so he dropped his gaze to her legs. "How's the knee?"

"It's fine."

"Can you bend it?"

"Yes."

"Let me see."

"No."

He wasn't going to go over there and manhandle her—she'd had enough of that lately—so he decided to trust that she was smart enough to see a doctor if she needed one. "I brought you a real ice pack." He lifted the flexible pack he kept in his own freezer. It glowed pale blue.

"Oh. Thanks."

He walked over and laid it carefully over the swollen knee, bending it into place, but careful not to touch her flesh with his bare hand. Then he backed away. "Can I get you a Coke or something?"

"I don't have any soda in the house."

"Oh. Some water? Tea?"

She smiled a little. "Thanks. I'm fine." She looked at him as he retreated to the entrance to her bedroom, half his body inside the room and the other half still in the hall.

"I'd like to talk to you," he said.

She looked a little wary but scrunched herself up higher on the pillows and put her book aside. She closed the cover and flipped it to its back before placing it on her night table, but not before he'd made out one word in the title: addiction. "Well, it's not like I have a lot else to do. What's on your mind?"

He decided to ease into this conversation sideways,

so he asked, "How's your cousin coping since the murder?"

"You work in the same building—wouldn't you know best?"

"I only see her when she has her public face on. I thought you might know more."

Gillian's laugh was low and bitter. "It's not like we're the best of friends. I turned to her for help and she called the cops."

"Maybe she was worried about you."

She shrugged and he saw her hands clasp tightly together. "Maybe."

"How did you get the black eye, Gillian?"

She blinked rapidly, twice. "I was angry. Upset. I walked into the door and fell down the steps."

And he was the First Lady. "I can't help you if you won't tell me the truth."

"You can't help me anyway." She sounded so . . . defeated.

He took a step into the room and then another and sat gingerly on a wicker chair upholstered in pale blue. Everything was neat, clean, orderly. "Try me."

Her gaze connected briefly with his and then away. "I don't think so."

"You asked me to believe you last night. I did. Why not give me another shot?"

He spoke gently, leaning forward in a casual pose and resting his elbows on his parted knees so his hands slipped between them. Since he'd seen the black eye last night, and the way she was fleeing town, a lot of things had fallen into place. But he couldn't put words into her mouth. This had to come from her. He was good and sure it was her bastard ex who'd hurt her, but until she went on record and admitted to spousal abuse, he couldn't touch the guy.

Besides, although in his gut he knew it was Eric, he

also had to clear her of any involvement with a recently murdered drug dealer. There was an outside chance that he was wrong and her supplier had decked her when she couldn't pay her bill. That they'd fought and she'd killed him. He didn't believe that's what had happened, but he'd like to clear her so everyone in town could believe her.

He glanced around. "You do a better job keeping things clean than I do."

"Well, it's not like I have a lot else to do." She shrugged. "I'll be moving out soon, anyway. We have to sell the house for the divorce."

"It's a nice house. Don't you want to stay?"

She shrugged again. "Can't afford it."

She seemed so lonely, sitting here in a too-clean house with a reference book that couldn't be a great escapist read for someone with her history. "Why don't you get a job?"

"Who'd hire me? Come on." She stared at him, one gorgeous eye so big and sad, the other half shut and badly bruised. "I know what everyone says. I'm a screwup. A junkie. Unreliable, com—"

"So prove them wrong."

Her mouth was still half open and she didn't bother to close it. "How? I tried to volunteer at the library, but that's not working out."

"Maybe you could start your own business."

"You make it sound so easy. But I think I need to get a paying job. I have no capital to start a business, and no ideas anyway. I'm moving into my grandfather's place temporarily. But eventually that will have to go, too. It's half Alex's. I'm going to have to support myself."

It wasn't his affair so he kept his mouth shut. But he wondered why she was so short of money. Forrest Art and Antiques seemed busy, and there was the stipend from Eric's gig as councilor. Eric Munn was probably doing pretty well for this part of the world. They didn't have kids or go on expensive vacations. He was going to have to have a chat with the bank manager real soon.

Things weren't adding up here, and there was one obvious reason why there wasn't enough money. Oh, hell. He couldn't dance around the subject. He decided to come right out and say what was on his mind.

"Gillian, if you have a drug problem, there are programs—"

A scream of such frustration howled out of the slim body on the bed that he felt for a moment as though he'd stumbled into a scene from *The Exorcist*.

Her head didn't spin off her shoulders, but she leaped off the bed, wincing as her sore leg hit the ground and said, "Let's go."

"Where?"

"Test me. I want the full range of tests. Right now. I am so sick of this." Tears spilled down her cheeks and she rubbed at them.

"Hey," he said rising from the girl chair and wishing he were miles away in a place that smelled of beer and sweat and guys were telling dirty jokes. A place he understood. "I'm just trying to help."

"You said you believed me last night."

"I did believe you. You weren't drunk. Doesn't mean you don't have a drug problem."

She turned to him and anger crackled all around her. "I am clean and sober!" She stormed as fast as her ungainly, limping gait would allow her to her dressing table, yanked out a drawer, and threw something at him.

She had terrible aim but he was a pretty good catcher. He blinked at the small, round disk in his hand. "What is this?"

"A progress pin from AA. And I'm almost at two years with Narcotics Anonymous."

He glanced up at her and she was standing there,

flushed and half angry, half hopeful. Suddenly he saw how difficult this must be for her, to ask a stranger to believe in her. But he knew those closest to her didn't. Sure, she could be cheating AA and NA. She wouldn't be the first.

But once, long ago, she'd given him a break. They'd shared a few fumbling kisses. Fumbling, because he was so excited to be touching her and so eager that she not think him foolish that of course he bungled the whole thing. Their teeth crunched, his nose struck hers so hard he made her eyes water and he'd been so eager to stick his tongue down her throat she'd almost choked to death. After he'd drawn back, she'd touched his face as though he'd made the earth move for her.

Instead of laughing at him or telling him where to go, she'd stroked his cheek and told him she'd leave her window open every night for a week. And he should climb up and visit her. The hottest girl in the world was asking him to come and have sex with her.

She'd offered him heaven and he'd been too scared to climb up there. So frightened it was a big joke and he'd be a laughingstock among her girlfriends. A girl like her? Known to be so experienced and into sex, what would she want with him? Probably the only guy his age who was still a virgin.

Now she was asking him to believe her. Begging him with her eyes, and he needed to give her that.

Because at the end of that week of torture, of gazing up at her window and wishing he was man enough to make the climb, she was the one who'd climbed out that window and down the tree at dawn, not him.

She'd left home.

He looked her straight in her good eye. "Congratulations on two years of sobriety," he said.

Her smile made her beautiful, so he didn't even notice the black eye.

"Thank you for believing in me," she said, and tottered over to give him a hug.

He didn't want a hug. He wanted to be eighteen and climbing the tree.

She stepped into his arms and snugged up tight and he dropped a kiss on her hair. As he'd hoped, surprise made her look up at him, and he took advantage of the posture by kissing her lips.

After a quiet gasp of shock, she eased right into the kiss. This time their teeth didn't grind. His nose didn't rearrange hers. His tongue went nowhere near her tonsils.

This time he wasn't a bundle of nerves warring with an overload of eager testosterone. This time he was easy with her, more interested in giving than taking.

This time, they fit.

He'd expected lust to blast through him when he kissed her and that happened, all right, but something else happened. She wasn't throwing herself at him like the wildcat he remembered. She was hesitant. Her lips trembled against his. In fact, she trembled all over.

Tenderness washed over him and he gentled his mouth, loosened his grip on her.

"I've wanted you for half my life," he admitted.

"But you didn't come to me when I invited you." She'd tipped her head so her forehead rested against his chest. Her voice came out muffled and he couldn't see her face, only the fall of blond hair down his front.

It wasn't easy for him to admit the truth, but he figured he had a small window of opportunity here to get this right. A little honesty wouldn't kill him. "I was scared."

She chuckled, still not looking up. "Scared of me? No one's ever been scared of me."

"You're wrong." His fingers traced patterns on her

back, silly loopy patterns that kept a little more of him in contact with a little more of her. "I was terrified you'd laugh at me. I didn't have much of a clue about what to do with a woman back then."

Gillian sighed and wrapped her arms around his middle. "I'm feeling scared right now."

He was puzzled. Was she still talking about them getting naked together or was she onto a whole new subject, like who gave her the black eye and why. He knew that as an officer of the law he should be delighted if she was about to give him any kind of clue as to what was going on around here. But the raging teenager who still lived somewhere inside of him had a one-track mind. He only cared about the getting-naked part. And what came after. "What are you scared of?" It couldn't be the sex. Why, she'd practically invented the act.

She pressed her forehead harder against him, as though trying to hide. "I'm not sure I'm ready for this."

Ready or not, he thought, *here I come.* But not while she was battered and bruised, and absolutely not in the home she'd shared with Eric.

"Come on," he said, walking her gently toward the bed.

She hesitated and the glance she sent him was part panic, part desire. He was going to have to rid her of the first emotion and overwhelm her with the second. Very soon, but not today.

"I'm putting you back to bed where you belong. With an ice pack."

She laughed softly, but he heard a measure of relief in the sound. "That's not very romantic."

"Wait until you're recovered, lady. Then you'll see romance."

He helped her onto the bed, wincing when she clamped her lips together as her knee bent. When he'd bunched those absurd mini-pillows behind her, he picked up the ice pack from the floor and resettled it, then dropped a quick kiss on her lips.

There was a phone by her bed, and he scribbled his cell number on the pad of paper beside it. "That number reaches me day or night."

"Thank you."

"When are you moving?"

She glanced at her knee. "A couple of weeks from now."

"You can't move out of this house soon enough for me."

Chapter 14

"Can I help you?" a mousy young woman asked Duncan.

He replaced the ornate silver fork into the faded and worn blue velvet lining of the walnut box where a twelve-piece setting of sterling cutlery resided. *Late Victorian. Circa 1890*, read the hand-lettered card bearing the Franklin Art and Antiques logo.

Duncan smiled at the woman in her navy skirt and white blouse, sensible pumps. Her face was pleasant rather than pretty and her brown hair was pulled back in some kind of bun.

She looked as though she should be around the corner working at the library, and he suspected that were the women to swap places, Alex would have sales of antiques skyrocketing.

"I'm interested in paintings," Duncan said, not bothering to keep his voice lowered since he was the only customer in the shop.

As he'd hoped, his loud pronouncement flushed Eric from a back room. "I thought that was your voice,"

Alex's former cousin-in-law said with false pleasure, putting out a hand to shake. "First time in the store?"

"Yes," Duncan lied. It was the first time during office hours. He'd had a good snoop late one night and found nothing more interesting than a large commercial safe which contained a few thousand in cash, and the smaller, expensive pieces that were displayed for sale during opening hours, such as an ancient burial mask from the Salish tribe, some sterling, and the best of the estate jewelry.

"We don't have much to tempt an art professor," said Eric with his glossy politician's smile, "but I'm proud of this one. I bought it as part of an estate."

He led Duncan to a small landscape. "What do you think?"

Duncan obligingly leaned closer and spent a minute contemplating the painting as though he'd never seen it before. If the price weren't so inflated, and he didn't hold an aversion to Eric . . . "Anna Hills. Looks to be from the twenties, painted in California en plein air style. I love her work." The oil wasn't large, measuring about twelve by fourteen inches, but the colors drew him, and the stylized trees against the water. "Very nice."

"We're open to offers," Eric said cheerfully, sending a wink to the mousy assistant, who'd followed them.

"I'll keep it in mind," said Duncan. "I love the American Impressionists, though I really prefer the Europeans. Gauguin, Monet—have any of those lying around?"

The three of them shared a polite laugh.

"My true favorite is Van Gogh."

Was it his imagination or did Eric's politico grin morph into a shark's grimace? "We don't get many of those around here."

Duncan let a beat pass. "You never know when a buried treasure will turn up."

There was a moment of absolute silence when he could hear the sonorous ticking of a two-century-old grandfather clock, almost feel the dust motes suspended in the suddenly thick atmosphere. Then Eric said, "Well, the Hills isn't going anywhere. Come on back anytime."

"I'll do that," said Duncan, and turning to the woman who'd first helped him, he said, "and while I'm here, I'd like to buy a small gift for a woman I'm seeing. I thought I saw a display case over there with some jewelry?"

He didn't look at Eric, but he'd just delivered his second message. In case Eric was in any doubt, he wanted it known that Duncan and Alex were more than librarian and patron.

He already knew what he wanted to buy her. He'd seen the platinum and onyx art deco earrings before. Sleek, geometric, and, like Alex, they managed to be both wild and elegant.

He followed the assistant—Sheri, according to her name tag—to a locked display case of assorted watches, jewelry, and pricey little knickknacks.

"The deco earrings," he said, pointing.

She unlocked the case and passed them to him. He studied them in the light and nodded.

As he was paying, Eric walked behind the counter. "I'll wrap them for you," he said to his assistant. From her glance of surprise, this wasn't his usual behavior.

"They'll look beautiful on Alex," Eric said as he wrapped the box in gold paper. "And are a better choice for her than, say, a heavy necklace." His gaze flicked to Duncan's. "You wouldn't want anything to disguise that fantastic beauty mark." He didn't mention the word *breast* in front of Sheri, but he passed his fingers over his left chest, exactly in the location of Alex's mole.

Duncan didn't think of himself as the jealous type. But at the words—and worse, the sly expression that accompanied them—he experienced a burning urge to knock this man's too-white teeth down his throat.

He hung on to his composure while Eric tied gold ribbon into a bow and slipped the package into a brown paper bag with the store's logo printed on it.

The man was scum and trying to cause trouble, Duncan told himself. But even as he sauntered out the door as though his blood weren't pounding against his temples, he knew that Eric had seen Alex's naked breasts. There was no way that mole would be revealed by clothing, not even the skimpiest bathing suit.

At the thought of that slimeball with his hands on Alex's naked body, Duncan wanted to go kick something. Hard.

As he strode down the sidewalk, he tried to convince himself that the Alex he knew wouldn't sleep with her cousin's husband, not even once they'd broken up. For all her wild clothes, and even wilder sex drive, he sensed she had a strong moral core.

Unlike Eric. He'd probably seen pictures of the two as little girls in the bathtub together in Gill's photo albums, and that's how he knew about the mole.

Since Duncan had dropped hints as subtle as a meteor shower, Eric was scrambling to fight back.

Well, Duncan wasn't going to give him the satisfaction of causing trouble between Alex and him. He wouldn't say a word to her.

Since she'd let him know she'd be out tonight at a birthday dinner with some women friends, he'd agreed to meet her at her place around midnight.

He grabbed some takeout and once home, decided to use the anger burning his gut for something useful. He pulled out one of his enlarged photocopies of the black-and-white photo of the missing Van Gogh.

He tacked the blurry photocopy to the wall above the table which was his temporary desk and rapidly prepared paints, brush, and easel. He dove in with enough emotional intensity for any tortured artist.

The black-and-white photo taunted him with its lifelessness. Van Gogh would have hated the idea of his colorful paintings being reduced to shades of gray. A line from one of the anguished artist's letters popped into Duncan's mind. *Trying to render intense color and not a gray harmony,* he'd written to his brother Theo.

Ironically, all that remained of *Olive Trees and Farmhouse* was this gray, lifeless photograph. But Duncan imagined those flowers there would be yellow, the bright, pitiless yellow the painter loved so much. And the tree in the foreground a sun-scorched, muted sage . . .

Duncan would never be an artist—he'd accepted that. He had technical proficiency but no elusive spark of genius, but he could draw and he'd learned a great deal about art by mimicking the best. At first his dad had held out hope he'd become a forger, but he'd let the family down again, using his talent only to help him re-create the colors of stolen pictures.

This painting had been done in the late summer of 1889 in the south of France. The light would be heavy and golden.

While he worked, he hoped his subconscious mind would also get to work. It wasn't just a search anymore. It seemed it was also a race. Accepting the unspoken challenge only sharpened his competitive drive.

He painted until almost eleven, then cleaned up and took a shower.

It was time to check in with one of his unwilling partners in this mission. He picked up the phone, calculated time differences, and placed a call to a London suburb crawling with row houses, factories, and Uncle Simon.

"Simon?" He said loud and cheerfully when an old man's grumpy voice answered. "It's Duncan Forbes."

"What in bloody hell time do you call this then?" the crotchety voice complained.

He grinned, pleased with his timing. Early enough to wake the old buzzard and before he got going on the booze or out bookmaking for the horse races. "Sorry, I must have miscalculated. How are you?"

"My back's bent like a bleedin' corkscrew, I've got bunions, and my head aches. What do you want?"

Simon and Duncan's dad had been business associates for years. Neither had yet recovered from the fact that Duncan had gone straight. To add insult to injury, he'd developed a fascination for art and antiques at his father's knee, and now spent his life getting back the very treasures that men like his dad and Simon stole.

But somehow, they'd developed a grudging respect for each other. Duncan would no more turn his father and uncle or their friends over to the law than he'd saw off his own leg. But the balance to that equation was that he was given information when he asked for it. And Simon, the fence, had worldwide connections.

His daily business was carried out in a jumble stall in Petticoat Lane, where it was famously known one could lose a wallet at the beginning of the lane and buy it back at the end. Simon sold a lot of second-string antiques and collectibles to tourists. His undeclared, and far more lucrative, income came from fencing the goods that men like Duncan's father stole. Simon was one of the best.

While he was less than thrilled when Duncan got involved in recovering recent thefts, Uncle Simon, having injured his back while he was working stationed on a minesweeper during the war, had as healthy a hatred for the Nazis as anyone.

He was also paranoid about getting caught and imprisoned, so Duncan had learned to be circumspect in their communications. "Heard any more about our friend Vinny?" he asked. Vinny was their code name for Vincent Van Gogh.

"No, lad, not since the last time he wrote."

"I'm out here at the address you gave me, and some of his friends from L.A. dropped by."

"I heard. Sorry to hear one passed on. They're no friends of Vinny's or yours," Simon warned.

"Do you think Vinny's moved? Maybe there's a new address?"

"No. That's the last I heard of him. The old bloke had been in touch."

"Well, the old bloke died. No one else has Vinny's address."

"If the fellows from Los Angeles are there, you leave it to them. They'll find him, all right." In other words, back off.

Duncan was frustrated, but not surprised. There were no new rumors about the Van Gogh. Nobody looking to sell, and Mendes was still on the trail.

"Simon, here's my number. I'll be here a couple of months. Call me if you hear anything."

"You take my advice. Pack up and go on home. Or come home and visit the family. I've got a nice Chagall etching you might like."

"Did it come in the front door?"

A heavy sigh. "Of course."

"Hang on to it for me. I can't leave yet. There's a woman involved."

"Isn't there always? You watch your back, son."

"I will. Say hello to Dad."

Ending the call, he grabbed the earrings he'd bought Alex and headed out. It had been sixteen hours or so since he'd last heard her crying out beneath his thrusting body. It seemed like a century.

As he'd promised, he was at her place by five to midnight. He saw her light and knew she was home. Eric's snide insinuation wormed its way into his brain and he forced it out.

She sounded breathless when she answered the intercom.

"Hi," he said, feeling breathless himself. "What are you wearing?"

"The dress I wore to dinner."

"That's a problem." A chilly breeze brushed the back of his hair as he stood outside talking on the intercom phone.

"Why is it a problem?"

"I bought you something to wear. I guess you'll have to get naked."

A beat passed. He felt her excitement, imagined the expression on her face. "Take the stairs instead of the elevator. I'll be ready when you get here."

He took the stairs, all right, but he ran, a shade embarrassed at his eagerness. He'd had lots of sex with lots of women, but no one had ever made him so absurdly eager before.

He knocked on her door and heard the deadbolt click back and then the door opened half an inch. "Duncan?" she whispered through the opening.

"Are you naked?" he whispered back, pressing his mouth to the crack in the door.

For answer, she pulled the door the rest of the way open, hiding herself behind it.

He entered her apartment, the small package from the antiques shop clutched behind his back. It was dim inside, with only a small lamp from the living room lighting the place.

He eyed her naked body. "How is it that every time I see you, you're more beautiful?" Her shoulders were so creamy, the arms so finely muscled, and her breasts would make a sculptor weep. Round and full, the tips rosy and tight, growing tighter as he stood staring at her, so her beauty mark stood out in relief, taunting him.

He transferred his gaze to the key she always wore on a chain around her neck.

When he finally tore his gaze away from her chest and let it slide down, he saw the belly he loved to stroke, the triangle of dark hair he loved to part to reveal her secrets, and her long, sexy legs.

"You know, your feet were the very first part of you I ever saw. You have great feet." Tonight the polish on her toes was paler, a deep pink rather than the crimson she'd worn that first day.

"You said you brought me something to wear," she reminded him, her voice already sounding thick and smoky with anticipation.

"Close your eyes," he said.

She narrowed them first, then complied.

He stepped toward her slowly, letting his eyes drink her in as she stood there naked before him. He could see them playing this scene over and over; he'd float a silk negligee over her head, or kneel before her to slip on a silver toe ring.

When he stood before her, he said, "Are your eyes shut tight?"

"Yes."

He ran his lips up her jaw and lifted her sleek black hair, tucking it behind her ear. Whatever earrings she'd had on earlier, she'd already taken off. He saw the tiny, dark hole. His earrings were clip-ons, luckily.

He ran his tongue around the shell of her ear and breathed softly onto the damp flesh. She shivered but didn't open her eyes.

Paper rustled as he ripped open the package and drew out the earrings. He opened one and carefully snapped it on her lobe. She gasped when the metal pinched, then grinned when she realized what he'd done.

"Earrings? That's what you bought me to wear?"

He clipped on the second one. "You can open your eyes now."

She ran to the full-length mirror in her bedroom. "Oh, Duncan, they're gorgeous." She turned this way and that, tilting her head so they caught the light. "I love art deco."

He nodded, pleased. "The look suits you."

Her gray eyes glittered like the platinum. "And I had to be naked to get earrings?"

"They would have clashed with your outfit."

"You don't know what I was wearing."

He rested his hands on her shoulders, watching her in the mirror. "They look great just like this." Holding her gaze in the mirror, he removed his clothes and kicked them aside, then he kissed her nape and they both watched his hands cup her breasts. His fingers played with her nipples until they swelled to hard, blushing points.

All he could see was the black beauty mark.

He rubbed his finger over it. "I'm crazy about this. I bet every man who's ever seen you naked loves it."

He kissed her neck, but his eyes stayed steady on her face in the mirror.

"Probably," she said lightly, but she'd caught something in his tone, and stared back at him, puzzled.

He stroked her belly, grazed her pubis, which made her tremble, and traced back up to cup her breasts. *Let it go*, but Eric had planted his barb well.

Softly, he said, "Did your cousin-in-law like it when he saw you naked?"

She wrenched away and turned to face him, an angry flush climbing her cheeks. "What is this about?"

"Your cousin's husband and you. Did you sleep with him?"

"What do you care?" she yelled. "Our relationship is all fun and games, remember? No commitments. We enjoy each other while you're in town and then you're back to teaching on the other side of the country."

"Did you sleep with him?"

"Go to hell. I hate jealous men. You have no right. Have I ever asked you one single thing about other women in your life?"

Anger shimmered all around her. Her eyes darted fire, the earrings glittered, her chain seemed to glow with it. She was so gorgeous he could hardly stop himself from reaching for her. And he was such a moron he couldn't believe his own actions. But for some reason he couldn't back off.

"I'll tell you anything you want to know about every woman I've ever known."

"Well, I don't want to hear about them, thank you very much." She stomped, naked, to her closet, pulled out a robe, and yanked it on. "I think you'd better leave."

He grabbed his clothes up off the floor and walked to the door.

Two sharp pains hit his naked butt.

"Ow!" He turned his head to see her earrings bounce off his flesh and hit the floor behind him.

"Take them," she said.

If her voice hadn't wavered, he would have kept on going, slamming the door behind him.

Instead, he turned all the way to face her, feeling like a fool with his bundle of clothes held in front his crotch.

This wasn't like him. He never acted this way with women. He was the cool one, always free and easy. No ties, no commitments, no recriminations.

He knelt slowly, picked up the earrings, and stood staring at them. "I feel possessive of you," he admitted, even though the words didn't come easily. "I've never been like this before, and believe me, I don't like it."

"I don't like it, either."

"Eric said something today, and I couldn't get it out of my mind." He took a deep breath and raised his head to look at her. Apology was right up there with commitment on things he wasn't good at. "I'm sorry. I have no right to question your past."

Alex stared at him, her arms hugged around herself. "No. You don't."

He thought that's all she'd say, but after a moment, she continued. "Gill and Eric had this very private patio behind their house. She and I sunbathed topless a few times." She stroked her bare foot back and forth across the carpet in front of her, staring down. "Eric came home early from work one afternoon and saw us. We all acted casual, like it was no big deal, but I didn't sunbathe over there any more after that."

He dropped his clothes and was in front of her in two strides. "I'm sorry. I've never been like this with anyone before. You drive me . . ."

"Crazy?"

"Yeah."

A small smile tilted her lips. "Me, too."

He kissed her and before she could think about protesting, lifted her in his arms and carried her to bed.

Too anxious even to throw back the comforter, he pulled the sash open on her robe and spread it out beneath her. She opened herself to him and he entered.

"It doesn't always have to be fun and games," he said, making love to her slowly, watching the play of expressions on her face as her passion built, letting her see his.

They came together, and he couldn't have said, in that one trembling moment, where his body ended and hers began. Never in all his thirty-four years had he known intimacy like this.

Even as their breathing slowed, they stayed locked together, kissing as though they couldn't bear to return to their separate selves.

Chapter 15

Six o'clock in the morning wasn't Duncan's favorite time of day. But to leave the bed of a warm and exciting woman to spend time with a guy who wanted to put him in jail added an extra layer of irritation to his mood.

There was no sunshine to tempt him outside, either—the sky drooped with heavy, gray clouds, but it seemed to do that a lot out here. He dressed swiftly in the clothes he'd tossed on the floor last night and headed out, giving Alex a quick kiss on her sleep-warm cheek.

When Perkins arrived to pick him up at his cottage forty-five minutes later, he'd had time to shower, had ingested some coffee and instant oatmeal, and felt half human.

Perkins looked more like a regular guy without his uniform, Duncan thought, as they loaded up and set off.

He didn't love the company, but he loved climbing, even if he imagined the climb might resemble a hunter stalking its prey. Him, unfortunately, cast in the role of prey.

He had one goal in mind. To find out how much Perkins knew, and to let him know he should direct his resources elsewhere to find Plotnik's killer.

"There's a nice face about an hour's drive away," Perkins said. "The routes are mostly 5.10 to 5.12. I'm thinking of starting on Devil's Advocate—it's a 5.11b. Is that all right with you?"

Duncan nodded. For two experienced climbers who'd never climbed together, who would literally hold each other's lives in their hands, it sounded like a good choice. The climb would be challenging, but not insane.

They drove out of town, through increasingly forested terrain. After forty minutes or so, they turned off onto a gravel road. About ten minutes further he glimpsed the rock face, jutting above the trees like a single giant's tooth. He flexed his fingers in anticipation.

While they climbed, enjoying the challenge of the craggy, jutting stone face, it was tough not to develop some kind of trust. Perkins climbed first, clipping into the route while Duncan belayed from below. While he held the anchoring rope, he watched the sergeant and was forced to admire the single-minded athleticism of his climb. They didn't compete, exactly, but there was nothing lazy about Duncan's ascent of the same route.

They were both sweating and panting by midday when they stopped for a break, sucking back water and chomping fruit leather, sandwiches, and trail mix.

Duncan figured this was Perkins's idea for them to climb together, so he let him start the conversation. Which he did, sitting back in a granite indentation that kept them out of the wind. "You're seeing Alex." It was a statement, not a question.

"Yeah. You planning to break my balls?"

A swift grin lit Perkins's face. "You can sleep with her. Just don't hurt her. Then I'll have to break your balls."

Duncan snorted. "When you first warned me off, I thought you had an interest there yourself."

"Nope. I have an interest somewhere else."

Duncan nodded. "Gillian. She's a beautiful woman, like her cousin."

He thought for a second that his climbing companion was going to topple off the ledge. "How the hell do you know that?"

"I saw you look at her in the library. It reminded me of the way I've been looking at Alex."

From up here, they had a view over the tree line. Heavy gray clouds brushed the tops of ragged, dark green cedars and towering Douglas firs. Duncan breathed deep and wondered what Van Gogh would have made of this somber palette.

"Well, it's complicated," Tom answered at last, "so I'd appreciate it if you kept your observations to yourself."

"No sweat." There was a pause. A Whiskey-jack landed near their feet and cocked its black-and-white head, looking for food. Duncan tossed a scrap of the fruit leather over and the bird squawked, presumably out of gratitude for the treat, and hopped higher to eat. "Gillian seems like she needs careful handling."

"What's your point?"

"Hurt Alex's cousin and I might have to break your balls."

The laughter they shared did as much as the physical exertion to ease the tension.

"Ready to try something more challenging?" Tom asked after they'd finished most of their food and caught their breath.

Duncan nodded, accepting that they'd moved beyond wariness to a measure of trust. They'd been swapping the lead back and forth. This time it was Tom's turn to go first.

When he hit the ground, Tom took over belaying duties while Duncan climbed. It was their toughest climb yet, and he exhilarated in hanging from burning fingertips as he edged his feet over, finding a small fissure, and jamming his toes in. By the time he'd reached the top of the climb, his blood was pounding and his breath coming hard.

He took a moment to enjoy the warmth in his muscles and the feeling of having conquered another route. He felt the rope quiver as Perkins took up the remaining slack.

He looked down to the small figure below and yelled, "I'm just going to rest for a minute before I start down."

He'd have to climb down the route, removing their clips as he went.

The breeze cooled the sweat on his face, the rope creaked as he swayed slightly. He heard the distant crack of a car backfiring in the parking lot.

A bee buzzed by his head. Even as he wondered what a bee was doing out here in February, he heard a small explosion against the rock face not a foot from where he hung, helpless, suspended in air.

Not a bee. A bullet. Years of experience dodging gunfire came into play. He didn't panic. A cold, icy calm enveloped him.

Get down. It was all he could think. *Get down those forty feet—and fast.*

He yelled to Perkins, "Lower me, now!"

Perkins didn't argue, ask questions, or say a word, simply let the rope out.

Faster, Duncan urged, when the sound he'd dreaded came again. He heard the whine and whistle of the bullet and hunched his head instinctively.

Even as he congratulated himself that the shooter had missed him a second time, he felt an odd shift in the rope, a tiny jerk. He glanced up in time to see that the bullet hadn't hit him, but the rope that held him aloft.

The nylon was severed, but not completely. He now hung from a thickness about that of household twine.

It would never hold.

There was a knob of rock five feet below, and a fissure he could jam his toes into. That became his immediate goal. All he had to do was climb down, nice and easy. If he didn't stress the rope, maybe everything would be fine. He hung there, concentrating on that jutting elbow of rock, and not the bone-smashing distance between him and safety.

He reached out for a handhold. It was an inch from his questing fingers when the rope snapped and hurled him into freefall.

All his attention was focused on that jutting piece of stone below. His climbing shoes hit it, and he used his feet to slow his fall. He had one chance. He humped his body and grabbed the rocky outcrop with his hands, using every bit of muscle, bone, and ligament to hang on even as the weight of his body and gravity combined to try and break his hold.

But it didn't. He hung on grimly until his feet stopped swaying. His own panting breath was loud, as was the frantic scrabbling below as his feet tried to find a hold.

"Hang on," Tom yelled.

Which was pretty much his plan.

He found a toehold. It would do. It had to.

"The rope snagged about four feet below you and two feet to your left." Perkins's voice was as calm as he knew his own would be if their positions were reversed. "If you can grab that, I can lower you down."

Not bothering to waste energy answering, Duncan

worked his way down, spiderlike. He put out of his mind all thoughts of bullets and the possibility of falling and concentrated on the next hold, and the next. His muscles screamed, adrenaline raced through his system, lending him the extra strength and focus he needed.

A toe crammed into a crack where moss grew gave him enough stability to reach for an elbow of rock. He saw the severed rope, which had snagged on one of Tom's clips, and he worked his way over to it.

Somewhere in the distance, he heard an engine roar and the squeal of tires. He fervently hoped it was the shooter, who'd seen him fall and assumed the worst.

"Almost there. Stay focused," Tom's calm voice reminded him.

And there it was, dangling before him like a broken promise. The severed rope. He grabbed it with both hands. "Okay," he called down, pleased with his own calm tone. "Lower me."

The trip down seemed to take a year, but at last his shoes hit the ground. His chest heaved and he fought the urge to collapse and kiss the ground.

"Thanks, man," he said to Tom.

His partner thumped him on the back. "Come on. I want to try and catch the guy."

They ran for the Jeep and threw themselves in. Tom took off at full speed and their vehicle fishtailed as it hit the gravel road.

"Hold on," Tom said, pressing harder on the accelerator.

Duncan picked up the rope and ran his thumb back and forth over the sliced end, brushing the frayed portion that had snapped under his weight.

"Who knew you were coming today?" Tom shouted over the noise of the engine and the scatter of pebbles against the undercarriage.

He shrugged. "Any number of people. It wasn't a secret."

"Can you think of anyone who'd want you dead?" Duncan stared out the window at the evergreens, thick as an invading army.

Yes. He could. His competition for the Van Gogh, that's who. He'd dropped some heavy hints at Forrest Art and Antiques. Seemed like they'd been picked up.

Eric, the bastard, must be behind this.

He could tell Tom about his real reason for being in Swiftcurrent and his suspicions about Eric, but he chose to keep them to himself.

First, because he had no proof Eric had tampered with his rope.

Second, because, even though he'd consulted with Interpol a few times, he was generally leery of cops. They tended to stick their noses in his business.

Third, and this was the strongest reason, he didn't have the Van Gogh yet. He was a big believer that possession is nine-tenths of the law. When he had the painting, he'd cooperate fully with the law. Until then, he preferred to work solo.

He seemed to have come out of this ordeal with two sore shoulders and some new information. Eric was also after the Van Gogh and willing to kill for it.

But if Mr. Franklin Forrest's golden boy knew about the picture, how could he not know where the hell it was?

By the time they'd rejoined the main road to town, it was clear that whoever had tried to kill Duncan had gotten clean away.

Tom didn't rant or swear, he simply eased off the speed and compressed his lips. After a moment he said, "I want you to come in and report that incident."

"No. It was probably a freak accident. A hunter with lousy aim."

"Somebody tried to murder you today. I don't want another dead body in my town, even if it's yours."

"Does that mean I'm no longer a suspect?"

Tom shot him a sideways glance. "It means I'm not arresting you today. But I will not tolerate anyone holding back information that could help solve a murder. What if you'd taken Alex climbing with you?"

Dark green trees flashed by the window like solemn warning flags. A few ferns drooped onto the roadside. The tires hummed over cracked pavement. A minute passed. Two. Duncan thought about Alex, the way she'd looked last night when they'd made love. How her lips tasted when he kissed her, and the way she sighed when he was moving deep inside her body.

"If I were you," he said to Tom, "I'd see if you can find a connection between Eric Munn, Jerzy Plotnik, and an art dealer in L.A. named Hector Mendes."

Alex pulled in behind the cottage where Duncan was staying. Down here by the river it was a bustling place in the summer, but in February it was rainy, dreary, and lonely.

Perfect for a writer in search of solitude and few distractions, she supposed.

She hoped he'd like her surprise—which would definitely count as distraction. Hating to think of him down here with nothing but a bare-bones summer kitchen after spending a day in the cold mountains, she'd decided to bring him dinner cooked by her own hands.

Maybe it was her way of saying everything was back to normal after their disagreement of the night before. She couldn't believe Eric would let on to the man she was sleeping with that he'd seen her naked breasts. It was so out of character for the man she knew.

If the FREE Book Certificate is missing, call 1-800-770-1963 to place your order.
Be sure to visit our website at www.kensingtonbooks.com.

To start your membership, simply complete and return the Free Book Certificate. You'll receive your Introductory Shipment of 3 FREE Zebra Contemporary Romances, you only pay $1.99 for shipping and handling. Then, each month you will receive the 3 newest Zebra Contemporary Romances. Each shipment will be yours to examine FREE for 10 days. If you decide to keep the books, you'll pay the preferred subscriber price (a savings of up to 20% off the cover price), plus shipping and handling. If you want us to stop sending books, just say the word... it's that simple.

FREE BOOK CERTIFICATE

Yes!
Please send me 3 FREE Zebra Contemporary romance novels. I only pay $1.99 for shipping and handling. I understand that each month thereafter I will be able to preview 3 brand-new Contemporary Romances FREE for 10 days. Then, if I should decide to keep them, I will pay the money-saving preferred subscriber's price (that's a savings of up to 20% off the retail price), plus shipping and handling. I understand I am under no obligation to purchase any books, as explained on this card.

Name _____

Address _____ Apt._____

City _____ State _____ Zip _____

Telephone (____) _____

Signature _____

(If under 18, parent or guardian must sign)

Offer limited to one per household and not to current subscribers. Terms, offer and prices subject to change. Orders subject to acceptance by Zebra Contemporary Book Club. Offer Valid in the U.S. only.

Thank You!

CN034A

THE BENEFITS
OF BOOK CLUB
MEMBERSHIP

- You'll get your books hot off the press, usually before they appear in bookstores.

- You'll ALWAYS save up to 20% off the cover price.

- You'll get our FREE monthly newsletter filled with author interviews, book previews, special offers and MORE!

- There's no obligation — you can cancel at any time and you have no minimum number of books to buy.

- And—if you decide you don't like the books you receive, you can return them. (You always have ten days to decide.)

llı..ı.lll..ıı.ll.ıl.ı.lı.ı.ıı.ll.ı.lı.ı.lll.ıl

Zebra Contemporary Romance Book Club

Zebra Home Subscription Service, Inc.

P.O. Box 5214

Clifton , NJ 07015-5214

To start your membership, simply complete and return the Free Book Certificate You'll receive your Introductory Shipment of 3 FREE Zebra Contemporary Romances, you only pay $1.99 for shipping and handling. Then, each month you will receive the 3 newest Zebra Contemporary Romances. Each shipment will be yours to examine FREE for 10 days. If you decide to keep the books, you'll pa the preferred subscriber price (a savings of up to 20% off the cover price), plus shipping and handling. If you want us to stop sending books, just say the word… it's that simple.

If the FREE Book Certificate is missing, call 1-800-770-1963 to place your order.
Be sure to visit our website at www.kensingtonbooks.com.

FREE BOOK CERTIFICATE

Yes!

Please send me 3 FREE Zebra Contemporary romance novels. I only pay $1.99 for shipping and handling. I understand that each month thereafter I will be able to preview 3 brand-new Contemporary Romances FREE for 10 days. Then, if I should decide to keep them, I will pay the money-saving preferred subscriber's price (that's a savings of up to 20% off the retail price), plus shipping and handling. I understand I am under no obligation to purchase any books, as explained on this card.

Name _____

Address _____ Apt. _____

City _____ State _____ Zip _____

Telephone (___) _____

Signature _____

(If under 18, parent or guardian must sign)

Offer limited to one per household and not to current subscribers. Terms, offer and prices subject to change. Orders subject to acceptance by Zebra Contemporary Book Club. Offer Valid in the U.S. only.

CN034A

Thank You!

lll..l..lll...lll..ll.l.l.l.l.l.l.l..lll.l..ll.l..lll..l

Zebra Contemporary Romance Book Club

Zebra Home Subscription Service, Inc.

P.O. Box 5214

Clifton , NJ 07015-5214

She'd have gone over to the store today and given him a piece of her mind if Duncan hadn't made her promise she wouldn't. He said he didn't want Eric knowing he was the jealous type, and he'd managed to convince her that nothing but awkwardness would arise if she challenged Gillian's ex.

He was probably right, but she was in no hurry to see Eric again.

Cooking was one of her passions and she'd enjoyed the homey smells of baking as she'd cooked coq au vin, simple and hearty. The smells of red wine, tomato sauce, vegetables, and spices bubbling around a free-range chicken had made her feel housewifely today as she'd completed her weekend chores around her apartment. The washing, ironing, and cleaning. She loved the smell of beeswax polish on her antique desk, the sparkle of windows when she cleaned them, the steamy, fresh laundry scent of ironing.

It had been her habit to cook her grandfather dinner once a week and deliver the meal with enough leftovers for a couple of days. Then they'd chat, play chess, or watch TV in the evening. It hadn't mattered what—it was the connection that was important.

No psychiatrist needed to tell her that she was recreating her ritual by cooking for Duncan. She grimaced as she realized she'd brought plenty so there'd be leftovers he could heat later in the week. She also had a crusty loaf of bread, a salad, a bottle of burgundy—and something she hadn't taken to her grandfather's—a raging case of lust.

Even as she put her feet to the gravel and gathered her bags, she was aware of the excitement in her belly—it had been simmering all day along with the chicken.

She only hoped Duncan would be as excited to see her as she was to see him.

A knock on the door yielded nothing. A tiny frown gathered. Duncan's beige rental was parked in its usual space so she'd assumed he was there.

Was he out walking? She glanced around her at the rain dripping from the dark green cedars and firs. A dense mist made the river ghostly and the path beside it anything but inviting.

She rapped louder.

Nothing but the depressing sound of rain dripping from the eaves.

She started to turn. Surprising him had obviously been a dumb idea. She'd call him on his cell and arrange something. Then she paused, hearing the low riff of a saxophone coming from the other side of the door.

Had he fallen asleep?

She stood there another minute outside the door while rain dripped off the trees behind her.

Pushing a plastic grocery bag over her wrist, she tried the door handle and it turned. She eased open the door and stepped inside.

She couldn't see Duncan, but above the sound of the CD she heard the shower, which explained why her knocking hadn't received a reply.

She thought about him naked and wet in there and contemplated climbing in with him, but first she needed to get her dinner organized.

The coffeemaker contained half a pot of cold coffee. There was a bowl of bananas and apples on the counter and the trash contained several scrunched takeout containers.

She opened the wine to breathe, stuck the chicken in the oven, and slipped the salad into the small fridge, where it joined an open quart of milk, a block of cheese, some olives, and half a dozen beers. He was such a guy.

She heard the water shut off. So much for joining him. Oh, well, she was certain they'd think of something. "Duncan?" she called. "It's Alex. I brought dinner."

"Great. I'll shave."

Good plan. Since she didn't imagine he was worried about giving the chicken whisker burn, she concluded she was dessert. More pleased with her surprise by the second, she returned to the kitchen to pour wine.

She wandered over to the adjoining living/dining area where an easel was set up. He'd shoved the dining table over to the wall and used it to store his paints, including the crimson tone she recognized from his shirt cuff the day they'd found the body.

She studied a half-completed painting that was a copy of a grainy black-and-white photocopy. Duncan Forbes was a derivative artist at best. The painting wasn't one she recognized, but it was clearly in the style of Van Gogh.

He was good, she thought. Technically very good, but she wasn't emotionally moved as she imagined she'd be if she were in the presence of a true Van Gogh.

When he emerged, in a towel that showed quite a bit of his mouth-watering physique, his hair springing in damp curls all over his head, his eyes warming at the sight of her and his face freshly shaved, she tried not to let her shiver of reaction show.

In a town like Swiftcurrent, a man like Duncan Forbes seemed like a mirage in the driest desert.

She passed him a glass of wine.

"Thanks," he said. He didn't lean over and kiss her as she'd half thought he might, but his eyes promised that and a whole lot more.

"I hope you didn't already have plans for tonight."

"Of course I did. If you hadn't come to me, I'd have come to you."

She sipped her wine. He was awfully sure of himself. Where did he get off thinking she was so hot for him? Unless the screaming orgasms had given her away.

"How was the climb?"

"Quite the workout," he said, rolling one shoulder as though it were stiff.

"Did you and Tom get on okay?" She'd had a tough time picturing them together having fun after the way they'd met.

"I was glad he was there," he said curtly. "Listen, I'm going to get dressed." And he disappeared into the bedroom. So much for *Hi, honey, how was your day?*

She stared at the shut door. "Don't dress on my account," she muttered. Had the climb tired him out? But if he was too exhausted for sex, why had he shaved?

When he emerged a couple of minutes later in a creased gray shirt, cargo pants, and bare feet, she gestured to the half-done picture and said, "You're quite the artist."

"I'm in my Van Gogh period."

She chuckled. At least he wasn't pretending. "It's very good."

"Thanks. You should see me with sunflowers."

"Is this an actual Van Gogh?" she asked, gazing at the photocopy.

"You've never seen it?" Duncan's usually lazy gaze sharpened and she felt him staring at her with keen concentration. Was this some kind of pop quiz?

She stepped closer for a better look. "I'm not much of an expert," she said. "I know the famous paintings. The sunflowers and the self-portraits and the fields at Arles, but apart from recognizing the style, no. I thought you'd created it yourself."

"Poor old Vincent would roll in his grave to hear you say that. It's his, all right. A lot of artists learn technique by copying the greats."

"So you're an Impressionist?"

"Not really. My own work is more realistic." He gazed at her, in that sleepy, sexy way that turned her to liquid desire. "But usually I wait for inspiration."

"Really."

He stepped closer. "I'm feeling inspired right now." He lifted her hair and kissed her neck. "Let me paint you."

This was more like it. Whatever strange mood he'd been in when she arrived had dissipated. She rolled her head to give him better access to her neck. "You want me to pose for you?"

"Absolutely—now take off your clothes."

She chuckled as his lips continued their lazy tour of her neck.

"You want to paint me nude?"

He grinned against her skin; she could feel it. "Every artist has his specialty."

She wasn't at all sure she trusted that grin or the twinkle deep in his eyes when she turned to stare at him, but who was she kidding? When she'd planned to come here, getting naked had certainly been on her mind.

His charm had her responding, just as her body reacted with a wash of pleasure to the idea of stripping before him, stretching out for his pleasure while he painted her.

She glanced around at the oatmeal-colored pull-out couch in front of the TV. What she needed was a dark red velvet divan surrounded by ruined pillars or something, not a Sears Special beige couch built for durability rather than beauty, pushed against a cedar-paneled wall.

"I don't know."

He caught the direction of her gaze and went to the closet and pulled out a white motel sheet, which he flicked so it billowed like a sail and drifted slowly to the couch, giving the practical furniture a dreamy look. He was an artist, she reasoned; he'd paint in whatever background his imagination suggested.

Turning back, she saw the challenge in his gaze and her mind was made up. But he didn't have to know that.

"How will you pose me?"

"I need to see you naked first—then I'll work with whatever inspires me."

"Does this inspire you?" Keeping her gaze on his, she slowly raised her hands to the first button on her shirt.

Duncan watched, half mesmerized as she slowly slipped the button free, baring an inch or so of flesh. Even that subtle gesture had the room temperature rising.

Based on the way he was reacting to her undoing a single button, she'd have him enslaved by the time she was down to her underwear. Especially as her lingerie was her secret weapon. She ordered it from an exclusive company in France at exorbitant cost.

The jazz was sultry and eased into her blood, so she swayed with the music in a slow, sliding way as she slipped more buttons free.

She didn't want bump and grind—she liked this pace fine. All she was doing was removing her clothes in time to the music. It wasn't a striptease, exactly, more like free movement. She'd taken dance classes in her college years, mostly to stay in shape, but she hadn't forgotten the moves.

The artist seemed to be gaining inspiration by the second, watching her unblinkingly from those deep blue eyes.

The buttons undone, she slipped the shirt from her shoulders and let it drop.

The groan he emitted when he saw her gauzy bra was worth every Euro.

Oh, she'd pose for him, all right, for as long as he could stand it. Based on the way he was shifting from foot to foot like a stallion pawing the ground, sniffing a mare in heat, she didn't think she'd be waiting long.

Her skirt was three-quarter-length, stretchy black wool and she put a little extra sway into her hips as she peeled it down her legs and then stepped out of it.

She rose and his gaze went immediately to the opaque silk panties held together with ribbon, then followed the path of her legs down to the thigh-hugging stockings and all the way down to her black heels.

"Do you want me to keep going?" she asked softly.

"Oh, yes."

She removed her bra first, and as her breasts spilled free she saw his hands clamp into fists.

She pulled a ribbon on each hipbone to release the bow and parted her legs so her gossamer panties floated dreamily to the ground.

Would he stop her now? But no. He watched as she turned a wooden dining chair toward her, stepped out of her right shoe and placed her foot on the chair seat. Slowly, she rolled down her stocking. Placing her bare foot on the ground, she repeated the procedure with her left leg, sliding her stocking down in time to a sultry piano scale.

Naked, she turned toward him.

His Adam's apple bobbed as he took in the sight of her and the knowledge that her body affected him so powerfully only added to her own excitement. He'd better be one fast painter.

"Lie down," he said.

She sat, the white sheet cool against her naked skin, and reclined, shivering when more of her encountered the cotton. She felt a little feverish. Cold on the outside, furnace-hot on the inside.

Stepping back, he narrowed his gaze and inspected her from top to toe. "Have you ever been painted before?" he asked softly.

"No," she whispered.

"Try to relax and follow my instructions. And stay still. It's very important not to move."

She cocked a brow. If he started issuing orders . . .

"I'm going to place your limbs the way I want them. Do I have your permission to touch you?" he asked as though he were a calm professional with nothing but the highest aesthetic ideal on his mind.

Okay, asking was better than ordering. "Yes, you can touch me." *Yes, yes, yes!*

His hands were warm and firm as they grasped her shoulders and shifted her toward the center of the room so her breasts thrust forward. He trailed his fingers down her arm as though contemplating, a slight crease between his brows; then, with a small nod, he picked up one hand and laid it beneath the jut of her breasts. She felt them rise and fall with her breathing. Felt the slight caress each time the underside brushed her knuckles.

Next, he touched her inner thigh, just above the knee. She was so sensitive, so keyed up, that she gasped softly. "Raise your knee."

She did.

"Beautiful," he complimented her in the tone she bet he used on his students when they got an A.

The curtains weren't closed on the sliding doors, so she could see her reflection in the dark glass, indistinct like a reflection on water, but clear enough that she saw the provocative pose.

He placed her second hand on her raised thigh, moving it until her fingers curled against the sensitive flesh of her inner thigh. She felt absolutely open, her whole attitude begging to be taken.

The pulse built, low in her belly, echoing in her throbbing nipples. The slight caress of her own hands only reminded her that she'd promised to stay still, remain on display for him, naked while he remained clothed.

"How do you feel?" he asked, so close as he studied and arranged her that she felt his breath on her belly, making her shiver.

How did he think she felt, contemplative? "Horny."

"Good. That's great. Now, let's help you project that feeling."

"Project horny?"

"Sure—great art comes from the subject as well as the artist, you know. Where would Da Vinci be if Mona Lisa was in a pissy mood that day? Would she wear the most famous scowl in history?"

She chuckled softly.

"Don't move," he admonished, opening her knee a little wider.

Chapter 16

He picked up a handful of brushes and glanced over at her, squinted, then grasped a tube and squeezed a blob of bright yellow onto what looked like a paper plate.

Bright yellow? What part of her was bright yellow?

"Tell me about how you feel at this moment."

"I feel like a woman who's about to get the best sex of her life." Sooner, she hoped, rather than later. She felt as though her entire body were a sex organ thrumming.

"You're a smart woman." Cocky bastard. "Now close your eyes and tell me how you feel about the way I've posed you."

She closed her eyes. Sure, he was a game player, but it was a lot of fun when she played along. She breathed in slowly and really concentrated. "You've placed my hands near my breasts and between my legs, but not close enough to touch myself, and that seems to focus my attention on my erogenous zones."

"That's exactly where I want your attention." She had

a damn good idea that—artist or no artist—his attention was firmly focused on her erogenous zones also.

"There's something about having my hands right there but being unable to move that makes me feel—constricted in some way."

"Constricted?" A thought interrupted her as she pictured herself, and imagined the resulting painting.

Her eyes flew open and she glared up at him. "Who will see this painting?"

"No one but me. It's for my private collection. Relax and go back to what you were saying. You feel constricted."

"Yes." She didn't dare shrug, heeding his reminder not to move. "I can't move. It doesn't matter that it's only my mind stopping my body from moving, I still feel—almost bound."

"Bound . . . like a slave?"

Her nostrils widened as she released a sharp breath. She imagined this would be how a love slave might feel, imagined herself the pampered object of desire, but still an object. As a modern woman and a feminist, naturally she found the very notion abhorrent—but as a momentary fantasy, playing a love slave was powerfully exciting.

"Yes," she whispered.

"Good. Work with that." He had a palette full of paint blobs now and brushes of all shapes and sizes thrust from his pocket. "I want you to close your eyes, imagine you're in that very position, lying on a . . ."

His voice trailed off and almost dreamily she finished the sentence. "A dark red velvet divan." She saw him, then, the dark prince whose slave she was, eyes narrowed, assessing his newest acquisition. He'd purchased her, or perhaps she was a gift. It didn't matter. In her fantasy she was helpless, belonging to him only for his pleasure.

She shivered at the thought, smelled incense, heard the soft swish of robes as her dark prince approached. Every nerve in her body tightened and her skin seemed to prickle with the knowledge that he would touch her any way he liked. But she must remain passive.

A moment passed, another. She felt the air shift, grow heavier; she was no longer alone in her own space. She wanted to open her eyes and yet didn't.

The incense smell faded, replaced by something . . . oilier.

Before she had identified the new scent, she felt the strangest touch on the upper slope of her breast. She would have jumped but remembered she mustn't move. The touch came again, a soft, slightly rough stroke, like calloused fingers soothing lotion onto her skin. Rough and smooth, cool and then warm where her body warmed the lotion.

And the scent was stronger now. Like a good olive oil on warmed bread.

Her eyes flew open and then her mouth.

Duncan was squatting beside her, a broad-headed sable paint brush in hand, a gaze of intent concentration on his face as he was brushing bright yellow paint onto her breast.

"What are you doing?" she shrieked.

He grinned up at her, all sexy mischief, his eyes twinkling with it. "I told you I wanted to paint you."

"But . . . but . . . I thought you meant a picture of me."

"I'm fresh out of canvas."

He didn't stop what he was doing and the sliding swirl of the brush spreading color on her sensitive skin was intoxicating. She shook her head, thinking back to the day they'd met. "You do pick the oddest materials to scribble on."

"Hey," he raised his head giving her a look of mock

hurt, "this isn't scribbling. I'm painting in the style of Van Gogh. And stop moving around."

"It was just my head." She could end this silliness anytime, of course, but instead of making her want to slap him and grab her clothes, his turning her body into an Impressionist painting had her so hot it was even more of an effort to keep still.

"This style seems to involve a lot of brushwork," she said, trying not to gasp as the brush swirled and dipped, tickling, soothing, arousing as it drew inevitably nearer her nipple, which appeared shockingly red against the sunshine yellow. In fact, she realized dimly, Duncan wasn't dabbing randomly, he was turning her left breast into an Impressionist's sun.

"He was manic, you know," Duncan said, closing in on the bright berry at the center of the sun.

"Bipolar. Yes."

"Painted almost eighty paintings in the last few months of his life. At one point he painted a canvas a day." He grinned up at her. "That's how I like to work. On one canvas until I finish the job."

The bright yellow sun did a flipflop as his meaning sank in and she gasped. He'd better finish the job, and fast. Get going south, pretty quick. Enough already with the sun—there were sky, trees, ground to cover and she wanted him hitting a certain spot and she wanted it badly.

"Are you a fast painter?"

"I believe in attention to detail," he said, as though he weren't picking up on her distress at all when she knew damn well he was. "Here, for instance," he said. "This raised area of the canvas . . ." He took a clean brush from his pocket and lightly traced the tip of her nipple. Sensation radiated all over her body and she bit back a whimper.

"Don't move," he warned softly, then brushed back and forth a few times.

"I am going to make you pay for this," she informed him from behind clenched teeth. She was going to think up something so diabolical, he'd barely be able to walk when she was done.

"Oh, I hope so," he replied, not looking at all frightened of the consequences. "Cadmium orange, I think," he decided, dabbing the fresh brush into a blob, "mixed with a little burnt umber to portray the weighty center of the sun in the south of France."

Like she cared. Her sun was going to implode into a black hole—poof!—if he didn't get on with it.

Then the soft, wet silky dab, dab, dab on her nipple. Her hand, which had been obediently lying slightly curled beneath her breast, flexed helplessly. He was driving her mad with a mixture of white-hot—well, deep orange—desire, need, and frustration.

He leaned back on his heels to admire his handiwork, then tapped the brush handle against his chin. "Can't have two suns," he said, focusing on the empty canvas of her right breast.

Good. Maybe he'd forget about the sky already and come down to earth.

"A cloud." He decided with glee, then took his time mixing white with blue and a little black. Once more, the brush swirled over her flesh, but quicker now.

"I've always been partial to landscapes," Duncan said, as he slapped blue across her diaphragm in bold sweeps.

Her belly button became the center of a sunflower. A big, crazy Van Gogh sunflower, a little wobbly where she giggled when the brush tickled her. As the stem of the sunflower headed into her pubic hair, her giggles dried up and all her tortured senses centered on that wide open space he'd created when he posed her with her legs apart.

"There," he said cheerfully, shoving the used brush to join the others in his pocket. "All done."

She emitted a wrathful gasp. He'd done all this and was going to leave her a wide-open, sexually unsatisfied sunflower? The hell with Van Gogh. She should have demanded she become a human O'Keeffe.

Never in her life had she felt this hot, this needy, this . . . frustrated.

His eyes gleamed with unholy delight and she knew he was as aware of her distress as though he shared it, which, quite possibly, he did.

Holding her gaze, he took a brand new brush out of his pocket with long strands of silky black hair. While she watched, hardly daring to believe he'd do it, he dipped the tip of the brush inside her and trailed the wetness up to her throbbing center.

Nothing, not all the will in the world, could keep her hips still. She jerked helplessly as he swirled the silky, soft strands around and over.

All her nerve endings, every scrap of sensation, was centered in her clit. She longed for the soft tease of that brush, knowing she was going to explode momentarily.

He cast a quick, intimate glance up at her face; then, with utter concentration, slowly brought the now-wet brush and flicked it back and forth across her hot button.

"Unhhhn" she cried.

"Shhh. Hold still," he answered. Oh, like that was possible.

The threat of death couldn't stop her moving when the agonizing delight of the soft, wet strands brushed across her again and again. So wildly did her hips buck that he ended up "painting" part of her thigh.

"Tsk, tsk. I usually keep a damp rag handy for little mistakes." He shrugged. "I don't have a damp rag, but . . ." And he leaned forward and licked her.

"Oh, oh, yes," she cried, as the soft, wet slide of his tongue rolled over her. There was no more teasing, no more torment; she knew he was as far beyond it as she when he cupped her hips in his strong hands and this time physically held her still as he licked at her with strong, regular strokes and she rose to a dizzying height.

She was going crazy as his tongue licked and then filled the empty, wet place that hungered until her head and shoulders came right up off the couch as she screamed, her entire body convulsing in climax.

He held her through it, sucking the last of her orgasm right out of her until she fell, limp and gasping, back to the couch. In seconds, he'd scrambled his wallet out of his pants and fumbled out a condom.

He was naked and sheathed before she'd come anywhere near back to earth, and, kneeling at the end of the couch between her thighs, once more he cupped her hips and lifted her. She put her forearms down and pushed, thrusting her hips up until he could slide in deep and hard. He hit the magic spot deep inside that was still throbbing while she wrapped her legs around his waist and rocked her pelvis back and forth against him, the sun, cloud, the crazy blue sky, and the wobbly sunflower all undulating as though a stiff breeze were blowing across the landscape.

He filled her all the way, stretching and fulfilling her until the dam burst again. As her inner walls clenched and kneaded him, she felt him go rigid, then the last jerking thrusts of release before he twitched a couple of times inside her and collapsed on top of her.

"Your shirt," she cried as he tumbled right onto the sun, the cloud, and the wobbly sunflower.

"My painting," he mumbled into her hair.

She turned her head and kissed his ear, letting a smug smile touch her lips. "You'll just have to paint another."

No wonder Duncan Forbes loved Van Gogh so much, Alex thought as she soaped herself thoroughly in the shower. They had insanity in common.

She'd come here intending to have sex, but wow! She hadn't had a clue he could tease her like that and she'd respond so wildly.

The water pounded against skin that was still sensitive, so she tipped her head back and enjoyed the warmth cascading against her breasts and belly.

Over the pounding of the water and her own erotic thoughts, she didn't hear the bathroom door open. Didn't notice the bathtub curtain pull back slightly. Didn't clue in that she wasn't alone until big, warm hands cupped her soap-slick breasts.

Her slight gasp of startlement turned into a sigh of pleasure as his fingers toyed with the soapy peaks and then slid down her belly.

Between the soap and the shampoo, the warm water and their hands and mouths, the shower took some time. By unspoken mutual consent, they aroused and teased but didn't take each other over the top. This time, they wanted to be in bed.

After the laughter and silliness, the paint and the torment, it was strangely intimate to slip naked between the sheets. She turned to him and he pulled her against him, so warm and strong. He smelled of soap and shampoo, of excited male and just a little bit like paint.

She smiled into the kiss, reminded of the brush when her nipples rubbed against his chest hair.

His gorgeous dark blue eyes were glazed with passion, the dark flecks crowding together, clouding as he began to lose control. This time, they took each other slowly, with soft caresses and barely intelligible whispers, and she wondered, with a stab of premonition, what she'd ever do without him.

This was the danger zone, she realized. Lying here, well-loved and floating, dreamily blissed out. This was where a woman could fall into stupid patterns, like imagining what it would be like to wake to Duncan every day. To pose for him regularly, to cook for him when she felt like it, make sure he did his share of household chores.

Inside, she groaned. A couple of earth-shattering orgasms and she was planning laundry day.

It had to stop.

She should get out of this bed and get back to their usual relationship of antagonistic, wild attraction. In his bed, warm and soft, with him playing with her hair in an absentminded intimacy made her throat ache.

Damn it. She never should have slept with him. She wanted to fall in love with a man who was home for dinner every night at six. She planned to marry a guy whose idea of adventure was two weeks a year at a lakeside cottage.

Duncan Forbes was not a contender. He had *wandering man* written all over him.

She sighed, turning to gaze at the tough profile on the pillow beside her.

"What is it?"

"You are so bad for me."

He sent her a look that reminded her she was still pulsing from a climax that had almost blown her head clear off.

She flapped her hand around above the sheet. "I have plans. A clearly mapped life path. You are a detour."

His expression was hard to read but she definitely

had his full attention. "I've traveled all over the world. I've always found the detours were the most fun."

Irritation tickled beneath her breastbone. "Detours slow you down. I'm thirty. I have this damn biological clock ticking. I want things. Normal things like a home and family."

His Adam's apple took a quick trip from the top of his throat to the bottom as he swallowed.

"Oh, I'm not suggesting you for the job." She laughed, a little breathlessly. "I know you're not the settling type. But I am. I get distracted when you're around."

"Well, I'm not sure whose time I'm beating. Sergeant Tom fits the bill but . . ."

"That's my point exactly. I need to move on, out of this town, and you're distracting me from my mission."

She'd half expected him to pull out of bed and sprint for his rented auto and the nearest airfield, so she was surprised when he pulled her in tight and kissed her lightly. "If there's a woman in the world who could make a man settle . . ."

He felt so good, right here beside her. Why did he have to be the last man she should want? Keeping her tone light was more of an effort than she liked. "I know. You're not the settling type."

"I never have been. I always wonder what's around the next corner. Or where the next adventure is. I've watched the sunrise over the Kalahari, sailed a felucca down the Nile, seen nearly every major artwork that's on public display and many that aren't. I'm not sure I can change."

"Maybe you've never had enough reason to stay before," she said softly.

"I know one thing. It's going to hurt to leave you." His fingers pushed the hair back off her temples and he stared at her face as though memorizing it. "Usually, I

have my adventure and I'm ready to move on." She
thought he was telling her one of his deepest truths,
and was grateful for his honesty. "If I asked you to come
with me when I leave here, would you?"

By prefacing the question with *if,* he wasn't asking
her, though, was he? She thought she'd love to watch
the sun rise over the Kalahari, sail rivers, and visit galleries around the world. But the difference between
them was she'd always want to come home, and Duncan
would spend the return flight planning the next escape. "I don't get as many sabbaticals as you do."

She thought a shadow of pain crossed his face, but in
the dim light it was tough to be certain. In an effort to
lighten things, she said, "I got a phone call today from
the family that lived next door to Grandpa. Some
friends of theirs are looking for a home and might be
interested in buying the house."

Duncan sat up in bed so fast he took the covers with
him and a waft of cool air hir her naked body. "You'd
sell that beautiful old house?"

"They have a family. They'd make a home out of it
again. Haven't you been listening? I'm going to leave
Swiftcurrent as soon as . . . things are straightened out."

"I think you should take your time. Don't do anything crazy."

Crazy was wishing for a future with a man who got hives
at the mention of marriage and permanence. *That* was
crazy. But, for now, he was helping her get through a
tough time while the murder investigation continued
and Gill remained needy. So they were using each other
for sex and, in her case, comfort. They were adults. They
knew what they were doing. If she kept her heart to herself, no one was going to get hurt, unless she developed
an incurable sex addiction.

Marvelous scents were wafting from the kitchen, and
she decided it was time to concentrate on a different

appetite if they were going to survive the weekend. She rose from the bed and shrugged into his robe.

She liked slopping around in his bathrobe fixing dinner. It seemed so intimate, with the candles she'd brought, the linen napkins she'd ironed earlier, the wine, and even the sound of the rain pattering outside, making her feel cozy and protected.

"So, how's your book coming?" she asked, once they were sharing the meal.

"Fine. Mmm. This chicken is fantastic."

It was, she had to admit. A little of her sexual anticipation seemed to have sneaked into her cooking—a secret ingredient that added extra flavor and richness to the deep, red sauce.

"Is it your first book?" Odd, she'd never really asked him about his work. They usually had other things on their minds.

"No. I published a book a couple of years ago about Gauguin."

"Really. How wonderful."

"Not wonderful enough for Swiftcurrent. It's not in your library."

She squelched the urge to smile. "Well, I'll have to look out for it next time I'm ordering books. And this one? I'm guessing it's not Gauguin the Second."

He helped himself to salad. "No. It's more of a general reference work about the Impressionists."

"And that's what you teach?"

He nodded.

She sipped her wine and regarded him. "Both undergrad and graduate level courses?" Why was he being so reticent? Most people loved to talk about their work.

"Sure. But, like I said, I'm on sabbatical right now to get the book finished."

"How's it coming?"

His gaze lifted to hers and regarded her steadily. "It

would be coming a lot faster if I weren't spending so much time trying to get you naked, getting you naked, or fantasizing that you're naked."

The moment stretched and she felt the invisible pull that had been there from the start, that only grew stronger the more time they spent together. What was she going to do when he left? She'd known the first day she met him that this man would be trouble. And yet, looking at his sensuous, intelligent face, she knew she wouldn't miss a moment with him, even though she sensed that more than her passion was involved. "You do that, too, huh?"

He reached across the table for her hand and brought it to his mouth. "Morning," he kissed her fingers, "noon," he kissed her palm, "and night," he kissed her wrist and just the soft brush of his lips had her pulse jangling.

Chapter 17

"I want you to do something for me," Duncan said as Alex finally left his place early Monday morning, tired from lack of sleep but sated from an early morning lovemaking session.

She glanced at him in surprise. Was there anything she hadn't done for him this weekend? The man was tireless. Good thing. Because so was she.

"Steer clear of Eric."

Frowning, she said, "I already told you I wouldn't mention the beauty mark incident."

"I want you to stay away from him altogether. He's trying to make trouble for us." He grinned at her, but the smile didn't reach his eyes. "Put it down to jealousy, but do this for me. Please?"

"Something's happened. Tell me what it is."

"Okay, I will." The hard look softened to the sly sexuality she was accustomed to. "Something's happened, all right. I've turned into a jealous monster and I don't want any other man near my woman. Promise me. You focus all your energies on keeping it hot for me."

She didn't have time to argue now—she had to get ready for work, and she wasn't prepared to promise until she knew what was going on. Maybe they could talk later. "You're working in the library again today?"

He leaned closer. "Have you ever been taken up against the stacks?"

She swallowed as a rush of lust hit her like a drug. Still, she had some standards. The library indeed.

"Certainly not."

"Good. I'll be the first, then."

"You will—" His mouth slapped on hers so fast she was sure she'd bruise.

When he'd kissed her breathless, he said, "You have got to stop making statements you know aren't true."

Before she could fully restock her verbal arsenal and really let him have it, he'd shut the door. Right in her face.

Well. Well! If he thought he was going to waltz into her library with that smug expression and . . . and . . .

Her inner librarian warred with her inner wild woman, and never had the two been more at odds.

Her inner wild woman was crazy about the idea of having noisy, wall-banging sex with Duncan against the stacks, so her carefully ordered books would tumble all over the floor, get hopelessly disordered, and take her days to reshelve properly.

Her inner librarian just about fainted at such an act of disregard for literature. Have sex right in front of Emily Dickinson? Mother Teresa? Anne of Green Gables? She didn't think so.

She ran home for a quick shower and a change of clothes. Checked for messages. Eric had called over the weekend. She did not return the call. Gillian hadn't called.

She bit her lip. She'd call her cousin later and offer to help her move her stuff to Grandpa's house.

She applied her makeup with more than usual care, feeling ridiculous even as she dithered over eyeliner, then made a kissy-face in the mirror to apply her favorite, sinfully expensive lipstick, knowing it made her lips look succulent and just-licked.

When she opened her closet door and began judging outfits on their ease of removal, her inner wild woman scoffed. *Are you kidding? Make him work for it.* And her inner librarian piped up, *Not work for it. Make it impossible.*

Pushing the one-piece sweater dress back, she dragged out the most severe outfit she could find. A dark navy suit she'd bought for her grandfather's funeral. In the end she hadn't worn it. It depressed her and it would have depressed Franklin Forrest, so she'd worn a bright, happy dress he'd always liked.

Hauling on the suit made her feel funereal. She hated everything about it. The color was drab, the fit baggy. If anything would put Duncan off his idea, this would.

But what the hell was she doing dressing down for Duncan any more than she should be dressing up?

Rolling her eyes at her own foolishness, she undressed and stuffed the suit into a bag. She was never, ever going to wear it so she might as well donate it to Goodwill.

She decided to dress as she usually did. For herself.

That decision made, she pulled out a soft red sweater with a heart-shaped neckline, black dress pants, and boots. Then she clipped on the art deco earrings Duncan had given her and decided her makeup was just fine.

At work she went through her usual morning routine while trying to ignore the flutters in her stomach as nine o'clock approached.

Five to nine. He'd be here in a few minutes. She checked her lipstick, fluffed her hair, and took a deep, calming breath. Would he try and take her against the stacks today?

Quivers danced over her flesh as she glanced out at the neat rows of books rising from the floor. So straight, so staid, so in need of a little shaking up. Like her life, she thought, before Duncan Forbes entered it.

Three minutes to nine and she was wandering the stacks, testing how well they were anchored to the floor while her belly grew heavy wondering . . .

A minute to nine and she was back at her desk, her first cup of coffee half gone, trying to look so absorbed in her computer screen that no one could ever think she was remotely interested in sex in her workplace.

At nine promptly she unlocked the front door of the library, her heart hammering.

No one waited outside. She put her head right out and glanced around, half expecting to see him running her way with a takeout coffee in one hand, his laptop in the other.

But no.

So much for his eagerness to see her.

She made her way back to her office and once more attempted to absorb herself in work.

She knew the moment he came in, about half an hour later. She felt it in every atom of her being.

Still, he didn't have to know that. Her gaze stayed riveted to her computer screen as she waited for the shadow at the periphery of her vision to pass.

It didn't. The shadow vanished and moments later the man appeared in her doorway. "The public is not allowed past the checkout desk," she told him in her best at-work voice.

He didn't look abashed or put out, merely mouth-wateringly sexy. "The public's probably not supposed to bang their brains out among the books, either, but it's going to happen."

"It is no—" She caught herself before she ended up one more time being kissed to silence.

The dancing lights in his eyes told her he knew just what she was thinking and why she'd cut off her own words.

She stared at him and he stared back. The office, already on the small side, seemed to close in on her, far too crowded with all the sexual electricity charging around. And Duncan seemed so large, blocking her exit, trapping her in here with her memories and her desires.

There wasn't another soul in the library—only the two of them, and all she could think about was his promise/threat. Instead of retreating, he propped a hip on the edge of her desk. "You won't be the first. I've seen the slogan on coffee mugs and t-shirts. *Librarians do it in the stacks.*"

"My life's dream is to act out a coffee mug slogan." It would probably be horribly uncomfortable; books could fall on her head, she could end up with concussion instead of orgasm, anyone could walk in, and that would be the end of her career and reputation. So why was she so turned on she had to force herself not to squirm?

"You're thinking about it," he said, his voice low and husky, so she knew he was thinking about the two of them up against the stacks in as much detail as she was.

"Thinking about what?" she taunted.

He took a step closer. "Me taking you up against those neatly ordered books out there, with your skirt up around your waist and your legs wrapped around me. We could do it in the history section, give those crusty old dead guys a thrill, or maybe in the cooking section. Something about cookbooks always makes me horny."

She rolled her eyes. "Everything makes you horny."

"Or, we could do it in the romance section."

Her first thought was that at least most of those books were paperback so if they came tumbling down it wouldn't hurt so much.

He angled his head so he could see her lower body behind the desk. "Pants? You're wearing pants?" He sounded outraged. "Where are those short skirts you always wear? This calls for short skirts." He wagged his forefinger at her in admonishment. "And no underwear."

"Maybe it calls for a little more ingenuity on your part." She crossed her legs. She wore boots under her slacks, a belt around her waist, and on top she wore the red pullover sweater. For her, this was like armor. She was a little overheated but his outrage was worth it.

She leaned back. "When are you planning this . . ." What was the word that was appropriate here? She had an excellent vocabulary but if there was a term for *taken up against the stacks,* she didn't know it . . . "assignation."

He grinned at her so wickedly that she could barely stop herself from drooling. "If I told you, it would spoil the surprise."

"If I made it easy for you, it would spoil the challenge," she taunted right back, hooking the chain of her necklace with her forefinger and running the gold key back and forth across the top of her breasts.

His nostrils flared as he followed the motion with his eyes. "Have lunch with me," he said in a tone she didn't at all care for. It was far too close to a command.

Ten minutes ago she'd have jumped at the invitation to have lunch with him—which undoubtedly meant a quickie at his place or hers, a rushed snack for sustenance, and then a race to get back here within her allotted hour break. But now he was playing control games, and she needed to let him know who was really in charge.

She'd let him take control of her when he'd painted

her on the weekend, and it had been wildly successful, but he was a man who'd dominate everything if she let him. "I've got an appointment," she lied.

If he suspected she'd invented her appointment, he gave no sign of it. "Too bad," he said. "I was hoping to take you to lunch." He removed his hip from her desk and headed for the door. "Or take you at lunch."

"Some other time." She smiled coolly.

He ambled in his unhurried way to his favorite spot, a table and chairs that gave him a perfect view of her sitting in her office. That table had never before been completely in her line of vision, which made her suspect either that the cleaners had become a whole lot more efficient and were now moving furniture to clean beneath it or that Duncan Forbes had moved the table for his own reasons.

Based on the dust on her light fixture, she knew it wasn't the cleaners.

She could have twiddled the blinds closed so Duncan couldn't see her anymore, but she sort of liked the fact that she could glance up at any time and see him pecking away at his keyboard or reading from any one of a number of books, some belonging to the library and some that were his own. She could make sure he had plenty of notepaper at hand and nothing more indelible than a number two pencil.

She felt his gaze on her, as surely as she felt her temperature rise, and lifted her eyes to find him watching her, his eyes heavy-lidded and brimming with carnal intent.

She held his gaze for a moment until a flash fire was imminent, then primly went back to her work. She'd never in her life had so much fun, or looked forward so to work.

Where on earth could she go in—she glanced at her watch—an hour and a half that would count as an ap-

pointment? Her teeth were recently cleaned. Even if
she could get in to see her doctor at such short notice,
being ten months early on her annual physical was obsessively organized, even for her.

She had nothing to discuss with the bank manager,
no one she really wanted to have lunch with. She'd seen
most of her friends at the birthday party Friday night.
Gill and she weren't exactly on lunch terms.

Duncan was the only one she wanted to have lunch
with. She glanced across the square. Katie's Kut 'n' Kurl
stared back at her balefully. She drew in a breath. Maybe
it was time to mend some fences.

She'd ask only for styling. No cutting, perming, color-
ing, or anything that wouldn't wash out. How bad could
it be?

Duncan smirked at her through the window when
she hung up from making her hair appointment, but
there was no way he could have heard her conversation.
He was guessing at what she'd done and she wouldn't
give him the satisfaction of knowing he was right.

She left her office and got busy checking in and re-
shelving all the books from the weekend drop box. Since
the murder, business was up in the library and she was
pleased to see some of the patrons she'd shamed into
taking out library cards or checking out books were
turning into repeat customers.

Duncan stood in front of the faded yellow Victorian
Alex's cousin would soon occupy. He'd already searched
it thoroughly and he'd found nothing. Unless the Van
Gogh was buried in the backyard, he doubted the painting was on the property.

Today, he planned to visit the neighbors.

The house on the left had a bike in the driveway

about the right size for a ten-year-old who was probably at school. There were no cars in the drive.

The house on the right looked more promising. Parked in the freshly swept drive was a sky blue sedan at least a decade old that glowed with regular waxing. Everything from the yard to the lace curtains in the window was neat and tidy.

Best of all, lights were on in the back of the house. He knocked at the solid front door and waited.

A dog yapped, growing louder until he heard the yapping interspersed with panting and snuffling against the bottom of the door.

"All right, Trixie, calm down," said an old man's voice. The door opened and the dog roared out, a fluffy white bathmat with the soul of a rottweiler.

While Fluffy sniffed his ankles, darted back and forth between him and the door, and barked some more, Duncan passed the old man his card. "I'm Duncan Forbes," he said. "I teach art history at Swarthmore and I'm writing a book. I'm interested in Mr. Franklin Forrest."

The old man shook his head. "I'm afraid Franklin passed on a few months back."

"Irving? If that's the Jehovah's Witnesses, tell them you're Catholic."

A small lady approached. She was all pastels, from the pale blue rinse in her hair, to her pink blouse and mint green slacks.

"He's not a JW, he's an author. He came looking for Franklin."

"Oh," she said. "I'm sorry, young man. He's passed over."

"I'm sorry to hear that. I was hoping to interview him."

They shook their heads, so he did, too. The dog barked a couple of times.

"I hope he didn't suffer."

"It was quick. Heart attack," said Irving, patting the left side of his own chest.

"Was his family with him or was he alone at the time?"

Daisy's pale blue eyes wrinkled around the edges as she squinted. "You're the first person who ever asked us that. We didn't say, because what was the point, with him being gone and no one could do anything by then, but we heard shouting that day."

"The day Mr. Forrest died?"

"Yes. I felt so bad that he should exchange harsh words with someone on his last day."

"I hope it wasn't one of his granddaughters . . ."

"Oh, no. It was a man's voice." He wanted to ask if she'd recognized the voice, but didn't want to push his luck. Daisy, however, once she'd started, seemed relieved to tell anyone at all, even a complete stranger, about the argument.

"I'd baked him a pie. He loved my apple pie, and after his wife passed, I used to take over some baking once in a while. I knew he was home, because his car was parked out front, so I went to the back door. We always used each other's back doors. Casual like.

"But when I got there, before I knocked I heard shouting. Awful shouting. Two men. Well, I knew Franklin's voice, of course, but not the other. It was a younger man, I'm sure."

"Just one man?"

"I think so."

"Then what happened?"

"I left with my apple pie. I didn't want him to know I'd heard anything. I came home and told Irving and we waited about an hour, then I phoned over, but there was no answer even though his car was still out front."

Irving picked up the story. "I went over and knocked. Nothing. We had each other's keys, of course. Have done for years. I let myself in and found him on the floor in his study . . ." He shook his head. "I called the police."

"We didn't want one of the girls finding him."

"I'm sorry I didn't get a chance to meet him. He sounds like a fine man."

"That he was. Him and his wife. You'd never know finer people."

"Thanks for your time," he said. "I appreciate the help."

So Franklin Forrest's heart attack had been provoked. By whom?

Chapter 18

Alex returned from lunch with a bouffant. An honest-to-God, backcombed until her eyes watered, sprayed until her hair had the shape and texture of a space capsule, beehive.

If she'd had time she'd have gone home and showered, but a forty-years-old hairstyle took time. This monstrosity had taken nearly a full hour to create so Alex hadn't even had time to eat anything. Now she was back, looking like a caricature of a 60s prom queen. She had a headache from the backcombing, incipient hairspray poisoning, and a stomach grumbling with hunger.

"Not one word," she said when Myrna opened her mouth.

"I couldn't think of one anyway," she said and disappeared down Textiles with a sound suspiciously like a giggle.

She glanced furtively around. Duncan's usual spot was still vacant, thank goodness, and there were only a few patrons visible. Before anyone could approach her, she made a dash for her office, where she snapped the blinds shut. More smirking and uncontrollable laughter she did not need.

She tried to get back to work, but her head felt strange—as if she tipped it to one side she'd need a crane to get it upright again—so she held it rigidly balanced between her shoulders.

At least no one could see her hidden in her office with the blinds closed. She only had to make it through another four hours and she could leave. With luck, no one but Myrna would ever know.

A shadow fell and every womanly particle of her being recognized Duncan Forbes.

"Go away," she said without moving her head.

"I heard you got a new look," he said, managing to keep a straight face.

"What do you think?" she asked sweetly. Let him think it was the latest fashion. With his rumpled, hiking-man dress sense he might not know Katie had paid her back for all the years of going elsewhere.

"You look like Marge Simpson crossed with Doris Day."

Okay. So he'd noticed she wasn't exactly *au courant* in the hair department; at least her coiffure of humiliation was giving someone pleasure. "Well, that should give your libido a rest."

"Are you kidding? I love those old Doris Day movies. I could go for that look in a big way. In fact," he said, leaning against her doorjamb and appearing to give the matter considerable thought, "I'd like to paint you like that."

"Well, I feel like I'm wearing the Statue of Liberty on my head, which is starting to pound. I am not in the mood."

"Should have had lunch with me. It would have been more fun."

Since she knew exactly how much fun it would have

been, and she knew she'd have ended up with something a lot more pleasant than a headache and a bill for thirty-five bucks, she scowled at him. "Out."

He went, whistling "Que Sera Sera."

She opened her top drawer for painkillers and all thoughts of Katie, Doris Day, and lunchtime frolicking with Duncan Forbes fled her brain.

There was a gun in her drawer.

A chrome-and-black, I-kill-people-for-fun kind of gun.

She must have made some sort of sound, for suddenly Duncan came pounding back and he wasn't whistling. "What is it?"

She swallowed, not lifting her head, as though the revolver might go on a shooting spree if she didn't keep an eye on it. "A gun."

"Bad idea to keep a firearm in an unlocked desk drawer," he said, coming around her desk to take a peek.

"It's not mine. I hate guns." Her voice wobbled a little and his hand dropped to her shoulder with reassuring warmth.

"Don't touch it."

An unnecessary piece of advice. She couldn't be more scared of that thing if it had fangs and snarled at her. She pressed her lips together, thinking that a mysterious dead man, a man who'd been shot, and a gun that certainly looked up to killing people being found in her library within the space of a couple of weeks had to be more than coincidence.

"I'll call next door," she said, pulling herself together with an effort and picking up her phone.

Luckily, Tom took the call.

"There's a gun in my desk drawer," she told him as calmly as she could. "It's not mine." And the subtext was clear. *Get it out of here.*

He said, "I'm there," and disconnected without any of the chitchat they'd have indulged in two weeks earlier. Funny how a murder changed things.

"Tom's on his way," she told Duncan, still unable to take her gaze off the black-and-silver object in her desk drawer.

"Good." He disappeared and she decided to be strong and not wail that she needed him beside her for this latest crisis. But he was back in less than two minutes with a mug of water and a bottle of pain killers in his hand. "Myrna's," he said when she glanced at him questioningly.

Gratefully, she swallowed the pills. It was pretty obvious he hadn't told Myrna why he needed them, or she'd be crowding in here, too.

Duncan moved behind Alex and rubbed her shoulders, as though he could feel the burdens pressing down on them. She touched his hand briefly. "Thanks."

He didn't ask what she was thanking him for, which was mostly just being there when she needed him. "You're welcome," he said.

Tom arrived in minutes. His eyes widened slightly when he took in her hair.

"Did either of you touch the gun?"

She shook her head. "No."

Tom glanced at Duncan, who also replied in the negative.

He came around behind Alex and stared at the thing in her drawer. "Jennings, nine millimeter, semiautomatic," he mumbled to himself.

"The murder weapon?" Duncan asked.

As though realizing he wasn't alone, Tom frowned. "I'd like you both to leave the office, please. Try not to touch anything."

"Yes, of course." *I know the drill,* she felt like saying. "Should I close the library?"

"Yes."

Tom pulled out a pair of surgical gloves and slipped them on, and she and Duncan left him to it. As they were leaving, he said, "Why don't you go next door and wait for me in my office."

Alex glanced at Duncan, feeling puzzled. "Both of us?"

"Yes. I want statements from you both."

With a shrug, Duncan fell into step and they went next door. She felt the stares of everyone she passed getting a load of the beehive and she thought as long as she lived she'd never forgive Katie for this.

It was a whole lot easier being mad at Katie than admitting she was terrified.

She got home after that awful day, wondering why she'd ever thought this town was dull.

The first thing she needed to do was shower, at least seven times, to get rid of the shellac feel to her hair. But once she got to the bathroom and caught a glimpse of herself, she clapped a hand over her mouth.

"Gill should see this," she mumbled behind her hand. They'd played hairdresser when they were younger, using their mothers' photo albums as a guide. She'd never been much good at playing hairdresser, but Gillian had a flair.

As Alex stared at herself, she could swear it was her mother staring back.

She didn't have a mother anywhere close, either geographically or emotionally. She didn't have any real family but Gillian. Since she'd called Tom the night she'd found her cousin with a black eye, well, she obviously hadn't had Gillian on her side, either.

Sticking out her lower lip, she blew out a breath. Her hair towered over her like a building had accidentally been dropped on top of her head, adding to the feeling of pressure she felt whenever she contemplated her cousin.

Gillian needed her. She'd realized that for a while, but tonight, when she was feeling alone and unsettled and wanting to share the joke of Katie and her hairstyle with someone who would get it, she realized that in an odd way, she needed Gill, too.

She stared at the phone for a while. Picked it up. Put it down. Put on the kettle for herbal tea and then never made a pot.

Finally, she grabbed her coat and car keys and left.

She reached Gillian's house long before she was ready to face her but decided she had to suck it up and walk up that path.

Even so, she spent a good two or three minutes out on the freshly swept front doorstep staring at a wreath of pinecones and winter greenery before she got up the courage to knock.

It took a while for the door to open.

"I know you're there, Gillian," she finally yelled. She could feel her cousin on the other side of the door.

It opened. "What do you—" The surly words were cut off as Gillian snorted. Then the snort turned into a giggle, which led naturally into a lung-endangering guffaw. "You look like your mother on her prom night," she shrieked.

"I went to Katie's K-K-Kut 'n' Kurl and ended up with a goddamn bee—"

"Hive."

The laughter felt good, especially today and especially with Gill. They hadn't laughed together for a long time. But it couldn't last forever. By the time they'd quieted to snickers, Gill managed, "So, why are you here?" She didn't invite Alex inside.

The hairstyle seemed even heavier as Alex tried to

figure out what she wanted to say. Finally she went with the simplest. "Gill, I'm sorry."

Her cousin nodded, waiting for more. But she didn't slam the door, so that was good.

"I shouldn't have said what I did the other night." She wasn't going to apologize for suggesting her cousin needed help, because she probably did. But, in retrospect, Alex could see that her behavior hadn't been completely warmhearted, not to mention tactful.

Gill stared at her. "You still think I need help?"

Alex stared back, looking into her pretty blue eyes, seeing that her hair was clean, her skin dewy, and that she looked—good. "Why don't you tell me what you need?"

The door opened wider. "Want some tea?"

Alex felt her eyes sting. "Yeah."

The funny thing was that they didn't end up talking about drugs, or murder, or failed marriage. They talked about their grandparents.

"Do you remember when Grandma caught us smoking?" Alex said as they sat over tea in the kitchen.

Gillian chuckled softly. "We wouldn't have gotten caught if you hadn't coughed your guts up."

"I couldn't help it. Smoking didn't come easily to me."

"Neither did sex."

They stared at each other and once more collapsed into giggles. "Oh, my God. I was such a geek." Alex dropped her head into her hands, and banged her hairstyle against the kitchen table which only made them laugh harder. "I'm getting brain damage!"

"You've got a long way to go to catch up with me," Gillian said, and the mood turned serious.

"Come back to the library," Alex said.

She touched her face. "I can't. I'd scare the kids."

"The bruise has really faded. Come on."

"I don't know. I've got a lot on right now. I'm moving this weekend, and I've got to start looking for a paying job."

Like that would be easy. If she, Gillian's own flesh and blood, had had a hard time allowing her cousin to volunteer, she couldn't imagine anyone in town paying her to work for them.

"You did a great job in the library, you know. Some of the moms have been asking for you. The little kids really liked having you help them."

"Let me think about it, okay?"

"Sure." To change the subject, Alex said, "The word in Katie's is that you're seeing someone." She'd been amused to hear that Tom Perkins was hot for her cousin, just because he'd been seen driving her home. Some people made gossip out of thin air.

But then she noticed that Gill had ducked her head so her honey blond hair spilled over her face, but not before Alex saw the blush.

"Oh, my God. It's true!"

"Nothing's happened. Yet."

"But you want it to?"

Gillian raised her head and pulled back her shoulders. "Yes," she said. "I want it to."

"I remember in high school you were—"

"Yeah."

"Wow. Okay."

"My marriage is over. I'm moving out of this house. It's time for a fresh start."

And, why waste time? Naturally, she didn't say that. What she said, rather surprisingly, was "Do you want some help moving?"

Gillian poured more tea. "Sure. That would be great."

"I could bring Duncan to help." She added milk and sugar to her tea so she didn't have to look at her cousin. "You met him in the library."

"I know who he is."

"Right. Well, we're . . . seeing each other."

"I'm not blind, Alex. I know. Is it serious?"

"Oh," Alex said, wondering if she'd also become fodder at Katie's. Guessing she probably had. "Of course it's not serious. He'll be leaving in a couple of months." And that was just fine with her.

Chapter 19

Tom waited until her moving day to approach Gillian. He'd thought long and hard about the situation and since he'd now cleared her of suspicion, and her divorce was well on its way, he could start on that romancing he'd promised her.

She looked like a woman who could use some romance.

He'd checked her story. She'd been going faithfully to AA meetings in a town about half an hour's drive, keeping her sobriety a secret the way some people keep their drug habits quiet.

He decided to show up, nice and casual, in a place where a strong back and a willing pair of hands would be of use. He'd start easy, and take it from there.

He not only felt an urge to pound the son of a bitch who'd blackened her eye into the dirt, he also felt a powerful urge to protect Gillian. When he'd held her in his arms, he'd felt a fragility he hadn't thought she possessed. To a guy who'd spent his life taking in strays and trundling birds with broken wings to the local vet, he acknowledged his own urge to heal even as he recognized there was something else mixed in with it. A possibility that sparkled.

Wearing serviceable jeans, a work shirt, and his steel-toed boots, he showed up at Gillian's house. The first thing he saw was a nice, trim ass bent over, the top half of the woman inside a rented U-Haul. But his blood pressure didn't spike, so he knew it wasn't Gillian's backside. Sure enough, the woman emerged and it was her cousin.

"Morning, Alex," he said.

"Hi." She eyed him, pretty surprised to see him there.

"I came to lend a hand."

"Gillian's in the kitchen, I think."

"Woman, would you get your ass back in here so the damn bookcase doesn't fall on my head?"

Duncan Forbes was also helping on moving day. He had to hand it to the professor—he'd gone from the man least likely to make Alex happy to see him, to top of her list in a couple of weeks. He only hoped he could move in on Gillian that fast.

He knocked on the open front door and called out as he strode down the hall to the kitchen, "Gillian? It's me. Tom. I came to help you move."

He heard dishes bashing together in the kitchen, and he figured she hadn't heard him, so he yelled some more. "I've got a strong back and a pair of—hey!" he yelled, as a frying pan came flying down the hall like a demonically possessed Frisbee and narrowly missed the side of his head. "What the hell was that for?"

Gillian looked mad enough to take him apart with her slender, graceful hands. He glanced behind him, wondering if some monster had wandered in, but nope. There was nobody else around. The flying pan seemed meant for him.

"Unless you've come to arrest me, get out of my house!" she shrieked.

"Are you deranged? I came to help move boxes."

"Is that why you canvassed the neighborhood asking if anyone had seen me the night of that man's murder? If they'd maybe heard shots coming from my house?" Her voice was rising with each word and by the time she got to *shots*, he was worried about his long-term hearing. He was also getting a bit hot under the collar himself.

"It's my job, Gillian. I was doing my job."

"Hah!" He'd heard of women being magnificent when they were angry. Gillian wasn't one of them. Her face was red and blotchy, and her pretty blue eyes were screwed up tight as though the less of him she had to see the better. "You didn't ask about one other single person in my neighborhood. Only me. Because I'm supposed to be the drugged-out loser. If there's trouble, come looking for Gillian."

She was starting to cry, but not sad, little weepy tears; these were more like poison sparks flying out of her eyes. Each one seemed to prick him with tiny stabs of remorse.

"I had to make certain."

"You said you believed me. For once, I thought someone I cared about really believed in me." Now she was crying real tears. Slow, rolling heartbreakers. "But you didn't." She shook her head violently when he made a move toward her. "You came in here to snoop around, didn't you? Looking for blood or bullet holes or something. I know you, Tom Perkins, and you don't have any guts."

"Please, Gillian, it's not like that."

"Go away."

"I'm sorry."

"Get out!"

So he did. And his heart felt heavier than an entire moving van of furniture.

Gillian ignored the pounding on the front door as she'd been ignoring it for the last ten minutes. She'd peeked out the upstairs window of her grandparents' house and recognized Tom standing there.

The bouquet in his hand made her soften for an instant, but not more than that. Flowers were easy to come by. Trust wasn't.

The banging continued.

She flicked on the TV.

"Gillian? I know you're in there," he yelled.

"Man's a genius," she mumbled, turning the set up louder. She didn't pay attention to the station. It was some kind of game show with a lot of clapping and electronic music.

It didn't matter. Nothing could drown out the noise. The pounding on the door echoed in her ears, seemed to pick up the beat of her heart.

It stopped and she breathed a long sigh of relief, only to jump half out of Grandpa's old recliner when a fist rapped sharply at the window.

Tom's face appeared, and he held up the flowers. "I'm sorry," he yelled. It must be raining, for his hair clung damply to his skull and water dripped off his ear.

She clambered out of the recliner, walked to the window. Saw him smile at her and pulled the blinds down so hard they sounded like a hailstorm. With a flick of her wrist she closed the louvers.

The sharp rattle of his knuckle on the glass set her teeth on edge. She ought to call the cops. Except that he was it.

"Damn small town," she muttered. Maybe it was time

to move on, to somewhere big and anonymous where a person's past mistakes didn't stick to them like some kind of visible skin condition. Was she the only person in the history of Swiftcurrent who'd been wild in his or her youth? She couldn't be, but perhaps she was the only one who tried to stay in the same town and live down a reputation.

The trouble was, the townspeople wouldn't give her a break. If she stumbled on a cracked bit of sidewalk, she saw the eye-rolls. *Drugged up again,* they'd be thinking. If she fumbled with her wallet in the supermarket or dropped her purse, she felt the weight of the town's disapproval heavy on her shoulders. And if her perfect cousin was anywhere near, she was worse. The harder she tried to appear in control and sane, never mind perfect, the more clumsy and inept she became.

She had a feeling she was lumped in the same category as old Earl Hardminster, who sat outside the liquor store wearing a torn hunting cap, some old clothes, and a guitar with a broken string. Didn't matter about the broken string. He never played the thing, only left the case open for money. As soon as he had enough, he went into the liquor store and stocked up.

He slept wherever he could find some shelter and on really cold nights, Tom sometimes found an excuse to arrest him so he could spend the night in jail where it was at least warm and dry.

Yep, she and Earl. They were quite a pair. The town drunk and the town druggie.

Maybe it was time to move on.

Except she didn't want to go.

She slumped back into the recliner and stuck her hands over her ears. She didn't want to go anywhere. This old house comforted her like the smell of home-baked oatmeal cookies, or the wrap of a faded quilt.

She had ideas, some energy seeping back now she

was no longer living with Eric, and the stubborn feeling that if she could prove herself here, where attitudes were already against her, she could somehow get back that long-lost sense of possibility, that she could be anything, do anything she wanted.

No. She wasn't running away. She'd done that once before and look how that had turned out.

Eventually, the banging, window-rapping, and the yelling ended. Good, she thought, as she crawled up to bed just after eleven. Tom had gotten her message. She didn't want his flowers, she didn't want his apology, and most of all, she didn't want him.

She readied herself for bed, slipped into her favorite gown. It was floor-length Indian cotton cut in a traditional style. She thought of it as hippie chick meets Victorian maiden, which summed up how she felt coming back to sleep in her old bedroom. The sheets were cool as she slipped between them, the comforter the same one with the faded roses that sort of but not quite matched the old wallpaper with a different kind of rose stamped all over it.

They'd never changed her room when she left, and now she was glad. If she could go back to where she'd first taken a wrong turn, maybe she could straighten everything out.

She settled down in the clean sheets that smelled of lavender and made her miss her grandmother, who'd been the only real mother she'd ever known. Minutes ticked by and sleep wouldn't come. She'd hurt her grandparents when she left, hurt them worse when she returned, but at least she'd been able to show them she'd cleaned up. They had always believed in her.

This bed was all lumps. She turned and fidgeted, yawned, and tried to figure out what kind of work she wanted. What did she know how to do? She didn't even have her high school diploma, so who'd hire her? She could cook, clean, garden. The great irony of her life was that she'd run away to the big city, only to discover eventually that she was a homebody. She was basically an old-fashioned woman who wanted to take care of a home and a family.

She punched her pillow and tried to make it less lumpy, while the sounds of the old house settling for the night jarred instead of soothed her. Rain pattering on the roof was normally as restful as a lullaby, but tonight it drummed like a headache. The chintz curtains flapped at the window, which she left open a crack to let in fresh air.

The thought of making a success all on her own, with her lack of education and her wild past against her, was not conducive to relaxation and sleep so she turned again in the single bed whose mattress hugged her with every turn. It didn't matter what she thought about, so long as it wasn't Tom.

Or Eric.

Or any human being on the planet with a penis.

There were definitely too many of those and all they ever did was screw up her life, she thought miserably. She'd never really been on her own. Maybe it was time to see what she could do.

The old house creaked and moaned around her. She still wasn't accustomed to the nighttime noises and they could be unsettling, reminding her she was all alone in a hundred-and-something-year-old house where her grandfather had died—and who knew how many others?

She knew her grandfather's ghost would only want to help and protect her, but even a benign spirit walking at night had her eyes opening in the dark, because it certainly sounded like something strange was going on.

There was a tapping, scraping sound that seemed to be coming from close by, as though bony fingers were tapping the wood siding outside her window.

She'd heard that sound before.

Sitting up in bed so fast she almost hit the dormer ceiling, she recalled those wild nights of her youth when she'd flouted authority every chance she got, going so far as to invite boys to climb right up into her bedroom.

Looking back now, she suspected she'd wanted to get caught, wanted to shock her grandparents in some way, perhaps punish them for giving her a home so her mother was free to abandon her. Whatever the reasons inside her seething teenage brain, her grandparents, as far as she knew, never found out about those boys who'd climbed the sturdy vine and shared her bed.

Alex knew, but she never said anything. Sure, she disapproved, even tried to read her a couple of lectures, but Gill wasn't going to listen to a nerd her own age who, she suspected, was jealous.

Maybe her grandfather had known all along. Maybe he was slapping the wisteria against the wall in some poltergeist punishment from the afterlife.

It wouldn't surprise Gill. Life seemed perpetually to punish her.

The last boy she'd invited to climb the wisteria, the one she'd wanted more than any other, hadn't bothered.

Tom.

She thumped back into bed. Well, she could forget that old fantasy. Tom hadn't climbed in her window when he was young and as foolish as a man like him would probably ever be. If he hadn't done it then, he wouldn't do it now.

Another rattling scrape.

What if he hadn't gone away? What if it was Tom out there now?

She jerked upright in bed and flew, barefoot, across the room to the window.

The warped wooden frame squealed and fought her as she yanked on it but finally she got it open and stuck her head out.

Surely, she was wrong.

Rain pelted the back of her head as she blinked down into the darkened garden. Sure enough, a bulky, dark shape was attempting to climb the wisteria, which was probably as old as the house and hadn't been pruned, fertilized, or cared for since her grandmother died.

She knew it was Tom climbing up. He clutched a bouquet in his teeth.

But it was raining hard, and he wasn't a nimble boy in his teens anymore.

"What are you doing?" she called to him.

"Mmmphingmmumnegguuu," he mumbled through the flowers.

Her heart stopped and then tumbled back in time and she was every towered princess from every fairy tale being rescued by her prince.

Except that this prince wasn't doing so well.

The old, gnarled vine was slick with rain, moss, and who knew what. It was also frail with age.

And Tom was a solid man. He climbed with rugged determination, but she could see he was having trouble hanging on. His boots kept slipping.

"Come around to the door," she cried. "I'll let you in."

He shook his head, the flowers flapping side to side.

"You're crazy. You'll get yourself killed."

"Mmmingelluuummmorrry," he said.

Knowing conversation was not only fruitless, but probably taking his concentration from his task, she shut up and watched, a ball of fear forming in her throat.

He managed a couple more feet. He had maybe four more to go and then he could hook his hands to her windowsill and haul himself in.

He planted a foot on a gnarly "V" of vine branches, put his weight on it, and raised the other foot.

A dreadful snap made her clamp down on a shriek. Oh, God, oh, God. He was going to fall and cripple himself, maybe worse, and it would be all her fault.

He hung there by his hands, and she could see the vine gleaming wetly, dark brown and gray. His hands curled tight and she prayed as she'd never prayed before that the vine would hold.

She heard his feet scrabble around and then a grunt and she felt rather than saw that he'd found another foothold.

Her heart was pounding, her hands clasped together, cold and shaking. Please, please let him hang on.

"Just a little more," she said.

He was making a hell of a racket and she had a feeling the wisteria would never recover, but she couldn't stop the tears stinging her eyes as she watched a stolid, respectable, community law officer trying a little B&E.

She'd never been so happy in her life.

Suddenly, a search beam seemed to hit her in the face. Tom slipped and scrambled not to fall.

"What in the Lord's name is going on over there?" Mr. Davidson from next door called out, a flashlight the size of a satellite dish pointed at them.

"It's me, Mr. Davidson."

"Gillian? Is that a burglar? You want I should call the police?" The Davidsons' little white dog, not wanting to be left out of things, started barking.

A bubble of borderline hysterical laughter formed in her chest and she fought it down. "This *is* the police."

"What are you talking about, girl?"

"This is Sergeant Perkins."

"Tom Perkins? Is that you, son?"

"Mmmummmpphm," said Tom.

For another excruciating minute the searchlight held them in blinding brilliance and she fought the urge to quote, *Romeo, oh, Romeo,* thinking it was a good thing Shakespeare set *Romeo and Juliet* in Verona and not in the rainy Pacific Northwest, where the lovers would have been more likely to expire of bronchitis than blighted love.

"What's that you got in your mouth?"

"Flowers," Gillian answered for him. And the flowers were as drippingly wet as everything else.

"Something wrong with your door?" Mr. Davidson wanted to know.

"No. This is more romantic," she explained, feeling her eyes begin to drip as she saw the expression in Tom's. He had just made a complete and total fool of himself in front of one of the biggest old busybodies in Oregon state, and he was doing it for her.

"Irving?" Mrs. Davidson's voice joined the night chorus. Tom sent Gill a desperate glance, but what could she do? He seemed incapable of moving, impaled by Mr. Davidson's flashlight.

"Um, Mr. Davidson? Do you think you could turn off the flashlight? We're fine."

After another moment, the light went out and it was blessedly black. "Irving? What's going on? What's all the noise next door?"

"Hell if I know," said her long-suffering spouse. "I expect it's one of those crazy sex games like you see on TV."

The thought of Irving and Daisy watching crazy sex things on TV—and worse, imagining Tom acting one out—was more than her already hysterical emotions could bear. She was laughing and crying at the same time, so hard she was having trouble breathing.

With a lot more speed than finesse, Tom made it the rest of the way. She held out a hand to help him but he shook his head and motioned her to move aside. So she did, snapping on her bedside lamp to help light his way as she watched him grab the sill, his fingers white as he gripped and hauled a leg over. He planted one boot, then ducked and swiveled the rest of his body inside. Then he rose to stand before her, dripping, cold, covered with broken twigs, bits of dirt, and the stringy gray remains of a spiderweb decorating one cheek.

He took the wet, bedraggled flowers out of his mouth and presented them. "I'm twelve years late," he said, "but I finally made it."

And if she hadn't been in love with him before, Gillian fell headlong at that moment.

Chapter 20

Gillian reached for the flowers and then threw herself into Tom's arms. He tried to hold her off, but she wouldn't be deflected. She plastered herself against every soaking, cold, shivery inch of him she could reach. She felt as though ice cubes were being rubbed on her breasts and belly and the sensations of pulsing heat and shocking cold pushed some long-forgotten wild button inside her.

She lifted her face, pulled his head down, and kissed him for all she was worth.

"Gillian," he said, pulling back, "I'm sorry."

Well, duh. Actions speak louder than words and he'd groveled all the way up that vine. "Apology accepted."

Her lips sought his again.

"I want to explain," he panted when he'd freed his mouth once more. "We should talk about this."

Gillian was as much into *we should talk* as any Oprah-watching woman, but there was a time for talk and there was a time for action. Right now, she wanted action.

She gagged him with the simple expedient of slipping her tongue into his mouth.

Once she'd shut him up, she made the most of her position. She licked deep into his mouth, tasting him, his heat and his need, feeling her own needs rise as he sucked greedily at her tongue, grabbed her hips and pulled her tight against his erection.

She gasped and jumped, feeling as though a sponge full of ice water had just been squeezed over her mound.

"Let's get you out of these wet things," she said, stepping back. As she did so, his gaze darkened and traveled her body. She glanced down at herself and saw that the sheer cotton was now plastered wetly against her breasts, the nipples hard and dark beneath the white gauze. The sides of the gown were dry and still hung loose at her sides but where she'd touched him the cotton was like opaque shrink wrap. Her breasts, belly, and the dark curls of pubic hair were on vivid display, while the glowing cotton around her gave her an ethereal appearance.

"You look like a sex goddess," Tom told her.

She decided she liked the image and right now, she felt exactly like she looked—all her focus and energy in her erogenous zones, everything else fading softly into the background.

He began to shuck his clothes, his eyes never wavering. It wasn't easy; the damp cloth clung and seemed reluctant to leave him. She didn't blame it. But he persevered until there was a soggy pile of boots and clothes on the floor by the window and he wore nothing but dark green plaid flannel boxers. They were so darling and old-fashioned on his young, virile body that she smiled.

He saw the smile and crossed to her. "Oh, great. One look at me naked and you'll be laughing your head off."

She ran her fingers lightly along the hard ridge that

rose in his boxers. "I can guarantee that is not going to happen," she promised. "You've filled out a lot in twelve years."

"I hope I've learned a thing or two as well. I hope I know how to please you."

He was half teasing but there was a hint of seriousness behind the words that made her gaze into his earnest green eyes and ask, "Is that why you never came when I invited you?"

In a dozen years she'd never thought that might be the reason, but she saw it was when he nodded solemnly. "Honey, I was a virgin. I didn't have the first clue what to do with a woman."

"You would have learned," she said softly. "I would have helped you."

"I would have made a fool of myself. You weren't some girl as clueless as I was that I could fumble around with and try to fit the right parts together. You were so experienced and—"

She turned abruptly. "A slut, you mean. That's why you didn't come to me. You thought I was—"

"No!"

He swung her around, holding her against all the hot length of his body by splaying his hands across her back so she couldn't avoid him. Not his touch, not his expression, not his eyes, which shone with the truth. "I thought you were amazing. Incredible. Sexy. And I figured you must think I was . . . in your league. But I wasn't. I wanted to climb that stupid vine so badly I hung around almost every night that week. Once I even made it into your yard. But I chickened out every time."

She felt like weeping for the girl she'd been then. So cocky, so goddamn sure of herself. When sex had been the easiest thing in the world.

She touched Tom's cheek with her palm. "I'm not that girl anymore." She'd tried to explain to him before, but she wasn't sure her message had been received. "Some things have happened to me since that time." How could she explain to this honest, uncomplicated man? He wouldn't understand the million subtle cruelties, and some not so subtle. The way Eric had done his best to humiliate and control her. In the early days, she could get high and go to a place where it didn't matter, but when she stopped escaping her reality, it became uglier. And, she now realized, Eric had punished her for cleaning up her act.

At first, she'd thought it was fun the way he'd make her beg before letting her come. Then it stopped being fun. And he started to hurt her. And then, after a while, she stopped coming at all. And he'd taunted her with that. Called her stupid, ugly names.

Now she faced having sex again—she didn't know what she was capable of, what she even wanted, apart from simply being held by someone good and solid. Someone she trusted.

And if this turned out to be a disaster, she wasn't sure she had the courage to try again.

"I want you to do something for me." She realized she was still gripping the flowers. "I should put these in a vase," she said.

Tom gripped her shoulders. "They were in the rain all night. They'll be okay. What is it you want?"

This was so hard. She was such a coward. She didn't want to explain, didn't want to admit she was scared and messed up and unsure of herself. She flicked a brief glance at Tom and realized that if he hadn't let fear stop him all those years ago . . .

Well, maybe nothing would have been different, but maybe something would have. She didn't want to be the coward this time. It was sex. A natural, normal human behavior and she'd get through this. Tom might not be exciting, but he'd be kind and the boy who'd rescued stray animals would never hurt her deliberately.

"I've . . . got some bad stuff I want to put behind me . . ." She trailed off, but he didn't push. He wore the universal cop face they must teach in law enforcement training academies all over America. The world, probably. He knew about violence against women.

Why had she stayed with a man for eight years if he'd been so bad for her? That was a question she didn't have an answer for.

Tom's hands gentled on her back. She felt his erection, as stiff as before against her belly, but the rest of his demeanor gave no clue to his arousal. It was hard not to respect that kind of restraint in a man.

"Do you want to talk about it?"

"Yes. Someday. But not today."

He nodded and ran his fingertips over the faded bruise on her face. "We will talk about this. I can't do anything until we do."

"But not tonight," she begged.

"No. Tonight there are only the two of us in this room. Agreed?"

She nodded, hoping she could manage it, hoping the demons from her past didn't insist on crashing the party.

He took a look around the room, which had never been redecorated since she'd lived there, as though her grandparents had somehow always known she'd be back. The single bed looked virginal with its white iron frame and faded chintz comforter.

"This is what your room would have looked like if I'd been brave enough to climb up here when you asked me," Tom said, as he took her hand and led her to her bed.

She nodded. Absurd to be trembling. He must feel it through their joined hands, but she had a feeling her entire sexual destiny would be mapped out in that narrow bed over the next couple of hours.

She was so nervous she was hyperventilating. Soon she'd faint. Just what Tom needed in his life. A naked, passed-out former slut.

She might as well give it up now and see if there was a convent in the world who'd accept a woman like her.

While these thoughts cascaded through her mind, Tom led her forward until her knees bumped the edge of the mattress.

She swallowed, as though seeing it for the first time and associating it with something other than sleep. She turned to him and raised a trembling hand to his face. "Be careful with me."

There was a serious light in his eyes when he said, "Always."

He kissed her, pulling her gently into his arms, and she thought, *Maybe this is going to be okay*. He didn't grab or grope, maul or shove, simply kissed her, leaving his hands loose around her waist.

She'd forgotten how nice simple kissing could be. His lips were warm and firm, his tongue subtle but masterful as he took possession of her mouth, then eased away, letting her take the lead.

She began, very slowly, to melt.

His skin was still damp in places, his hair in wet curls against his scalp, but he was warm. So warm. He eased her onto the bed, not even attempting to take off her night dress. Maybe it was the way they seemed to have gone back in time, but she felt like a girl again, as though she were just starting out. Each touch felt new. Each caress surprised her.

"Would it be all right if I touched your breasts?" he asked softly, his lips kissing her ear after he whispered the words.

She was charmed. If anyone had ever asked her, she

didn't remember it. Romance, he'd promised her. It seemed she was getting it.

She appeared to consider his request, and saw that for all his careful wooing, he was half crazy for her. Which was good. She was gaining confidence and taking back control of her body. The years fell away along with her bad memories. Maybe some people thought rewriting history was cheating, but Gillian decided if it had been botched the first time around there should be rewrites allowed.

"Yes," she said equally softly. Then trembled, her breasts pulsing and throbbing with the knowledge they were about to be caressed. And when it happened, when his hands touched her there, she discovered the anticipation had made her response that much richer.

"I'd like to kiss your nipples, if that would be okay?"

She moaned, as the heat scorched her.

"I'll kiss you through your night dress. I promise," he said. He was sweet and careful with her, but he wasn't a boy. There was nothing fumbling, groping, or adolescent about his moves. She began to realize she was in the hands of a sexually confident and experienced lover.

"All right," she said, her own voice shaking, with need now more than nerves.

As his mouth closed over her nipple, she felt the hot wetness of his tongue as well as the abrasion of wet Indian cotton on her sensitive skin. It was quite possibly the most erotic sensation she'd ever experienced. She knew his tongue would feel smooth and luscious on her naked skin, but the barrier of wet cotton kept up a maddening scratching, scraping that wasn't painful, merely different. He sucked a nipple into his mouth, cotton and all. As he lifted his head, the cotton quickly cooled, making her nipple ultrasensitive, so she felt it puckering along with the wet fabric.

She didn't want any barriers between them. She wanted his tongue on her nakedness.

All of it.

But Tom was in no hurry.

His hands might not be quite steady, but they were slow, smoothing the cotton against her sides as he stroked her. Kissing her breasts for so long, her lower body was in torment.

She tried to give him a hint that it was time to speed things up, gripping the waistband of his boxers and attempting to yank them off, but he stilled her hands.

"Please," she gasped.

"Not yet," he replied softly.

How could he not understand that she needed to get this first time out of the way? That she wanted to replace Eric with Tom as the last man who'd been inside her body. Then, she squeezed her eyes tight shut, realizing she'd let Eric into the room, after she'd promised both of them she wouldn't.

Breathing deep, she concentrated on the feel of Tom's body against hers, on the smell of his skin and rain-washed hair. She played with his hair, learning its texture, loving the way the damp, short curls brushed her fingers. Following his lead, she took the time to learn his body, his textures and his most responsive zones, while the urge to get on with things grew thicker and hotter within her.

Once she'd finished with his hair, she moved to his neck, his shoulders, his torso. Maybe he was only upholding the law in a podunk town in Oregon where nothing much ever happened, but he stayed in shape. If muscle was ever needed, Tom Perkins was your man. His shoulders were hard, his neck muscular, and his torso—well, that looked like something you'd see on an infomercial for some ab- and chest-strengthening device.

He seemed as interested in her torso as she was in his.

He toyed with the ribbon that held her bodice closed. His eyes were dark and his face achingly familiar as he asked, in his slow way, "Could I untie this? I want to see you."

She gulped and a tremor shook her. She couldn't speak over the ache in her throat, so she nodded slowly, wondering if she'd ever felt this special. She didn't think so.

Suddenly, she wished she'd thought to switch off the lamp, but it was too late now. Her heart was having trouble finding a rhythm as Tom's big fingers made clumsy work of untying the pale blue silk ribbon. It was the first awkwardness he'd shown. He really was as anxious to see her naked breasts as she was suddenly shy about displaying them.

He parted the fabric slowly and she held her breath, feeling his gaze on her almost as real as the soft slide of cotton.

His breath caught as at last, at long, long, last, he bared both breasts.

Her flesh shivered. He didn't go straight for her nipples, or palm her entire breast, but propped himself on one elbow and with the index finger of his other hand traced the outline of her breast.

The move was subtle, her reaction anything but.

She felt warm, pulsing waves of desire—and this was from his fingertip tracing her left breast. Her trembling began in earnest as she contemplated what he could do to her if she were naked and he really put his mind to it.

Her breasts were generous in size. At eighteen they'd been as high on her chest and perky as twin balloons. At thirty, some of the air had leaked out of the balloons. She reached a hand for the lamp and he stopped her.

"You are so beautiful," he said.

Chapter 21

She stared up at him and drew in a shaky breath. "I'm afraid of what you're going to do to me."

And on one level that was truer than she could have believed possible. A man like this could steal all her love and never give it back.

He lifted her hand and placed it over his heart, so she felt the solid thump against her palm, and he placed his hand over her heart, which was bouncing with nerves and excitement. "I promise I will do my best never to hurt you."

As they stared at each other, she knew he'd keep that promise.

Maybe she was being given a second chance, she thought, as her eyes drifted shut and the sweet balm of desire warmed all her cold, numb places. Her fingers danced over his chest, and his also got busy.

From tracing her breasts, his hands moved slowly but surely to her nipples, palming and cupping them, along with the full part of her breasts so they warmed to life and began to spread pleasant, throbbing sensations to the rest of her body.

Relaxing into the slow, easy seduction, she found herself lying pliant and warm, nothing on her mind but her own pleasure. When she felt the warm, wet heat of his tongue on her nipples, a sound escaped her lips, part sigh, part moan.

"Too rough?" Tom asked, raising his head.

"No," she said breathlessly. "Perfect."

Part of her wanted to rip their clothes off and get on with it, but a truer part of herself, one she hadn't always listened to in her life, wanted to stay with this slow pace, wanted to enjoy every minute, to savor and prolong. She'd had a lot of sex, but she'd known very little of making love.

That's what Tom was doing to her and she found she liked it a whole lot better.

He went back to her breasts, lapping, kissing, suckling a little, and meanwhile his hand traced her belly through the cotton. As he hit the base of her belly, the pressure changed so he just brushed her pubic hair through the cotton gown.

At first she thought it was accidental, then after the not-quite-caress left her with the suggestion of a touch rather than the touch itself, and that only upped the anticipation, she realized he was doing it deliberately.

Her exploring fingers had made it down his back— the plaid boxers were a serious impediment to any further shenanigans. Plus, she wanted to see him, feel him, taste him. She let her fingers toy with his waistband for a minute, held back a gasp of frustration as he airbrushed her crotch once more.

He brushed her again, not so lightly this time and she touched him just as softly through the boxers.

His breathing rate upped as she caressed him slowly.

Meanwhile, he reached down for the bottom of her gown and raised the hem an inch at a time, all the while continuing to play at her breasts with his mouth.

She slid her thighs apart the minute the gown passed her knees. She felt an orgasm in her imminent future as sure as she'd smell rain in the air on a gray, cloudy day. She wanted that orgasm so fiercely she trembled all over with the wanting.

Of course, Tom didn't know about her recent troubles. He couldn't know that she, who had never previously grasped the concept of a vibrator, now wondered if even one powered by a super battery could bring her body back from the dead zone.

And here was the elusive orgasm tingling in its possibilities, hovering just out of reach.

If Tom tormented her much longer it was going to take off for greener pastures.

How she'd gone from being unsure about even being touched to burningly close to climax, she couldn't quite fathom.

Whether Tom had picked up on her distress or had simply reached the end of his own tolerance, she didn't know, but suddenly things seemed to speed up.

His lips brushed her inner thigh, her nightdress was slipping deliberately up over her hips, which she raised to aid the operation. She was mostly naked before him, apart from the gown rucked around her waist, but damn it, he was still wearing his boxers. What the hell was on his—

"Aaaah," she cried aloud as his mouth found her sweetest place and he licked at her with the same focused effort he put to every task.

After all the waiting, the slow seduction, the may-I-put-my-mouth-on-your-nipple, to have his tongue swirl right up inside her and then slide slickly over her throbbing clit was a joy to her love-starved body. She rose, slowly, as he played his tongue with gentle deliberation over her most sensitive flesh.

There was no hurry, no pressure. She felt his pleasure in his task and believed he'd be happy to stay there all night, so she relaxed and gave herself over to the relentless heat building slowly but surely.

She heard panting, and knew it was coming from her throat, heard the springs of the old bed creak, and knew that was caused by her lower body, which was starting to thrash.

Reaching back over her head, she grasped the metal posts of the bed frame, feeling she needed to anchor herself.

And she was right. In a move as mind-blowing as it was unexpected, he sucked her clitoris right into his mouth, maintaining a gentle suction. And just like that, she flew apart.

By the time she floated back to earth and her heart seemed to be back in her body, she discovered that Tom's boxers were nothing but a tartan heap at the end of the bed.

And he was slipping a condom onto a penis as rock-solid and reliable as its owner. The jingle of a truck commercial flashed through her mind. Something about being made in America and built tough. That was Tom.

As he slipped between her legs, she opened for him and then he was there, entering her body slowly and deliberately as though he'd be in no big hurry to leave again.

With a sigh of pure bliss, she wrapped her legs around his hips and rose to meet him. Their gazes caught and held and as he began to thrust she felt, absurdly, as though she were starting all over again.

In all thirty years of her life, she realized, she'd never been intimate with a man she truly loved.

Until now.

She kissed him, tasting herself on him, and his own heat and need.

The speed increased and she discovered safe, reliable Tom had some moves on him she'd never have guessed, including a delightful habit of hitting her g-spot with each deep thrust.

She'd had her orgasm and was happy to ride along with him, enjoying her own aftershocks and ready to enjoy his pleasure almost as keenly as she'd experienced her own.

She had no idea quite how he did it. He changed the angle somehow and seemed to stretch her in some new way that had her gasping and forgetting all about climaxing vicariously through him as a second orgasm exploded through her. She was clinging to him, arching to receive each thrust as he took her deep and hard and to some new place she'd never been.

On the echo of her own cries she heard a deep roar and felt his explosion somewhere so deep she suspected it might be her heart.

"Thank you," she said softly, much later when they lay twined and ridiculously crowded in her old single bed, the mattress so giving they were like a human California wrap.

He smiled at her but didn't answer, tucking a strand of hair behind her ear and following the length to smooth it over her shoulder and all the way to the end, which happened to be mid-breast. Once he was there, her hair was promptly forgotten and he toyed with her breasts with sleepy sexiness.

"I . . . I felt almost as though that was my first time," she said, knowing she was now at the Oprah-watching woman's-need-to-talk part of the program.

"It *was* our first time. With each other."

"So, I was a virgin for you and you were a virgin for me?"

"Yeah."

Tears stung her lids, but they weren't the tears of misery that had been her constant companion the past few months. They were tears of hope.

Eric had come into her life when she'd been vulnerable, young and weak. He'd used her, introduced her to drugs, and then talked her into bringing him to her home. In Swiftcurrent, he'd gone from being the failed rock singer she'd first hung with, so cool and exciting with his long hair and his drugs, all the way to a pillar of the establishment.

Gillian now realized that Eric had craved respectability the way she'd craved love. They'd been disastrous together but in one way they'd both sucked what they'd needed from the marriage. Her grandfather had helped Eric become a respected business owner in this town, and Eric had brought her back home, where she was loved—by her family, if not her husband.

Well, she wasn't quite so young, but she wasn't as weak and foolish, either. She wouldn't settle for so little ever again.

She kissed Tom long and deep and his attention to her chest grew instantly less lazy. An insistent nudging against her thigh told her that all of him had sprung to attention.

Sighing, she rubbed against him, as aroused and ready for round two as he, and no longer inclined for talk.

"If I have to roll around on this old mattress again, I'm going to put my back out," he complained. So he hauled her off the bed without ceremony, pulled the mattress, its bedding clinging as best it could, to the floor and got down onto it.

Once she was standing, her nightie started to slip; feeling his gaze, hot and focused on her, she let it go. Maybe she wasn't one of those gym-obsessed hard bodies, but she spent an hour a day doing yoga and she walked most places. Her body was trim and flexible and Tom obviously had no complaint.

He eyed her from the floor, his gaze sliding hotly up her body from her feet to her chest. It seemed to snag there, but eventually kept going until their gazes met. She'd never seen a longing so fierce and she shivered in reaction.

"Come down here," he said hoarsely.

"If you're a restless sleeper, I'm going to end up tossed on the floor," she complained after they'd made love again, simple and straightforward and sweetly satisfying.

"I can't stay," he said.

"Why not?" She hadn't meant to sound so distressed, but she hated the thought of him up and leaving right after what they'd shared. Or had she made a big deal in her mind about something that meant much less to Tom?

Probably. With her usual knack for throwing herself into things long before she was ready, she'd obviously made more of the Tom thing than he had. She'd imagined him climbing her wisteria had been a sentimental and highly meaningful gesture, but perhaps he'd just missed his workout and used the side of her house as a temporary gym.

"I've got to get home to Lucky," he said about the same time she concluded she was a total idiot.

"Lucky?"

"My dog."

"I thought you had a cat." She knew he did. A tiny, scrawny kitten he'd rescued years ago. She saw it at odd times hanging out around town wherever it felt like. It was the size of a small sheep, a natural redhead, and snooty as a spoiled princess.

"I do have a cat. Lucky's more recent. He's a Lab red setter cross and very smart. I found him out on the highway, lost or abandoned. He's still young and can't make it through the night without accidents."

"Okay." She tried to keep her voice pleasantly neutral. No problem, buddy. *Come on by anytime, screw me and leave me for a Labrador cross.* She supposed women had been left for less.

"Come with **me**."

"Pardon?"

"I'm not near finished with you. And," he tweaked her nose, "I have a big bed."

Chapter 22

"There's something serious I want to talk to you about," Eric said on the phone. It was Sunday night and Alex was preoccupied planning her week's wardrobe, so she hadn't checked her call display, assuming it would be Duncan on the phone. The minute she heard Eric's voice, annoyance filled her.

She wished she hadn't made that promise to Duncan. She wanted to yell at Eric for telling Duncan he'd seen her half naked. Still, even though she'd promised not to confront Eric, she didn't have to be sweet to the man. "I really don't think—"

"You've had so much on your shoulders lately. I've tried to be there for you, to help you, but that fellow is always around."

"Which fellow?" Alex asked through gritted teeth. She was getting close to breaking her promise to Duncan and giving Eric an earful.

"The man who calls himself a teacher and who haunts your every waking moment."

A lot of sleeping ones, too, but she decided not to share that information. "If you mean Duncan Forbes, he *is* a teacher and he's using the library for research purposes and a quiet place to write."

"Alex, he arrived here the day before a man was murdered. He was in the library the morning a gun showed up in your desk drawer. Has it occurred to you he isn't all he seems?"

She tried not to let the doubts creep into her mind. Eric was trying to make trouble between her and Duncan. She had no idea why, but she didn't like it.

"It's late, Eric. I think I'd better—"

"Wait." She heard him let out a breath. "I'm sorry. I've no right, I know that. It's just that I feel like the closest thing you have to a brother. I'm trying to watch out for you."

Abruptly she softened. "I appreciate it, but I can look after myself." And yet, for all her feelings of self-righteousness, what did she know about Duncan? She'd believed everything he'd told her.

"Well, your grandfather wanted me to keep an eye out for you. I have to respect his wishes."

Her anger dissolved. "I understand."

"How are you doing with those tapes?"

If she weren't spending so much of her time playing private games with Duncan, her grandfather's memoirs would be coming along a lot faster. "Fine. I've got most of them transcribed now."

He seemed to consider his next words for a moment, then said, "Look. This may sound crazy, but I got the feeling your grandfather had something special that he wanted you and Gillian to have. Did he ever tell you anything about that?"

"Yes," she said. "Grandpa talked to me a few months before he died about a special bequest, but there doesn't seem to be anything other than the house and some small savings."

"What did your grandfather say specifically?"

"Nothing. He said he was leaving a letter with his will, but there wasn't one."

"He said something to me a few months ago, also. I got the feeling there might be some art work involved."

"Really? That's more than he told me. You mean a special piece from his collection?" She thought about it and shook her head. "I don't think so. You've seen his paintings. There are a couple of nice ones, but nothing very valuable."

"Maybe he forgot to write the letter, but the . . . special bequest is hidden somewhere. Can you think of any locations where it might be?"

"Eric," she said, feeling her irritation return, "he was an old man. He probably meant those godawful brasses from India. The tiger and the dancing woman and the gong. I know they're ancient, but they are ugly, and not exactly worth a fortune."

"Your grandfather was a shrewd art dealer. If he said he had something of value, he did. It doesn't matter to me, obviously, but Gillian is going to need money. Rehab is expensive."

A frown pulled at her forehead. "Rehab?"

"I'm worried sick about her. She's getting worse. She may have to be put away for her own good."

"Put away?" The term conjured grim images of a Victorian mental hospital.

"I don't think she can go on like this much longer. God knows I can't."

"But she seems so much better." Alex was getting a sick feeling in the pit of her stomach. She knew already that she wouldn't be a party to putting Gill into rehab unless her cousin wanted it. And the bright-eyed, shiny-haired woman she'd shared tea and laughter with didn't look in imminent need of forceful confinement. She remembered Gillian's bitter claim that she always believed Eric. And she had, she realized; maybe from now on she'd be more careful to pay attention to what he said.

"Alex, some addicts never recover." He sounded so sad as he said it.

"Maybe we need to give her another chance."

"Oh, I agree. I'm just saying it would be easier if there was money for her care. Or money to get on with her life. Your grandfather wanted you to have something special. It would be a shame for it to stay hidden when you could both benefit."

"Maybe we'll dig up the backyard and find buried treasure," she said lightly.

"Maybe," he laughed, but not very humorously. "If I can help at all, call me. You know I only want what's best for you and Gill."

Did he? She wasn't so sure anymore. "Thanks. I appreciate it."

"I'm on my way out of town for ten days or so. There are some auctions coming up in Eugene and Portland, and some clients I need to see. Before I leave, I wanted to warn you to watch out for that professor. I don't trust him."

She suspected his warning about Duncan stemmed from the same source that had urged him to tell Duncan he'd seen her beauty mark. And yet, even as she tried to dismiss his words, they hit home. How much did she know about Duncan Forbes? She'd pretty much taken him at his word.

Enough of that. She was a librarian, wasn't she? Maybe it was time to do what she did best. Boot up her computer and research the man. If only to disprove Eric's hints.

It didn't take her any longer than a Google search. The name Duncan Forbes produced a gratifying number of hits. Of course, there could be a lot of guys named Duncan Forbes. That didn't mean anything.

She scanned the listings. Immediately her attention was caught by an article from the *London Times* dated just over a year ago.

Stolen Gauguin Returned. She clicked on that, surmising that since Duncan was an art historian he might have helped authenticate the work, or perhaps he had an esoteric comment to make about the importance of Gauguin to the art world.

> *A Gauguin painting, valued at ten million pounds sterling, has been returned to Lord Hooting, from whose fifteenth-century castle it was stolen three months ago.*
>
> Women Bathing *was stolen in broad daylight on one of the public visiting days at the castle.*
>
> *Professor Duncan Forbes, nicknamed "the Indiana Jones of the art world" for his record of recovering stolen and lost works of art, was the principal figure in the art work's recovery . . .*

She almost choked on her water. "The Indiana Jones of the art world?"

Article after article cited Duncan as a paintbrush-wielding bounty hunter, tracking and retrieving stolen art works all over the world.

Immediately, she recalled that the dead man in her library had been a fence. Could there be a connection? And if so, why had Duncan never said a word to her?

"You lying prick!" she shouted as she finished the search.

She wanted to kick something very hard. Preferably Duncan's face. Instead she kicked the wall, not willing to move from her computer until she'd read everything she could find about Mr. Duncan "Indiana Jones of the art world" Forbes.

Wait, calm down, she told herself. He hadn't lied. He was a prof, and, according to a review that came up among the Google hits, the author of a seminal work on Gauguin, which he'd mentioned.

He'd told her he was writing a book while he was here, so there was no reason to tell her about his other life. But he was sleeping with her so there was no reason to keep it a secret. She recalled how reticent he'd been when she asked him about his work. He could have told her about his lucrative sideline, but he hadn't.

Why?

The more she thought about the way he'd kept secrets from her, the less she liked his reasons.

She'd told him all kinds of things about herself. The man had been inside her body. A little honesty didn't seem too much to ask in return.

She grabbed her phone. She'd call his cell and yell blue murder in his ear.

The phone was back in its cradle before she'd pushed a single button. No. She wanted to do this in person.

Five minutes later, she pulled out of her parking space and headed to Duncan's cottage. Her temper did not improve when she discovered his car wasn't in its usual spot.

He wasn't inside the cottage, either. The door was locked, so she pressed her face against the windows. All was dark.

She felt like a hunting hound who thinks it's got its prey cornered, only to find the animal had gone to ground. No wonder hounds bayed. She felt like doing a bit of baying herself.

Typical male behavior to disappear off the planet whenever a woman wanted a good fight.

Oh, and she did want a fight. The more she thought about how he'd been lying to her the whole time he'd been here, the more angry she became. She wasn't a stupid woman and while she sat, freezing in her car, waiting for Duncan, she began to see his presence in Swiftcurrent in a new light.

The dead man who'd turned up in her library had been a drug dealer; they'd all glommed onto that piece of information and assumed that drugs had been involved in his death. But he'd also been a thief.

She tapped her gloved hands against the steering wheel in a mindless rhythm.

Duncan, according to her Internet search, spent a lot of time tracing stolen goods, mostly art. Was there a connection? Was Duncan not only involved in recovering stolen goods but in stealing them as well?

Getting both ends of the business?

She didn't like to contemplate the possibility, any more than she liked the logical connection between Duncan and the dead man. She couldn't believe she could show such poor character judgment that she'd sleep with a man who'd turn out to be a thief.

She wasn't going to believe her lover was a killer on such circumstantial evidence, but neither was she going to hang around in this dark, secluded area to confront him with her findings.

Tomorrow would be soon enough. She'd meet him someplace with a lot of people around. In daylight.

And she would not spend any time at all wondering where he was at nearly eleven o'clock at night.

Duncan took a deep drink of his second pint of draught at Sailor Ernie's Pub, which he'd rapidly discovered was guys' gossip central in Swiftcurrent just as

Katie's Kut 'n' Kurl was the women's. He'd learned nothing new tonight, but he hadn't expected to.

He was really here to sort out his feelings over an ice cold beer.

He'd almost begun to believe that Plotnik's death was drug-related. A bizarre coincidence, and he was no closer to the Van Gogh than he had been when he first arrived.

Then the gun showed up in Alex's drawer.

The gun he strongly suspected was going to turn out to be the murder weapon. It was a message for somebody.

It seemed to be for Alex.

But why? Of all the things that didn't make sense, only one thing did. Alex was in danger.

Maybe this quiet little gig didn't involve chasing down the streets of Lisbon or payoffs in the back alleys of Rio, but this was Swiftcurrent, so sleepily law abiding that it seemed like hard work would be required to nab a parking ticket.

Something was going on, though, and it seemed Alex was the key. It was time to do what he'd been putting off and tell her the truth about himself. He swallowed hard, hoping the beer would lend him some courage. He wasn't sure he wouldn't prefer shady Russian mob figures in a dark alley in Moscow to an angry Alex.

He was doing a crap job of coming up with the painting on his own. Coming clean with Alex was not only the clearest way to finding the picture, if Franklin Forrest had ever owned it, but it was also the best way he could see to protect Alex, and that was more important than anything.

The noise level was a constant dull roar punctuated by raucous laughter, the smell of spilled beer, and incipient-lung-cancer-level cigarette smoke. From his perch at the pock marked, stained oak bar, Duncan could see everyone from loggers to farmers to the local bank manager. He wondered where their women were.

He knew where his woman was. At home, since she liked to spend Sunday nights obsessively organizing everything from her pantyhose to her hair clips for the week ahead.

If he hurried, he could watch, and maybe throw in a few suggestions for the week's underwear. He found he could watch her do the most mundane tasks and get a kick out of them. He took pleasure in simply watching her, being with her, loving her.

A choking sound was loud in his ears and he discovered it was him doing the choking. Love? Was that what this was?

The truth was there in front of him like a hidden picture he'd uncovered—as beautiful and as magical as any of his finds. Hard to believe, but he was in love with A. M. Forrest. He loved every rule-obsessed, ultraorganized, sexy, gorgeous inch of her. He loved her sophisticated demeanor and the small town heart he doubted she knew she possessed. He loved her laughter and her openness, her intelligence, wit, and basic goodness.

He needed to trust her fully with the truth of who he was, why he was here, and, most frightening of all, with his heart.

Instead of filling him with terror, the truth brought a warm glow to his chest.

He paid up and left, so anxious to get to Alex he damn near sprinted to his rental.

A glance at the car's clock told him it was getting on for eleven. She usually watched the eleven o'clock news and then went to bed, so if he hurried, he wouldn't wake her.

Of course, there was always the possibility that she'd refuse to let him in so late, but he knew her weaknesses.

All he had to do was mention a couple of things he planned to do to her that she wouldn't be able to resist. When she'd taunted him with how much she loved sex, he'd assumed she was exaggerating or making it up to torment him. He'd been wrong.

He'd never known a woman who flat-out loved sex as much as Alex did. Raunchy or gentle, noisy or silent, lights on or off, in bed, or anywhere. It didn't matter. He hadn't found a position she didn't respond to or a time she didn't feel like it.

He grinned to himself in the dark. She was a dream come true.

Of course, he had no idea how they were going to work out the future, but he assumed if they put their minds to it they'd work something out.

He stopped grinning twenty minutes later when it was clear she wasn't home. Where the hell was she at this time of night?

Frowning at the intercom wasn't helping. He could get into her place easily enough, but if she was ignoring him for some reason, or asleep, she was not going to be thrilled to find him breaking and entering. However, if she was in some kind of trouble, he couldn't break and enter fast enough.

He rang her apartment again. Still nothing.

Ten minutes later, he was getting ready to break in first and think of a good explanation later when he heard a car. Sure enough, it was Alex's, driven with unseemly haste for such an orderly woman.

He sprinted after her and was in time to watch her speed into her parking lot and miss hitting the building's siding by an inch.

Now what was that about? And where the hell had she been?

"Hey!" he said when she stepped out of her car.

"What?" she snapped.

"Alex, it's me. Duncan."

"Of course it is. Who else would bother me at midnight? I do not want sex and I certainly don't want you. Go away." She stomped to the side door and stuck her key in the lock.

"Now, that's two lies in a row. You should be ashamed—" She entered and slammed the door behind her.

What bug had climbed up her ass?

He jogged around front and called her on the intercom, knowing the buzzer was going to drive her nuts until she answered it.

"Will you stop bothering me?" was his greeting when she picked up.

"I want to talk to you." He wasn't a fool. It was obvious she wasn't in the mood for declarations of love and devotion, but would a simple conversation kill the woman?

A moment's silence. He waited in faint hope for the click that meant she was letting him in. "I want to talk to you, too. Tomorrow."

"Look, it's import—"

Once again, he was talking to himself. With a muttered curse, he stomped back to his car. The woman he'd just this evening learned he was in love with didn't want to talk to him. Right now, he felt like yelling. While disappointment settled heavy in his belly, he realized he'd have to leave things until tomorrow.

Nothing life-changing was going to happen in one day.

The next morning, Alex woke to sunshine. As was her custom when the weather was fine, she walked to work, track shoes on her feet and a pair of heels in her bag.

Well, *walk* would not be quite accurate. She stomped to work, wishing she could squish beneath her feet the feeling that she'd been made a fool of by Duncan Forbes.

Of course, not even a towering rage would cause her to cross against the light, so she waited, in spite of the fact there wasn't any traffic in the area, until the neon sign across the street flashed that it was her turn to walk.

He'd lied to her by omission and what he'd omitted suddenly seemed to have significance precisely because he'd kept his moonlighting business secret.

Stomp, stomp—she reached the next sidewalk and kept going, working her heart rate good and hard as her pace increased along with her frustration.

It had seemed too good to be true to find a man like him in Swiftcurrent. Or anywhere, come to that. He was the kind of man she'd planned to move to a big city to meet. He was athletic but intellectual, good-looking but not narcissistic. And he was the best sex she'd ever had. Not that sex was everything—she'd learned long ago to be discriminating and that it was better to do without than to sleep with men she couldn't respect.

Which immediately took Mr. Forbes off her list. How could she respect a man who was dishonest? She couldn't. Maybe sex with him was fantastic, but sex wasn't everything. Although even the idea of never sleeping with him again seemed to burn a hole right through her, she had to admit the possibility that she'd let him make a fool of her because she was in a dry spell.

Even as she rolled her eyes, she noticed a beige sedan very much like Duncan's.

"Oh, give me a break!" she yelled at the oncoming car. The sun was in her eyes, and the driver had the sun visor pulled down, so she couldn't even see his face, but she glared at him good and hard anyway.

The car wasn't slowing. It was heading right for her.

She gasped as she watched the car cross the yellow line onto her side of the road.

It was aimed right at her like a large beige bullet. *Oh, my God,* she thought, *he's going to kill me!*

She heard the engine race and that's when her adrenal glands yelled, Hellooo!!

She screamed and instinct took over. She dove over the scrubby hedge of azaleas. She heard the roar of the engine loud in her ears, then a cacophonous shriek of tires.

She hit the ground and for a couple of seconds she didn't know anything. Was she dead? But her body hurt too much to be dead.

Can't just lie here. He'll come back.

She tried to pull herself to her feet and gasped as the big pain flowered into a hundred smaller pains. Hauling herself up, she found she was clinging to the granite base of Swiftcurrent's war memorial.

She held on to it, fighting nausea. She only seemed able to hang onto one clear thought at a time. *Have to get to the library.*

Her side burned where she'd hit the ground, her hip felt like all bruise and no bone, and her head ached. But the panic trying to choke her was the worst sensation.

She had a good two blocks to go until she hit the town square, and never had they seemed longer. She didn't have her cell phone with her to travel between home and work. Never had she regretted its absence more bitterly.

When she heard the sound of a car behind her, her muscles, every one of which was already in full fight-or-flight mode, tensed further. A glance over her shoulder confirmed the worst.

A tan car was following her.

She reached down, picked up a rock, turned, and threw it as hard as she could at the car window. She bent to reach for another, still trying to run.

"Alex, what the hell's going on?"

At first, relief washed over her when she recognized Duncan's voice, then she backed away.

By this time he was pulled up beside her, the passenger window rolling down as he stared.

She ought to hit him with the rock first and ask questions later, but she was trembling so badly, she couldn't quite manage it, and the throbbing in her side was turning into the mother of all cramps.

"Get in the car."

"No. I'm fine. I'll walk."

He was out of the driver's side in an instant and rounding on her. She tried to step back and stumbled.

"Hey," he said, with a voice a whisperer probably used on a nervous mare, "let's get you sitting down."

That sounded reasonable and a very good idea, seeing as how none of the parts of her body that were designed to hold her upright seemed to be doing a very good job. In fact, she was going through reverse evolution as she stood there. Bending, hunching, losing basic language skills—soon she'd be on all fours and gibbering.

Duncan took her arm, still speaking softly, though what he was saying she couldn't fathom, and easing her into his car as though she were a very frail person. If he was going to murder her, she realized she was going to let him. He buckled her seat belt for her, shut her door, got in the driver's side, and started driving.

"Are you planning to kill me?"

He glanced at her sharply. "Alex, I'm trying to keep you alive."

"Oh. Good. Just checking."

"Is that why you threw a rock at me? You thought I—"

"It was the same car."

"The same car as what?"

"Your car is the same as the one that ran me off the road a few minutes ago." She glanced around and realized they weren't near the library. "Where are we going?"

"The hospital."

"No. I have to open the library at nine."

"Alex, did you hit your head?"

She touched her aching scalp. "I'm not sure. I might have."

"You probably have a concussion. You have to get checked out. Plus, you're bleeding."

She hadn't even noticed, but sure enough, when she glanced down she saw red liquid oozing through the blouse she'd ironed to white crispness not sixty minutes ago. "I'm sorry, it's going on your upholstery. The rental company will charge for cleaning."

"I'll survive." He sounded curt, but she thought his anger was directed at something other than her for bleeding on his car. When her head didn't hurt so badly, she'd think about that.

In the meantime, he was pulling out a cell phone—it figured he'd think to bring one with him—and punching buttons.

"Don't you know it's dangerous to drive and talk on a cell phone at the same time?"

"I'll be very careful," he promised. "I want Tom Perkins," he said into the phone. "Tell him it's an emergency."

She sighed, thinking if Duncan were calling Tom about this, then he wasn't going to murder her.

"Tom? Duncan Forbes here. I've got Alex with me. Somebody tried to run her down this morning," he said in a voice that was a little calmer than she liked. Maybe she wasn't the love of his life, but a little panic, a little, *Oh, thank God you're all right,* would have been nice.

"She says it was a car like mine," and he gave the make and model. "One driver." He glanced at Alex and she nodded confirmation.

"Male?" She thought back and realized she'd seen nothing but the blur of a head. "Couldn't tell," she said and he relayed that information. "License plate?" This time she shook her head. All she'd seen was the blur of the thing coming at her. She couldn't have even said what state the license plate advertised, never mind the number. But she'd noticed it had a rental sticker, like Duncan's.

"It was a rental, like yours," she told him.

"She says it was a rental. I suggest you get an APB out and try to catch the bastard," Duncan said savagely and she decided that maybe there was more than one way to say, *Oh, thank God you're all right.*

"No, she's not okay," he yelled. "She's bleeding, concussed, and limping. I'm taking her to the hospital—see you there."

"You made me sound like a total mess," she complained. "And you should have told him to get Raeanne to open the library at nine."

"I'm sure it's top of his list. Now relax."

"I feel kind of sick."

"Hang on," he said. "We're almost there."

But she couldn't hang on, and with the hospital in view, she had to make him stop the car. One glance at her and he pulled over. He bolted out of the car and opened her door just in time for her to vomit into the gutter, narrowly missing his shoes.

"Oh," she groaned. "I'm sorry."

"Ssh, it's okay," he said, smoothing back her hair. "Feeling better?"

She nodded miserably and eased back into the seat.

He shut her door again and rounded the car and got back into his side. Before she'd had time to stop feeling embarrassed or to start feeling sick again, they were at emergency.

Chapter 23

"Hi. How are you feeling?"

Alex felt her eyes fill with tears as her cousin appeared at her hospital bedside that afternoon with blueberry muffins. Her favorite.

"Gran's recipe?" she asked hopefully, knowing her concussion couldn't be too serious if she could still remember these.

"Absolutely." Gillian smiled at down at her. "You look like hell."

She chuckled weakly. "Thanks. That's how I feel."

"I spoke to the doctor. They're keeping you overnight but she says you can go home tomorrow if you have someone to look after you."

"I can take care of myself."

"Alex. Come home. I'll look after you."

"You will?" It was such a foreign concept, to have her cousin the one doing the nurturing and her the needy one, that she smiled.

"I can cook, water all these plants," Gill gestured to

the greenhouse that Alex's hospital room had already turned into, "and make sure you get some rest."

"One thing I'd really appreciate you doing."

"What?"

"Keep Duncan Forbes away from me."

"Alex, he's out there right now. They'll only let one of us in at a time, even though it's visiting hours. I pulled family connection and outranked him, but it won't be easy to keep him out."

"Please?"

Gillian was smoothing her sheet and tucking it in, the way she preferred her bedding. Funny she'd remembered that. "I thought you liked him."

"I'm mad at him, but I have such a headache that if I see him I'll start to cry."

Her cousin patted her cheek. "You never would let anyone see you cry. Unlike me. Okay, I'll keep him out."

Alex didn't hold out much hope that her soft-voiced cousin could keep a determined Duncan Forbes out of hell itself if he had a mind to go there.

But, amazingly, she managed it. Gillian, she was beginning to suspect, had hidden resources.

So, when Alex was released the next day, it was her cousin who helped load all the flowers into the car and who drove Alex back to their grandparents' home.

"Thank you," she said as Gill brought in her lunch on a tray. It was the very same soup their grandmother used to make them when they were sick as kids—Campbell's chicken noodle, and egg salad sandwiches with the crusts cut off.

"Making your meals is the easy part," Gillian said, pushing her long blond hair behind her ear. "Keeping Duncan Forbes out of this house is the Herculean labor. The man won't take no for an answer."

"Tell me about it. He's the pushiest guy I've ever met."

"If you ask me, he's in love with you."

Alex laughed, but it sounded a bit like a sob. "I can't believe you are still such a romantic."

Her cousin blushed like a teenager. "I am a romantic."

Well, maybe Alex's own love life was a disaster, but it seemed somebody was having more luck. "So, this whole thing with Tom, it's . . . ?"

Gill fussed with a flower arrangement, snapping off a few dead roses and sticking her finger into the florist's foam to check for moisture. "I . . . we're trying to take things slowly."

"I remember when you had a crush on him in high school."

"I don't think it was a crush," her cousin said in a voice so soft Alex could have imagined it.

"Wait a minute? What do you mean?"

Gillian put her face in her hands. "Oh, forget it. I don't know what I'm saying."

But Alex had had a lot of time to think while she'd been lying here, and she'd heard Tom Perkins's voice downstairs several times. Those visits weren't all to check up on her. He'd taken her statement at the hospital, and they were trying to track down the car that had tried to run her down. "You're in love with him."

"Stop it."

"Is he in love with you?"

"Alex! Give me a break."

And suddenly, the past fell away. "Oh, my God. That's why you ran away, isn't it?"

Gillian dropped her hands from her face, and it wasn't a crazy woman with a history of drug abuse staring at her, but an adult who'd made mistakes and accepts them.

Her cousin didn't speak, as though words were too precious, or too painful.

She nodded.

It wasn't fair that she should have to intercept Duncan, not when she had such a promising love affair on her hands. Besides, Alex was feeling stronger by the minute. She could fight her own battles now.

"Tell Duncan I'll see him tomorrow, anytime after lunch."

"I am so angry with you."

It wasn't as though Alex needed to say the words; anger vibrated in the air around her, glared at him through her narrowed eyelids, snarled at him through her pursed lips.

But at least she was finally talking to him. After banging down the door every day for the three days she'd been home, he'd finally convinced Gillian to tell her stubborn-ass cousin that he wasn't going anywhere until they'd talked.

He wasn't the most even-tempered man in the world; he was the first to admit that, and Alex was a recovering attempted murder victim, but that couldn't stop the annoyance. "You don't think I was trying to kill you, do you?" he shouted.

She looked at him the way she'd look at a dung beetle. "No. I don't think you're trying to kill me. But I think there's more than murder going on in this town. And you've been lying to me."

Now, when a woman said *you've been lying to me*, there were a lot of possibilities, but in this case he suspected only one. "You checked up on me?"

She nodded. "I admit to being criminally slow. Every thirteen-year-old with a crush checks out their intended on Google. Me, I trusted what you told me."

"You have a crush on me?" In spite of the fact she was sleeping with him—well, *had* been sleeping with him, he was flattered about the crush business.

"Could we stick to the point, please? You deliberately withheld the real purpose of your visit here."

His eyes narrowed in frustration. "That's what I wanted to talk to you about the other night. I was coming to tell you everything."

"Sure, you were."

"There is a missing Van Gogh hidden somewhere in this town. I believe your grandfather brought it into the country during World War Two. What was I supposed to do? Blab it all over town?"

She raised both hands and started rubbing her temples. As a stalling-and-hoping-for-pity tactic, he had to give her full marks. It was a good one. He felt like an asshole for yelling at her when she had a headache. "My head is a little fuzzy, but what is this about a Van Gogh?"

"Look, Alex," he said gently, "I know this isn't your fault. It was your grandfather who took the painting a long time ago. But I have to find it and restore it to the rightful owners."

When he started the speech she looked puzzled; by the time he finished, he wasn't entirely sure why her face was suffused with red verging on purple.

She rose from where she'd been lying on the couch in Grandpa's study, crossed the room, and slapped him across the face, looking all the world like a furious female from the movie screen.

"Ow," he said, putting a hand to his cheek.

"You think . . ." She opened and closed her luscious mouth a few times as though gasping for breath. "You think my grandfather was a thief?" He winced as it rose another decibel. If she got any madder, crystal was going to start shattering all over town. "And you didn't tell me why you were really here. Why? Because you think I'm a—a—thief's accomplice?"

"No. No! Well, maybe at first I thought that, but not since I got to know you better."

"Would that be before or after you started sleeping with me?" She looked pale. He wasn't sure if it was shock, anger, concussion, or a combination of all three. So, even though her question enraged him, he kept his voice calm.

"Now, that's not fair."

Since she still appeared to be in a state of semi-shock, he decided to tell her the entire tale and see what she could make of it. It wasn't as if she could get any angrier with him, and maybe, once she calmed down, she'd help him find the bloody thing.

"Alex, I am here to write a book, exactly as I told you. But, as you no doubt discovered Web surfing, I also help locate stolen treasures, mostly art. I have a lot of sources and I heard a rumor that your grandfather had been the last person to see the former owner of a missing Van Gogh alive."

She glanced sharply his way and her brows drew together, so he knew she was listening.

"He was a Frenchman. His name was Louis Vendome. Ever heard of him?"

She shook her head, giving him the dung beetle look again.

"Your grandfather never mentioned the name?"

This time he got only the *you are the bottom of the insect totem pole* expression. No head shake.

"It was right before France fell in World War Two."

This time her nostrils flared. She knew her grandfather had been there when war broke out. He suspected Grandpa's war stories filled at least one of those tapes she was transcribing.

"Louis was killed fighting with the Resistance and the

painting disappeared. A lot of treasures disappeared during the war. Looted or destroyed by Nazis, or hidden by their owners, who never had a chance to go back and find them. Every once in a while another one turns up. Found in an attic, buried in a wine cellar." He shrugged.

"Or in St. Petersburg."

"You did do your research on me."

"You were one of the team who discovered that some of the art stolen by the Nazis was 'liberated' by the Russians and ended up behind the Iron Curtain, not seen again by the west until Glasnost."

He nodded. "A lot of families have contacted me over the years hoping I can help them get their families' treasures back. Sometimes I can help, most times not. The Vendome family was one. After hearing their story, I told them their quest was probably hopeless. Then a few months ago I heard a rumor that a man called Franklin Forrest had been studying art in Paris and knew Vendome and his family's famous painting. The rumor suggested Mr. Forrest might know how to find the painting. *Olive Trees with Farmhouse.*"

She blinked. "The black-and-white photocopy that you were painting that day when I . . . brought you dinner."

"Right. I decided to try and interview your grandfather and see if he could tell me anything that might help. Frankly, I probably wouldn't have done more than give him a phone call if I hadn't also wanted a quiet place to write where I could also do some climbing."

"So you came here."

"That's right."

"And when you found out Franklin Forrest was dead, you decided to seduce his granddaughter for information." Her voice was calm enough but her eyes burned with fury.

"No!"

Her brows flew skyward. "We didn't exactly hit it off, yet you pursued me until you got me into bed."

The room seemed to grow uncomfortably warm. "I'm not saying I didn't want to see if you knew anything about the painting, because I did. Maybe I would have taken a brush-off better if I wasn't thinking you were the last hope for finding that Van Gogh. But I swear to God I didn't sleep with you for information. I wouldn't do that."

She did not look convinced.

"Alex, I'm not the only one who thinks you have that painting, or know where it is."

She gasped as the truth hit her. "The dead man in my library?"

He nodded. "He's been known to work for a dealer in L.A. who doesn't do all his deals on the floor of his gallery."

"But, why did they try to kill me?"

"Not to take away from your ordeal, but if they'd wanted to kill you, you'd be dead."

She was pale, but he could see she was reasoning through what he'd already concluded. "Yes. Of course. They wanted to scare me into giving up the painting, I suppose. Except that I don't have it. My grandfather never would have done a thing like that."

"I never knew him, so I can't comment, but he may not have stolen the picture." He began to pace the study. "Think about it. The Nazis had truckloads of stuff they took off the Jews and sold in Europe. That was before war started. Then, once it did, they looted Poland, Italy, Holland, France, and Belgium of its treasures. Desperate owners and gallery managers tried to smuggle or hide art works to keep them out of the hands of the Third Reich. Because they didn't only confiscate what they wanted, they had a nasty habit of destroying art they thought was degenerate. That included some of the great modern masters. Maybe your grandfather smuggled the picture out for safekeeping."

"And never gave it back?"

Duncan shrugged. "His friend was dead. Maybe he didn't know about the family. He never sold the painting in his lifetime, so he didn't profit himself."

"But why would he hang on to it all those years and never say anything to anyone?" She stopped. Blinked. "Oh, my God." She put her fingers over her lips as though trying to stifle her words, but then she dropped her hand and spoke clearly. "He kept saying he had a special bequest for Gillian and me. He talked about a letter that went along with his will. But after he passed on, and we found his will, there was no letter."

"I'm guessing somebody has it."

She swallowed audibly. "Who?"

"Isn't *that* the ten-million-dollar question."

Chapter 24

When Alex showed up at his door later that night, Duncan could see she'd been crying.

"Come in," he said, pretending he didn't notice the damp patches on her cheeks and the red-rimmed eyes. "Let me take your coat."

"No. Thanks. I can't stay." She hugged herself into it as though it could protect her from the ugly truth.

"How are you doing?" It was a stupid question, since it was painfully obvious she wasn't doing all that well, but he sensed she needed to unload.

"How am I doing?" She walked past him and stood facing the sliding doors, so all either of them saw was her wavy reflection in the darkened glass. "I'm thirty years old and I just found out my grandfather might be a thief. How do you think I feel?"

He guessed it sucked to find out at the ripe old age of thirty that your grandfather was a thief.

"I couldn't say. I've known my grandfather was a thief ever since I understood what a thief was."

She turned from the window, shock and suspicion staring at him. "Your grandfather was a thief?"

He nodded and went to the fridge for a bottle of wine. While he uncorked it and poured two glasses, he said, "I come from a noble line of thieves. My great great grandfather was a highwayman. They hanged him. I've got family in Australia, who got there on a convict ship," he said cheerfully. "They ended up with their own cattle station."

"I can't believe this," she said.

"My Uncle Simon was another black sheep. It's a veritable herd. He became the family fence. But I really let down the family tradition. I went straight."

"Your entire family are thieves?"

"Not the women. We're traditional like that."

"So, that's a cozy little system you've got going. They steal the goods and you conveniently find them for a nice, fat fee? Is that how it works?"

"No. That is not how it works. I stay out of the family business altogether except we have an understanding that they'll pass on any rumors or information that might be useful in my work. In return, I keep my mouth shut about their businesses." He shrugged. "We're no more dysfunctional than a lot of families in the world."

Only Duncan had let down the tradition. His relatives still shook their heads over him.

"You're an absolute abe-r-r-ration, laddie, that's what ye are," his Uncle Patrick was fond of saying.

"Are you saying that to make me feel better?"

"Yes. But it also happens to be true."

She chuckled, a bit wetly, but it was a start. Her coat was still on, but she accepted the wine he passed her and sat.

"If my grandfather had something to do with that painting, then I want to help you find it," she said, "because it needs to go back to its rightful owners."

He nodded and wondered why he hadn't confided in her earlier. Had he really thought she had something to do with concealing stolen property? This woman who wouldn't jaywalk in a ghost town?

"Okay," he said. "From now on, we work together."

She settled back, looking much more like a sexual fantasy come to life than a co-solver of crime. But, at the moment, she was the best co-solver he could imagine. "What do you know so far?"

He winced. "Not a lot."

"Well, things should go quicker now that you're no longer convinced I have the painting." She gave him a snooty look. "I assume you are no longer convinced I have the painting?"

He glared. "Give it a rest, Alex."

"Well, because your apologetic demeanor leaves me speechless, I will agree to help you. On one condition."

He was pretty sure he wasn't going to like this. "What's the condition?"

"Neither my grandfather nor anyone else in this town is to be named as being involved in any sort of criminal action."

It went against his nature, but, on the other hand, given his family background, he wasn't a stranger to re-shaping the truth like so much pizza dough into a more convenient shape. He'd presented pizza in every flavor and shape imaginable and his clients and the media ate it up, so long as the missing item was on the table as well.

"Agreed. But you have to promise me in exchange to share any information, no matter how small a tidbit, that could help."

She thought about it for a second, then nodded. She shucked her coat, pulled out a spiral-bound note-book—a brand new one with the cover still shiny—and a ballpoint that he would have guessed was also new from the way its blue plastic cap gleamed. Then he noticed the ink was half gone. She'd used half the ink and still had the cap? And it wasn't dulled, scratched, or chewed?

"So," she said, "what do we know?"

"We know your grandfather leaked information about the Van Gogh—an easy thing to do with his connections. I'm assuming he planned to sell it."

She looked as though she might argue, then dropped her gaze to her notebook and began drumming her pen against the paper.

"We know that Jerzy Plotnik was killed in or near Swift-current and the body dumped in your library. Plotnik worked for a guy in L.A., a shady art dealer named Hector Mendes."

He caught her quick glance. "What?"

"You knew who the dead man was all along, didn't you?"

Promising to be completely open with Alex had seemed like a good idea when he'd proposed they work together. Now he wasn't so sure. "Yes." He held up a hand. "Spare me the good citizenship speech."

"Do you know who killed him?"

He didn't think he deserved that. "No. If I did, I'd tell the police."

She sniffed. "And we know that the gun was put in my drawer."

"And we know someone tried to run you down in a car that looked suspiciously like mine."

She nodded.

"It's probably the most common rental and the most common color, but I don't think it was a coincidence. Someone is trying to stop us from working together."

"You did a fine job of that all by yourself," she reminded him.

"Someone tried to kill me, too, by the way."

Her nose came out of the air in an instant as concern lit her face. "What?"

"When Tom and I went climbing. Somebody shot at me. They missed, but hit my rope."

"You never told me."

"I wasn't hurt. And believe me, that night when you came over with dinner, I had other things on my mind."

A little more color highlighted her cheeks. "And all this, this murder, shooting, and running people over is for a painting?"

"Yep. Or for the money it will bring."

She rose, then sat again. "None of us is safe until that painting is found."

"Agreed."

"So, if we think the dead man, Plotnik, stole Grandpa's letter, then someone else took it from him when he died since it wasn't found on his body."

"Or he never got the letter."

"Or there is no letter. Think about it. If someone stole the letter, they'd have the painting."

She went back to drumming her pen on the notebook, and he did a little pacing. "Who is the executor of the will?"

"I am."

"No safety deposit box?"

"Yes, but it was a small one. With the deed to the house, some stock certificates, that kind of thing."

"No paintings."

She shook her head.

She ran a thumb along her fingernails as though checking her manicure. Still, it wasn't as irritating as turning her notebook into a bongo drum.

"Where was the will kept?"

"At home. His home. So, if it was stolen, it must have been taken by someone with access to the house," she said. "There haven't been any break-ins."

He took a deep slug of wine, knowing he had to tell her something she wasn't going to like, but he felt he owed her his honesty. "Actually, there have been break-ins."

"What do you—" Her eyes opened wide as she put together his statement with what he'd just told her about his family. "You broke into my grandfather's home?"

"I could hardly ask permission to search for a missing painting when I suspected you of harboring it."

Alex wasn't stupid and after staring at him for another long moment, she said, "Where else did you search?"

He rubbed a hand over his face, half wishing he'd kept his mouth shut. "Forrest Art and Antiques. Your place." He ought to apologize. He knew that, but *sorry* didn't come easy.

She rose and once more stared at the dark glass sliding door. "You have betrayed my trust on every level," she said, her voice shaking.

"Not every level," he said, rising to his feet and joining her at the window, standing behind her so both reflections were visible. "I've been intimate with you in a way I never have with another woman." He wanted to tell her he loved her, and now that he felt he was close to losing her, the need to share his feelings grew desperate. "Alex, I—"

"No."

She swung to face him and he saw tears trembling on her lashes. "I can't even think about that right now. I want to find that painting so I can help right a wrong. Once you've got what you came for, you leave town. Understood?"

It was exactly his plan in coming to town, so why should he suddenly feel so desolate at the idea?

"Alex, please, I need to explain." Although he wasn't certain himself that he knew what he wanted to tell her, except that he couldn't stand the way she was looking at him right now, and he wanted to be able to pull her into his arms and the hell with everything else.

He must have telegraphed his intention, for she stepped around him. "Fun and games," she reminded him. "That's all we were to each other. And now the fun and games are over."

She reseated herself, once more staring at her notebook.

"It's not over. You know that as well as I do."

"Maybe Grandpa meant to write the letter and never got around to it, or he misplaced it. Years from now it could turn up," she said, getting back to the facts and away from any personal discussion between them.

All right. For now, he'd let her avoid the personal stuff, but he wasn't going to lose her easily. He brought his mind back to the puzzle at hand. "Maybe. Or we could go looking for it."

Her gaze was cool and level. "The letter or the painting?"

"Hey, a letter's paper and ink. That Van Gogh is—"

"Canvas and oil."

"You know better than that. It's art. It's history."

"It's loot. And if you find it, you get a fee."

"That painting belongs to someone else. If it's in your grandfather's house we have to find it and return it."

She nodded. "Okay. What do you suggest? You've already searched the house."

"Yes, but I don't know it the way you do, and it's the obvious location."

"Let me call Gillian. She's staying in the house—I want to make sure she's okay with us going there."

He felt his jaw tighten. "She could be involved."

"No, Duncan. She's not involved. She's been looking after me for the last three days. She's not getting drunk or high or visiting a stolen Van Gogh. She's been cooking me soup and baking goddamn muffins."

"And sleeping with the town detective," he admitted.

"Maybe Grandpa went to these L.A. people and died before he could hand over the painting. They came to the same asinine conclusion as you did and went after me."

"Maybe." But he didn't think so. "I dropped some heavy hints with Eric about the Van Gogh the day before I went rock climbing."

She gasped, paling before his eyes. "And it was Eric who put enough doubts in my mind that I researched you on the Internet. He knew I'd be so angry I wouldn't let you sleep over."

"That bastard. So he knew you'd walk to work alone the next morning and he could conveniently terrorize you and make it look like I did it." He strode to the phone. "I'm calling Tom."

"Eric said he was going out of town. To Eugene for an auction."

"I bet if somebody checks all the car rental companies in the area, they'll match him to a tan Taurus."

He made the call, passed on the information, and when he finished, Alex was gone.

"Alex!" He ran for the door, sprinted out into the rain in time to see her rear lights disappear. "Damn it, woman. Wait!" But he was shouting to himself.

Guilt wasn't an emotion that troubled Duncan overmuch—well, coming from his family background, it had pretty much been bred out of him. But tonight, after the way Alex had reacted when she found out he'd broken into her place and searched it, he felt small and dishonest.

She'd left a couple of hours ago and he'd spent the time staring out the darkened window at the raindrops chasing each other down the pane. He thought he'd go insane if he had to listen to the sound of that drip, drip, drip much longer. Hadn't anybody here heard of cleaning out the eaves trough?

He'd hurt the woman he loved.

If she pulled that you've-really-let-me-down routine when she was a mother, she was going to have the best-behaved kids in the Pacific Northwest. He hoped to the bottom of his soul that he'd be their father.

His own mother, now departed, must have passed on whatever guilt gene Duncan now possessed, for it was her voice he heard in his head. *Apologize.*

Tell her you're sorry.

He grabbed a jacket and raced over to Alex's place.

He called her on the intercom and she answered so frostily she had to know it was he. "I'm sorry," he said.

A nice older couple who lived in the building came past him and the man opened the front door with his key. He raised his brows at Duncan and held the door for him as Alex said, "What did you say?"

He grit his teeth. He'd been prepared to apologize—did he have to grovel in front of a couple of seniors? "I said I'm sorry!" he yelled.

"You'll never get anywhere yelling, young man," the older woman admonished him. "You should have brought flowers and chocolate. That's what Harold always does when he's in the dog house, and we've been married forty-eight years."

"Is there someone there?" Alex said.

"Yes, Harold and . . . ?"

"Daphne. Roland."

"Harold and Daphne Roland. They think you should forgive me." He winked at the woman, sensing an ally.

"Do they know what you did?"

"Do you want me to tell them?"

With a curse that would have had Daphne Roland turning pink if she could hear it, Alex said, "Come up."

"Thanks," he said with real gratitude as he walked in behind Daphne and Harold. He kissed the older woman's cheek. "You got me past the first hurdle."

"My advice is, whatever she calls you, agree with her."

"Okay." Duncan took mental notes, figuring a man who'd been married forty-eight years must be an expert groveler. "Then what?"

"Why, then you kiss her."

He liked that part of the advice, so he thanked them and left them at the elevator while he ran up the stairs.

Alex let him in, but reluctantly. "You have five minutes," she said.

"I'm sorry," he said. That was a good start and he was proud he'd gotten the words out, not once but twice. And with an audience. Didn't seem like she was ready to fall into his arms, though.

His father would curse him for a fool for ever admitting he'd been in her place at all, but his mother—what would she advise?

"Why are you screwing up your eyes like that?" Alex asked him.

"I'm wondering what my mother would tell me to say."

"Your mother?"

He nodded. "She was a good woman. She'd be horrified at what I did, breaking into your apartment and searching it."

"She was married to a thief."

"Yes, but that was business. You don't steal from people you care about."

"Well, it's twisted logic, but your mother's right."

"I know. And my dad would curse me for ever letting on I was in here in the first place. Don't I get any points for honesty?"

She was wearing a red silk kimono that just begged to whisper down her soft skin as it fell to the floor. But her eyes still looked sad and disappointed and the red silk might as well have been sprayed to her skin for all it was coming off for him. He thought he'd do just about anything to get her to look at him the way she had before she'd searched the Internet the other night. "One point for honesty. Ten demerits for destroying my trust."

"I don't know what else I can do but apologize and tell you I'll never do anything like that again. Please, Alex. Don't end things between us. Not like this."

"You've disappointed me."

He was getting pretty near the bottom of the groveling barrel. "Have you ever had the key to a man's place, or stayed in bed when he went off to work?"

"Ye-es. But I don't see—"

"And you never snooped?"

"Well, I might have—no. Not the way you did it."

"You never, oh, I don't know, checked out his medicine cabinet to see what stuff he used? Checked his computer for e-mail from other women?" She was starting to blush and he knew he'd nailed her.

"It's different if you've been invited to stay and the person knows you're there. That implies a level of comfort with . . ."

"Snooping?"

"Healthy curiosity."

He smiled, knowing he had her. "But Alex, you offered to let me stay behind the first time we slept together."

"You said no."

"But if I'd said yes, you'd have been tacitly accepting

that I might show some 'healthy curiosity' about you and your life."

She fiddled with the cuff of her kimono but he knew from the way she was biting her lip that she was thinking about what he'd said. Finally, she glanced up. "What you did was still wrong."

"I know, and I humbly apologize."

She nodded once. Sharply.

"You know, I don't apologize. It goes against my nature."

"That must be why you do it so badly."

"Wench," he said pulling her against him. "Am I forgiven?"

"Well, it seems we both have larceny in our family history. I suppose I'm going to have to become more broadminded."

"I need to be inside you right now more than I need my next breath," he said against her throat, knowing how special she was since he'd been so damn close to losing her.

He slipped the tie from the silk kimono and kissed her. Because she was still sore in places, he kissed her all over, careful, gentle kisses that eased into careful, gentle loving.

And with every kiss, he tried to let her know his feelings. He wanted to ease into the big declaration slowly.

Chapter 25

"I should go home," Gillian whispered, snug against Tom's chest. It was getting to be a habit.

"Don't."

"But, if I wake up with you every morning, leave with you, then people are going to think—"

"That we're sleeping together. Do you have a problem with that?"

Was he kidding? She'd been wanting to get him into bed since she first started thinking about sex. Now she knew why. She must have had the intuition that they were meant for each other. She sighed.

"What is it? Do you have a problem with people knowing about us?"

She shook her head, burrowing into his chest as though she could hide there.

He didn't let her, though, and tilted her chin until she was looking up at him. The planes of his face were so cleanly sculpted. He was so serious and straight and—unmessed-up.

"I was just thinking my self-destructive streak must have started in high school. Maybe if I'd run for the school council, or hung out at the library instead of sneaking away to smoke dope and have sex, maybe we could have dated and history might have been different."

"Can I tell you a secret?"

"Sure." Like she wasn't baring her soul.

"Those school council and library girls kind of bored me."

A delighted giggle shook her. "Really?"

"Yeah. I know I'm straight and pretty boring myself. And with a girl like that . . . I'd have ended up in a Friday night bowling league, making love to my wife three times a week after the eleven o'clock news."

Actually, that sounded like heaven to her after the roller coaster her life had been—except three times a week was never going to be enough with Tom. Based on the way he was with her, she didn't think it would be enough for Tom, either.

"You mean I'd have bored you if I was one of the good girls?"

"Frankly, I don't think you have it in you to be boring. Don't hit me or anything, but I don't think you have it in you to be a good girl, either."

"But I've changed."

"Sure you have. You've grown up. But I suspect there's a part of you that will always dare the devil."

"I'm not going back to drugs and booze. Not ever." She felt as though she was always trying to tell him and she wondered if he would ever truly believe her. And if he didn't, what future could they possibly have?

"I know you're not." He sounded irritable. "You talk about me trusting you. What about you? You have to trust me to believe in you."

She blinked. She'd never thought of it that way before, but he was right. Maybe she didn't have to carry the burden all alone. Trust was a two-way street.

She drew in a deep breath. "Okay. I believe you. But if you don't think I'll go back to drugs, what were you talking about?"

"Well, let's see. Suppose we joined the Friday night bowling league, right?"

"Mmm-hmm." She kind of liked the image of the two of them bowling on Fridays. It felt so . . . permanent, so small town, so . . . everything she wanted.

"And let's say, for instance, I'm overcome with a desperate urge to take you, right in the bowling alley."

She giggled, feeling her belly squirm with delight. "Does this often happen to you when you're bowling?"

He dropped a hand to her butt and squeezed. "I've never been bowling with you." After a few minutes of kissing and silliness, he continued. "So, I'm in the bowling alley, overcome with lust."

"Right."

"What do we do?"

"We could go home?" Home. She liked the sound of that, especially in connection with Tom.

He shook his head. "Can't go home. We're in the ninth frame. I've got a strike, you've got two spares. We're about to break the club record."

"Right," she nodded, though it had been so long since she'd bowled she really didn't know what he was talking about.

"Can't leave then. But there's a room behind the shoe rental place, a small storage space where they keep supplies and extra shoes. If I had needs, could we go in there for a quickie?"

"Well, I suppose so. You're the cops. You probably wouldn't arrest yourself for indecent behavior."

"You see? You didn't hesitate." He grinned at her

and his face lit up, as it had been doing a lot lately. She got the feeling she was loosening Tom up a little. With a jolt of pleasure, she realized she was good for him, just as he was good for her. "Admit it. The idea turns your crank."

"A quickie with you in a bowling alley?" She sighed blissfully. "I'd love it."

"Well, most of the girls who hung out at the library and were on school council wouldn't love it. You see what I mean? I'd be lost with a woman like that."

Tears were starting to blur her vision, softening his gorgeous, safe, trustworthy face. "Yes, you would be lost with a woman like that. Is that why you never married?"

"Yep."

She was silent for a few minutes, blissed out on the picture he'd painted of them. "So, you're saying you want to go bowling with me?"

"Yeah."

"When?"

"I don't know. Friday night?"

"This Friday?"

"Sure. Why not?"

She rolled away from him to lie on her back and stare at the ceiling. "What about Eric?"

"I wasn't planning on asking him along, if it's all the same to you."

"You know what I mean. It's not going to be easy, is it?"

"Look, this is a small town. If you're not sure about splitting from Eric, then this is the time to tell me."

"No." She reached for him, touching his face, running her fingers over his lips. "I would never go back to Eric. But . . . he could make trouble."

Tom shrugged, but he didn't deny the accusation. "Sometimes when trouble comes, you have to stand up to it, and it goes away."

"Maybe we should take this slowly."

"I don't want to take it slowly. Hell, we've taken twelve years to get this far. I don't want to wait any more."

"Okay." She was tired of waiting, too. "Hey, guess what?"

"What?"

"I got a job today."

"You did? That's great." He knew how scared she'd been of being rejected, so his hug held meaning and support. "I knew you could do it. Where's the job?"

"Green Thumb."

"The plant nursery?"

How many places in Swiftcurrent were called Green Thumb? "Yes, the garden center."

Tom was starting to chuckle. "Who hired you?"

Sometimes it was great knowing each other's histories. She was starting to grin herself. "Old Mr. Stokes."

"The same old Mr. Stokes who tried to have you put in jail when you were seventeen for stealing all his roses?"

"We planted them along the highway as a statement against roadside litter," she told him piously.

"It was a drunken lark."

She snorted with laughter. "That, too."

"And you got that old coot to give you a job?"

"I told him how sorry I was for what I'd done, but also pointed out that those roses are still thriving, so obviously I knew what I was doing, even back then. We planted and fertilized them properly."

"You're making this up."

"I'm not. He was pretty shocked at first. He said, 'Young lady,' like I was still seventeen, 'those roses cost me two hundred dollars wholesale.' "

"And he tried to make the council pay for them, since they ended up on municipal property."

"My grandpa ended up paying for them, and I had to work every penny of it off in the garden." Which she'd loved, except for the humiliation of knowing she'd let her grandparents down, again.

"Go on."

"So I said to him, 'Mr. Stokes. I've grown up and I've changed. I'll work for free until I've paid off the two hundred dollars,' pretending I didn't remember it had already been paid off."

"The old bugger probably took you up on it, too."

"You know what he said?"

"Plus interest?"

She laughed. "Yes. And I said sure. But once I've paid that off, if he's satisfied with my work, he lets me stay on."

"And he agreed?"

"He sure did. Part-time, and at slave wages, but it's a start."

"I am so proud of you."

"Thanks," she said, and kissed him. She felt as though she could never get enough of kissing him.

He turned their bodies so he was leaning over her and the bedside lamplight fell on her face. "Your eye's almost completely healed now."

"Yes." She didn't want to talk about this. It was from another lifetime, so she tried to roll him back, but he was a solid man and when he decided he wasn't budging, not much was going to move him.

He traced the faded bruise with a gentle finger. "My first guess was that a drug dealer did this to you—that's why I had to canvass your neighborhood."

"I told you, I fell," but she didn't look him in the eye when she said it.

"I'm a pretty good law enforcement officer for a small town. I'll never be one of those brilliant minds that get hunches and solve complex crimes in a second.

I'm a little slower, pretty methodical, and I do things by the book. Once I realized it wasn't a stranger who did this to you, there was only one other possibility."

She shifted. "You're heavy. Let me up."

"Did he ever hit you before?"

"It was the goddamn door!" she yelled.

"It was Eric!" he yelled right back.

A sob broke from her throat and she turned her face. He let her go then and she rolled to her side.

Tom rubbed her back, slow and gentle. "You have to stop covering for him."

"You don't get it. You don't know what he's like. Eric told me he'd get me using again and force me into rehab. And he has the stuff to do it anytime he pleases." Her voice was rising and her chest felt tight. "I can't ever go back there. I don't know if I could clean up a second time."

"My God. That's evil."

She had to make Tom understand. "There's something wrong with him. Something twisted. He can be so charming and sweet, but at his core I think he's sick."

"Honey, I can help you, but you have to be willing to go on record—otherwise I can't touch that bastard."

"I can't take the risk. Please understand. I'm finally starting to feel like my life can be good again. He'd destroy it if I tried to get the police involved."

"But I'm—"

"Please."

He kissed her. "In this bed I'm your lover, not a cop."

"And what does my lover think?"

"That it's time for lights out."

She fell asleep happier than she'd felt in years. Maybe, just maybe, her life was about to get better.

* * *

She awoke with a smile on her face. It was early and Tom was still dead to the world.

She was filled with energy and purpose, however. Today was the day she'd finish moving all her stuff out of the house she and Eric had shared and turn over her keys. It seemed a symbolic gesture, as well as a practical one. When Eric found out about her and Tom, he was not going to be happy. She didn't want any of her stuff held hostage, even something as mundane as an old tube of lipstick.

Then, once the house was sold, and the assets—such as they were—split, she'd be free of Eric. She had to believe that.

She puttered around happily in Tom's kitchen, wondering if he liked a big breakfast. She shrugged and decided to get started on coffee. While that was brewing, she checked out his fridge. Pretty good for a single guy, but then Tom had been alone for enough years to have grown out of frozen dinners and takeout.

There was fruit, fresh vegetables, eggs.

She heard him go into the bathroom, whistling.

Coffee was ready. She placed it, along with a pitcher of milk and his sugar pot, on the table.

When she heard him rummaging around in the bedroom, and guessed he was dressing, she called out. "Hey, bring my bag in with you, will you?"

"You leaving already?"

"No. I need my artificial sweetener."

"That stuff will give you cancer."

"It keeps me thin. I'll take the risk."

"Exercise will keep you thin."

"Just bring it."

"Sure," he rumbled in a just-awakened voice. In her state of bliss she imagined hearing it every morning of her life. Imagined all the tiny things they'd get to know about each other.

She was at the counter, chopping leeks to go in her omelet. She figured a single man who kept leeks in his fridge was going to take his fair share of kitchen duty, and being on the receiving end of his cooking probably wasn't going to be a hardship.

She felt him in the kitchen, even though she hadn't heard him. He was soft-footed for a large man—she wondered if it was more cop training.

She waited for him to kiss the back of her neck; the possibility seemed to shimmer. But after a minute, when his lips hadn't fallen there, she wondered if maybe he wasn't much of a morning neck-kisser. She could live with that.

"Gillian," he said, and the neck that had seconds ago quivered with anticipation, now prickled with foreboding. It was his cop voice.

She put the knife down slowly and turned.

"How would you explain this?" he asked, holding out a small baggie of white powder that wasn't sugar substitute.

Her gaze flew to his as despair filled her. This was it. The end of the line. She'd told him she was clean. He'd said he believed her.

"You're the detective," she said, crossing her arms to keep the trembling from showing. "You figure it out."

"Gillian, I am asking you for an explanation."

"You're not going to get one," she said and walking to him, took the purse hanging off his other arm and turned on her heel and walked out of the kitchen.

"Wait!" he yelled from behind her.

His phone began to shrill in the sudden silence. "I'm on call. I have to take that. Don't move."

She turned, crossed her arms under her breasts, and gave him her best tough-girl glare. "Are you going to arrest me?"

"You're pissing me off. Don't move."

He picked up the phone. "Yeah." His glance shifted from the wall to Gillian, standing in the doorway watching. "Yes, Bert. Uh-huh. Which judge? Yes, go on."

She turned and walked down the hall and out the front door.

She dug in her bag for her cell phone, disgusted to see her hand was shaking.

Maybe she'd made a fool of herself again, but this time she wasn't going to fall apart. She punched in the number from memory.

"Hi, Gill," Alex said when Gill identified herself. "You must be psychic. I was going to call you."

Well, she couldn't return the compliment about her cousin's extrasensory powers. Alex in chitchat mode was obviously clueless about the fact that her cousin was walking up the rutted lane that led to the main road back to town center.

"What's up?" Gillian asked, mimicking Alex's bright tone. The hell with it. She was tired of leaning on Alex. She'd walk into town. It wouldn't kill her.

"I wanted to show Duncan the house where we grew up. Would that be okay?"

"It's half your house. You don't have to ask."

"Well, with you staying in it, I figure you have squatter's rights."

Gillian chuckled dutifully, but her stomach felt like she'd snacked on aluminum siding. Her rosy dreams of cooking breakfast and bowling into the sunset with Tom were up in smoke. This was where she'd ended up. A charity case. Squatting in her dead grandparents' house because she didn't have anywhere else to go. "I'll get my own place as soon as I—"

"Hey, don't worry about it. Is it okay if I bring Duncan with me? He's interested in seeing the house."

"Sure. I won't be home, anyway. I have to clean the rest of my stuff out of our old house."

There was a small pause. "Do you want me to come help you?"

"Thanks," she said, feeling a little less alone. "But I'll be fine."

And, she realized, she would.

She heard the rumble of a male voice in the background. Alex wasn't alone.

"I forgot—you called me. What did you want?"

Well, not a ride, now she knew the sexy professor had stayed the night with her cousin. "So, Professor Sexy just dropped by for breakfast."

"Actually, I'm at his place."

From Alex's laugh, she knew she was blushing. On the spur of the moment, she said, "Let's get together for dinner one day soon. There are some things I need to tell you." It was time, as Tom had said, to stand up to trouble. For her, maybe that meant telling Alex about Eric, and trusting her to see the truth.

"Yes. I'd like that."

Gillian smiled at the quick *yes*, though there was no one to see her but a crow staring at her greedily from a fence post, obviously hoping she was going to break out food and share.

"Great," she said. "I'll see you later."

She put her cell phone back in her bag and started trudging. She had a long walk ahead of her.

Chapter 26

The sound of a car behind her made Gillian grit her teeth. Sure enough, she recognized Tom's dark green Jeep as it edged ahead of her. With a mechanical whir, the passenger-side window rolled down. She didn't bother turning her head.

"Get in the car."

She stuck her nose in the air and kept walking.

"Gillian, will you please get in the car."

Hysterical barking made her turn her head and there was Lucky, sandy red head stuck out the window, pink tongue hanging out, doing his best to encourage her. If she weren't so mad she would have smiled. What kind of cop brought an overgrown mutt on an arrest? But she was mad. Angrier than she'd been in a long time.

"Don't make me get out the cuffs."

"I'm resisting arrest," she told him. If he wanted to make her life more of a hell than it already was, he was going to have to work a little harder at it.

She expected a little more yelling back and forth through the open car window, but she should have remembered his training. The Bronco's nose jutted in front of her, about six feet from where she stood, cutting off the gravel shoulder. He cut the engine and was rounding the back of the SUV before she'd recovered her wits enough to start stalking to the other side of the road. She wasn't going to run; she wouldn't give him so much satisfaction. But she wasn't going to stand here waiting for him to arrest her, either.

He caught up to her before she made what would be the middle line if this road were important enough for middle-line paint. He spun her around and, to her surprise and shock, pulled her into his arms and kissed her fiercely. Her squeak of surprise was swallowed by his mouth, but this wasn't a tender, sweet kiss like she was used to with him—it was full of burning anger.

She had plenty of her own burning anger, however, and it didn't manifest itself in kissing. She wanted to hurt him.

Since she was trying very hard to cope with her emotions in a more mature way, she restrained the knee that was itching to thump him in the balls and contented herself with putting her palms on his shoulders and shoving.

Tom was about seventeen times stronger than she was, but he let her go as she pushed away from him. With their faces a couple of feet apart, his green eyes still furious and his lips wet from the kiss he'd forced on her, she felt like weeping. Why couldn't he be the man she wanted him to be?

He crossed his arms, making him appear even tougher and more unapproachable. "Are you going to spend your whole life running away from me every time I make you mad? What kind of future is that?" he bellowed.

Had she stumbled down the lane and into some alternate universe? "You said you'd believe me and you never—"

"I did believe you." His face was grim, the jaw close to cracking from the tension he was holding there. "I do believe you."

"But you said—"

"I asked you to explain what a bag of cocaine was doing in your purse. I think you know."

She blinked. "But you don't think I bought cocaine for my own personal use?" She had to be absolutely certain about what she was hearing before the bird of hope lodged in her chest took flight.

"I know you don't do drugs anymore." His voice gentled and hearing his faith made her knees wobble.

"Then why did you get so mad when you found that stuff in my purse?"

"Because somebody's setting you up. Possibly both of us. I don't like it and I want to know why."

It hadn't occurred to her that Tom was a possible target as well, but of course it made sense. She swallowed. "Oh, Tom, I'm sorry. I never thought he could hurt you as well."

"Eric?"

She swallowed, dropped her gaze to the ground, and nodded.

Tom put his arm around her and led her back to his vehicle. Lucky was so happy to see her, she could have been gone for a week. She hugged the dog, accepting the drool along with the happy, wriggling, hairy body.

She didn't ask where they were going and was only vaguely surprised when he turned around and took her back to his place.

"We never did get those eggs," he reminded her. She knew he wanted the whole story of Eric and his drug problem and, with a pang of regret, she knew she was going to give it to him.

As much as she'd like to rationalize that her ex-husband was only doing this to get her back, or out of jealousy over another man, she knew he'd gone too far. When he set her up in front of Tom he must have hoped she'd be charged with possession. Why would he do that?

Maybe he counted too much on her loyalty. Or, worse, on the fact that no one would believe the truth.

She shook her head sadly as she poured more coffee once they were back in Tom's kitchen. Lucky was flopped under the table, his big body leaving so little room that she slipped off her shoes and rested them on the warm, soft back. It was comforting to get that warmth in her feet and the press of a loving dog's coat while she told her unpleasant story.

Tom finished cooking the omelet and she was shaken up enough that she let him. "I'm sorry you got stuck finishing my breakfast."

"You can cook next time." It was so matter-of-fact that she had to restrain the urge to fly out of her chair and hug him. He still wanted her, still believed her. She hadn't been wrong. Tom Perkins was a man who'd stand by a woman. He was solid and steady enough to lean on, but somehow in the last few months she felt much less inclined to lean. She was going to make it on her own, but a big granite boulder of a man who believed in her was going to make the standing on her own that much easier.

So she told him. "Eric's a high-functioning cocaine addict," she explained to him, quoting the term she'd read.

"How much is he using?"

"I don't know." It wasn't much of a lie. Since they'd stopped living together, she really didn't know how much he used. "A hell of a lot, though, and it's been taking most of our money."

"Is that why you left him?"

She blinked. "The story I heard is that he left me."

"Because you're a hopeless drug addict. I warned you I'm slow, but I'm not stupid."

"Tom Perkins, I love you."

That earned her one of his sweet smiles. "Back at you. Now get on with your story." But he stretched his hand across the table and she grasped it.

"I left him because he was seeing another woman."

"Who?"

"I never found out. I don't even want to know. I found a pair of panties that weren't mine in our bedroom. Then I started looking. He hadn't even tried to hide it. There were credit card receipts for a motel outside of town, a bill for lingerie I never got. You know."

Tom nodded.

"It was the last straw. I told him to leave."

"Must have shocked the hell out of him."

"Out of both of us. I've never been any good on my own, but suddenly I thought, I'm thirty—is this what the rest of my life is going to be? So I told him to leave. Do you really love me?"

"Till death do us part. Did he try to get you back?"

"Briefly. When he came to tell me we had to sell the house and I was going to have to move, I got mad. I knew he'd spent all the money on drugs and I lost it. Which was stupid, because I could see he was high and he had a crazy look in his eyes. Anyhow, he hit me. It was the first time he ever did that."

"I'm sorry."

"Don't be. It made me realize it was completely over."

Tom placed her omelet in front of her, and one at his own place, then sat. On her plate was an omelet approximately the size of a space ship. His was even bigger. She dug in, thinking she was going to have to remember he had a big appetite.

"What do you know about his supplier?"

Her fork jabbed into the eggs. "Nothing. There was a guy who called the house a couple of times, but Eric's out of town a lot with his business. That's when he stocks up."

"L.A.?" Tom posed the question casually, but she wasn't stupid.

She put down her fork. "You think Eric had something to do with that man's murder?"

"It makes sense. The guy's got drugs. Eric needs them but doesn't have the money. They argue. A gun gets involved. The dealer winds up dead. Eric has the keys to city hall."

She felt as though the eggs were crawling back up her throat. "Why would Eric implicate himself by putting the body near city hall?"

"Who knows?" Tom shrugged powerful shoulders. His omelet, she noticed with a certain detached awe, was half gone. "Maybe he was so whacked he didn't know what he was doing."

She tried again. "Eric wouldn't kill anyone."

"They said that about Ted Bundy. I think maybe I should have a little talk with Eric when he gets back from his business trip."

She heard the cheerful tick of the kitchen clock. Beneath her feet, Lucky's flank rose and fell in a contented sigh. She didn't want to say the next words, but she had to. "Eric couldn't have killed that man. He was with me that night."

The line sounded like it came straight from one of those black-and-white movies, but corny or not, it got Tom's attention and she didn't like the way he was looking at her.

"Are you still trying to protect the bastard or is that the truth?"

"It's the truth," she said, wishing it weren't. She hastened to explain.

"He showed up at the house that night. He was sneezing and his nose was all red so I knew—"

"My God. The allergies . . ."

"The only thing Eric's allergic to is a twelve-step program."

"It's been hell for you, hasn't it?"

After a moment, she nodded.

"So he showed up loaded."

"Yes. I think he'd been drinking, too. He was sort of rambling. He went on about Grandpa's will, and what did I know about it. I got the feeling he was desperate for money and grasping at straws. Grandpa's estate was split between Alex and me and we're not going to get rich off it. And it will be months before it's all sorted out."

"What time did he show up?"

She thought back. "Around ten, I think."

"Then what happened?" This felt altogether too much like an interrogation but it was happening on two levels simultaneously. Sergeant Perkins wanted to know about timing and the actions of a possible murder suspect. But, while the calm, detached voice was that of a police officer, the eyes burning with intent belonged to Tom. He was jealous of her former husband.

"Like I said, he wasn't himself. He talked about getting back together, and about us moving into my grandfather's house."

"And then what?"

"And then he passed out. I know I should have kicked him out, but I put a blanket over him and left him on the couch."

"The M.E. put the time of death at midnight to one A.M. Are you sure he didn't leave the couch?"

"Positive. When he's been drinking, he snores. I couldn't sleep with the noise even though I was in my bedroom with the door closed. I could have used my earplugs, which I did when we were living together, but—"

"But what?"

She stopped eating and pushed her plate away. "I wanted to hear if he tried to come in the bedroom."

Tom nodded and she saw his Adam's apple bob as he swallowed. He wasn't enjoying thinking about that night any more than she was thrilled to be telling it.

"I was kind of upset, too. Riled up about everything so I couldn't sleep. I read until around three and then I dozed for a while. About five I heard him leave."

"He left at five in the morning?"

"He wouldn't want the neighbors seeing him and I suppose he wanted to get back to his place and shower and change for work."

Tom, whose plate was cleaner than bleached bone, seemed to be taking a short mental health break. He gazed out the kitchen window with a faraway expression. He didn't fidget or tap, simply sat there with his body and mind clearly in different places.

Gillian rose and cleared off the table but he didn't seem to notice.

She scraped a good chunk of her breakfast into Lucky's dish, figuring that living with Tom, Lucky probably didn't get a lot of table scraps. Then she put the dishes in the dishwasher and mopped the counters.

Tom rose, suddenly back in the present. "What are your plans for the day?" he asked.

"I'm going to finish getting my stuff out of the house."

"You're not going in there alone," he said, and she glanced up, startled at his fierce tone. "I've got to go into work today. I'll give you a hand when I get off shift."

She kissed him. "Eric's out of town and I've got my cell phone. I'll be fine."

He drove her back to her grandpa's house and then took his time kissing her good-bye. "I'll see you tonight," he said when they were both breathing heavily.

"Yes." Tonight and every night.

Chapter 27

———————————

"Do you really think this is what the real painting looks like?" Alex stared at the canvas Duncan had completed from the black-and-white photo, using a sort of paint-by-number technique, only with no numbers and no color chart to recreate the Van Gogh.

The artist himself came up behind her and set his chin on her shoulder, his body just brushing hers from behind. "What do you think?"

"You're no Picasso."

He nipped the side of her neck. "I did my best work when I painted you."

He was squeezing up behind her in a very suggestive way, but she hung on to her composure by a thread even as desire came along with garden shears. "How accurate are these colors?"

"I hope to God I get a chance to find out," he said. "You have a great ass. I'd love to paint it."

She wasn't going to get caught by that one again, but she couldn't deny the warmth percolating through her system at the thought of what this man could do with a paintbrush. There were artists, and then there were artists.

His hands slipped under her shirt and up, warm over her belly, hot when they closed over her breasts.

She turned in his arms, or he turned her, it didn't matter; all that mattered was that she was now facing him.

"Here, hold on to this for a minute," he said and placed her hands back over her head and onto the towel holder on the wall where he kept paint rags and a couple of old towels. He'd moved the table under the towel rack so she found herself arched with the back of her thighs at table height and her spine forming a bridge that was graceful, thanks to her years of dance class.

"How long do I hold on to it?"

"Until I tell you to let go."

Then he pulled her t-shirt up and over her head, stopping when it wrapped around her elbows. She rolled her eyes at him. "Is this your idea of bondage? It's pretty feeble."

"I left all my black leather at home." Then he dipped his head and licked the top of one nipple. Her arch took on balletic proportions as her body tried to follow his retreating tongue. Another lick on the other nipple and she felt tiny shudders already starting. She'd never known a man who could take her from zero to the-earth-moved in so short a time.

But he was never in a hurry. His technique was more to get her from zero to oh-please-hurry and then toy with her until the pressure reached dangerous levels. She'd complain, except that when she finally came it was an orgasm of epic proportions.

She had a little game she liked to play right back. It was to try and fool him into thinking she wasn't nearly as close to blowing as he thought, then sometimes she could sneak one in early.

So, she said in as bored a tone as she could manage, "I'm really very uncomfortable in this position. With my spine bent like this, I could get rickets."

He probably knew as well as she that rickets was caused by a vitamin deficiency but he simply said, "Don't move" and went to fetch a pillow. He pushed the pillow beneath her hips, which was, in fact, wonderfully comfortable and also put her at the perfect height for him to make a meal of her.

She hid her grin of satisfaction and tried to imagine how she must look to him. The picture excited her enough that she made a kind of growling sound when he sucked on her breast. This was a mistake because it was a cue he was bound to pick up on, so she grabbed her blasé tone back again.

"I think there's a cobweb in the corner above the TV. You should tell housekeeping."

"I forgot my gags at home, but I could use an old paint rag," he said conversationally.

"You wouldn't."

"Don't push me."

He grinned down at her and she couldn't stop the answering grin. They had so much fun together. It was too bad he'd be leaving soon. She wanted to savor every minute they had together, so she lifted her head, parting her lips in clear invitation.

He leaned slowly forward and their gazes locked. Something happened. She felt her heart start to pound and a longing swept through her so intense it made her want to cry. Why did he have to leave?

His mouth was warm and firm when their lips met and his arms came around her to cradle her as he stretched his body over hers. The emotion sweeping through her was as sweet and poignant as perfect music.

She wanted to hang on to it, to stay in that moment, but she knew it would pass.

I love you. The knowledge danced through her as she recognized the emotion.

She knew it was true the minute the thought took hold. She loved him.

What an idiot. They had fun and games. That's what they were good at. Sexual silliness, absurd erotic dares, laughter and teasing. They weren't serious. They couldn't be. Duncan was a pirate, a wanderer, the freakin' Indiana Jones of the art world. For a man like that, there would always be another treasure hunt.

Even if, by some amazing coincidence, he returned her love, he wouldn't stay put any more than her father had, and she wouldn't live a nomad's life again, wouldn't take second place to any man's egotistical quest.

She didn't know if he looked at her again when he pulled away from her mouth because she'd closed her eyes. Bad enough she'd fallen in love with the man. Worse if he should read the truth in her eyes.

His lips traced the curve of her throat when she tipped her head back once more. He followed the line to her breast and she felt the chain of her necklace shift across her skin so she raised her head to look.

Perhaps he'd caught it up in his mouth by accident, perhaps on purpose, but he was using the chain to tease her nipples, wrapping the wet links around her, flicking her with the key itself.

Maybe it was his innovative use of the jewelry, maybe it was her newfound knowledge that she loved him, but her whole body was crying out for him and for once he didn't tease her beyond reason. He hooked a chair with one foot, dragged it behind him, and sat, pushing her thighs apart as he did so. Spread out on the pillow, she felt like dinner on a platter.

And he acted like a very hungry diner.

He devoured her with more need and a lot less finesse than he usually showed. Her hands gripped tighter against the towel bar as he licked and suckled until she exploded.

Usually he brought her down slowly, gentling his tongue, but not today. She was still on some fuzzy cloud somewhere when he thrust into her with deep, driving strokes. She wrapped her legs around him and arched against him, being driven up again almost before she'd come back down to earth.

Once more he leaned forward and kissed her hard while he pumped into her until they both cried out.

The moment was so intensely intimate that she tried for a light tone. "Can I let go now?"

"No," he said and raised his head once more to eye her naked torso. He picked up the key idly and then said, "Didn't you tell me this was a special gift?"

"Yes. For my twenty-first birthday. My grandfather said it was the key to his heart."

"Well, his heart wasn't pure. The gold's wearing off."

"What?" She let go of the towel bar and shoved and pulled until she had the t-shirt off; then she picked up the key. Sure enough, a patch of silver showed at the bottom edge.

Duncan was staring at it with as much intensity as she was. She'd never really looked at it that closely before, or considered that it wasn't simply decorative.

"Do you think it opens something?" she asked, even though she knew they shared the same thought.

"Something big enough to contain a painting."

"Let's go," she said.

Gillian found there wasn't much she still wanted from her old home, after all. Half a dozen liquor store boxes held her old photo albums, some Christmas wrapping, a few garden tools. The clothes she hadn't already taken over to her grandpa's were mostly things she was never going to wear again. They no longer fit, they reminded her of Eric, or she didn't like them anymore. Those she left. He was the one who wanted to sell the house. Let him seek out somebody to haul away the junk.

Her childhood doll collection and the pieces her grandmother had left her were still at her grandparents' house. Odd that she'd never brought everything over to this place. Had she somehow always felt this wasn't home?

The remaining furniture could go with the house or be sold separately. She didn't want it.

She walked through a last time, checking closets and drawers for anything she might have left behind.

The hall closet contained her raincoat and an umbrella. She pulled them out. Eric's jacket was hanging in there and she wondered why. He'd moved all his clothes out months ago. Puzzled, she pulled it out and then remembered he'd worn it when he came to call the night of the murder. When he'd snuck out at dawn he must have forgotten it. He would have been in no state to remember where he left it. She could be a nice person and take it to the store and return it to him or she could shove it back in the closet.

She shoved it back in the closet.

But as she did, she noticed an envelope sticking out of the pocket. Okay, she had only so much mean in her. If this letter was something important, she wouldn't want to pretend she hadn't seen it.

She slipped the envelope out of the coat pocket and her eyes widened as she instantly recognized the handwriting on the front. It was her grandfather's. It gave her a pang to see it, as though he should have taken all his handwriting with him to the grave. She couldn't imagine how Alex could stand to listen to his voice when she transcribed those tapes.

It seemed odd for Eric to carry around a letter her grandfather had written him. And why write a letter to a guy you see all the time? By this time her eyes had taken in the fact that the letter was addressed to Alex and her. Eric's name was nowhere on it.

Alex had mentioned a letter Grandpa was supposed to have left with his will. She'd wanted to know if Gillian had seen it, which she hadn't. She was certain she'd asked Eric also and he'd denied all knowledge of it.

Was this the letter?

Only one way to find out. It was already open, so she didn't hesitate, but pulled out the single sheet of paper. It didn't crackle in her hands like an ancient pirate's map, but something about it didn't feel all that new, either. The glue on the envelope was yellowed and the ink seemed kind of faded. How long ago had the letter been written?

Oh, there was the date, right at the top. Nine years ago. She read on. *Dear Alexandra and Gillian, I suppose every family has secrets.*

Her eyes misted. That sounded so like her grandfather, and she could see him sitting at his desk writing those words almost a decade earlier. At the time she'd still been in L.A. being a screwup, and Alex would have been close to finishing up her first university degree, piling success on top of success.

She fought down the usual bitterness, knowing it for what it was. Jealousy. Alex had handled her life better. But it wasn't too late for Gillian to start following her cousin's example and make something of herself and her life. Hell, she had experiences and had learned compassion that maybe they didn't teach in library school. Plus, she had a job now.

She sighed and went back to the letter. Family secrets. God, she hoped he hadn't left a letter behind him to let her know he'd heard those boys in her bedroom. Shame washed over her as she thought about what she'd put her grandparents through.

> *I want you girls to know how proud your grandmother and I are of you both. Gillian, you are a searcher. You've got the courage of an adventurer.*

Courage? Her?

> *And a heart easily bruised. We pray for you nightly, but we are sure you will find your way home.*

She sniffed, barely realizing a tear had rolled down her cheek. Home.

> *Alex, you've the intellect and the drive to go far. I worry much less about you, but don't be too independent. Gillian and you haven't always been the best of friends, but you're family and deep down I know you love each other and will always be there when needed.*
>
> *Alex, you haven't made any mistakes yet, or if you have they've been minor ones. Gillian, you'll understand what I'm about to reveal better, and I hope you can explain human frailty to your cousin. For I did make a mistake.*
>
> *If you are reading this letter, then I haven't yet been able to rectify my error.*
>
> *But, I must go back. All the way to what must seem distant history to you girls.*

Gillian rolled her eyes, recalling how her grandpa had that irritating way of older people of treating her and Alex like simpletons.

> *As you may recall, I was in Paris in the last*
> *days before Hitler's army invaded and France fell.*

If the letter hadn't been pretty short, Gillian might have given up right there. It wasn't like they hadn't heard their grandpa's stories fifty million times. And his days as an art student in Paris were right up there with his faves.

> *I had a good friend, Louis Vendome. His family owned, among other works, a Van Gogh, and he and I had spent many a night over many a bottle discussing the techniques. Both of us did our best to copy the painting as a way of understanding Van Gogh's brilliance. We were art students—wine-swilling, Gauloise-smoking students. Hitler and the Nazis were nothing to us until we heard they were clearing their museums of "degenerate artists" like Gauguin and Klee, Picasso and Van Gogh.*
> *To us, the greatest crime of the Nazis was that they destroyed some of these works, and mocked the rest. Even when Poland fell, our talk was maybe ninety percent art and ten percent war. Then the Nazis marched through Europe. They were closing in on Paris and now our talks were ninety percent war, ten percent art. Louis joined the underground resistance. As an American, I knew I had to leave. When I said good-bye, my friend gave me the Van Gogh, and asked me to take it to America for safe-keeping until the war was over, when we would once again be free to drink wine, smoke cigarettes, and talk about our great love, the Impressionists.*
> *But Louis didn't live long enough to see the end of the war.*
> *I waited, and no one contacted me for the painting. I waited several years and it was clear no one knew I had it. All these years I've had it. I could have given it back*

*to France, but what would the French government do
with it? If I hadn't saved it, perhaps the Nazis would
have burned it anyway. So I rationalized my decision to
hang on to a valuable object that didn't belong to me.*

Now it's yours.

*I'd hoped to be able to return the painting somehow
and collect a reward, but of course, they'd know I was responsible for taking it and I'd receive contempt and
ridicule instead of any reward. But, once I'm gone, you
two will be able to say you stumbled across it. My reputation won't matter to me when I'm six feet under and it
will give me pleasure to know that the reward money will
give you girls a decent start in life.*

*If I were a banker, I'd say the key to your heart is in a
vault. But I'm a painter, though sadly I was never a
very good one. And I say the key to your heart is a blank
canvas.*

*Paint your canvases well, my darling granddaughters.
The future is yours.*

> *Your loving grandfather,*
> *Franklin George Forrest*

Gillian sat blinking for a moment, then leaped from
the couch, her boxes forgotten. Her mind was over-
crowded with new information and the unpleasant
thoughts that accompanied them. *Tom,* she thought.
Tom has to see this.

Tom knew that doing the right thing was sometimes
difficult, but he discovered that doing the wrong thing
for the right reasons was even worse. He knew that what
he was about to do could cost him his job, possibly even
the woman he loved.

He was planning to execute a search warrant of Eric

Munn's premises, even though the information Gillian had shared with him this morning meant her ex-husband couldn't have killed Plotnik.

However, he was convinced that even if Munn hadn't committed the murder, he was somehow involved. The warrant might turn up something useful, and for that reason alone, Tom would keep his mouth shut.

It was amazing that Gillian should arrive at his office just as he was about to head to her ex's place, as though he'd somehow summoned her by thinking about her so much. "Hi," he said, trying not to sound guilty.

"Hi," she said. "Raeanne told me I could come right in."

"Sure, yes." He rose and came forward to greet her. "What's up?" She was flushed and her eyes appeared a little wild.

Her mouth opened and then shut. "You'd better read this." She disentangled one hand and pulled an envelope from her pocket.

He let go of her and read the letter. Once rapidly, in gathering amazement, and then again, slowly, as more pieces of the puzzle fit themselves together.

Gillian stared at him anxiously the entire time.

"Where did you get this?"

"It was in the pocket of Eric's coat. He must have left it at my place the night he came over—the night that man was killed."

"Do you still stand by your story that he was snoring in the front room until three A.M.?"

She glared and started to form words he knew were going to be nothing but mouthing off and he didn't have time for that.

"Yes, or no."

"Yes." She glared.

He was tired of telling her all the time how he trusted

her, but he was a cop and doing his job here. He was also a man facing a woman whose self-esteem was frail at best. His trust was a big deal for her, he understood that, but there must be a way to make it clear he would always believe her.

She was standing there, both belligerent and vulnerable. And then suddenly the words were there. The words he needed to say and that she needed to hear.

"I love you. And I want to marry you," he said, and kissed her.

"I love you, too," she said, her eyes as bright as stars. "And yes, I'll marry you."

He gave her shoulders a quick squeeze. "We'll figure everything out later. Right now, I have to go." He took a step away from her and then turned, knowing he had to tell her. "We've got a search warrant for Eric's apartment. When he gets back to town, I'm hoping we'll have reason to arrest him. I'm sorry, Gillian."

She blinked at him, and he realized she was suffering major information overload. Then her eyes widened. "Eric's back in town. I passed his car on my way here."

He tapped the letter. "If he passed you, then he knows your grandpa's house is empty. He's probably there snooping. Does he have a key?"

"No. Unless . . ." She gasped.

"What is it?"

"That must be why he wanted me to move into Grandpa's house, so he could have a reason to go over there. He told me he'd forgotten his house key one time and borrowed my set. He could easily have had one of Grandpa's house keys copied."

"I want you to go to my place and stay there. Eric's probably running scared. I'm going over to have a talk with him."

"Oh, my God! Alex. She's at the house right now."

"I'm on my way." He pulled out his house keys and the Bronco keys. "Go to my place and lock the doors."

"My cousin's in danger. I'm coming with you."

It was pointless to argue when she was hanging onto him like a burr.

Chapter 28

_____

"I am so tired," Alex said, straightening her back. They were trekking up from the basement—spider heaven, as she'd discovered as she poked into every dark corner and in every murky cupboard down there. They emerged into the dazzling brightness of a kitchen in daylight.

"You're sure you never saw him with a safe?"

She shook her head with the exaggerated patience of someone who's been asked the same question fifty times and given the same answer to every one. "No," she reminded him in case he'd developed amnesia since he'd asked the question half an hour earlier. "There was the safe at his shop, but Eric has that."

"I checked that safe. No Van Gogh."

She rolled her eyes. "Of course you did."

"The painting has to be here somewhere."

"Well, it's not in the attic or the cellar—there isn't a wall safe on the main floor." Or if there were they'd failed to locate it despite combing every inch of wall, looking behind every painting, and even moving furniture.

Duncan closed in on her and picked up the chain around her neck with one finger. He smelled of dust and sweat and if irritation had a scent, it was liberally spritzed all over him. "Maybe he was just cheap with his birthday gifts."

"Of course not," she said huffily, snatching back her chain. "It was my twenty-first birthday present—he wouldn't give me gold-plated jewelry." She thought hard, running the key back and forth on its chain for inspiration.

"Key to your heart," she repeated. "Maybe that's a clue." Her eyes widened. "Wait a minute! My grandmother's sampler." She ran into the living room, Duncan's heavy tread thumping behind her, and took the sampler that her grandmother had stitched years earlier off the wall.

The heart of the home is family was cross-stitched inside a border of twining hearts.

"We already looked behind it."

"I know." She turned the sampler over and tried to remove the small nails that held the backing in the frame but they were jammed in tight. "My grandfather hated all those cutesy sayings my grandmother embroidered." She damned near snapped a fingernail trying to pull out a small black nail. "Get some pliers from the basement," she told Duncan.

"Maybe he was sentimental," he said, pulling the frame out of her hand and opening one of those Swiss Army Knife gadgets with enough thingies on it to ensure a Swiss soldier's survival whether stranded in the middle of the forest and in need of a tiny saw, or at a party with no corkscrew. Of course, it had mini-pliers and he went to work carefully extracting the tiny black nails.

"He kept her picture in a silver frame, but he took

down the cross-stitched sheep from the kitchen that said *Somebody Loves Ewe* and the one in the bathroom about cleanliness and godliness.

She was really babbling to let off some nervous steam while she watched Duncan slip the backing off and then ease out the cross-stitched sampler. It was done on cream-colored linen which was tacked onto a stretcher board. Duncan turned it to the back but all they learned was that her grandmother was such a meticulous needleworker that the back of the piece looked almost as neat as the front.

Then he turned it to the side and there, in black ink, was a series of four numbers.

3578.

They looked at each other and she felt the excitement fizzing in her belly. "Three-five-seven-eight," she said aloud, "and the key." She lifted it almost to make certain it was still there.

"It must open a safety deposit box somewhere."

"But where?"

"Right here at the Evergreen Savings and Loan," said a voice from the hallway.

She started and turned, recognizing the voice. "Eric, you startled—" She petered out when she saw that Eric was holding a gun and it was pointed in their direction.

"What are you doing?" Alex shrieked, feeling as though she'd stumbled into the last scene of a murder mystery without having sat through the first part.

Both men ignored her, seeming to be intent on each other, like one of those nature shows where the alpha reindeer circle each other before locking horns. Of course, on a nature show, it was antlers only. One of the reindeer wasn't normally packing heat.

"Did you kill Jerzy Plotnik?" Duncan asked.

Eric sniffed, and she noticed his nose was bleeding. He pulled a handkerchief from his pocket and staunched the flow. "No. Some friends of mine did. I promised to sell them the Van Gogh, but your grandfather died before he told me where it was."

"You knew about the Van Gogh?"

Eric nodded. "The old man got the guilts about a year ago. He decided he wanted to return the painting quietly, collect a reward that he'd pass on to you. He didn't want you to know that your dear old grandpa was a thief."

"I don't believe he stole that painting," Alex said.

She noted that Duncan was closer to her than he had been before and realized he was surreptitiously moving. She suspected he had some kind of heroism in mind and for some reason that made her tremble more than the sight of the black gun staring at her with its one round eye.

"Believe what you like. He said he had it in a safe place and as soon as I made the arrangements to return it and get the reward, he'd give it to me. But I got to thinking that there was a lot more money to be made selling the thing. I've got a friend in L.A. who knows some people. We had a deal. But when I told your grandfather I had everything arranged," he shuddered at some memory, "he turned suspicious. I lost my temper. We shouted at each other . . . right here in this room. He said he'd changed his mind. He'd return it himself, or if he died first, he'd left instructions for you, Alex. And he suddenly keeled over. Dead."

"No," she moaned. Her grandpa shouldn't have died like that. It should have been peaceful, not angry.

"Meanwhile," Eric continued, "I already had a deposit that I couldn't return."

"It went up your nose?"

Eric ignored Duncan's interruption. "To remind me of how serious they were, my connections in L.A. killed my buddy."

"Jerzy Plotnik," Duncan said, and Eric nodded.

"In my apartment," he shuddered with distaste.

"And you moved him to the library?"

"Your grandfather said you'd know where the painting was, so I put Jerzy in the library. We were always good friends. I thought you'd turn to me when you got shaken up. You should have come to me instead of him." Eric jabbed the gun toward Duncan.

She recalled the second horrible incident, when she'd found a gun in her desk drawer. One that looked similar to the pistol now pointing at them.

"And you planted that gun in my desk."

"Right again. I figured if you thought Duncan had put it there, you'd come to me for sure."

"And when that didn't work, you tried to run her down in a car just like mine," Duncan said.

"I never tried to kill her. I was just going to scare her. It was better for her if we worked together." He turned and blinked a few times, as though trying to bring her into focus. "You should have trusted me, Alex."

That was so blatantly absurd that she almost laughed. But things didn't seem all that amusing when a gun was staring you in the face.

She felt movement beside her but determined to keep Eric's attention on her. She'd seen the Swiss Army gizmo was still in Duncan's grasp. He was no doubt trying to open the mini-bayonet. It was up to her to keep Eric talking.

She tried to focus on something apart from the fact that she and Duncan were in serious trouble here. If she could keep him talking. But her mind was whirling at the knowledge that this man she'd trusted was behind the wheel of the car that had run her off the road.

"It was you who shot at Duncan when he was climbing, wasn't it?"

"Well, I had to do something. Your boyfriend came

into my store and basically told me he was looking for the Van Gogh. I phoned Hector Mendes in L.A. and he knew all about Duncan Forbes. Told me to get rid of him." Eric sniffed.

"How could you?"

"Alex, do you have any idea how much money that painting is worth? There are millions of bucks at stake. Enough to kill for."

"But Eric, think what you're doing. You haven't killed anyone yet. You've barely broken the law. We can return the painting like Grandpa wanted and no one will ever know you were involved in all this." She tried to keep her tone calm and reasonable and ignore the fact that a man who was high on drugs and looked a bit of an emotional wreck was pointing a loaded gun at her. "I promise. And we'll get you help. There are programs—"

"You don't understand, Alex. My friends are going to kill me if I don't get them that painting. And it won't be a pretty death. I figure I've got another week, tops. I'm sorry, honey. I hate to have to do this, but it's you or me."

"You're planning to kill me?" She could not believe this.

"Well, officially, Duncan will kill you. He'd do anything to get that picture. I'll make it look like you stole the gun, Alex. You threatened him. He overpowered you and killed you. Then he escaped. With the painting. Pretty good, huh?" He looked as though he expected praise for his clever plan.

"Are you insane?"

Eric smirked. "Of course, you won't really escape with the painting. The Van Gogh and you will both disappear and never be seen again."

Alex felt as though she might vomit, except her muscles were all so paralyzed by fear that they wouldn't obey the distress message from her stomach.

"I'll need you for a while yet, Alex. The letter your grandfather left? It was impossible for me to understand. You'd have got it right away. But he was telling you to go to the bank in town. They won't let me in to his deposit box, but you're the executor. They'll let us in together. We get the painting."

"Why should I help you? You're going to kill me anyway."

Eric blinked. He'd obviously never looked at this from her point of view. He was high enough on drugs to have confidence in his crazy plan.

It was small comfort to think he'd be bound to get caught when she and Duncan would unfortunately be dead by then.

"I don't want you dead, Alex. I never wanted you dead. I'll take you with me. With money, there are places in the world where you can disappear. Poof. We'll live like royalty."

Until the last of his fortune went up his nose. Still, maybe playing along with him would buy her a little time. She was off the hook for now, but Duncan was of no use to him. She had to think. There had to be a way to stop him from killing Duncan.

"I need you to draw the living room curtain—*now, Alex,*" Eric said in that overfriendly voice that was starting to jar.

He was going to kill Duncan the minute she'd closed out any possibility of a neighbor seeing the murder.

But he couldn't kill Duncan. She loved Duncan and hadn't even had time to tell him.

"Eric, please. There has to be another way."

"Do it," Eric said, and pointed the gun at her.

"Do what he says, Alex," Duncan told her. She glanced at him and saw the same message in his eyes that must be burning in hers. He loved her. She was as certain of that as she was of her own name. Tears burned as she thought of how foolish they'd been to be given the precious gift of each other's love and not to have shared it openly.

Duncan sent her the ghost of a wink and she blinked, pulling herself together as best she could. If they were going to die, at least they knew they loved each other, even if the words remained unspoken.

"I'm sorry, Duncan," she said, putting defeat into the slump of her shoulders. "I'll close the curtains now, Eric."

She turned away, as though not wanting to witness Duncan's demise, took one step toward the window, thinking all they needed was a tiny break. Please, let someone be outside coming up the path. But there was no one.

"Hurry up, Al—" She heard the beginnings of a sneeze and knew this was the biggest break they were going to get. Before the *aah* had given way to the *choo*, she flung her grandmother's needlepoint sampler on its wooden stretcher frame at Eric.

Eric was in the process of honking into his hankie while still leveling the gun at Duncan. He started as *The Family is the Heart of the Home* missile came flying his way.

Duncan wasted no time. He launched himself across the room.

He wasn't going to be fast enough. Eric was already repointing the gun. Unable to bear it, she threw herself into the fray, even though she was certain she'd be too late.

The sound of the gunshot blasted through the room.

She screamed, in fury and fear.

Duncan was on top of Eric, holding a Swiss Army Knife corkscrew to his neck. He was alive, was her first thought, but she saw the grim look on his face and then noted the bloom of red widening on his shoulder.

"Oh, God. You're hurt."

"I could use some help here, Alex," Duncan said,

and she realized that Eric still had the gun in his hand, that he was struggling madly, and that Duncan couldn't hold him with his wounded arm much longer.

She had her grandfather's ancient brass gong in her hand. She had no idea she'd picked it up. She ran forward and banged the struggling, swearing man as hard as she could over the head. In spite of the satisfying *thunk* and small gonging noise, he still held the gun.

Knowing Duncan was weakening fast, she stepped on Eric's arm and ground her Blahnik stiletto heel into his wrist.

Eric screamed just as another shot was fired and the front door blasted open.

Her first thought was that Eric's friends had arrived and, knowing Duncan was hurt and Eric was dangerous, she grabbed the gun that had rolled out of Eric's hand.

She was shaking all over, the gun wavering crazily, when Tom and Gillian rushed in.

Tom took one look at the room, pointed his own weapon at Eric, and scooped the gun out of Alex's hand as he went by.

While Tom held the gun on Eric, Alex threw herself to the ground beside Duncan, who slumped on the floor, his back against a blue velvet wing chair. Tears were blinding her vision. "Are you okay?"

"Yeah. He got my shoulder. Nothing serious."

"I love you," she said, so glad she could say the words aloud.

"I know. I love you, too," he said softly, and she could see he was going gray around the mouth.

"You're bleeding," she said through her tears. She put her hand on his shoulder and felt the blood oozing, warm and sticky. Of course he'd pretended it was nothing. What action hero ever admitted he was badly hurt?

She pressed her hand against the wound, ignoring her lover's swearing as he protested.

"Gill, I need some cloths to stop the bleeding."

Behind her, Tom was calling for an ambulance. Gillian ran out of the room and returned with a stack of tea towels. She folded two and passed them to Alex. "Thanks," she said, and pressed the pad against Duncan's shoulder as hard as she could.

"How long till the ambulance gets here?" she yelled to Tom, who was on the radio to someone or other.

"Don't fuss," Duncan said, his forehead damp and his breathing shallow. "I'll go to the doctor and get a few stitches. I'll be fine."

"You're going to be difficult about this, aren't you?"

"And you're going to be a pain in the ass."

They smiled at each other and she kissed him softly, feeling her own tears wet his cheeks.

Of course, she got her way and she had the satisfaction of seeing Duncan still yelling at her as he was hauled into an ambulance.

"He can't be seriously hurt if he can still call you a know-it-all bookworm," Gillian said.

"No. I think he's going to be okay," and with that, Alex lost it. She threw herself into her cousin's arms and burst into tears. Gill hugged her back.

"I was so scared, Allie," she used a nickname she hadn't used in years. "When I heard that shot, I thought I'd lost you."

Alex cried on her cousin's shoulder, finding it had a comfortable feel. It felt almost as good as her grandmother's shoulder had felt when she was a kid and needed a safe and loving place to go.

"I'm sorry," Gillian said, rocking her back and forth. "I knew Eric had a drug problem, but I didn't tell anyone."

"Why would you?" Alex sniffled. "I believed his lies, and I didn't believe you. I'm sorry, too."

"Maybe it's time we got to know each other again."

She sniffed. "Come on. I'll drive you to the hospital so Duncan can yell at you some more."

"Thanks. What about Tom?"

"I'm guessing he'll be busy for a while."

"Eric turned me against you," Alex admitted.

"Then he almost killed you."

"And the man I love."

Gillian sighed blissfully. "It sounds so good, doesn't it? To say 'the man I love'? "

"Mmm-hmm. You and Tom?"

"Yes. We're getting married."

"I'm so glad."

"Me, too."

As they drove to the hospital, Alex said, "Hey, Gill?"

"Mmm-hmm?"

"Tom's going to be working late tonight, right?"

"I think so."

"And Duncan's going to be in the hospital overnight at least."

They grinned at each other in perfect understanding. "I'll bring the Chinese takeout."

"I'll bring the bridal magazines, and I am choosing my own bridesmaid's dress."

And then they started to laugh.

Chapter 29

A lex had her arm around Duncan as they stepped into the locked cubicle behind the bank employee who placed the gray metal box on the table and left.

She told herself she was helping to support Duncan, though in truth his bullet wound was healing nicely. Mostly she liked to have her arms around him. When she thought about how close she'd come to losing him, she needed to reach out and touch him. He'd been out of the hospital for ten days, with a sling that made him look unbelievably romantic—when she could bully him into wearing it. She doubted wound and all, if he'd still be here had it not been for the sting operation he'd helped mount, which had led to the arrest of Hector Mendes, the man who'd threatened and killed for a Van Gogh.

In order to keep absolute secrecy about the actual location of the painting, they hadn't been able to come to the bank and see it for themselves. Not until today.

"Well," she said, pulling the key from around her neck, "here goes."

Duncan kissed her. "For good luck."

She threw her arms around him and kissed him back, deepening the kiss until they were both a little unsteady on their feet. "For more luck," she said.

Her hand wasn't quite steady as she opened the box.

"Would you like to go first?" she asked Duncan, seeing the light of anticipation in his eyes.

He shook his head, jutting his chin in the direction of his sling, which he'd finally agreed to wear when she told him she wouldn't take him with her to the bank without it. "You do it," he said.

So she reached in and removed the single item. The canvas was tacked on a board, but the frame had been removed so it would fit into the safety deposit box, she assumed.

They stood staring at *Olive Trees and Farmhouse* and all the colors jumped out. The burnt orange of the heavy, south-of-France sun, the dull green of late-summer olive trees, the golden stone farmhouse.

And the simple signature. *Vincent.*

For several minutes they stared at the painting, neither willing to speak and break the spell of holding a long-lost masterpiece.

"To think a man was murdered over this, and Eric almost—" She still couldn't bear to think of it. "As soon as he was clear of the drugs, I know he never would have—"

"I think he'll have some time in prison to dry out."

"And he'll get a much lighter sentence for helping out with the sting on the Mendes operation in L.A."

"My phony Van Gogh got Eric and his FBI handlers into that shark's private sanctum. A few stolen treasures were returned as a result."

"You sound pretty pleased with yourself."

"I am." She had a feeling he was as chuffed that his painting had passed for a real Van Gogh as he was that they'd arrested a vicious criminal—and in the process, liberated a few more stolen treasures that would now be returned to their rightful owners.

"Gillian and I talked it over. We don't want any reward. We only want this painting to go back where it belongs."

"I'm waiving my finder's fee, too," he said.

"But it's how you get paid. It's different for you."

He shook his head. "The family isn't keeping the painting. They've decided to donate the picture to a gallery, in memory of Louis."

"Oh, that's so wonderful. Maybe we could go and see it sometime. I mean," she mumbled, cursing herself for the 'we,' "maybe I could . . ."

"Alex?"

"Yes?"

"I got my own treasure," he said. He touched a finger to her cheek. "Marry me?"

"You're proposing to me in a bank vault?" She tried to laugh but it came out sounding like a sob.

"Vincent's here. He was a pretty romantic guy."

"But," she took a deep breath, "I love you, but I don't know if this can work."

"I love you. You love me. What's not going to work?"

She touched his cheek. "I spent so much of my life moving around because of my father's job." She shook her head. "I can't do that again. And then, ever since my grandfather died, I've been thinking about moving away, but I—"

"You're a homebody." His blue eyes twinkled at her and she saw so much understanding there that her heart squeezed. "If you can't see this is your home and the place you belong, you're probably the only one who can't."

"What are you saying?"

He leaned against the wall of the small room. "I

haven't worked out all the details, but I know that in spite of the fact that you stick out like a call girl in a nunnery in this crazy town, this is your place. I had some time to think in the hospital. I can get a job teaching out here."

"What about your adventurous life chasing stolen art?"

He shrugged, then winced with pain. "I'm giving it up. I'll stay home with my wife—and hopefully, my family."

"You'd give up chasing stolen art for me?" Her heart was beating so hard she was amazed she didn't hear it echoing around the tiny space.

"Alex, we both almost got killed. It makes a man think. My life is nothing without you, and you don't want a wandering man."

She wiped her eyes with the back of her hand. "Will you have enough to do?"

"Well, there's also my painting career," he said, shooting her a teasing glance that had warmth spiking, even through her tears.

"Of course, we'll have to find somewhere to live. Your apartment's too small for a family."

"Gillian and I have talked a lot lately." And she realized how much they enjoyed each other, now that they'd accepted who they were and that the past was done. "As soon as she and Tom get married, they're moving into his place. We could . . ." As she started to articulate her idea, she realized it wasn't new. She'd been toying with this in the back of her mind while Duncan recovered.

"We could what?" His good hand reached out to rub her arm lightly, encouraging her.

"I was wondering how you'd feel if we bought out Gill's half of Grandpa's house and lived there?"

"It sounds perfect," he said, as though there was nothing he'd rather do than live in a house that needed renovating, decorating, and a new roof.

A man who was willing to go through so much for her deserved something in return.

"You know, if you give up being the Indiana Jones of the art world, I'm going to start wearing Laura Ashley."

"You wouldn't. I love the way you look. It's part of who you are."

"And tracking down treasure is part of who you are. We'll work it out. Maybe I can go along sometimes. Maybe you don't have to take on so many quests."

He kissed her again, a deep, sweet kiss that promised so much. She doubted theirs would be a smooth ride, but she thought it would be a passionate and primarily happy one. "Have I told you today that I love you?"

She kissed him back, and leaned in so she could whisper in his ear, "Have I ever told you about this fantasy I have?"

"Refresh my memory."

"I'm working in the library, returning a book to a high shelf, and I notice a man looking up my skirt."

"The dog. I hope you kick his teeth in."

She smiled slowly, running her tongue around the edge of his ear before continuing. "No. In this fantasy, I part my legs so he can see my panties."

"Tell me you're wearing the black thong. I love that one."

"You're very good. That's exactly what I'm wearing."

"Then what happens?"

"I don't know yet. As soon as your shoulder heals, we've got a date at the library, and we'll both find out."

"I'm going to take you up against the stacks. You know you've been longing for it." He nuzzled her neck and she smelled dust and paint, and she was almost certain she could smell lemon and bougainvillea, lavender and the heady scent of grapes heavy on gnarled vines. One of these days, they were going to make their pilgrimage to France and see this painting hanging where it was meant to, in a public gallery to be enjoyed by everyone.

"Alex?"

"Mmm?"

"I'm a fast healer."

Dear Reader,

Drive Me Crazy is about love and lust, stereotypes that are meant to be broken, and the people in our lives who make us nuts but are deep down always there for us. We don't walk through this life alone and everyone who becomes important influences us in some way. I really enjoyed exploring and interweaving three critical relationships in this book. There's Alex and Duncan who spark off each other in all the best and worst ways from the second they meet, to Alex and Gillian—cousins with the love/hate relationship of sisters—and Gillian and Tom, who have to go back before they can start over. I hope you enjoyed their stories.

In the continuing theme that love pretty much makes people crazy, next month will be a brand new Brava called *Turn Left at Sanity*. What happens to a Manhattan workaholic who thinks he's got it all together when he lands in a dinky Idaho town where most everyone is eccentric, to say the least? When he falls for the owner of the town's former brothel, now the Shady Lady bed and breakfast, Joe starts to question his own sanity—especially when he realizes he's happier than he's ever been. But is he crazy enough to choose love over business?

I love hearing from readers. Come visit me in cyberspace anytime at http://www.nancywarren.net. Check out the virtual book signing. If you'd like a signed bookplate, I'd be happy to send you one. And I always run a fun monthly contest. Be sure to enter.

Happy Reading!

Nancy